FRONTERA
STREET

FRONTERA STREET

Tanya Maria Barrientos

Written by today's freshest new talents and selected by New American Library, NAL Accent novels touch on subjects close to a woman's heart, from friendship to family to finding our place in the world. The Conversation Guides included in each book are intended to enrich the individual reading experience, as well as encourage us to explore these topics together—because books, and life, are meant for sharing.

Visit us online at www.penguinputnam.com.

NAL Accent
Published by New American Library, a division of
Penguin Putnam Inc., 375 Hudson Street, New York, New York 10014, U.S.A.
Penguin Books Ltd, 80 Strand, London WC2R 0RL, England
Penguin Books Australia Ltd, Ringwood, Victoria, Australia
Penguin Books Canada Ltd, 10 Alcorn Avenue, Toronto, Ontario, Canada M4V 3B2
Penguin Books (N.Z.) Ltd, 182–190 Wairau Road, Auckland 10, New Zealand

Penguin Books Ltd, Registered Offices: Harmondsworth, Middlesex, England

Published by New American Library, a division of Penguin Putnam Inc.

First Printing, July 2002
10 9 8 7 6 5 4 3 2 1

FICTION FOR THE WAY WE LIVE

REGISTERED TRADEMARK—MARCA REGISTRADA

LIBRARY OF CONGRESS CATALOGING-IN-PUBLICATION DATA
Barrientos, Tanya Maria.
Frontera street / Tanya Maria Barrientos.
p. cm.
ISBN 0-451-20635-5 (trade pbk. : alk. paper)
1. Mexican American women—Fiction. 2. Female friendship—Fiction. 3. Ethnic relations—Fiction. 4. Single mothers—Fiction. 5. Texas—Fiction. I. Title.

PS3602.A837 F76 2002
813'.6—dc21   2002022784

Printed in the United States of America
Set in Adobe Garamond
Designed by Ginger Legato

Printed in the United States of America

To my parents,
who built the ladder for me

Acknowledgments

My endless gratitude to Judi Kauffman, who believed in Alma and Dee even when I didn't; Elinor Lipman, for being such a great role model; and Lauren Cowen, who is always an inspiration. A heartfelt thank-you to my family of friends—Jeff, Chris, Lil, Dave, Ellen, Janice, Stephanie, Karen, Wendy, Annette, Macarena, and of course, Ted—who took this long trip with me, and to current and former colleagues at the *Philadelphia Inquirer,* especially Maxwell E. P. King and Avery Rome. A prayer of thanks to the late Josie Gimble, who selflessly shared her magical place in the mountains, and the late Alethea Glimp, who is always in my heart.

A special thanks to James Rahn and the Rittenhouse Writers Group, for welcoming me into the fold; the Pennsylvania Council on the Arts; and the Pew Fellowship in the Arts.

Besos to John M. Talbot, the agent from heaven, and editor Genny Ostertag, who groomed my work with loving precision.

And finally, a loving embrace to Jack Booth, the strong and sturdy anchor of my life.

Muchismas Gracias.

Part One

Chapter 1

DEE

THERE ARE FOURTEEN VERB TENSES IN SPANISH, SO MUCH MORE than the past, present, and future. That's what it said in the first sentence of the paperback I bought, thinking I just needed to brush up.

Speaking real Spanish never mattered much before. Any kitchen-scrap approximation got me, and everyone else in Los Cielos, what we wanted. It got the beds made. It got the lawn mowed. And when we sat inside restaurants across the border, it got us private stock tequila instead of the watered-down stuff pawned off on the *turistas*. But the more I read, the more I realized that what I'd been speaking most of my life wasn't Spanish at all. It was nonsense.

Real Spanish has verb tenses that English never even considers. Like the imperfect subjunctive, which is all about uncertainty. *Esperaba*/**She hoped**/*que aprendiendo español*/**that learning Spanish**/*cambiara todo*/**would change everything.**

All the fear and anxiety, all the cloying expectation of not knowing what's ahead, are stuffed into the verb like the springy plastic grass inside a wicker Easter basket. There's no hesitation, either, no little dance around the possibility that a thick, dark cloud of risk might be hovering over everything. In Spanish the imperfect subjunctive assumes that it probably is.

There should be a verb tense like that in English, because those are the only kind of words that could fully describe what happened today when I found myself standing at the button counter of Frontera Street Fabrics, handing the HELP WANTED sign to a salesgirl.

"It fell?" the salesgirl asked.

"No. I took it down."

She glanced over my shoulder toward the front door, where bits of dried-out masking tape still clung to the glass.

"I'll put it back," she said, stepping out from behind the cash register.

"Wait. You don't understand." I stopped her. "I want the job."

She leaned toward me, as if getting closer might help her grasp the situation. Black-handled scissors tied around her neck with a narrow strip of red grosgrain ribbon dangled between us like a silver exclamation point.

"I'm sorry . . . my English . . ."

I pulled the cardboard sign out of her hand and pointed to the hand-lettered message.

"*El trabajo*," I said. My West Texas accent made the word "job" sound like "backhoe." I pointed to myself. Then to the sign, and back to myself.

"I want the job . . . Me . . . *El trabajo*."

"Yes? Sure. Okay," she stammered. "I'll get the manager."

I don't know how I ended up at the fabric shop, or what I was even doing in that particular part of town. I bought the Spanish book thinking I could use something to occupy my mind. But the rest happened in a fog, like everything that's taken place in these hazy weeks after Mitch's death. The first few pages said that Spanish has two past tenses. The simplest is the preterit, also called the "definite" past. Direct and unchangable, the preterit gets right to the point. *Mitch died three months ago of a cerebral aneurysm.* It's a verb tense as honest as bleached bones in the desert. *I buried my husband on my twenty-eighth birthday.* An action completed. Bones picked clean.

I've been back in Los Cielos for twelve days, and I'm still not sure what I'm looking to find. On most days I simply wander and, after buying the book, I suppose I wandered right into the barrio, where normally I'd never go. People say I haven't been myself, which could very well be true, because inside I haven't felt like anyone at all.

In a border town people stay on their own sides of things. Living near each other has nothing to do with living together. That's the way it has been since the city of Los Cielos rose out of the sandy banks of the Rio Grande, and most folks in my hometown—Mexican and white alike—could never picture a day when things might be different. I couldn't either, but something made me pick up that Spanish book anyway. The same muddy logic that took me to Frontera Street, I suppose.

Everybody on our side of Los Cielos was supposed to learn basic Spanish in grade school, as a nod to the fact that we lived on the line. But nobody took the weekly *yo hablo español* classes seriously. By seventh grade anyone with ambition transferred over to French. Speaking French proved to college recruiters that even though you lived in West Texas, you might be smart enough to get out. I was, and except for the usual holiday visits, I stayed away until Mitch died. That was when I came back, unsure why and unsure for how long. Since the funeral, just getting through the wide desert of a single day seemed like success. I marched through the motions like an ant in an ant farm, separated from the world by a dull wall of numbness.

She drove to the bank. She made herself lunch. She cut the sandwich in a pretty diagonal, as if there was somebody there to care about the presentation.

She threw it away.

I watched myself go places I had never been and do things I would never do. So winding up inside Frontera Street Fabrics, on the wrong side of town, speaking bad Spanish and asking for a job in a place I didn't belong, made as much sense as anything else.

She did it and I watched her.

I looked around the shop. Bolts of fabric were perched upright and arranged in wagon-wheel circles on top of six huge tables that flanked the main aisle. There were cotton, and wool and jersey knit, every common fabric in every color imaginable. In the back, next to the button and ribbon counter, was the fabric too good for everyday clothes. Back there nothing was peppered with flowers or polka dots or zoo animals. Everything was plain and beautiful.

To my left were eight bolts of China silk that was woven so tight it glimmered. To my right were long rolls of heavy satin, in no fewer than seven shades of white and ivory, extra wide for wedding dresses. Rolls of upholstery vinyl, in tans and reds and greens, were tethered to the wall like ladder rungs stretching to the ceiling. And tucked into bins that were squeezed in between everything else were precut lengths of tulle, lamé, and velvet.

Women walked through the store touching everything. I watched one take a fistful of a plaid-patterned rayon and squeeze it tight. She opened her hand and watched the fabric spring back to life and slither out of her grasp. She was testing for wrinkles.

There was no music, which made the rasp of the customers' shuffling feet and the rustle of their shopping bags punctuate their moves. Every few minutes I heard the heartbeat thud of a heavy fabric bolt being rolled out, the wool or organza being stretched and measured along the yellow wooden yardsticks that were nailed to the edge of the cutting table. That was followed quickly by the high-pitched squeal of scissor blades slicing through the weave in one quick sweep.

I heard English only here and there.

It was the sort of place my husband, Mitch, always wanted to find when we visited Los Cielos, an instant photo of border life developing into sun-drenched sharpness in front of his eyes.

"*Ando buscando* terry cloth, *y unos* hook and eyes," one customer told a saleswoman, pointing to the backside of the Butterick pattern she'd just picked up.

"*Por allá*, over there in notions," the red-aproned clerk replied, waving her hand in an arc toward the rotating racks of snaps and zippers.

When the store owner, Septima Guzman, came out to meet me I offered bits of truth about myself, hiding my lies in the pieces I left out. I told her my husband was gone, and she didn't question how or why.

Septima was about twenty years older than me, judging from the hint of fatigue around her eyes. Middle age was robbing her round face of the plumpness of youth, but there was a serenity that seemed to keep the sharpest angles at bay. I saw strength in her hands as she wrote my name on a bright yellow job application. We were seated at a card table near the back of the store.

"Dee— Dee Paxton," I answered her first question.

"Your address?"

Septima's accent was a thick mix of Mexico's quick music and Texas's slow drawl. I gave her a post office box instead of a street. She stopped moving the pen and looked at me straight on. There was something about her soft gaze that, for an instant, delivered me out of the fog. For the first time since Mitch's funeral I wondered what I looked like. I couldn't remember if I'd bothered to brush my hair, or for how many days I'd been wearing the same sloppy combination of clothes.

Normally, I would have shrunk from such directness, but Septima's face served up the stillness of a church altar, and even if it lasted only for a moment, I wanted to let the fresh air of clarity wash over me like cool water. I took a deep breath and Septima smiled.

"You know how to sew." She made it a fact instead of a question.

"Sure," I said.

It wasn't exactly a lie. My mother had taught me the essentials, and when I was thirteen I'd made a pair of pumpkin-colored culottes with a zipper down the front. Of course, I'd only worn them once, because when I sat down the crotch cut deep between my legs and the back ballooned out like a parachute.

"I know how to knit, too." I went ahead and gilded the lily.

Septima said I could start that afternoon. Six dollars an hour and one Saturday off each month. She folded the application and stuffed it into her apron.

"You speak Spanish?" she asked.

"I'm learning."

She stood up and slowly made her way back to the cash register, instinctively tidying this and that. She stopped only once, looked back at me and said, "I know."

A saleswoman named Alma passed me a red apron sealed inside a plastic bag marked "medium." She was the same person I had handed the sign to when I wandered in.

"You can decorate it any way you want, as long as you put your name on the left. Up here," she said, pointing to just below her collarbone. On her apron "Alma" was spelled out in rolling cursive letters made of the tiny pearl buttons that used to be standard on ladies' kid gloves.

"You're going to start in buttons, with me," she said.

Her English was full of fat vowels and abrupt stops. It sounded as if, were it ever allowed off its leash, it might bound away and turn into a language without rules.

"I'm Dee," I told her.

"Okay." She nodded.

I got the feeling that Alma didn't understand if Dee was actually my name, or some letter of the alphabet I pulled out of the air. And the tone of her voice made me think that she didn't really care. I decided to try again, drenching my words in as much friendliness as I could muster.

"That's my name . . . Dee."

"Okay," she said again. "I'm Alma. That's Pilar." She pointed to a reedy young woman plunging scissors across a wide stretch of dark green denim.

Alma was small, with curvy hips and gently sloping shoulders. Her clothes—faded gabardine pants and a thin white schoolgirl-type blouse—fit as if she had once weighed more, and her long black hair cascaded over the back of her apron in a thick braid that reached the middle of her back. She was closer to my age than Septima was, and distinctively attractive. Her skin was the color of twine, and her face was dominated by a pair of amazing eyes, cut-glass starbursts of golden brown that played beautifully off her slim terra-cotta lips and smooth cheekbones.

I pulled the stiff red apron over my head and tied the side ribbons into loose bows.

"I can start now," I announced.

Alma walked up and down the store aisle filing dozens of cards of buttons between her outstretched fingers with incredible speed, instantly categorizing them by color and size. When her hands were full, she turned to face a wall of drawers that rose up behind us. Each drawer had one button glued to its front, and from a few steps away they looked like the mosaic ruins of Pompeii. The top row, just above Alma's eye level and too high to reach without the help of a footstool, was devoted to white rounds. At the far left were the tiny glove buttons that Alma had used to decorate her apron. Drawer by drawer they grew in diameter, expanding from seed-sized shirt buttons to nickel-sized smock accents and, eventually, to wide coat clasps requiring the heaviest of thread.

The row under the whites was for the yellows, and then black and dark blue, followed by red and green. There was a row for brass and one for silver, which somewhere down the line switched to copper. After that came the novelty buttons—the toggles and rosebuds, the carved-brass lion faces and glow-in-the-dark goblins.

Finally, there were the expensive "selects," the shimmering wafers of mother-of-pearl, the heavy sterling silver drops made by the Navajos, and the hand-cut Austrian crystals, each sold separately and laid out in front of a customer like jewelry on black velvet.

"Somebody has to be in buttons all the time. Okay? You can't leave without getting Pilar to stand in for you," Alma instructed in a flat voice as she grabbed more button cards out of a red plastic bucket marked with a sign that said: PUT UNWANTED BUTTONS HERE.

Once again she fanned the cards out like a poker player checking her hand. Then she proceeded to match each card to its proper drawer.

"*Oiga*, Alma!" A woman approached the counter holding a colorful bouquet of filmy chiffon.

"Get ready, *tú*, it's that time of year again!" the woman exclaimed as she placed five squares of the sheer fabric in a line on the counter—two shades of rose, one violet, an autumn gold, and a black. The woman was dressed in a red velour sweat suit that had a wide green ribbon around the middle and made her look like a lumpy Christmas present. She had bifocals pushed far up on her forehead and was carrying a huge black tote bag with straps mummified in masking tape.

"*Ay mijita*, already?" Alma began, welcoming her overdramatic customer.

"You believe it?" The woman rubbed her temples.

The woman fished a stack of fashion magazines out of her bag and Alma, for the first time in forty-five minutes, stood perfectly still, leaning on the counter with her elbows.

"*Y, esta?*" The woman nodded her head in my direction, allowing her eyeglasses to sink back down to her nose. She pushed them into their proper position while giving me a quick inspection. Her bag fell open on the countertop.

"Dee, this is Lettie Sanchez." Alma gestured toward me and then back toward Lettie. "She makes the wardrobes for a lot of the Miss Sun Carnival pageant girls."

"Twenty years now," Lettie added, as she licked the tip of her thumb and index finger and paged through a well-worn *Modern Bride*. "I've dressed four Miss Suns and two Miss Texases. Remember Laurita Caldero, Alma? The one who made top ten at Miss America?"

"That's before I lived here," Alma answered.

"Well, she would have gone further if she'd listened to me and put her hair up when she wore the halter-top gown, instead of letting it flop around like a kitchen mop."

Lettie smoothed out a page in the wrinkled magazine with a swipe of her thick palm. "Okay, here. *Mira!*" She slapped the magazine onto the counter in front of Alma.

"*That's* what I'm going to put Socorro in one day." Lettie's flamingo-pink fingernail landed on a photo of a burgundy velvet sheath with an off-the-shoulder shawl collar.

"*Qué te parece?*" Lettie asked.

Alma took the magazine in both hands, looked at the pale, red-headed model in the picture, and laughed.

"Look, I haven't even started talking to her about the *quinceañera.* Don't be putting ideas in her head already," she warned. "She doesn't have enough to hold up a dress like that, anyway."

"Just wait, *tú*, she's filling out good," Lettie teased, giving me a wink.

"Who's Socorro?" I wanted to catch up with the conversation before it rolled on to the next topic.

"Oh," Alma said, giving me more than a glance for the first time all day. "That's my daughter."

In Spanish there is one pronoun set aside for formal relationships. *Usted.* Every conversation between strangers begins with it, out of respect. *Cómo está usted? Muy bien, y usted?* Young people use it to speak to their elders, and maids use it to speak to their employers' entire families, even the ones in diapers. *Usted* establishes distance.

If a conversation is going well, one speaker will quickly slip out of *usted* and into *tú.* It's a linguistic welcome mat, a door swung open. *Mi casa es tú casa.* There's nothing like it in English, but that didn't stop Alma from letting me know she hadn't offered me the friendly familiarity of *tú.* She didn't need Spanish to shut her door.

There was something about me that hit Alma all wrong. We both felt it immediately, and while I tried to wade through the rough water, Alma let it rise until there was a wide, choppy river between us.

Chapter 2

ALMA

SOCORRO HEARS NO HARSHNESS IN THE BULKY WORDS OF ENglish. She believes the American legend of George Washington and his tree of cherries. *Y por qué no?* She's an American. She knows nothing about the *brujas* who live in the invisible winds or the spirits who hide in the coyotes' eyes. She believes the stories her teachers tell about a shot heard around the world, and Abraham Lincoln returning a library book in the snow. She is *pura Americana*—red, white, and brown.

As a little girl she was satisfied with the flimsy family history I provided, a past that did not go beyond the happy stories of my childhood Christmases, and quiet summers in the cool Mexican mountains. She believes her grandparents are in heaven, because that is what I've told her. As she grew older, she asked to know more. I said God had led us out of Mexico just before she was born, and when she asked about her father, I told her that his name was Paul Walker and he was a good man. Now, almost fifteen, she is demanding to hear the rest. I know the day is coming when I will have to tell her my whole story, *mi cuento Mexicáno,* including the sin and sorrow that brought us to this side of the border and left us *perdidas y encontradas*, lost and found. But, I hesitate because it is full of so many shortcomings, regrettable truths that are bound to change how she feels, about him and about me.

I had no idea why Septima hired the *gringa* when it was clear she didn't belong with people like us. Blond and tan, she looked more like a wife from the west side of town than a worker from our neighborhood.

She needed help, Sepi told me, but people like Dee have their own places to go when their lives fall apart, clinics with pretty lawns and exercise rooms. What was she doing at a fabric shop in the barrio? She had to be in the kind of trouble that makes a person want to hide from the world. And I, for one, didn't need that kind of mess in my life. So I ignored her as much as I could, figuring she'd be gone in less than a week.

That Saturday morning, as I got ready for work, I heard Socorro talking on the telephone in a groggy, slow-motored meter. With her back to me and the phone cord coiled around her shoulders, I could see Paul Walker's outline in my girl's long legs and the way she leaned into one hip more than the other. I watched her fidget inside the oversized T-shirt she wore as a nightgown. As a little girl she was all angles and sharp edges, but now her corners were melting into curves and she wasn't quite used to the new softness. Lately I'd found myself staring at her, silently celebrating each step of the amazing change and wondering how different we'd both be when it was finished. She felt my presence and turned to look.

"Peeps is going to that thing today. Can I go with him?" She tossed the question over her shoulder. Peeps, who lived two doors down, got his nickname because of his bad eyesight. He and Socorro had been playmates since before they could walk, and sometimes Socorro used me as an excuse to avoid doing boring things with him. So I wasn't sure if yes was the right answer.

Socorro kept the phone to her ear and pumped her head up and down, prompting me to approve.

"What's this thing again?" I asked.

"Mom, it's Peeps's audition at Arts High?" Her tone questioned how I could have forgotten such an important occasion. It was true, Peeps had been practicing for months, filling Frontera Street with the low moans of his French horn, giving us all a crash course in Mozart whether we wanted it or not. Nobody in the neighborhood knew if he was any good, but according to his orchestra teacher, he had natural talent.

The teacher was a young man who, like most of the new ones, attacked his job like a calling from God. Before the school year even started he'd walked from door to door on Frontera Street, introducing himself to parents, ducking both the beer bottles and the insults that the teenage boys threw at him. We'd seen so many do-gooders come through the neighborhood before, each of them preaching that one person could make a difference. Then we'd watched them abandon the difference-making when a better job came along. So the young teacher's plans seemed like nothing more than empty talk, until the kids told us that he'd fought the school district to get more than drums, flutes, and trumpets for the orchestra.

When the new instruments arrived, Peeps traded in his trumpet for the French horn because, to him, it looked like a coiled lasso and sounded like something that might have announced duels between knights in armor. Other kids walked home with trombones, saxophones, and cellos. Socorro's best friend, Cece Cardenas, even played the English horn for three weeks, until she decided the bleating-goat sound that it made had nothing to do with England and she quit.

"Richard is driving," Socorro said, using the teacher's first name, the only one he went by.

"Okay," I answered, still not sure why she wanted to go, since she had never shown much interest in music.

"Okay," she repeated into the phone before hanging up and heading to her bedroom to change.

When I got home from work late that afternoon she was still away, and that's when I got the phone call.

"*Una vaca! Una vaca!*" Richard the orchestra teacher was shouting into the receiver, thinking the louder he spoke the more sense he'd make. "Arts High. They want to give her *una vaca!*"

"A cow?" I answered. "Somebody wants to give her a cow?"

"Ummm. No." Richard reined his voice back into normal speaking range. "*Una* . . . what's the word I'm looking for?"

It was always a toss-up with the new teachers. Either they insisted on speaking to us in rickety Spanish that they learned in one week from a cassette tape, thinking that whatever they came up with had to be better than our English or they refused to utter a single syllable in Spanish. Those were the ones who believed Latinos held on to their language only out of spite, and if we would just stop being so disrespectful and start speaking English all of the time we'd see how much more America had to offer.

I usually let the Spanish speakers tie themselves into knots while I gave them puzzled looks. Then, when I felt they'd embarrassed themselves enough, I would very softly say: "Maybe it would be easier for you if we spoke in English."

Not that my English was perfect, but I'd been studying it since elementary school and having grown up in Cuernavaca, a town famous for its language institutes, I'd been surrounded by it most of my life. And Paul, of course, had taught me plenty.

As for the English-only types, I usually answered them in long, rambling Spanish sentences that made their blood boil.

Richard the orchestra teacher was different, though. He spent afternoons and some weekends on Frontera Street talking to entire families, respectfully apologizing for his Spanish even though it was pretty good. He was trying to learn something about each of his students' lives and, while some people thought he was just being nosy and self-righteous, I liked him because Socorro respected him. So instead of leaving him dangling on the other end of the telephone, I used the clearest and slowest Spanish I could offer to help him out.

"I think you mean *beca*. Right, Señor Richard? Do you mean *beca*?"

"*Sí, sí, beca*, not *vaca! Beca*. A scholarship. *Beca, beca*."

He repeated the word in Spanish, and then in English, hammering it into his head and, eventually, into mine.

"A scholarship?" I asked, realizing that our little word game had kept me from concentrating on what he was actually saying. "An *art* scholarship?"

"You should take the offer seriously," he said.

I wanted to know how it happened. What sort of art did Socorro know about? She couldn't draw a straight line, that much I knew from her Mother's Day cards. And what about Peeps? Wasn't he the one looking for a scholarship? What happened to him at the audition?

"Look, I don't want to steal Socorro's thunder," Richard replied. "Let her tell you when she gets home. We can discuss the details later. Here's my number."

That night La Llorona appeared. It wasn't a dream. I felt her presence in the wind that rushed through my window and quickly built into an angry sea of mist around my bed.

She is supposed to be a fable, a folk tale rolled out by the fireside like bedclothes. The story says that La Llorona—the wailing woman—was a plain and humble village girl who fell in love with a nobleman. He bought her a house. He gave her his love and, in time, made her the mother of his two children. But because of his high social position and her deep poverty, he never married her. And one day he told her that his family had arranged for him to marry someone else. She would have to learn to live without him.

She grew enraged and consumed by jealousy. Unable to cope with her bitterness, La Llorona tossed her children into the river. Then she drowned herself.

At God's feet, the young mother was told she could not enter heaven until she found her children's lost souls. So she searches eternally. Children are told that La Llorona roams the earth looking for naughty youngsters to snatch and claim as her own.

That's the myth. The truth is different. It is not the children whom La Llorona haunts. It is their mothers.

The first time she came to me was in Mexico. I was twenty years old, still unmarried and secretly carrying Socorro in my womb. At first I was convinced the vision was a nightmare, a shadowy hallucination fueled by fear of my father's anger and by guilt over my mother's humiliation. But when the Dark One spoke, I knew she was more than a dream. Her voice dripped with venom, and her breath rose like steam from the cradle of Satan's lair.

"This child was conceived in the filthy sweat of sin and passion," she bellowed. "It will be born with a red stain of lust. Give it to me, now!"

She stretched her hand toward me, her jagged fingers glowing like the desert sand in a full moon's light. I curled into a ball, pulling my knees close to my chest, but I couldn't stop her from reaching inside.

I looked at the little statue of La Virgen de Guadalupe that I kept on my dresser.

"Maria Purísima!" I pleaded. "Save my baby! She is tearing it right out of me!" Deep sobs racked my shoulders, and screams strained my throat. I clutched the gold crucifix that my grandmother had brought to me from the Vatican on my first Holy Communion. "Hail Mary, full of grace . . ."

La Llorona laughed at my desperation, and I prayed louder. She cackled, rattling the windows and shaking the walls. Didn't Mami and Papi hear me?

I don't know how many hours I pleaded with God, or how long I fought La Llorona's grip. But just before dawn, when the promise of daylight seeped through the window shades, I opened my eyes and saw my little Virgencita standing strong beneath a crown of the purest light I have ever known. My blessed saint was the only one who didn't judge. She stood beside me when I told my father that I didn't need a husband, her loving embrace protected me and my baby when we left, and she gave us the strength to cross the border. She continued to watch over us as we planted roots in this new soil and began a new life.

But suddenly La Llorona was back. Why, after so many years? Socorro was not a baby anymore. Far from it. What could the dark witch want with her now?

"This time Socorro will come to me on her own," La Llorona thundered. Her growl was so deep it shook the floor. She laughed when I reached for La Virgencita, who seemed too old and fragile to protect us.

"She will turn away from you and come to me." The spirit's words rushed toward me like a mad dog, and I could taste the sour mash of my own fear rising in the back of my throat. What had I done to bring her back?

Chapter 3

DEE

"THIS IS YOUR THIRD WEEK, AND IF YOU'RE GOING TO STAY YOU have to take this off."

Septima peeled back the strip of masking tape that I'd been using as a name tag since my arrival. Everybody else had their names sewn permanently into the left side of their red smocks, and it was clear they had put considerable thought into the designs. Septima had created a large *S* out of baby rickrack and had embroidered the rest of her name between the curves. Pilar had wrapped yellow ribbon around a needle and, with a few nips and tucks, had made a vine of roses bloom in a wavy border around the five letters of her name. Alma, of course, had used buttons.

I hadn't considered what I was going to do—whether I should use colored thread or simple white stitches, whether I should brighten the apron with sequins or get creative with patches and rivets. None of the options had occurred to me because, when I began working at the store, I was convinced the same stray wind that delivered me to Frontera Street would just as unexpectedly carry me away. But I kept coming back. I kept parking my car in the underground garage near the bank and walking five blocks to the fabric shop every morning. Soon I was a regular on the sidewalks near the downtown plaza, such a regular that the kids waiting for the school bus didn't even look up when I walked by. Such a regular that I knew exactly when the smoky smell of the breakfast chorizo sizzling on the greasy grill of La Indita luncheonette would lead me off Main Street, across Empresario Avenue and straight into the heart of a neighborhood I had ignored, or at least conspicuously avoided, for most of my life.

On my way to the shop I walked by Flores by Dolores, where the front window was decorated with a selection of cemetery wreaths and Barbie doll centerpieces with puffy gowns made out of pink and yellow chrysanthemums. I passed an appliance store that kept two loud air conditioners displayed on the sidewalk. The owner tied red and white ribbons to the machines' plastic grilles, and they flicked and snapped at passersby like lizard tongues.

Half a block from Septima's shop I passed the blind man selling Mexican lottery tickets on the honor system and the Quick Snap Photo Studio, offering a green-card-and-passport-picture package for twelve dollars.

It was the same every morning, and it wasn't long before I began to chuckle at how my momma used to say the barrio had nothing to offer people like us, except trouble. The fabric shop seemed like the perfect place to start over. Nobody there needed to know more about me than what they saw. Septima and Alma must have thought I was divorced, or even abandoned by a lover, and I didn't bother to tell them otherwise. I felt safe leaving their unspoken questions unanswered, and I wrapped the silence around me like a big black cloak.

Officially, of course, Mexico doesn't begin in downtown Los Cielos. It starts a few miles away, where the Monterey Bridge straddles the Rio Grande. Halfway across that uninspired arch of concrete a sign reads: YOU ARE LEAVING THE UNITED STATES OF AMERICA. Two paces farther a different sign offers: BIENVENIDOS A MEXICO. Nobody is sure who owns the steps in between, but just like that, the nations divide.

Anyone who has ever lived in West Texas knows the real border has nothing to do with that bridge, or the Rio Grande, or even the government. People have drawn their own lines for as long as they've been able, and in Los Cielos the true border has always been at some invisible point near Frontera Street, just past Schuster's Department Store, directly across from the downtown plaza.

That's where shop names abruptly change from Bobby O's Factory Discount Boots to Castillo de Zapatos. It's also where, every weekday as the first red ribbons of daylight stretch across the shallow Rio Grande, four tired Mexican buses limp over the Monterey Bridge's hump, down Texas Avenue, and across Main Street, hauling cheaper-than-American day workers from *el otro lado*, the other side. Like old horses following a well-worn trail, they pull up to the south side of San Elizario Plaza, where shimmering purple oil stains coat the hot pavement like melted wax. The engines shudder and sigh, as weary of the repetitive route as the dozens of dull-eyed passengers riding inside.

It is the same scene every morning. You can set your clock by it, and for decades lots of people have. Especially the Westside ladies who drive down to the plaza for the Pick-and-Pray. That's what the housewives call the once-a-week trips they make to fetch their maids. Pick a woman and pray that she won't steal the family silver.

The caravan begins early on Tuesdays with the wives rushing out of their front doors by six-thirty in order to make it downtown by seven. Any later than that and all the good ones will be gone. Plus, nobody wants to be on the road at eight o'clock, when the men get tangled up in rush hour. The entire thing is so precisely timed that by half-past seven they will all be home again and the maids will be busy stripping bed linens. Then the mothers who don't have toddlers tugging at their knees will fill their long days with round robins of tennis or golf at the Westside Country Club, or luncheons sponsored by groups that pride themselves on their devotion to civic duty.

Whenever a new family moves to the neighborhood, the Westside wives fill them in on the going Pick-and-Pray rates. Forty dollars a week from Tuesday to Saturday afternoon. Saturday evenings are negotiable, especially if there is entertaining involved. But all the *muchachas* are to be back home by Sunday morning, in plenty of time for church. Because there is, after all, a right and wrong way of treating people.

My family's longtime maid, Serita, used to stand just beyond the four iron benches at the north side of the plaza. I can't remember a time during my childhood when she wasn't there, waiting for us. As a girl I loved Serita's sturdy roundness for the comfort it offered. Her ample shoulders melted directly into the folds over her elbows, and her generous hip line was as inviting as a feather bed, especially when she sat down and offered her lap along with a blanket and her soothing Spanish lullabies.

The downtown plaza started out as the throbbing heart of a hopeful frontier town. The men who founded it set out to create a sophisticated cross between a Mexican *zócalo* and a Victorian town square. Old photos show them wearing black suits, tall black hats, and fine pocket watches, their faces weathered but triumphant, as they dedicate their creation to the blue skies of the future. They show lots of trees, too, probably the same sun-bleached and water-starved cottonwoods that the maids lean up against now. But in those photos from 1864 the trees look lush and shady, and underneath them, in the center of the old plaza, stands a glorious fountain made of hand-painted Spanish tile. Momma used to tell me that even when she was a little girl, entire families would stroll down Main Street to gaze at that fountain after Sunday services at First Baptist. Restless children would climb onto the iron fence that surrounded it with curls and dips that looked like a fine lady's handwriting. She said most folks let the children play, assured that the swirling iron gate was strong enough to keep even the rougher boys away from the two Louisiana crocs that crawled around the bottom of the fountain bowl. The plaza has never looked like that again, not since the 1950s, when the better neighborhoods of Los Cielos migrated westward and left the founders' little piece of determination behind.

By the 1970s, when I was growing up, the fountain was long gone and the plaza had become the meeting place of *los Mexicános*, with Spanish being tossed across the scrappy lawn in rapid fire and tinny radios blaring music that was broadcast from the other side of everything. The Mexican songs would seep into our cars when the maids slid into the backseats, and for a few moments the rushing currents of sad ballads, weeping accordions, and trembling voices clinging to a single note would wash over us.

Mitch grew up in New Orleans, where the past and present were allowed to simmer into a rich gumbo, and he never understood why one side of Los Cielos pretended that the other didn't exist. He always wanted to visit the plaza, to take a walk into the neighborhoods I'd never been allowed to enter, saying that I'd left the best part of my own hometown undiscovered. I let him go on his border safaris by himself, and my family would chuckle when he would return and tell us about discoveries that he believed were cultural diamonds but we knew were just mangy pieces of the barrio.

*   *   *

Not long after Septima told me to decorate my apron she announced that Alma was going to be late getting to work and that Pilar was going to be busy all morning stocking the new polyester blends.

What she was saying—without coming out and actually saying it—was that for the first time since I was hired, I was going to be alone in buttons. I walked behind the counter, but instead of feeling comfortable, I felt like I had wandered into someone else's house. For three weeks Alma had allowed me to stand back there with her, but she always made it perfectly clear that I was an uninvited guest, taking up room that could have been put to better use. Without her there, the narrow space suddenly seemed big enough to get lost in.

Selling buttons wasn't a hard job, we both knew that, but it did require a certain eye for detail, and Alma took pride in her ability to complement a fabric's weave and pattern with her selections. She could convince even the most skeptical seamstress that choosing the best buttons she could afford would make her feel better inside her clothes.

I looked for something to do, but there were no button cards in the plastic tub for me to return to the drawers, and there were no customers waiting for service. For a moment I considered taking the time to study more Spanish verbs and grammar from the little book I kept in my handbag, but when I saw Septima glance over her shoulder, checking on me, I gave up on that.

Alma kept a scrap of last year's green Christmas velvet around to use as a dustcloth. I pulled it out of the cardboard box she'd tucked under the counter and wiped everything around me. I dusted the craft magazines featuring do-it-yourself pillows covered with buttons and wiped down the diameter display cards taped to the countertop.

When I put the dustrag back under the counter, my hand brushed against something pushed far into the corner. It was a square box the size of a notebook, made of wood. I pulled it out and saw that the lid and sides were decorated with uneven carvings, vines and flowers that someone not at all comfortable with cutting tools had sliced into the grain. The tiny brass clasp—a latch shaped like a question mark—was bent and, instead of sliding into the hook underneath it, passed just over it, keeping the lid slightly ajar. I knew the box probably belonged to Alma and she was keeping it secret for a reason. Still, I opened it.

Septima was at the other end of the shop, holding a clipboard and checking off each bolt of polyester blend that Pilar pulled out of a shipping crate. Only two customers were in the store, and they were sitting at the tables near the Ultra Suede, slowly leafing through pattern books.

Inside the box I found some unopened letters, two photographs, and a tarnished silver *milagro* medal shaped like a tiny hammer. I'd seen the miniature medals before, nailed onto crosses and, more recently, decorating high-priced furniture that designers sold as Santa Fe style. But I knew Alma wasn't using this one as a piece of art. In Mexico the medals are used as religious charms, a cross between a voodoo doll and a prayer card. People find a medal that represents whatever they are praying for and when their prayer has been answered they nail the medal onto a crucifix in their home, or they sometimes place it at the feet of their favorite saint.

Lots of crosses for sale in antique stores along the border are encrusted with a lifetime worth of prayers, in the shapes of arms and legs and houses and baby carriages. But I couldn't recall ever seeing a tiny hammer like the one Alma had stored away in the box, clearly still waiting for an answer.

I put the medal down and picked up the sealed envelopes. They were all addressed to the same person.

Paul Walker, P.O. Box 529, Scottsdale, Arizona.

The handwriting on the blue-tinted paper was cramped and lurched to the right. I had never heard Alma mention the name, but that didn't mean anything—she never told me about her life anyway.

I wanted her to like me, and I think that is why I kept coming back to the fabric shop, why I stood behind the button counter and kept quiet when she spoke to her friends as if I weren't there. It was why I asked her if she would explain some of the more confusing rules of Spanish grammar that I came across in the paperback that I carried around like a worn Gideon's Bible. And why I didn't push when she refused, saying that people who grow up speaking a language don't ever know the rules, they just speak.

It wasn't unusual for us to get through an entire day with conversations built on two words or less.

"Black crescents?" I'd ask.

"Wood or plastic?" she'd answer.

"Glass."

"Fifth row."

At first I thought she was shy because her English wasn't very good, but I learned soon enough that she both spoke and understood English better than she let on. She wasn't shy around her friends at all. When they came into the store her entire bearing changed. She gossiped with gusto, and as she spoke I watched her shoulders soften and her cold glances thaw.

Of course, I knew she wouldn't appreciate that I was poking through the contents of the little box. I was trespassing on property that I wasn't even supposed to know existed, trampling a trust I hadn't even won yet. I knew I should stop. But I couldn't.

I picked up the photographs. One curled in on itself like a cocoon. I smoothed out the corners. It was an old black-and-white snapshot of two people—a dark-skinned man with a heavy mustache in a crisp, dark suit with a rosebud pinned onto the narrow lapel and a delicate-boned woman in a satin Marilyn Monroe–type dress that pinched at the waist and clung all the way to the middle of her calves. The woman had her hair up in what must have been a loose French twist, and her hands were clasped around a limp pair of white gloves. Uneasy in front of the camera, the young couple were touching only at their elbows and shoulders, yet their eyes were electric with emotion. Something important had just happened, but neither the man nor the woman managed to smile about it. It was, I decided, a wedding portrait, taken at the very instant the young lovers conceived the enormity of the promises they'd made. I recognized the look in their eyes.

The second photograph was lodged inside a small frame made out of Popsicle sticks held together by dried clumps of schoolhouse glue. Bits of green glitter shed onto the counter like dandruff as I pulled the color snapshot out of the box.

I'd never seen Socorro, but I knew the picture was of her. She was beautiful and completely different than I had imagined. I had envisioned a wide-bodied girl because of the stories I'd overheard Alma tell her regular customers—stories about her headstrong daughter's adolescent stubbornness, her unpredictable moods, and her drive to shove harder, shout louder, and even fight tougher than the neighborhood boys. Yet the child in the photo was hardly more than a puff of smoke.

She was looking over her shoulder at the camera, as if somebody had just called out her name. A breeze had lifted her long hair and sent it flowing around a Valentine-shaped face. Her skin color was what people called olive when they didn't feel like saying dark brown. She looked like lots of other Mexican American girls, except for her eyes, which set her apart. They were clear instead of dark, not a gem green but the wintry tint of sagebrush leaves, surrounded by thick crowns of dark lashes.

Alma had, of course, never spoken directly to me about Socorro. But she told Septima everything, from what Socorro did or didn't eat for breakfast, to how she found her in the kitchen late one night, shaving her legs for the first time with one foot propped up against the kitchen sink and a handful of green Palmolive liquid smeared from ankle to thigh. Her stories were buckets full of pride and exasperation, pulled up daily from a deep well of tenderness.

The most recent news I'd heard about Socorro was that she and a boy named Peeps had been awarded scholarships to Arts High School. Alma mentioned it to Septima on a Monday morning, and by that same afternoon she was accepting congratulations from customers who came in to say they'd heard all about it from their children, who had heard it from someone else's kids.

"Elena *me dijo* that Socorro sang with a voice *tan fuerte* that all the windows rattled," one customer boasted.

"No! That's not the story," another one argued. "I heard that she sat down and sketched a bowl of fruit so detailed that you could see the juice inside the green grapes."

Alma and Septima laughed at how the simple facts had been passed from one woman to another and whipped like a bowl of egg batter. Out of politeness, or maybe curiosity, Alma patiently listened to every version of the story, no matter how exaggerated, before setting the record straight.

"What else did you hear?" Septima prodded.

"She has a full scholarship, that's what I heard," yet another customer reported, adding: "Richard the music teacher said he already has plans to try and get more scholarships next year. And Benita Quintanilla says her daughter, Norma, is practically guaranteed a spot because she cleans house for the vice principal. But I don't know who she thinks she's fooling, because that girl walks like an iguana, and is starting to look like one, too!"

"Well, I don't know about that," Alma jumped in, rescuing the discussion from sliding into a debate over what other reptiles poor little Norma might favor. "Most of what you heard is right," she confirmed, "except her scholarship is for dance."

"Dance?"

Alma nodded.

"I didn't know Socorro could dance."

"Me either," Alma answered, raising her eyebrows and throwing her hands open.

She explained that Socorro had gone to the audition only to keep Peeps company. He had asked her to be there because whenever he gets nervous his lips go numb and he can't press them together properly to play his French horn. He thought if Socorro could be in the audience he might stay calm, but when they got to the school Peeps was told to line up with the other musicians and Socorro wasn't allowed to even stand next to him.

Alma had everyone's attention as she continued to tell, in both English and Spanish, how it happened.

A teacher told Socorro that she would have to wait for Peeps outside, and got another student to walk her to the door. On her way out, Socorro glanced back over her shoulder and saw poor Peeps standing at the end of the long line of trumpeters, trombonists, and baritone players, smacking his lips in sheer terror.

Socorro had never seen a school like Arts High. The buildings were spread out over a huge island of green grass, watered by automatic sprinklers, and tended so carefully that if it weren't for the dusty desert hills just across the street, you'd never know you were in West Texas. There were tennis courts and greenhouses and even a swimming pool with not just one but two diving boards.

Inside each building, different auditions were in progress. Socorro walked from one to the other, observing. She saw students pacing in the hallways as they mumbled lines from plays they had memorized. She heard waves of violin solos and snippets of piano pieces escaping from behind closed doors. Alma said Socorro eventually walked into the gymnasium to take a seat in the bleachers and wait for Peeps. There, she saw girls in pink tights and black leotards taking turns leaping and twirling diagonally across the floor. The teacher was dressed in the same outfit, except hers included a black chiffon skirt that brushed against her knees. She walked from one end of the gym to the other, keeping time by pounding a black cane against the floor.

The teacher stopped in mid-beat when she saw Socorro walk in. "You're very late!" she yelled at her.

Socorro tried to explain that she wasn't there to audition, but the teacher, who spoke with a heavy Russian accent, didn't understand.

"Shh. Shh. Shh. Clothes? Shoes? Where are they?" the angry teacher demanded.

Socorro walked down onto the dance floor to try and explain, but the teacher hooked her walking cane into the crook of Socorro's elbow and pulled her into line with the other dancers.

"Take off shoes. Take off! Take off!" the teacher commanded, clapping her hands impatiently.

Socorro tried to speak up.

"No. No speak. Shhh. We continue," the teacher said, resuming the steady pounding.

Going through the movements, Socorro felt like a cow on ice compared to the other girls, who not only could slide their feet into awkward positions without falling over, but could move their heads and arms in different ways at the same time. The only two things Socorro was good at were the split-legged leaps and a balancing exercise that required her to stand on one leg while raising the other as high as possible.

After each exercise the teacher walked up to one or two girls, tapped them on their shoulders with her cane, and said, "Thank you." They left the floor immediately and either sat in the bleachers silently watching the rest of the audition or dashed into the locker room, crying. Socorro said she waited for the Russian to tap her on the shoulder, but that never happened. Every time the teacher dismissed somebody else, Socorro felt that girl aim a dirty look her way. At one point, according to Alma's version of the story, Socorro tried to walk off the floor. She'd had enough. But the teacher scolded her again.

"No. No quit. You dance now!"

The audition took an hour, and in the end Socorro was left standing with five other girls. The sweat she'd worked up made her shorts and T-shirt cling to her back and thighs.

"Congratulations," the teacher told Socorro and the five other finalists, handing each of them a manila envelope filled with forms.

"Fill out. See you in class," the teacher said before she turned and walked away.

The other girls squealed and hugged one another. Socorro took her envelope and went to find Richard and Peeps.

She found them standing by Richard's car, worried that she had gotten lost. Peeps had an envelope in his hand, too.

Richard told Alma that the ballet teacher believed Socorro had enough natural talent to catch up with the rest of the dancers within a year.

"All I know," Alma told the customers listening to the story, "is that Socorro wants to go, so I'll let her."

I looked at the photograph of Socorro in the Popsicle stick frame and understood what the dance teacher saw—a willowy strength coiled up like a tight spring inside elastic arms and legs. She was the kind of daughter Mitch and I used to whisper in the dark about having—chosen by God to move like a melody. I studied her picture closer and began to hear Mitch whispering something to me that I couldn't make out. His voice was tempered, deep and low, but his words were as murky as unsettled water.

"I said, what are you doing with that?"

It wasn't Mitch who was speaking to me at all. It was Alma. She was standing at the far end of the counter, her arms crossed and her face raw with anger.

Her eyes dared me to explain why I had her things spread out like a casual game of solitaire.

"What the hell are you doing with that?" she demanded as she snatched the photograph out of my hand.

"I found it," I murmured in weak defense.

"You think you can walk in here and do whatever the hell you want, don't you?"

She grabbed the wooden box and glared at me as she put each of the items back inside it.

"Septima might feel sorry for you, but I don't. You got that? I don't give a damn what sort of trouble you got yourself into. We've got plenty of our own troubles around here. So don't think I'm going to protect you *para nada*! If somebody comes in here looking for you—I don't care what sort of *cabrón* he might be—I'm just gonna point straight at you and say, here, you can have her."

Startled and unsteady, I stood back as Alma pushed her way behind the counter to put the box back where she'd hidden it.

"Around here you're not better than anyone."

I thought she was going to slap me, and I prepared myself for the sting.

I backed up against the button drawers and saw her raise her fists.

I gulped mouthfuls of air to try and stop the wrenching sobs that made my rib cage ache. I wiped my face with the tail of my red apron, and then I felt my knees give way as a tidal wave of nausea swept over me. A sharp pain in my abdomen knocked me to the ground.

The vomit burned like acid and then everything went black.

Chapter 4

ALMA

SEPTIMA RUSHED ACROSS THE FLOOR AND ORDERED PILAR TO call an ambulance. The two customers who had been thumbing through pattern books stopped, packed up their belongings, and left. They kept their eyes away from the spot where Dee had curled herself into a ball, as if by not looking they might be able to keep out of it. Part of me wanted to run out with them.

"Two blocks off Empresario Avenue, on the busy end of Frontera . . ."

Pilar was giving directions over the phone.

Septima knelt down and removed the stained apron from around Dee's neck. She lifted Dee's head into her own lap and gently brushed the tangled knots of blond hair away from Dee's face.

"Tell them she's breathing, but she's barely conscious!" Septima shouted to Pilar.

Dee groaned. Her eyelids fluttered. I had no idea what was happening. If she had fainted her body would be limp, her breathing steady. But she was rigid, her muscles tense. I wondered if I had brought on the attack. I hadn't hit her, but I knew I'd scared her pretty good. I listened to Pilar's voice on the phone. She was saying everything twice, answering questions from the other end. The situation was serious. Dee wasn't reacting to Septima's attempts to get her back on her feet. Pilar put the phone down and stood frozen in place. None of us knew what to do next.

"Alma, get a wet paper towel," Septima said.

My heart was pounding in my head. I couldn't swallow, and instead of racing, my mind was slow. I tried to move as fast as Septima's voice demanded, but my body was trapped inside an invisible net. I looked down at my shoes and silently ordered them to move, but nothing happened. I clutched my thighs and squeezed them to make sure they hadn't gone numb. I had to will my heels to move.

When I finally reached the bathroom I didn't bother to yank the silver chain that would switch on the bare bulb dangling between the sink and the toilet. It seemed like too much effort. Dee was hurt and, from the sound of her cries, in serious pain. I had been only two steps away from her when the spasms threw her to the ground. I watched as she crumpled, her back and shoulders heaving from the nausea. I should have felt bad. I should have felt scared. Even sorry. But I felt nothing.

For the first few moments I actually was happy she was hurting. It wasn't until Septima and Pilar began to snap like electric wires that I thought Dee might be in real trouble.

"Alma!" Septima called out again. "Get two towels! Hurry!"

My right hand reached for the sink, and the rest of my body dragged behind like a weight. I nudged one of the faucet handles, and a bullet of cold water shot out, hitting the pink porcelain bowl and exploding like a firecracker. The stack of stiff paper towels that I plunged underneath the steady stream of water softened and darkened as it soaked up all it could hold. Water pooled up to my wrists and helped clear my head. I knew I would be blamed for whatever happened to Dee, but it wasn't my fault. She was rummaging through my personal things, sticking her nose in places she wasn't invited.

None of us even knew where she came from, and there she was, helping herself to my secrets. She reminded me of the *gringas* like Mrs. Campbell whom I had to work for after Paul left me, back when I had to stand in the middle of the dirty downtown plaza with all the other maids, swallowing my self-respect. I had to lower my eyes and act grateful when those ladies handed me two twenty-dollar bills as payment for spending the day on my knees, cleaning their Mexican tile floors and their French antiques. They would tug at the other end of the bills before handing them over, warning that next time I should be more careful when dusting their precious crystal goblets.

I told Septima that people like Dee had their own places to go when their lives fell apart. But Sepi was the sort of person who was willing to look past unanswered questions. She was more forgiving than me. I let my suspicions pile up into a big mountain of distrust.

I could have crept out the back door of the shop right there and then, and believe me, I thought about it. But I owed Septima more than that. She was the one who hired me after Mrs. Campbell accused me of stealing. And I knew she did it out of mercy, because she had already promised the job to Lettie Sanchez.

Working for Septima was a badge of pride because she and Dolores of Flores by Dolores were the only women from the barrio with businesses downtown, and Septima was as devoted to the shop as she was to the church. She considered the fabric store a direct gift from God, and that was the only reason I had kept my mouth shut about Dee for so long. Out of pure respect.

I turned to walk out of the bathroom clutching the dripping paper towels in my hands, but when I got to the door I saw La Llorona's shrouded body blocking my way. The witch had never before appeared to me outside of my bedroom, or in the light of day. For an instant I thought I was out of my mind, but she was as sharp and as real as the ambulance siren wailing in the distance. My hands began to quiver, and an intense wave of heat swept over every other part of me. I concentrated on the sound of the siren, closed my eyes, and hoped the hallucination would disappear.

I spun back around to face the sink and dropped the paper towels into the basin. I shut my eyes and tried to steady my breathing.

La Llorona said nothing, but I felt her poison leaching into the room. Suddenly it was all clear. The dark spirit was behind what had happened. She had thrown Dee to the floor and twisted her insides into a knot, and now she had come to see how her drama would end. I was certain of it.

I held on to the smooth sides of the sink and pressed my palms against the cold porcelain, curling my fingers around its rough edge. I wondered if La Llorona would let me pass.

"What is taking you so long?" Septima complained from the other room.

Pilar rushed into the bathroom and grabbed the limp towels out of the sink. She hurried back out, through the empty doorway. I followed behind her, wondering where La Llorona was hiding now.

I scanned the corners of the store, searching for the dark spirit. I could still feel her pressing over me, but I couldn't see her anywhere. I knelt down next to Septima, who was rubbing Dee's stomach and telling her everything was going to be all right.

Pilar ran outside to flag down the emergency crew. They rolled a stretcher through the front door and set down several cases of equipment on top of the button counter. Dee opened her eyes as they strapped an oxygen mask over her nose and mouth, but then she slipped back into semiconsciousness.

"It's her stomach," I told the two paramedics, who took her pulse and spoke to one another in one-word sentences.

"Is she allergic to any medication?" the one in charge asked me.

"I don't know," I said, looking at Septima.

"She's a new employee. We don't know much about her," she explained.

The paramedics exchanged a quick glance, then lifted their patient onto the padded stretcher. Dee stirred.

They began to roll her out of the store, and the three of us followed. When the stretcher reached the ambulance door, Dee pulled the oxygen mask away from her mouth with a clumsy swipe of her hand. She reached out to grasp my arm, but her grip was feeble.

I noticed she was trying to say something. I leaned closer to her face, and she placed my hand on the white sheet covering her abdomen. Then she whispered into my ear.

"We have to go now, ma'am," the paramedic said, brushing my arm away from Dee's body. "Get back."

Dee locked eyes with me, silently asking if her message had been clear. I reached for her hand again, to let her know that I understood, but the paramedics pushed me aside and lifted her into the back of the ambulance. The one in charge hopped into the back alongside the stretcher while the other one ran around to the driver's seat and started the engine.

"Wait!" I shouted. My words were barely audible over the shrieking siren. "She's pregnant!"

To get to the hospital we had to borrow a car from Father Miguel and the Holy Sisters of Saint Joseph. Septima's husband, Beto, owned a truck, but he was already at work and he didn't like it when Septima called him there. So we locked the store, picked up Dee's handbag, and quickly walked over to the church.

Septima and Father Miguel had been through a lot together, and she knew that he would hand over the keys to his old Mercury, or even drive us to the hospital himself, no questions asked.

Pilar and Septima rushed inside the church, calling out for the priest. I stayed on the sidewalk. I hadn't stepped inside a church for years. Not since I'd learned that there are invisible forces in the world—like the sweet mercy of La Virgencita and the vicious stare of La Llorona—that slip right through God's hands. There is wicked sorcery swirling inside the desert's dust storm clouds, and mighty curses cast every day through the haughty scowls of house cats. There are all sorts of powers that church people pretend don't exist while they are sitting in front of an ornate altar. But ask Milflores, the *curandera,* and she'll tell you that when God can't handle a situation, the church people show up at her door asking for magic potions, *jabónes* and *polvos.*

I liked Father Miguel very much, but I knew that he was just a regular man like every other priest, and I had learned the hard way that no regular human can ever be God's honest messenger. Except for Septima.

Everyone on Frontera Street knew she had a special link with heaven. That was made pretty clear years ago when the miracle of the muffin occurred.

News of the *milagro* was on CNN and in the newspapers for a few days. It brought hundreds of people from all over the world to tiny Frontera Street, and straight to Septima's front porch.

She didn't own the fabric shop back then. That came later. She was working as a nurse's assistant at Baldwin Memorial, and she spent her free time helping Father Miguel at the church. Septima was the person who dusted the blessed *santos* every Thursday evening and made sure they had new velvet robes to wear every Christmas Eve. She also was the one who always volunteered to keep the dogs and cats from fighting during the springtime blessing of the animals, even when it meant standing between Joe-Joe Gallego's pit bull and Willie DelValle's one-eyed doberman with a garden hose at the ready.

But the week that the muffin *milagro* happened Septima was taking a little break from her church chores, getting ready instead for a visit from her daughter, Elena, who was a sophomore at San Marcos State and the first one in her entire family to go to college.

The story goes that Septima went to the Safeway to pick up some *torta* rolls, but the bin was empty. Nowadays people say the empty bin itself was a sign from God because there had never been a time before, or since, when the Safeway was completely out of *torta* rolls. Septima could have just ignored the sign and moved on to the produce section, or even left the Safeway entirely and picked up some *pan dulce* from the Jimenez Pasteleria.

But she wanted something to toast for Elena's breakfast, so she went over to aisle seven (breads and crackers) and reached to the top shelf to grab a loaf of Sunbeam Vitamin Enriched White. That's when some unknown—but what Septima insists was a holy—force slid her hand to the left, where she found a box of Thomas's presplit English muffins.

It's true that the only ones who actually saw the miracle unfold were Septima and Beto, but a film crew from *Unsolved Mysteries* showed up a few days later and got Septima to reenact every move. So it wasn't long before the entire neighborhood could tell the story.

Septima told the *Unsolved* viewing public that normally she would have been at church on a Sunday morning, but Elena was home and any good mother would want to make her daughter a decent home-cooked breakfast.

"*Quien sabe* why I picked up the English muffins?" she said straight into the camera. "I'd never tasted them before."

Since Septima doesn't have a toaster, she set the muffin down on her tortilla iron. On the show she slapped a reenactment muffin onto the cast-iron circle heating up over the blue flame of her gas Kenmore. The film crew got a close-up.

"I made some eggs," Septima went on, "and when I picked up the muffin, I saw it."

At this point in the show the camera zoomed in on the *real* miracle muffin that Septima kept in a Ziploc. Some eerie music played as she gasped in total reenactment surprise, and then the show broke to a commercial before revealing to the audience exactly what Septima saw.

Septima said they taped a segment in which she explained that she wasn't expecting a sign from heaven at all and was humbled by the Heavenly Father's decision to speak to her through the bread. She said that she told the producer she wanted to make that clear because she was beginning to worry that some people might think going on TV was a vain and boastful act. The producer let Septima film the statement, but it was edited out of the final version.

After the commercial the camera showed Septima examining the muffin like she was seeing the holy vision for the first time all over again. There, toasted to a glorious golden brown, were the sacred feet of Jesus Christ walking on water. The waves were seared into the bread in even peaks across the bottom of the muffin, and the Son of God's heels were toasted to a perfect hue of chestnut, making them stand out from the rest of the pale dough.

"You can even see his toes," Septima pointed out. But that wasn't all. No, above the feet and waves, above all that, near the crumbly crust, was a tiny crevice branded with the image of a soaring dove.

"That's what convinced me it was a sign from God," Septima whispered as the camera got a good shot of her kneeling down in front of her kitchen sink. Some people who eventually saw the muffin said the dove looked more like the Holy Cross, or even the star of Bethlehem, but Septima insisted that it didn't matter if other people didn't see the Bird of Peace, the toast was blessed no matter what it looked like.

Beto admitted that he wanted to eat it. He said Septima had to snatch the muffin out of his hand before he ripped it in two and used it to sop up the last bits of *huevos con chorizo* left on his plate, because at that point he had no idea how that piece of bread was going to change his life.

Septima woke up Elena and showed her God's holy sign, and Elena immediately called Father Miguel, who brought over some of the sisters from Saint Joseph's. The sisters believed in the *milagro* instantly, but Father said he didn't know if Jesus' feet in toast qualified as a true Catholic miracle.

"Are you sure you didn't do this yourself, Septima? With a lighter?"

That was what he asked his best and most devoted parishioner. It was wrong, he's admitted as much since then—but at the time he couldn't help but doubt.

"Ay, Padre," Septima pleaded, "why would I do such a thing? Don't you believe that God can speak to someone like me?"

She had served Him, and now He was thanking her. That was how she saw it. Father Miguel didn't answer her, except to say that he would contact the cardinal, or somebody even closer to the pope, to find out what to do. Not that that stopped Septima from calling all her neighbors, who didn't need anybody from Rome to convince them that they were in the presence of God's loving touch. They were the ones who alerted the local TV news, and *Unsolved Mysteries,* and even Cristina from Univision, who eventually came out and did a whole hour live from Septima's front steps!

After Septima appeared on television the first time, people started traveling from all over to see the muffin. It wasn't too long before reporters in trench coats were standing in front of our little box houses on Frontera Street, speaking into microphones in all kinds of different languages, via satellite.

Hundreds of believers found Septima, too. They came knocking on her door early every morning, begging her to let them see the holy muffin. She had to start calling in sick so she could stay home and lead visitors through her kitchen.

The muffin sat on a platter that Septima positioned on top of a purple velvet place mat. She stationed a silver crucifix where a spoon would normally go and crowned the *milagro* with an arch of seven white candles.

Septima said that she knew she was doing the right thing, even if Father Miguel had doubts. She knew God wanted her to bring people inside. He wanted her to be there when they received their own personal message from heaven through the muffin. Sometimes, Septima said, people broke into tears when they saw it, and she would hug them and let them become as small or silent has they needed to be in His presence. The only thing Septima never let anybody do was be alone with her muffin.

A few weeks after Septima first cooked that muffin, there were so many people crowded in front of her house that Beto couldn't park his truck in the driveway. If he had tried, he would have run over entire families kneeling and praying on his pavement. So he parked down the block and walked up to his own home, watching kids climb the brick walls like lizards just to get a peek inside the kitchen window.

He decided things were getting out of hand.

"*No más!*" he told Septima one night. "I don't care if God Himself decides to come and see that piece of bread. He's not walking inside my house!"

Septima said it took her a while to calm Beto down. She said he went on and on about how a man should be able to do certain things in his own home, how he should be able to be alone with his wife without people lurking outside the windows.

Now, Septima didn't tell any of the television people how she coaxed Beto, but she told us that she rubbed his back and crooned some sexy Spanish into his ear until she had his full attention. Then, when he was still drowsy and warm, she told him that God didn't want her to stop. Not yet.

Beto was too sleepy and satisfied to argue. To be fair, Septima agreed to set firm visiting hours (9 A.M. to 6 P.M.), and she talked Beto into making a special box for the muffin that would allow her to show it off on the porch instead of in the kitchen. That way she could keep strangers out of Beto's house and still fulfill her covenant with the Lord.

For a while everyone in the neighborhood enjoyed the attention that the muffin generated. Even Father Miguel, who saw it as a chance to spread his teachings further than usual. Some of the teenage boys made extra money by waving visitors' cars into empty lots and then charging six dollars for parking, and Anita Suárez, who worked part-time in a printer's shop, came up with a bumper sticker that read, I SAW THE HOLY TOAST.

The crowds got bigger every day. They pitched tents on Septima's lawn and camped overnight. Pretty soon there weren't enough empty parking spaces left, so they began parking in neighbors' yards and playing loud music at sunset and leaving bags of Fritos and cans of sardines and paper cups and plastic knives all over the street. Sometimes Beto had to park his own truck four streets away, and it wasn't long before neighbors started to complain.

Septima believed it would be a sin to make money off the muffin, but Beto told her that he had to raise at least a little something to keep the porch painted and the street clean. Septima didn't like the idea, but she agreed on four dollars to see the muffin and five dollars to take a picture of it. And she stopped feeling bad about it when she saw that people still sought out the *milagro* no matter what Beto charged.

Elena took a leave from college and stayed home to help. She tried to keep up with the trash that the pilgrims left behind, but she noticed that the leftover hot dogs, sold by the Chaparral High cheerleaders on Saturdays, the tossed bags of chips, and the spilled sodas had started to attract ants. Not little sugar ants, either, but the big red and black fighter ants that practically jump out of the way when you try to step on them.

Elena spent half an hour every morning tramping over crumpled sleeping bags and smoldering campfires, shutting off forgotten tape players that were churning out everything from the pope's high Latin Mass to Lola Beltran's lonely *canciónes del rancho*.

Septima didn't seem to notice that the neighbors were getting tired of all the commotion. She still loved listening to the visitors tell her how they found their way to the muffin. She kissed pictures of the devoted worshipers' sick nieces and dying husbands who couldn't travel. She held the hands and tapped the heads of people who asked for her blessing. She even paid Lettie Sanchez two hundred fifty dollars to sew a white silk chiffon gown for her, exactly like one she had made for a Sun Carnival queen, except without the sequins and the low-cut back. Septima wore the gown on Sundays when she stood next to Father Miguel, who had started celebrating Mass on the porch because more people were there than at his church.

He told her he still hadn't heard anything from the Vatican, but he was becoming very uncomfortable with what she and Beto had done.

"It's time to put this thing aside and get back to your life," he urged.

That made Septima pretty angry, especially since she had gone out of her way to thank God for the miracle every day, and to make sure that Father Miguel had center stage every Sunday. She told Father that the money she and Beto had made was God's way of helping her start her own business, and he could see for himself how she had already filled an entire grocery bag with thank-you letters from people who said the muffin had changed their lives. If that wasn't God's work, she said, she didn't know what was.

"I don't think you really believe in this *milagro*, do you?" she challenged Father Miguel. "Who has done God's will here, *dígame*, you or me?"

Septima said Father mumbled something about pride before the fall, and told her she had better take a look at who she was really serving. Then he quit coming to her porch to say Mass.

That didn't stop Septima. She started holding her own kind of services in her white gown, and the people loved her.

A few weeks later, Father Miguel approached Septima again, saying the neighbors were demanding that he do something to stop the muffin madness. But Septima wouldn't even speak to him until he admitted that what had happened was a true miracle.

"I don't care what Rome says, and neither should you. Why don't you just ask God?" she challenged.

Father knew that was going to be the only way to get Septima to put her muffin away, so he agreed. He said he would spend an entire night praying and fasting on the porch with the muffin, asking God for guidance. But he made one thing clear: Septima had to leave him alone with the muffin.

"Fine," Septima answered. "Go ahead, keep the muffin out here, Father. Pray. Maybe it will teach you religion."

The news of Father Miguel's holy test spread through the neighborhood, and when the special night arrived, he decided not to do anything about the crowd his vigil attracted.

I was there, and it was a beautiful sight. People lit candles and stood silently as Father Miguel recited prayers and wiped his brow and made the sign of the cross over the muffin. The night pushed on, and it was hard to stay awake, watching Father do nothing except kneel in front of the muffin, which he had perched on a little altar he brought from church.

At dawn Septima came out of her house. Those of us who were awake saw Father Miguel seated against the porch railing, his prayer book open and his chin bent over his chest. His breathing was slow and steady.

Septima shook him awake and offered him some coffee.

"Go wash up," she said. "I'll bring in the muffin."

That's when it happened, when what she saw made her gasp so hard that she almost fell over backward. I was close enough to see the disaster, too.

Ants. Hundreds of them were swarming all over the *milagro* muffin. There was a long chain of them stretching from the muffin's box, down the carved leg of the holy altar, across the porch floor, up one side of the railing and down the other. Like soldiers destroying a city, each of the red invaders was carrying a chunk of the muffin on its back.

"*Dios mío!*" Septima screamed, waking up all the other pilgrims asleep on the lawn.

"Get away! Get off!" she shouted as she tried to brush the ants off the muffin. But even I could see that they had already destroyed the apparition, that they'd reduced the Master's holy feet to nothing but a heap of stale crumbs.

Most of the pilgrims packed up their things and left by noon. Septima gathered whatever bread bits she could salvage and put them in the box. She told Father Miguel that it was his fault, that if he had believed from the beginning the horrible attack would never have happened. Father Miguel argued back, saying that maybe God had seen enough of Septima's false prophesying and had decided to put an end to it His own way.

That's when Septima slapped Father, and when he took his altar and left without saying one more word.

The incident split the neighborhood in two. There were people who believed that Septima was right, and those who sided with Father Miguel. But after a while it didn't seem to matter which side folks were on, because nobody was seeking out Septima's porch anymore, even though she continued to wear her gown and wait for worshipers.

Finally, two days before Christmas Eve, Father Miguel came over to ask Septima if he should get somebody else to dress the *santos* for midnight Mass.

"I'm sorry I got so angry," she said. He apologized too.

"Will you come back?" Father Miguel asked, adding that he would let her teach adult Sunday school if she wanted to.

"And," he said, "you can set the muffin box on the communion rail."

So that's where the crumbs of the Holy Toast have been ever since, its box filled, Septima has told me, with *milagro* medals that people have placed inside of it. In gratitude.

When Septima and Pilar walked out of the rectory, they motioned for me to follow them to the driveway. Septima was the only one of us who knew how to drive, so she navigated the big brown car down I-70 to the hospital exit. The radio was set on a country-western station, and I wondered who had borrowed the car before us.

Neither Septima nor Pilar spoke during the ten-minute drive, and

I suspected they were blaming me for what had happened. I told myself I didn't care what they thought. But the silence started squeezing me.

"It was La Llorona," I blurted, as Septima pulled up to the emergency room entrance. "I didn't touch her."

"You two get out and I'll find a parking space," Septima answered, as if I'd said nothing.

Pilar hopped out of the backseat and headed straight to the wide glass doors.

"Sepi?" I hesitated, my hand on the door handle.

"She needs our help," Septima said, keeping her gaze steady over the car's hood. "That's what's important right now."

"I saw La Llorona in the shop. Didn't you feel her there?"

"I was busy with Dee."

Septima didn't like to hear me talk about La Llorona, or any other *espíritus*, for that matter. Talk of spirits not recognized by the church made her nervous.

"I swear, Sepi, it wasn't me. I didn't hurt her."

Septima eased her foot off the brake pedal and the car began to roll forward.

"I'm parking the car. Are you going in?" Her voice was as hollow as a tin cup.

I stepped onto the curb as she began to pull away. When I got inside, I saw Pilar standing at the nurses' desk, where she had spilled out the contents of Dee's handbag.

"This address is an apartment in Dallas," the impatient nurse behind the counter complained. Pilar was holding Dee's wallet in one hand, and she had Dee's driver's license and credit cards spread across the countertop like pieces of a jigsaw puzzle.

"That's all that's in here," Pilar told the nurse as she slid her finger through the wallet's empty compartments.

When Septima walked in, the nurse let out an exaggerated sigh of relief, recognizing her from when she had worked as a nurse's assistant.

"Do *you* know this lady's address?" the nurse asked.

"No, she only gave me a post office box when I hired her," Septima answered. Pilar was already scooping up the tubes of lipstick and gum wrappers and the wire-rimmed sunglasses and placing them back inside Dee's limp leather purse.

"License says she's twenty-eight," the nurse announced to nobody in particular as she pressed her pen down on the documents attached to her clipboard.

"And," the nurse said, lifting her eyebrows, "she's an organ donor."

I noticed the stern nurse had a tiny toy koala bear clinging to the collar of her pantsuit uniform, and I wondered if she had any children.

"Know anything else about her?" she asked Septima dryly, holding her pen at the ready.

"No, not much more."

"She's pregnant," I added, too much like an afterthought.

"Yeah, I already got that from the paramedics."

"Is she okay?" Pilar finally asked.

"Haven't seen her since they brought her in. You can wait over there." The nurse pointed to three rows of orange plastic chairs, and we all followed her gesture with our eyes.

We sat down. Pilar's attention was immediately drawn to the television set hanging from a pair of brackets in the corner. There was no sound, but the picture was clear. A close-up of Erica Kane, and then a string of commercials.

The doctor came out and looked around for someone to update. Septima rose. He fiddled with the stethoscope around his neck as the three of us made our way to his side.

"Are you family?" he asked. "She said her mother is traveling."

"She works for me," Septima said.

"Well, we're looking at a bit of break-through bleeding," the doctor stated.

He was thin and bald and wore the sort of glasses that tinted automatically and cast a dark green shadow over his eyes. He had stubby fingers and nails that were trimmed shorter than they had to be.

"Is it serious?" Septima asked.

"Well, this early in the pregnancy it's probably just hormonal, but she needs to get off her feet for a few days," he explained. Septima nodded.

"I don't suggest she go home alone," he advised, scanning each of our faces to see who was going to take Dee in. "We need to keep an eye out for any more bleeding, and I should be contacted immediately if cramping reoccurs."

He rested his gaze on Septima.

"Maybe Father Miguel could . . ." she began.

"She might feel more comfortable with a woman," the doctor suggested.

"I can't, Doctor," Septima said apologetically.

I knew why she was saying no. Beto had put his foot down after the miracle. He'd told Septima she could do as much church work as she wanted outside the house, but he was done with soul saving at home.

I knew Pilar wouldn't volunteer. She still lived with her parents and five brothers.

"I don't have room," I protested to Septima.

"Socorro won't mind using the couch," she rationalized.

"Give the nurse your address," the doctor said flatly. "What's your name?"

"Alma," Septima said, closing the deal that I hadn't agreed to.

"Cruz," I finished. "Alma Cruz."

"Fine, Alma. I want to keep her here for a few more hours. I'll discharge her tonight."

"Can we see her now?" Pilar pleaded.

"She's sleeping," he said. "It'd be better if you came back later."

I wanted La Virgencita to show me the truth. I knelt before her, kissed her blue veil, and prayed the rosary in a whisper, hoping she'd shine some light on what was happening.

Had I been wrong?

"You saw La Llorona too, didn't you?" I asked the Holy Mother. "You heard her. What was I supposed to think?"

Ever since I was a little girl, I had been good at reading signs from the spirits. I trusted my instincts. I knew, for example, that when someone dropped a knife it was best to stay away from the person that the blade pointed toward, because he was a back-stabber. I also knew that finding a lost earring, or any other misplaced thing, in a place you never left it was a wink of protection from a kind spirit watching over you. I knew that a stray dog wandering into your yard was always a spirit messenger delivering a powerful blessing, or a potent curse, and it was up to you to decide whether to take the risk of looking the creature straight in the eye to receive it.

I knew those things, and when I first met Dee I was sure that I had felt gusts of unsettled winter air swirling around her, so I had kept my distance.

"But, Maria Purísima, I didn't know she was carrying a baby," I told La Virgencita.

Maybe La Llorona had tricked me.

I thought of how Dee had collapsed in the store, how she had doubled up in pain, fighting to protect her baby from whatever had reached inside her. I knew exactly what that felt like.

"Maybe the witch wanted me to think Dee was evil so I wouldn't help her," I reasoned out loud.

I searched my sweet saint's eyes for a hint of understanding.

Then I asked, "Have you been trying to tell me that?"

Chapter 5

DEE

I TOLD THE DOCTOR THAT SENDING ME TO ALMA'S HOUSE wasn't necessary. I'd call if I felt the slightest tug or kick or cramp. I'd stop by once a week, put myself on a regular prenatal schedule.

"Is your mother getting back from vacation in the next couple of days?" he asked.

"Not that soon, but soon enough," I assured.

The doctor moved as if every muscle in his body wanted to sit down and rest.

"Ms. Paxton," he began, "this is a serious situation, and if you don't . . ."

His words piled up inside my head like cars in a crash. I slammed on the brakes after I heard him call me Ms., stopped by how ugly it sounded, sawed off like a rotten tree stump. I'd always hated that word, hated the way the brash female lawyers in Mitch's office used it like a sword, sticking it in people's faces to prove how tough they were. I'd wanted to be a Mrs. since I was six and my mother brought home a pulpy coloring book called *Rose's Garden Wedding.* After I colored Rose's bridal gown ecru and tinted her bouquet a light shade of geranium, I tore out the page that showed her and her tuxedo-clad groom breezing along the flower-flanked garden path. The caption at the bottom, written in a slanty script, said: "The minister presents Mr. and Mrs. David Johnson."

I loved being Mrs. Mitchell Paxton, and I didn't care if other women crinkled their noses when I said so. I was delighted to make dinner reservations under his name and took pride when I wrote it across the bottom of my checks. I especially enjoyed watching the law firm partners break into broad smiles when I stood next to my husband and introduced myself at cocktail parties. I wore his name like it was an expensive fur coat. I wanted it to sink into my skin and down into my blood so I'd always be a part of him. And as far as I was concerned, I was still Mrs. Mitchell Paxton, even though the rest of the world was ready to erase my marriage and declare me a Ms. with the flick of a pen.

"Mrs.," I said, so softly that I almost didn't hear it myself.

"What?" the doctor asked.

I felt tears welling in my eyes. "*Mrs.* Paxton," I muttered. "I'm *Mrs.* Paxton."

The doctor continued with his lecture, pushing my words aside with his own. "Let's get back on point here . . ."

"It's Mrs. Paxton!" I shouted, stunning him into silence.

"Excuse me?"

"Put that on the chart," I demanded. "Mrs. Mitchell Paxton. Write that down there. Write it down . . . Please."

The doctor's face softened. He removed his glasses and held them with one of his large hands as he wiped his forehead with the other. He sat down on a stool and rolled it so close to me that his knees were almost touching mine. Then he closed the chart and handed me a box of tissues. I saw his gold wedding band and automatically reached up to touch Mitch's ring, which I wore on a chain around my neck, tucked under my collar like a crucifix. I thought how this doctor had a wife who loved him no matter what kind of mood he carried into their house each night. And I wondered if he knew how lucky he was. Did he realize that in about one minute everything he thought was permanent could fall and shatter into a million pieces? Even though he worked in a hospital, even though he thought he could handle death well, I looked at him and knew he wasn't ready. Nobody is.

He was eager to be done with me, but I was crying and I could tell he didn't want to seem insensitive by walking out on a distraught patient. What had begun as a timid shedding of tears had suddenly turned into a jag of deep, wrenching sobs that sounded more like pain than sorrow.

"I don't think you are in any shape to be alone right now, Mrs. Paxton," he said as he inched toward the door and, finally, slipped out.

He never changed the chart like I'd asked.

I sat with my legs dangling over the side of the hospital bed, the ends of my thin hospital gown crumpled inside my sweaty palms. A nurse carried a plastic bag filled with my clothes into the room. When she set it on a chair next to the blood pressure machine, I heard the hollow clop of my wooden clogs.

"Take your time," she said. "The doctor will come back to sign the discharge forms when you are dressed and ready to go."

I pulled on my jeans and blouse, and they felt like they belonged to somebody else. Just getting them on made me tired, so incredibly tired. And when I heard the doctor walking down the hall, I could muster only enough energy to sit down and close my eyes.

"We both want to do what's best for the baby, don't we?" the doctor murmured. "That's what's important here, hmm?"

I nodded.

"Believe me, Mrs. Paxton," he said, "you need some rest."

Mitch collapsed on the sidewalk two miles from home, in front of the wine shop where he had picked out a bottle of champagne for my birthday. I can't remember what the young doctor told me after he mentioned a cerebral aneurysm and said he was sorry, and I'm not sure what I said back. The only thing that's clear in my memory is how cold Mitch's hand felt when I rubbed it against my cheek and how some part of me believed he'd wake up if I kissed the bruise flowering on his forehead. I waited for the miracle, whispering to him that everything would be all right.

When the nurse came to take him away, I wouldn't let her leave until I wet a tissue and washed the blood away from the small cuts made by the broken bottle.

Mitch's mother took care of the funeral details, silently growing more and more annoyed when I couldn't choose an outfit from the three dark suits and six neckties she'd laid out on our bed.

"He was wearing a T-shirt and shorts," she repeated, as if the untidiness of her son's death embarrassed her.

"You pick," I said, knowing she already had.

I saw the anger building in her eyes. She was blaming me because she couldn't blame anybody else, and I didn't have the energy to fight back. My own mother, who'd come to help, tried to calm her. But Mrs. Paxton looked at her as if she were a stranger and Momma quietly backed away.

"Do you want his wedding ring? Because if you do, you'd better tell them now, Dee. Can you at least do that?"

She had wrestled with every detail since walking off the plane from New Orleans, piling appointments at the mortuary on top of discussions with the florist and meetings with the organist. She'd laid each errand over the other like a mason setting bricks, and by the end of the funeral she'd built a wall around herself that was impenetrable and complete.

I don't know how I got to the service or how I even got dressed. I don't recall the faces of anybody there. My only memories are of lips, men's dry and cracked lips hiding in the tangled nests of mustaches or hideously exposed on the wide pale beaches of chins, moving like eels washed ashore. I remember women's lips stamping tight pink O's on my cheek, and I remember that when I closed my eyes all I saw were red and purple lines floating in a sea of black.

At the funeral words were spoken, prayers were said, but none of them were powerful enough to pull me up from my own darkness. When everyone else walked away from the grave, I stood and watched the blanket of shivering yellow roses that was draped over Mitch's coffin drop deeper into the dirt. I heard car engines cough and heard people pick up conversations that they had started sometime before the funeral, first in hesitant whispers and then in full voice. They'd put their lives on hold for two hours to acknowledge the certainty of death, but they didn't want to linger too close to it for too long. I couldn't move. Slowly the flowers disappeared into the jagged gash cut into the cemetery's green lawn. Two of the rosebuds fell over the side of my husband's coffin as it scraped against the bottom. My knees buckled.

Someone, I can't recall who, took my elbow and led me away, but I didn't want to go because it seemed wrong to leave Mitch there, in a space too small to hold a man for eternity.

For the first few days after the funeral the partners' wives came by to give me platters heaped with family recipes and quick offerings of polite sympathy. It was all they knew to do. They didn't know what else to say, or even where to look when they spoke to me. So we usually stood in awkward silence until they felt they had fulfilled their obligation.

Two weeks later the food was still in the refrigerator, untouched. I never returned the platters and no one ever came by to collect them.

A month after the services, the law office called wanting to know when I'd be back. Nobody wanted to rush me, they said, but the temp was having trouble with my filing system and if she was going to stay she wanted to change it. I told the voice on the other end that I'd be back the following Monday.

On that morning I pulled a tan cotton suit out of the closet. It was still wrapped in a plastic bag from the dry cleaners, and when I removed the thin cover, I found a pair of Mitch's summer wool pants tucked in between the blazer and the straight skirt. My stomach churned.

Suddenly, the thought of doing anything routine felt like committing a crime. What was I thinking by turning on the television to watch the traffic report? My husband was dead. Why was the newspaper still sprouting up on my front step every morning? Mitch was gone. The world was not the same, and it was an insult that people were carrying on as if it were. I called the office and quit.

That same day I took all of Mitch's clothes out of the closet, emptied every drawer of his socks and T-shirts and piled the garments onto his side of the bed. Then I took off all my clothes and laid down next to the mound of jeans and shirts and ties and jackets. I pulled the sweaters and sweatshirts close to me, slid my arms through the tangle of sleeves and inhaled the ghost fumes of musty aftershave buried in the fibers of his shirt collars. I stayed there all day, clinging to the warm scarecrow body I'd made out of Mitch's things, pulling them over me like a blanket and wondering if I'd ever have the strength to get up again.

When I finally did get up, I did nothing but play the piano. Only pieces by composers who could take me down the darkest corridors of sound. I pounded my hands on the keys, slamming one note against the other. I churned what should have been soothing tempos into chaotic cyclones, letting the notes careen out of control. I shot out A-flats and C-sharps written by Schumann, Mahler, and Bartók, and blasted volleys of assaulting sound into every inch of space around me.

I wanted to kill whatever killed Mitch. I wanted to throw knives and scratch and claw and bite. I wanted someone to blame, but there was no one to accuse. I played for days, until my fingers ached, and then I prayed to God to show me that somewhere inside the crashing waves of crescendo, or beneath the avalanches of sixteenth and thirty-second notes, I would find a calm sea of silver light that might offer me some rest, if not understanding.

I hadn't considered going back to Los Cielos until my mother suggested it. Dallas had never meant much to either Mitch or me. We were there because it was a necessary step on his career ladder. So Momma was right when she told me there wasn't a reason for me to stay.

She had moved to an assisted-living center about forty-five miles outside of Los Cielos, in Tres Cruces, New Mexico. She said her house on the Westside had become too big to handle, especially after Serita died with no daughter to inherit her duties. She'd tried a series of new maids for a while but caught them stealing and decided she didn't have the time, or energy, to go through the long search for an honest one. It was easier for her to just pack up and leave. So, she told me, if I wanted to move back to Los Cielos, she would take her house off the market and give it to me for free. She would also open a bank account in my name and put enough in it so I wouldn't have to worry about money for a few years. That way, she said, all I'd have to do is heal.

When I got there, my mother's friends dropped by all the time, treating me like I had the flu. They brought blankets and cups of soup. It would have made things easier for them if I had had bandages wrapped around my arms, or a pair of crutches. That way they could have seen the wounds. The problem was there wasn't anything they could do for me. Even the words they offered scraped instead of soothed. They leaned over my shoulder and whispered that, eventually, I'd move on. And to me that wasn't a comfort at all. It was a life sentence.

A year ago I would have laughed at anyone who would have pictured me back in Los Cielos, wandering through the desert with no Moses to follow. It would have been an absurd scenario, because our entire lives were headed away from the border's fixed horizon. The state's biggest law firms were courting Mitch, and we were looking at lakeside property in the beveled hill country outside of Austin. He had planned on working for the state attorney's office, and I had planned on using my degree in modern English literature to have his babies.

When I returned to Los Cielos, I thought I'd find some comfort in the irrigated cotton fields that stretched across the Westside like patches of thick-ribbed corduroy, and the dry desert's watercolor sunsets that trigger the crickets' serenade of the moon.

I thought I'd feel closer to Mitch if I spoke to him through the bright West Texas stars, instead of the gray headstone at his grave. But I was wrong. When I got to Los Cielos I couldn't find him anywhere.

Alma's house was tiny.

Built of stucco, it was shaped like a graceless version of the Alamo and stood out from the rest of the modest brick ranches that lined the far end of Frontera Street. The door had three locks that took three separate keys, and when it opened it swung directly into the living room, stopped only by the arm of a dark brown sofa placed beneath the wide front window. There was no front porch. No entryway. No coat closet. A single step took you right into the heart of Alma's home, and ten more would lead you straight out the back door.

The television was on, but there was nobody watching it.

"Socorro!" Alma called out, competing to be heard over the fast-talking television lawyer promising big checks to regular people. I followed her inside, even though she didn't invite me. I didn't have anything with me except my handbag, and I began to wonder why I hadn't asked Septima to drop me off at my car. I knew that once we were inside the dim underground garage, sitting elbow to elbow, with the engine of Father Miguel's car grumbling like fast-moving thunder, I could have convinced both Alma and Septima that they didn't have to carry out the doctor's instructions. I could have told them that I felt much better and there was no reason for me to intrude on either of their very busy lives. I think Alma would have welcomed an easy out like that. Septima would have protested a bit, but eventually I would have won her over as well.

Instead, there I was, standing next to Alma's stiff vinyl sofa, unsure if it would be rude to take a seat. I noticed that a blanket was draped over the back of the couch and I instantly recognized the fabric, a silver-colored velveteen with a fleur-de-lis pattern. Alma, or whoever made the throw, had trimmed its edges with strips of bronze moiré and had attached silk tassels to the corners. It was too much for such a tiny place.

"Socorro!" Alma shouted again. This time she shut off the television just as Oprah welcomed back her audience.

I heard somebody hang up a telephone in the kitchen and then saw Socorro step into the main hallway. She was taller than I expected, a good three inches taller than her mother. Her legs, sheathed in black dance tights and covered down to the middle of her thighs with an oversized T-shirt, were long and lean. Her thick hair was pulled back into a tight ponytail set high on her head, allowing her green eyes to dominate her slender face.

"Richard's driving me to . . ." she started to say, before she saw that Alma had not come home alone.

She stopped midway down the hall and gave me a quick once-over, then cast her eyes toward Alma, waiting for an explanation.

"This is Dee Paxton," Alma said. "From work."

I stepped forward and put my hand out like I was meeting one of Mitch's law office associates. I didn't know how else to handle the situation. There I was, wearing wrinkled clothes, my wrist still cuffed with a plastic hospital bracelet, shaking hands with a young woman who couldn't care less.

Socorro stepped forward and met my handshake with a quick tap of her fingers against mine. Then she leaned against the wall and crossed her arms, waiting for more information.

"She's going to stay here for a few days. Until she feels better," Alma informed her. Socorro raised her eyebrows and Alma began to speak in Spanish. They spoke so fast that I could only catch the meaning of the few words that mirrored English. Doctor. Hospital. And a couple of other simple ones like *peligroso* and *sola*. Patching them all together, I gathered that Alma said the doctor had deemed it too dangerous for me to be alone. Socorro let the news roll over her with no visible reaction, until Alma told her something about *la cama tuya*.

Socorro suddenly shot me a perplexed look and frowned. That was enough for me to figure out that Alma had just told her daughter that I was going to be taking over her bedroom.

"Oh, no, no!" I fussed, finally moving far enough into the house that I was in the middle of things. "Really, I'm fine on the sofa."

It was bad enough that I was going to be sharing a house with people who were opening their arms out of a sense of obligation. There was no reason to make things even more uncomfortable.

Socorro looked at her mother hopefully.

"I'm serious," I insisted.

That sealed the deal for Socorro, who was already bored with the negotiations.

She hurried to change the subject. "I'm going back to school for pointe class," she announced, ducking into her room and closing the door. "Richard's picking me up."

That left Alma and me standing in the hallway in awkward silence.

I decided to just go ahead and say what I knew we both were thinking.

"I don't know if it was fair for Septima to put you on the spot like this. Tomorrow I'll just tell her that I think I should go home."

Alma walked into the kitchen as I spoke and I followed her. She filled a glass with tap water and handed it to me across the L-shaped breakfast counter that extended from the sink. As I took the glass our eyes met.

"Why didn't you tell anybody you were pregnant?"

I wondered if she was asking out of sympathy or out of judgment.

"What for?" I shrugged. "So all my close friends at work could throw me a big party?" My answer sounded more sarcastic than I intended.

Alma leaned her elbows on the counter and shook her head. She fixed her eyes on mine just long enough to let me know that she could have hurled an insult right back at me, but didn't.

I took a long drink from the glass, wishing I could swallow my regret as easily as the water. What was wrong with me? Alma was making an effort, trying to set aside the grudge she'd held against me since the first day we met, trying to make motherhood the one thing we could have in common. I handed the glass back across the counter, and she let her fingertips rest on mine when she reached for it.

"You don't want to go through this alone," she said, "believe me."

I could tell she was speaking from experience, and I wanted her to go on, to tell me about herself and Socorro, but she didn't. She simply opened the cabinet over her head and produced a jar of peanut butter and a loaf of bread.

"Richard's here!" Socorro announced, leaning into the kitchen, but clearly on her way out. She had twisted her ponytail into a bun and surrounded it with a wreath of tiny silk flowers. She also had changed into a violet-colored leotard with a surprisingly graceful V-neck that she'd created by feeding folds of fabric into a safety pin.

"Take this," Alma said, slapping the sandwich shut and slipping it into a plastic bag. Since I was standing between them, I passed the lunch to Socorro, who stuffed it into a lumpy backpack that she slipped off her shoulder.

"And this," Alma said, handing over an apple.

There was a knock at the door.

Socorro dashed to answer it and Alma, wiping her hands on a dish towel, followed.

"Pase, pase!" Alma invited Richard inside.

"Mom, I have to go," Socorro protested.

"We've got a minute," the teacher said as he took a couple of steps into the living room. "How are you, Señora Cruz?"

"Ay, Señor Richard, you know to call me Alma."

The man was slender but not what you'd call slight, wide in the shoulders and solid in the torso. He wasn't extremely tall but still seemed a bit uncomfortable with his height around Alma, who, at five-foot-two, didn't even come to his chin. He looked to be in his mid-twenties and was handsome in a bookish way that must have worked against him during his teen years, and probably even through college. His smile tilted to the left, and the moment he flashed it Alma got flustered and began to search around the room for something else to focus on. She settled on me.

"Oh, Señor Richard, this is Dee," she said, stepping to my side. I extended my hand.

"Mommm!" Socorro groaned.

"You don't have to take her . . ." Alma began.

"Don't be silly," Richard balked. "I'm heading home and it's on my way. I'm happy to do it. I could bring her home, too, if you'd like."

"What? Come all the way back down here and then drive all the way back? No, no, Señor Richard."

"I'll catch the eight o'clock bus to the plaza. No problem," Socorro interjected. "Umm, can we go now?"

Socorro's plea pulled both Richard and Alma back to the moment, and he looked at the car keys he held in his hands as if they'd suddenly appeared there by magic.

"Right," he said. "Let's head out."

He turned toward the door, which Alma was now also walking toward, and hesitated just before he stepped outside.

"Nice to meet you," he said to me. I lifted my right hand to wave good-bye and when I saw the plastic hospital bracelet still around my wrist I called out to him.

"Wait!"

He stopped and looked over his shoulder.

"Could you give me a ride to the parking garage at Los Cielos National Bank?"

Alma shot a disapproving glance my way, and I couldn't tell if she was angry that I was going to attempt to drive by myself or if she was just perturbed that I was asking Richard to make an extra stop.

"No problem," he said.

I told Alma that I would go get my car and then run to my place and pick up a few things.

"Where do you live?" she asked.

Luckily, I didn't have to answer because Socorro, who was now sitting inside Richard's gray Toyota, honked its tinny horn, leaned out of the passenger-side window and yelled, "I'm going to be really late!"

"Okay, okay!" Richard answered, taking wide strides toward the curb.

I grabbed my pocketbook and slid out the door behind him.

Chapter 6

ALMA

As the car pulled away from the curb, Socorro and Richard waved good-bye, but Dee didn't even glance my way. The moment she got inside the Toyota she began busily digging for something inside her handbag. I got the feeling she wasn't coming back, which was fine with me.

I closed the front door and looked inside my little house. I could tell the *gringa* hadn't thought much of it, but to me it was everything. Socorro and I would never have made it without this place, and the neighbors who surrounded it. I honestly didn't care where Dee was headed now, but if she planned on raising that baby by herself she needed to find a place where she felt safe, and a circle of friends she could count on. There's no way for anyone to fully prepare for what's in store, but from the little I already knew about Dee's character, she seemed even less equipped to handle the single-mother thing than I was. She had never told Sepi or me exactly what happened to her husband, but whatever it was, it had shattered her world. The same way Paul had shattered mine.

When I was a girl, it was not unusual to see Americans walking through the streets of my hometown. They sought out the hilly mountain village that the Spanish conquistadors deemed the "land of eternal spring." Three hundred years later, the city's businessmen were still using that description as a slogan to attract Americans and their money to Cuernavaca's popular Spanish language schools.

The *gringos* would arrive at all times of the year, older couples in the winter and aimless college students in the spring and summer. They usually lived in the hotels near the center of town, except for the college students, who often stayed with families willing to give them a room for a modest rent.

When I was in high school, a letter arrived at our home requesting that we join the list of families hosting American visitors.

Although they dress like paupers, many of the young Americans come from fine families. It is important that they leave Cuernavaca with the knowledge that Mexico is home to refined and respectable people. That is why we hope you, Señor Cruz, as one of the city's business leaders, will consider the possibility.

My mother liked the idea, as long as the school sent us only middle-aged spinsters or widows. My father threw the letter in the trash.

"If they need to tromp through my house, eat my food, and dirty my linens to learn that there is more to Mexico than *burros* and *frijoles*, then how educated can they be?" he snorted. "If they come from such fine families, then let them pay for a hotel room. They can practice their Spanish on me when they come into my store to buy a proper suit."

I learned to stay away from the American boys, and it wasn't just because my father threatened to lock me in my room at night if he ever saw me out with one. No, I could see for myself how some girls smeared their family names with their reckless behavior around the foreigners. They would let the long-haired and stubble-faced Americans parade them through the *zócalo* on Sunday afternoons, holding them too tight and kissing them on the mouth in front of decent people. At night, they'd go to the bars and discos and let the crude young men buy them drinks and touch them as the liquor fueled their own fire. Sometimes the girls would even follow the boys back to their rooms.

And for what? Far away from home and free of the burden of their own families' reputations, the Americans made tequila-inspired promises of love and new lives across the border. Girls from Cuernavaca's poorer families often took them up on their offers, willingly trading their own respectability for more immediate profits. They knew marriage was rarely part of the bargain but, like gamblers, they played out the odds, lured to the game by the glitter of the prize.

They flirted and cooed. They dressed in tight skirts and high heels and let the *gringos* climb all over them as long as they paid for it with new clothes and expensive jewelry.

Sometimes I envied those girls and their freedom to smoke and drink and parade their power of seduction. But I knew the cost was high. Mami once told me that for girls like that brashness turned into bitterness as soon as the light of youth faded from their faces.

After high school, I wanted to go to the university in Mexico City and study archaeology. But my father said digging for bones in the dirt was no way for a young lady to spend her eligible years, and he refused to pay my way.

To get out of the house I took a part-time job in a neighborhood juice store, a tiny garage-like café with walls painted a bright lemon yellow and stenciled with drawings of apples and mangoes, guavas and bananas. It was a place where ladies met to gossip after their shopping sprees, where the American students gathered to study.

My job was to make *refrescos,* frothy cocktails of fruit, powdered milk, and dark vanilla extract whirled in a blender. The job required little skill and even less passion. And, at the time, that suited me.

The day Paul stepped into the shop I could tell he was different from the other Americans I'd seen. He walked with a purpose, which instantly set him apart from the *gringos* who haphazardly sauntered around town with no particular place to go. Students considered themselves instant locals even when they'd been in town for only one week. They hid their maps and tour books in the satchels that dangled from their shoulders and mistook our polite endurance of their fractured Spanish for proof that their steep tuition and heavy textbooks had made them fluent.

Paul, on the other hand, came into the store and immediately asked for directions to the bus station. It was late morning, and I had my back turned to the front door. I was chopping oranges and strawberries with a dull knife that squashed more than sliced, making the berries bleed all over my fingers.

His Spanish was excellent. That's what made me turn around so fast, with the long knife still clenched in my hand.

"Don't kill me. I'll find it on my own," he joked, raising his wrists over his head and taking a step backward in surrender. I wiped my hands, more for him than for me. I'd already tried everything to remove the red stains, even lemon juice and baking soda, but nothing worked. Suddenly, the red seemed brighter than ever, almost fluorescent, and I plunged my hands into my pockets.

He stepped up to the counter, plopped a worn map in front of me, and said, "I know I'm close." His hair was short, unlike the bushy mops of most of the students, and his hands were rough and strong, as if they had done much more than turn the pages of countless textbooks. I looked at his square face and was instantly drawn in by his sea-green eyes. As he spoke, I felt them stroking me as surely as if he was running his hands over my shoulders.

"You're two blocks away," I chirped, using the knife to point out his destination. Then I quickly added, "You don't have much luggage for somebody leaving town," hoping to make the conversation last longer.

"Oh, I'm not leaving. I just got here. I wanted to find out about weekend buses to Taxco."

"Are you a language student?" I pressed, giving him a reason to explain why he'd come to Mexico and how long he intended to stay.

He smiled. "No, not exactly. I never was good at that sort of thing. Worked most of my life, you know." His accent was strong, but his grammar was flawless and he spoke without hesitation.

"In Mexico? Your Spanish is perfect."

"Perfect? Well, you wouldn't say that if you knew me better. But I get along." He began to look around the store, and at the same time he folded his map and guided it into his back pocket.

He seemed to have set aside his plan to get to the bus station quickly, and I wasn't in a hurry for him to leave. The store was empty because the language students were on a one-week spring vacation and there was about an hour before the local lunch crowd would begin to trickle in.

"Can I get you some juice?" I invited him to sit down and told him I'd join him for a few minutes, if he'd like. It was unusual for me to be so bold, but there was something about him, and I couldn't think of any other way to keep him from walking out the door.

"Yeah, sure," he said, looking around at the empty tables. He chose one close to the counter.

I hurried to get the *refrescos* ready, and caught a glimpse of my own reflection in the glass door of the fruit case. I pulled off the dress-length apron that was permanently wrinkled at the knees because I bunched it up to wipe my hands hundreds of times a day. The dress I had on underneath wasn't much more attractive, a plain blue shapeless cotton shift that I'd yanked off a hanger without even thinking. It hid more than it accented, and usually that was what I aimed for. I'd learned my lesson after wearing slacks a couple of times and having to put up with the rude slaps and pinches from a few of the insolent students. In my own defense I started wearing clothes I thought would help me melt into the background.

That morning I regretted all my choices—the old wrinkled apron, flat shoes, my hair pulled back severely. I yanked the rubber band out of my thick hair, wincing as it raked its way down the length of my ponytail and snapped against my finger with a punishing sting. After taking a deep breath and closing my eyes for a few seconds in an attempt to get my pounding heart to quiet down, I delivered two glasses of frosty pineapple-strawberry *refrescos* to our table. When I put the drinks down I noticed he had run a comb through his own hair. Then he stood up and pulled out a chair for me.

He said he was in Cuernavaca for a couple of weeks to outline plans to change one of the last private Spanish villas into a hotel. Most of the red-roofed haciendas had already been converted into language schools, restaurants, and dance clubs. The families who owned them took the money and built new houses outside of town, away from the tourists they'd made room for.

"You work here?" he asked, even though the answer was obvious.

Suddenly the mindlessness of the job embarrassed me. My hands. My clothes. He must have thought I was a peasant. Uneducated and poor.

"I teach, too," I lied.

"Oh?"

"Yes, Spanish," I went on, trying to shore up my wobbly story. "Private lessons."

"Man, that's great!" He overreacted.

"Well, I'm not really—"

"No, it's great," he insisted. "And this juice is really good, too. What's your name?"

"Alma."

He thought for a moment and said, "Soul?"

I nodded to let him know the translation was right. Neither of us said anything for a few minutes.

The traffic on the street outside increased as lunchtime approached. The whine of motorbike engines rose and fell as they zipped up the steep hill toward the supermarket or down toward the post office. We could feel the earth rumble as the city buses barreled along the same route, and the sensation must have pulled Paul's mind back to his original destination. He looked at his watch and frowned when he saw that half an hour had passed.

"I've got to get back to work," he announced, slapping his hands on his knees.

"Me too," I said, gathering our empty glasses and heading back toward the counter. I looked at the small mountain of oranges and strawberries heaped on the cutting table, still uncut. I was going to pay dearly for our little chat. Now I'd have to race the clock to get everything ready before the flood of impatient lunch customers rushed in. I still had two dozen ham sandwiches to prepare and three cakes to slice.

He said good-bye as he walked out, and I didn't turn around to watch him leave.

I thought about him the entire day, fighting the urge to ask some of my regular customers if they knew anything about him or the new hotel. One thing I knew for sure was that in a town as small as Cuernavaca, where people knew each other from cradle to grave, any question I might ask would get right back to my father before the cathedral bells called the old ladies to six o'clock Mass.

Still, I spent hours eavesdropping on my customers' conversations, hoping to get some useful information. I lingered longer than usual when I served them drinks. I came back too many times to ask if everything was all right, and I wiped down empty tables within earshot of any loud talkers.

I heard plenty. I learned that Lupe Sameniego was at church with her husband acting like Carmen Pacheco hadn't already stolen him right out from under her nose, and I learned that even though Raul Moreno told the judge he wasn't the one who shot Francisco Monzon's yellow-eyed dog, everyone in the neighborhood knew Teza Ramos paid him to do it. But nobody said one word about the new American in town, not even the group of rich shopping ladies I was certain would have already noticed him.

I decided that after I closed the shop I would walk past the hacienda on my way home, even though it was a quarter mile off my regular route. But I promised myself I wouldn't stop, even if I saw him there, even if he asked me to.

The hours crawled. When five p.m. finally arrived I started to sweep and wash the blenders and knives. I took the trash out to the alley, and when I walked back into the front room I pulled out my key ring and headed for the door.

He was standing under the arch of the doorway, the evening sun throwing a long shadow from his feet to mine.

"By the way"—he spoke as if our conversation had never ended—"my name is Paul. And I sure could use some private lessons."

I chuckled to myself as I recalled how hard I fell for Paul the instant I met him. Then I shook the memory off before it took me back to the heartbreak.

I started thinking about Dee again. How she seemed to walk around in a permanent fog. And that's when I realized that I knew exactly how she was feeling when she climbed into Richard's car. Alone, overwhelmed, and scared to death. What if she really didn't have any place to go? I should have made her feel more welcome. Rescued. The way I felt when I discovered Frontera Street.

Chapter 7

DEE

I SET MY HANDBAG DOWN ON THE CREDENZA IN THE FOYER and looked around the house that I'd grown up in. I barely recognized it. My mother had had old walls torn down and new ones put up to make the floor plan more modern. After Mitch and I got married she changed most of the furniture. She put the old stuff in storage, waiting, she said, for us to settle into a place big enough to accommodate the mahogany table that seats ten (without the two leaves) and the fourteen hardback chairs that go with it.

My mind was in such a haze when I moved back to Los Cielos that I hadn't noticed that almost every stick of new furniture in the house was rattan. There was white rattan in the kitchen and dark brown rattan in the living room. In addition to the rattan sofa that creaked when you lowered yourself onto it, there were two rattan rockers with armrests wide enough for a drink *and* a magazine. The coffee table was made out of a rectangular piece of tinted glass that sat on top of a tightly woven bed of rattan, and the centerpiece on the table was a hideous porcelain monkey holding out a candy bowl made of woven straw. The place looked like the lobby of the Honolulu Hilton. I wondered what in the world had clouded my mother's good taste. The only things I recognized from my childhood were the framed family photographs that were propped up here and there, the collection of Gorman artwork still hanging on the walls, and the baby grand piano positioned by the sliding glass doors.

When I was little, I hated sitting in front of that keyboard, perfecting scales. But I knew that thirty minutes of practice every day, six baths a week, and homework done by eight o'clock would add up to a movie on Saturday afternoon and three dollars allowance. And it seemed like a good trade, especially since I was the sort of girl who liked to follow rules. It was a talent I nurtured.

Sit up straight. Cover your head in direct sun. Say li-brar-y, not li-berry. Commands like that never chafed me the way they did other kids. I didn't see them as reins pulled tight; I openly craved them.

Change your clothes after school. Never wander aimlessly outside, like a stray dog. Always wear a slip.

Maybe it was because I was an only child and accustomed to constant attention. I was Poppa's girl and Momma's pride. I was their miracle baby, sent by God to prove it was never too late. Momma was already forty-one when I arrived and fastidiously overprotective. Poppa was fifty-two and completely overwhelmed.

From the moment I could walk, the three of us negotiated my behavior like clauses in a legal contract. I was not allowed to sing or shout or be rambunctious during Walter Cronkite or *Meet the Press.* If I kept my fidgeting to a minimum during all of Momma's auxiliary meetings, I'd get a tiny cup of coffee with cream and two cubes of sugar to sip alongside the ladies. When other kids were presented with similar lists of rules, all they could see were limits. I saw the space in between.

My talent for conformity dazzled adults. During my parents' dinner parties I was never exiled to the TV room or thrown into the yard with the boys and dogs. I was allowed to stay with the grown-ups, quietly refilling the hors d'oeuvre tray or parceling out tasteful coasters. When some adult would ask me to play a spot of Strauss on the Steinway I would modestly comply, and afterward I'd stand as still as a marble statue next to the piano bench. My parents politely deflected their friends' flattery, but I knew they loved it.

It never took more than three meetings with any of my parents' acquaintances before they would invite me to call them Ted or Gloria or Annabelle. And, just as I was instructed, I'd say I wouldn't feel comfortable showing them such a lack of respect, but thanks just the same.

Rise when an adult enters the room. Cross your legs at the ankles. Never lift your own fork before the hostess lifts hers.

The formula seemed simple enough, and I wondered why other kids were blind to the power hidden inside good behavior. Couldn't they see how far a bit of obedience would get them? How it all came back around?

Other kids might have considered a skinny cheeseburger out of a paper bag a fun dinner out. But because he knew I would behave like a perfect lady, Poppa treated me to a real restaurant date once a month. Momma would fix my hair and slip her pressed powder compact into my little handbag before presenting me to my "gentleman caller," saying, "Sir, may I introduce your date for the evening?"

Poppa, who always wore a dark suit and shiny black shoes for the occasion, would take my hand and kiss it. I loved sliding into the car next to him, watching him remove his suit coat and carefully place it on the backseat before he climbed in. His crisp white shirt would glimmer, and the dim green glow of the dashboard would smooth the deep lines on his face just enough to show me how handsome he must have been when he and Momma met.

Every date was the same. We ordered steaks and Shirley Temples in the formal dining room of the Westside Country Club. The waiters called me *mademoiselle* and we had baked Alaska for dessert. Poppa asked me about school and I asked him what it was like to be a cotton broker, a job I didn't understand for a very long time.

I was allowed to stay up past eleven.

When I turned twelve, we stopped the dinner dates and Poppa started letting me come with him to his Sunday night poker games instead. He sat me by his side and taught me the difference between a full house and a straight flush. And he told me that knowing how to bluff was a skill no girl should be without.

By the time I was fourteen, I was stirring pitchers of martinis at my parents' cocktail parties and smiling obligingly as Mr. Schuster and Mr. Duffy told me, once again, that I made the best Manhattans this side of Central Park. Poppa laughed when the men asked him when I'd be old enough to marry, and Momma scolded, saying they should be ashamed for even thinking that way. They all had created their own truths about me, visions of my true character that fit whatever mold they wanted, and I was smart enough to know that was good.

In high school, my friends thought that drinking kegs of beer in the tall grass by the Rio Grande and smoking dope at Willie Nelson's annual summer concert and picnic in Austin were acts of outrageous rebellion. They were convinced that our behavior was setting shocking new lows in the history of adolescent depravity and were, of course, gloriously proud of it. But there was nothing original about what we were doing. I could see that, even if they couldn't. We played our music loud, we drove our cars fast, and whenever we got a chance we did lots of backseat groping. On Saturday night, girls with paperback notions of romance wiggled themselves out of their brassieres, and on Monday morning their clammy-palmed boyfriends bragged about what had happened after that.

Our rebellion was completely by the book, and our parents were grateful. When we were seventeen our entire world stretched no further than our narrow interests, and it certainly didn't include the poorer parts of town. The only time I'd spent in the barrio before Mitch died was when the rougher Westside boys cruised through the neighborhood on a dare or a lark. They would only go at night, leaning out their car windows to hurl foul language at the Mexican prostitutes lingering near the square. Sometimes the boys would lure them up to their car doors with whistles and fists full of cash, only to stomp on their gas pedals and pull away at the last second. They made a raceway out of the narrow streets and aimed their empty beer bottles at the walls of tiny stucco homes that had no shrubbery or fencing for protection. They'd scare their dates by telling them lies about murdered teenagers killed by dangerous drifters, and brutal gang stabbings that left even the most fearless young men disfigured for life. If the girl protested too much, the boys would threaten to leave her stranded there, in the menacing dark, where God only knew what would become of her before sunup. It was all part of the teenage ritual. Raising hell at the Mexicans' expense was the sort of thing that all our daddies had done. And when they saw that their sons were beginning to follow suit, they winked and grinned and bragged about how their boys were, sure enough, finally becoming men.

It never occurred to me that the barrio might be a place where families just like mine actually lived and shopped and sent their kids to school. We never thought about the people who lived there as individuals, just Mexicans. We didn't care if they might have been American-born or how much schooling they might have had; they were Mexicans, different from us in every conceivable way. Nobody, of course, really cared how they lived or what they did, except when they were working at our homes as Pick-and-Prays or gardeners. And even then, as long as they were respectful we kept our distance. It was best for everyone, we were told, to mind the borders between brown and white. That way everyone knew what was expected. That was the rule we all lived by, so, naturally, I obeyed.

After high school, I went to college at the University of Texas and did what everyone else did. I avoided adulthood for four years and fit some studying into a busy social schedule. My sorority sisters and I would start our weekend on Thursday night by smoking menthols and sliding our fancy-stitched ostrich boots in two-step time over sawdusty floors in smoky honky-tonks. We judged how attractive men were by how low they wore their Stetsons over their eyes and how firm their grip was on our backs as they led us through country waltzes, accordion polkas, and rockabilly swings. We let the sweet-talking, dangerous ones coax us into sex on the first date, but turned right around and played hard to get with the ones who mattered.

After graduation I worked answering phones at a Dallas law firm that had lots of clients in state government and plenty of young, handsome attorneys. That's where I met Mitch, who was fresh out of law school and determined to prove to his daddy that someone in his family could make a living away from the filthy muck of Louisiana's oil refineries. Mitch, whose Cajun accent made legal words sound like zydeco music, was all about dark blue suits, middle-of-the-road politics and ten-year career plans. Unlike some of the other young lawyers, he didn't have blood relatives in the state senate or old family friends in CEO positions who could cement his future over a three-drink supper with the senior partner. Mitch had to lay his own track, and he knew he'd have to work harder than some of his privileged colleagues to keep the political sand from shifting under his feet. His passion for firm ground attracted me, so I let him know that I was smart enough to take seriously but not as aggressive as the female associates he had to compete with.

I knew that those women talked about me behind my back, harping about feminism as they huddled in the ladies' room, smoothing out the seams of their boxy pinstriped suits. I knew exactly what they were saying about me, and they were right. I was looking for a husband. And I found one.

In bed at night I would slide my body up against Mitch's, close my eyes, and plan the rest of my life to the steady rhythm of his lovemaking. I knew marriage with him would lead me straight to routine happiness. We'd get some land, have two kids, and plop our little family in front of a camera every November to make a stilted Christmas portrait that we'd mail to all our friends. *Season's Greetings from the Paxtons.*

To me the future was clear and comforting, and even though Mitch sometimes teased about how conventional I wanted to our lives to be, I knew he wanted the same thing. There was nothing left for us to do but walk down that road. Nothing until the bomb lodged behind Mitch's beautiful brown eyes exploded and ripped our pretty picture apart.

What set of rules was I supposed to follow after that? I needed a regimen, but nobody seemed to have a prescription for widowhood at twenty-eight. Momma tried to help by explaining what she went through when she buried Poppa two years ago. She said some part of Mitch would always be with me, and I'm afraid I frightened her when I laughed in her face. What part would that be? I wanted to know. What specific part of the healthy, handsome young man buried under a ton of hard Texas clay did I get to keep?

It had been more than three months since I had buried Mitch and everything else I had planned for my life. Sometimes, mostly at night, it felt like I'd been alone for ages, and at other times I was certain that the whole horrible thing never really happened. I would be reading the newspaper and I would look up expecting him to be there. I'd be at the grocery store and would absentmindedly reach for his brand of shaving cream. I'd walk along the sidewalk downtown during my coffee break and turn around when I heard a voice I thought was his. I'd walk past young couples out for a stroll and my stomach would turn when I saw how happy they were in each other's company. Where did they get the right to wrap their arms around each other like they'd never have to let go, lording their this-will-last-forever attitudes over everyone like they had bottles of a secret potion hidden in their pockets?

Instead of getting better with each day, the emptiness I felt inside my own skin was growing deeper. Every morning I stood under a spray of hot water and remembered that whenever Mitch was running late he would climb into the shower beside me, steal shampoo suds from the top of my head and press his body against mine so we could both rinse clean.

There were still days when I would find myself sitting on the floor of the shower long after I had planned to step out, hugging my knees and crying so hard that my ribs ached. I would rock back and forth in a cloud of steam and stroke the tiny mound that my abdomen had become. I'd ask Mitch if he could see what was inside. I waited for an answer, listening for his voice to break through the steady *ssshhhh* of falling water. More than a few times I sat there until my toes turned blue and my arms began to shiver, realizing that I had no idea when the hot water had begun to run ice cold.

I had no intention of going back to Alma's. I suspected she was only being nice because Septima had pressured her to take me in. And even if I was wrong, I wasn't ready to let anyone get so close.

I made my way to the rattan-laden bedroom, stripped off my dirty clothes, and slipped into a cool cotton nightgown. It was only about five in the afternoon, but I crawled into bed and promptly fell asleep. When I woke up it was seven-fifteen and I heard the unusual sound of a hard, steady rain rapping against the bedroom window. I turned over and pulled my knees toward my chest. But instead of drifting off, I began to replay what had happened between Alma and me that afternoon. What was it about that box I found underneath the button counter that could give rise to such a strong reaction? Old pictures, grade school craft projects pasted together years ago by Socorro's little-girl hands, unopened letters. I couldn't imagine how any of it amounted to a deep dark secret.

I began to think about what Alma had told me in her kitchen and, more important, what she hadn't. She was alone, like me, when Socorro was born, and I wanted to know how and why. Was she a widow too? Was she divorced? If Socorro's father was alive, did he know that he had a beautiful daughter growing up on Frontera Street? I thought of my growing belly and imagined every pulse of my own heartbeat sending a river of blood to the tiny tips of my baby's hands and feet, dark blue pools of life pouring into the thousands of cells bonding together to create a perfect child.

I prayed the baby would have Mitch's gentle eyes. I sat up in my bed and listened to the rain wash away the last bits of evening light. It was early September and the afternoon temperatures were still climbing past one hundred degrees. But what made living in the desert different from living in any other part of Texas was that the daytime heat sank right down into the sand after sunset, and the rain would certainly make the temperature tumble even quicker. I thought about the people who might be caught in the sudden downpour: softball teams of stiff-legged, middle-aged men scrambling to the dugout; Westside women stranded at the beauty parlor, trying to decide whether to make a mad dash to the car or just sit down and get a pedicure to pass the time. I'd never known a single soul in Los Cielos who owned an umbrella. It rained so seldom that I don't think the stores even stocked them.

A clap of thunder rattled the bedroom window and sent a shiver down my spine. Suddenly I remembered that Socorro was out there, waiting for a city bus. I looked at the clock and saw that it was twenty minutes before eight. I rushed out of bed, threw on some jeans and a sweater, stuffed a couple of skirts and tops into a bag, and grabbed my toothbrush and cosmetics. I got into my car and pointed it toward Arts High School, which was less than two miles from my front door. The rain fell in a diagonal across the headlight beams and the low, lumpy clouds made the sky exceptionally dark. I circled the campus several times, slowing down to take a good look at every teenage silhouette I passed. There were spindly-limbed boys sauntering through the downpour as slowly as plowhorses, unwilling to let anything like a little rain break through their adolescent indifference. There were tight knots of girls who were screaming and giggling and holding book bags and spiral notebooks over their heads as they pranced from one dry stairwell to another. I didn't see Socorro anywhere. I drove toward Main Street and then about half a mile toward downtown. There, on the right, I saw a solitary figure standing next to a metal pole that had a bus stop sign on top of it—a perfect target for a spear of desert lightning. I pulled over to the curb and rolled down the passenger window. Socorro stepped away from the car instead of toward it. She didn't recognize the vehicle, or me.

"Socorro!" I yelled, straining to keep my voice from being drowned out by the rain. "It's Dee. Mrs. Paxton. From this afternoon."

She put her hand on the roof and peered into the open window. Her cheeks were wet and her nose was red.

"Get in."

She opened the door and dropped her backpack onto the floorboard before stepping inside.

"I'm all wet." She shut the door and ran one of her hands over her dripping hair. She began to sit back, but stopped short, afraid to dampen the upholstery.

"It doesn't matter," I said, as I pulled back into traffic. "Dig through that bag in the back and dry yourself off with one of my shirts or something."

"No, I got it," she replied, unzipping her backpack and pulling out a yellow hand towel. She wiped her face and her arms and then placed the towel against the back of her seat.

"The bus was coming in a minute."

"I know, but I was heading this way anyway."

Socorro looked at the bag on the backseat.

She looked at me as if sometime during the ride with Richard she'd figured out that, despite what her mother had said, I never planned to return to her house. Now she was confused.

"Where are you going?" she asked.

"Same place you are."

I continued to drive for a few moments, and we both kept silent. She settled into her seat, and I smelled the musty combination of wet clothes on wet skin. It was such a human scent. Intimate.

I remembered how Mitch used to shave first thing every morning and how he let the hot water run until thick clouds of steam had lathered up the air. I remembered how I'd roll over to his side of the bed and lie perfectly still in the warmth he'd left behind. At that instant I knew how incredibly lonely I had become and how much I wanted to find a place to belong—anyplace.

As my car neared downtown, Socorro said, "You can just drop me off at the plaza. You don't have to go all the way to Frontera Street."

"You know what?" I replied. "I do."

Part Two

Chapter 8

SOCORRO

MOM PULLED OUT THE SOFA BED AND SET THREE FOLDED TOWels on top of the television while Mrs. Paxton sat quietly in the kitchen and drank a glass of milk.

I could tell something was off. My mother would never abandon a girlfriend like that, leaving her alone at an empty table while she silently slid the corners of the narrow sofa mattress into the elastic pockets of a blue fitted sheet.

When Mrs. Paxton and I walked into the house, Mom had thanked her for picking me up from school, but neither of them acted like they were really friends. Mom had politely taken the overnight bag out of her guest's hands, and then practically pushed her toward the kitchen with a sharp order to get herself some milk. I didn't know whose idea it was for this lady to stay with us, but on that first night it sure didn't seem like a good one.

I felt sorry for her.

I slid my backpack onto the floor beside Mrs. Paxton and pulled out my textbook. "Know any French?" I asked. She smiled and nodded her head.

"You do?"

"Well, a little," she said softly. "It's been a while."

"These are dance terms, mostly," I said, moving my chair around to her side of the table to show her my book. On each page were photographs of young dancers dressed in black leotards with white ribbons around their waists. They were demonstrating *plies, tondues,* and *arabesques,* and underneath the French name of each step was the English translation.

Mrs. Paxton took the book and flipped through it. She seemed nice enough.

"We have a test every week," I said. "It's so weird."

"Weird?"

"Yeah, we have to sit outside in the hall and my teacher, Mrs. Polikoff, calls us in one at a time. She holds out a bowl that has all the vocabulary words for the week inside of it, written on pieces of paper that she's folded into little squares."

"How many words do you have to know?"

"It's like ten a week," I said. "So, you pick a word but you can't look at it. You have to hand it to her and she reads it out loud and you have to spell it and then do the step for her."

"What if you get it wrong?"

"Well, it depends on what you get wrong. You get some points taken off if you don't know the translation, but you get more points taken off if you can't spell it."

"Really?" she asked, looking surprised. "I would have thought knowing how to do the step would be worth more than anything else."

"I thought that, too, when I first started. But we do lots of these steps about a million times a day in class."

Mrs. Paxton nodded her head and directed her attention back to the book. I wondered what Mom was doing in the living room. I didn't hear the television, and I knew it didn't take that long to put sheets on the sofa bed.

"So, we're on this page, here," I continued, turning to the section on *barre* exercises. I walked over to the kitchen counter and held on to it with my left hand. I set my feet in fifth position, with my right arm out to my side, slightly below shoulder level and said, "Okay, pick a step."

"Ummm, lots of these are several words put together," she warned.

"Yeah, I know."

"Okay, let's see. How about *developpe, plie, releves?*"

"Easy!" I spelled each word slowly and then stretched my right leg in front of me, keeping my pointed toe parallel to the floor. As I held it about hip high, I bent my supporting knee and then straightened it out again. I rose onto my toes.

"You call that easy?" Mrs. Paxton chuckled.

"My leg's supposed to be a lot higher, but I'm just fooling around."

"Showing off is more like it." It was my mom's voice, coming from the kitchen doorway.

Mrs. Paxton and I both looked over to where she was standing, her arms crossed in front of her.

"She looks beautiful," Mrs. Paxton offered. "Her back is so straight and her arms are so graceful."

"She's turned my kitchen counter into her personal ballet *barre*, swinging her legs all around." I couldn't tell if Mom was actually angry or just pretending to be.

"You have to watch out when you walk through here. You might get kicked in the head, or end up with a ballet shoe in your mouth!" Mom chuckled, and we both followed her lead.

I continued to show Mrs. Paxton the difference between a *ronds de jambe d' terre* and a *ronds de jambe en l'air* and spelled every single step right, except I forgot the "d" at the end of *sur le cou de pied.*

"You're spelling it like *pie* in Spanish," Mom pointed out. She had moved to the other side of the kitchen counter, where she was making sandwiches for the next day's lunch.

"Why don't you think of 'ped'—like pedestrian?" Mrs. Paxton suggested.

"That's good," Mom said, clearly pleased. "Do that."

It was ten o'clock by the time we finished, and Mrs. Paxton looked exhausted.

"You should stay home from work tomorrow," Mom advised. "Septima won't mind."

Mom took a long shower and I finished my homework, and I guess by eleven we both assumed that our guest had gone to bed. But when I got up around midnight to get some water, I noticed that the living room light was still on. I walked toward the front door to shut it off and saw Mrs. Paxton curled up on top of the sheets with all of her clothes still on, even her shoes. She was crying, but as soon as she sensed that somebody else was in the room she tried to stop by pulling in air and not letting it back out.

I pretended not to hear any of that and walked down the hall to my mother's bedroom.

"Mom?"

Slowly reaching her arm up from her pillow, she switched on the reading lamp next to her bed, bathing the little Virgin Mary in a narrow beam of light.

"Are you okay?" she whispered, lifting herself onto her elbows. She slept on the right side of the bed. Never in the middle and never on the left, where the sheets were always smooth and cool. I crawled in beside her and she put her hand on my forehead, testing for fever.

"It's that lady," I said, keeping my voice as soft as possible.

"Is she throwing up?" my mother asked, immediately tossing the covers off of her legs and getting up.

"Maybe," I said. "She's crying."

My mother glanced over her shoulder at me as she pulled on her bathrobe and headed into the living room. I followed her a few steps down the hallway and stopped at a point where I could see Mrs. Paxton but she couldn't see me. I leaned against the wall and listened.

"Dee?" my mother said softly.

For a moment there was no sound, and I saw how my mother hesitated before sitting herself on the edge of the sofa bed. I couldn't see Mrs. Paxton's face clearly, but I could tell she had turned to look at my mother, stretching her arms and legs out of the tight ball she had rolled herself into.

Neither of them said a word for a long while. I heard the refrigerator humming in the kitchen, and when my mother turned off the living room light, I saw a beam of yellow moonlight skim the windowsill below the drawn curtains. I slid down against the wall until I was sitting with my knees in front of my chest. I was incredibly sleepy, but too curious to go back inside my room.

What was Mrs. Paxton doing here? That's what I wanted to know. My mother wasn't the sort of person who invited people in. In fact, I couldn't remember anyone but my best friend, Cece, ever sleeping in the fold-out bed. We didn't have any family who might come to visit for Thanksgiving or Christmas, and the only other guests we'd ever had in the house were Septima and Pilar, who sometimes dropped in on their way to or from the shop.

Recently, I had tried to get Mom to invite the orchestra teacher for dinner, but even though she had said it was a good idea she hadn't actually asked him over.

She wasn't mean, or shy. It was just that Septima was the one whose house was always open. Even before the miracle of the muffin, Septima's front porch was where everybody ended up on summer nights. And during the winter, at least a few neighborhood ladies met in Septima's kitchen every Sunday after church to make fresh tamales, while the men watched sports.

Mom was the only single parent on the entire street, and she once told me that she didn't need any more friends than she already had. Which, as far as I could tell, meant she only needed two—Septima and Lettie Sanchez.

"Let's get you out of these clothes," Mom said to Mrs. Paxton.

She looked over to see if I was still in the hallway, and then she called me into the living room to look inside Mrs. Paxton's bag for a nightgown. I found one and laid it at the foot of the bed.

Mrs. Paxton had stopped crying for the moment, but seemed too weak to help Mom undress her.

"Maybe a warm bath?" Mom asked.

She shook her head no.

"You go on to bed," Mom said to me. But instead of stepping back into my room, I sat against the wall again and watched.

Mrs. Paxton slid the straps of her bra down over her shoulders and Mom undid the hooks in the back. Mom worked the nightgown over the lady's head.

"My back hurts so much," Mrs. Paxton groaned, barely getting the words out before she started to cry again.

"It's your body getting ready," Mom said, moving closer to her. I could tell she didn't really know what else to do or say. Mrs. Paxton was lying on her side, clutching her pillow, and Mom reached over and began to rub the small of her back.

"Lie on your stomach," Mom suggested. She turned over, and Mom began to knead her muscles with the heels of her hands, pressing hard.

I'd never heard anyone cry the way Mrs. Paxton did, with moans so full of pain that they sent shivers down my arms. Mom put all her strength into her massage, leaning into each each stroke with her own back and shoulders. Eventually, Mrs. Paxton's breathing slowed down and evened out.

When she finally sat up, she didn't look at my mother directly but sat next to her, as if they were in a darkened movie theater. I saw my mother move her hand to touch Mrs. Paxton's.

"I'm so scared."

"I know," Mom replied quietly.

"What am I going to do?" The lady's voice started to break again, and she put her hands over her face. "I'm all alone."

"No," Mom said in a tone so stark that it startled me. She turned and grasped Mrs. Paxton's chin in her hand. "Dee. Look at me," she ordered. "You aren't alone. You hear me?"

Mrs. Paxton draped her arms around my mother's shoulders and said something I couldn't make out. Mom hugged her, and they rocked back and forth in the middle of the bed.

That night, my mom fell asleep on the sofa bed next to her houseguest, and I slept on the floor next to them both.

The next morning, Mrs. Paxton slept right through the chaos that began at six-thirty with my clock radio shouting, *"KCLS! Music so hot it rocks your mama's jalapeño cornbread!"* and blaring accordion-heavy Tejano tunes through the house. She didn't stir as I tripped through the hallway, into the shower and back into my room to get dressed. And she continued to sleep soundly as I put my hair up and packed my ballet bag with enough leotards and tights to get me through my three daily dance classes and an evening rehearsal.

Mom made me a couple of quesadillas for breakfast, and at seven-fifteen Peeps knocked at the front door, which finally caused Mrs. Paxton to awake.

I told Mom that going to Arts High was great, and that I was having lots of fun. I told Richard the same thing, too.

It made them happy, even if it wasn't true. The truth was that from the day we started at Arts, almost all the kids in the neighborhood, except Cece, had stopped talking to Peeps and me, unless their parents were around to make them. But I couldn't tell Mom and Richard that. Nor could I tell them that the rich girls in my dance class laughed at me the first time I put on my toe shoes and tied the ribbons into a big bow. Or that they still laughed, even after the teacher told them not too, whenever I walked by them in the halls. I couldn't tell them that Lucinda Herndon was the only friend Peeps and I had, and that even the bus ride to school was awful, and had been from the very first day.

Every kid on Frontera Street rode bus number 837 from the time they started kindergarten until they graduated from high school, or until they bought a junker car. Its bumpy route was so familiar to all of us that we anticipated every turn, leaning toward the windows and back toward the aisles to keep our balance, like sailors at sea.

Usually the noise level inside 837 was deafening, with fifty different conversations crashing into each other at top speed. And that first morning Peeps and I went to Arts High, everything was the way it had always been. Francisco, the driver, made all his normal stops, and kids slid in and out of each other's business, until the bus began to veer off in a different direction. That sudden change stopped conversations in midsentence. Francisco rolled right past the squat houses and sun-scorched lots that had become the wallpaper of our lives and then picked up speed as he cruised toward unfamiliar territory. A tense wave of whispers rose from the seats as he chugged past the downtown plaza, past the Catholic boys' school and beyond the tiny taco takeout place inside what used to be a drive-up photo lab. When he passed the edge of what we considered our part of town, Francisco shifted gears and the bus wheels began to whine like guitar strings rubbed the wrong way. Some of the little kids ran to the back window and pressed their teeny hands against the glass as they watched the only neighborhood they'd ever known get smaller and smaller.

We headed toward the Westside, past four-story office buildings and fancy funeral homes along Main Street, past movie theaters with six screens and neighborhoods called Tierra Nueva and Parque Vista, where joggers bounced along the smooth sidewalks in expensive running shoes.

Francisco kept driving, past old churches with wide lawns and a firehouse where men in folding chairs waved at us as they sat, fat and happy, next to their shiny red trucks. Eventually Francisco pulled the bus into an empty parking lot in front the Westside Skating Rink and Video Arcade. It was early on a Monday morning, and the lot was littered with stray bits of torn wrapping paper, empty soda cans, and the other scraps of somebody else's weekend fun.

He settled the engine down to an uneven idle, and then he reached for the big lever next to his right elbow, flinging the front doors open with a clang. He lifted his foot off the big black gas pedal and swung both his knees around until they were facing the main aisle. Then he stood up and yelled: "Arts High!"

The school was actually at the top of the next hill, but Peeps and I could tell by the way Francisco was standing—his legs apart and his arms pressed against his chest—that the skating rink was our stop, whether we liked it or not. Every pair of eyes was parked on Peeps and me, blaming us for leading them into uncharted waters.

Peeps lugged his bulky French horn case down the aisle toward the front doors. It was shaped like a big dog in the sit position and was as heavy as a sack of fertilizer. He waddled past the cold stares of at least forty resentful eyes, and he flinched when he was hit with a sudden wave of hoots and laughs and rude noises. Cece squeezed my wrist as I got ready to slide out of my regular seat and join him.

Cece, Peeps, and me. We had grown up together on Frontera Street, running in and out of each other's houses without ever knocking, sharing balls and bikes and skates and staying for supper so often that we each had a regular place at each other's tables. We clung together at school, too. In first grade we played the Three Wise Men in the Christmas pageant, and one Halloween we dressed up like the Three Little Pigs, with snouts made from an egg carton and three broom-handle hobo sticks slung over our shoulders.

When we were small, Cece and I looked like China doll twins, with identical bowl-style haircuts and bangs hanging straight down into our eyes. Peeps wore his hair in a cactus-needle crew cut until he was eleven, and he always had a narrow strip of black elastic stretching from one ear to the other that was supposed to keep his heavy glasses from sliding off his nose whenever he shook his square head. It was called a sports strap, but everyone on Frontera Street knew from pretty early on that sports would never be Peeps's way.

Our three birthdays weren't close together on the calendar, but we had joint parties anyway. It made things easier for our parents. It tripled the amount of food and the number of presents piled up on the specially decorated table, so our fiestas became the sort of celebration the entire neighborhood looked forward to each year.

The best part of our joint parties, of course, was the piñatas. There would be three of them, dangling like doomed prisoners over all of our little heads. Peeps always picked a block-chested superhero with black boots and a cape that would flap in the wind. Cece and I went with whatever was our latest obsession. Magic ponies. Blue-skinned Smurfs. Turtles. Every year the three of us trooped to the *mercado* across the river in Mexico to pick out our favorites, and on the way home we'd carry them onto the city bus with us, laughing when the driver threatened to charge an extra fare. We'd sit down next to our paper playmates, giving them the window seat.

At our parties we would impatiently endure endless rounds of pin-the-tail, and drop-the-clothespin, and whatever other stupid games the grown-ups set before us. We ate cake and opened presents and marched like happy little soldiers through every birthday party drill, knowing that each ritual brought us closer to the funnest part of all.

Finally, near the end of the afternoon, we'd all line up—youngest kids first, tallest kids last—in front of the three piñatas, and one by one we'd step out in front of the gathered crowd and bask in that glorious moment when one adult would hand us a baseball bat and another one would tighten a blindfold over our eyes and spin us around until we didn't know which way was forward. And then we'd swing.

"Left! Go left!" the kids would holler, guiding the would-be basher closer to the tissue-paper victim. The boys in control of the wire would tease the batter, lowering the piñata so far that it would be dangling right behind the blindfolded hunter's head, swishing and bobbing and making everyone laugh.

Of course, each kid was aiming for the tummy, where the piñata makers hid a brittle red clay pot filled with candy. After one lucky batter applied the perfect whack, Tootsie Pops and peppermints would tumble into the grass, alongside handfuls of butterscotch drops and packets of Sweet Tarts. Cece's dog, Chato, who came to every party and sat on the sidelines waiting for that very moment, nosed his way through our legs, sometimes knocking down the little kids, hoping to beat us all to the sweet, scattered treasure.

But that morning on the school bus, every kid who had come to our parties since we were five, and their cousins and sisters and brothers, glared at Peeps and me like we were from another planet. They were the exact same people who smiled and laughed and felt lucky to live on Frontera Street when we were bashing our piñatas, but now they looked at us with cold, blank faces, like those fiestas had never happened.

I stepped into the aisle and swung my backpack over my shoulder, grateful that I could hide my pink ballet slippers and my leotards inside the book bag. Not like Peeps, who had to wrestle with his French horn in front of everyone. I debated whether to lift my chin or keep my eyes pointed toward the floor as I made my way down the aisle. It was so quiet on the bus that I would have bet every single kid could hear the crazy argument going on inside my head. Look up, look down, look straight ahead.

My eyes ended up following the midair arc of a rubber eraser sailing through the air toward the back of Peeps's head. It hit him just above his right ear, knocking his glasses halfway down his nose. The direct hit was the spark everyone had been waiting for, the trigger pulled. The next thing Peeps and I knew, all sorts of trash was flying our way: pencils, wadded-up pieces of paper, rubber bands, even some lunches. We were the bull's-eye targets for our entire neighborhood's confusion and restlessness, and in a strange way, I wouldn't have expected anything else. I didn't feel so bad about it, personally, but I felt real sorry for Peeps, because in the middle of all the ruckus he started smacking his lips the way he always did when he got nervous. Even after I shot him a look that warned him to stop, and stop damn quick, he kept on smacking and smacking like an old woman who'd lost her false teeth. He shut his eyes tight, and I thought he was going to cry when a cluster of boys in the back began to imitate him, making wet, puckering noises by sucking in their cheeks.

Where was I supposed to look now?

We both hurried past the middle seats until we got to the wide front doors. We raced down the three steep steps and landed on the pale, sun-washed sidewalk. I heard Peeps take a deep breath as he set down his horn and turned his back to the busload of hecklers, who were still all worked up and shouting like crazy. Francisco shut the doors about half a second after we stepped off the bus and began to glide his gloved hands over the hula hoop of a steering wheel. He pulled the bus into a wide U-turn, pointing it back to familiar territory.

I looked up and tried to find Cece in the row of faces pressed against the windows. I finally spotted her. She must have been standing on her seat because she had managed to stick her head and shoulders completely through the narrow opening. She was looking straight at me, getting ready to say something.

With a jab to the gas pedal Francisco fed the engine, and it droned and rattled, growling so loud that I couldn't make out what Cece was shouting. As the bus pulled away I saw her pitch something toward me. I lunged to catch it, a lump of white tissue paper tied up with string.

When I lifted my head back up, the bus was already belching black smoke and picking up speed. I opened the tiny packet and found a delicate silver chain balled up tight. I slipped my finger through one end of the necklace and raised it up out of my palm, uncoiling it like a charmed snake. Dangling at the end of the chain were two miniature ballet shoes, crisscrossed at the ankles, frozen in fifth position.

I knew it was Cece's prayer for good luck, the only way she could make the trip to Arts High with me. It meant everything.

"I'll help you put it on," Peeps said. His voice startled me. For a moment I had forgotten all about him, forgotten that I had promised that we'd face whatever happened at the new school together. I could tell by the look in his eye that he thought I might abandon him. I handed him the necklace and turned around so he could put it around my neck. I bent my knees to even out our differences in height.

"Lift your hair," he instructed as he fumbled with the tiny clasp. I felt his fingers twitching, his hands still trembling from the incident on the bus. I reached back and patted his hand, leaving my fingers on his until the shaking stopped. He fastened the necklace and then leaned his forehead into my shoulder blades, depending on me for support.

"What are we doing?" he groaned.

I told him to remember what Richard told us: that being different isn't bad. That, really, it's good. I told him that our first day would be the worst and the other days would get better, even though I didn't believe that myself. If our brown skin didn't brand us as total outsiders, the fact that we were the school's first scholarship students surely would.

I told Peeps we'd meet at the cafeteria door at lunchtime, just like we'd promised, and eat together every day no matter what.

"You came here to learn to play that thing, right?" I asked, giving his horn a kick with my toe. "You're not going to learn back at Chaparral High, that's for sure. Back there, you know what would happen? That stupid Joaquin Ramirez would steal your horn and cut it up so he could have some shiny brass to make bracelets out of. And then he'd go around telling his fat, stupid girlfriends that they were pure gold."

Peeps began to laugh. "Yeah," he said. "Or I'd end up in a mariachi band trying to figure out how to work a French horn solo into 'El Rancho Grande.' "

The joking helped Peeps pull himself together, and I was glad of that. I needed him to rely on his own strength, because I knew that I didn't have enough for both of us.

On the second night of Mrs. Paxton's stay I came home from rehearsal to find her and my mom sitting at the kitchen table together. They were going through a pile of books about pregnancy.

"The second trimester may be the most enjoyable," Mrs. Paxton read out loud.

"Indigestion, constipation, varicose veins, nosebleeds, hemorrhoids," Mom read from another.

"That sounds really enjoyable," our guest said.

They read each sentence in a sarcastic tone, giggling between the words and laughing even harder at the drawings. They were having so much fun they didn't notice I had walked into the room.

"My gums bleed after I brush my teeth," Mrs. Paxton mocked. "What does that mean?"

"It means your teeth are going to fall out of your head!"

"My urine leaks when I laugh, sneeze, or cough. How can I stop this?"

"Listen to Mrs. Reynolds and Mrs. McCarton tell boring stories in the shop!" Mom could barely get her punch line out before they both exploded into laughter, pounding the table with open palms and wiping tears from their eyes.

I stood outside the kitchen and tried to imagine what my mother had looked like when she was pregnant. For the first time in my life I noticed how the swell of her chest narrowed like a funnel at her waist and how the arc of her hips balanced everything out again. I looked at the shape of her face and wondered if she had lost the delicate point of her chin when she was carrying me.

I thought back to the few photographs I had seen of my mom and dad together and how happy they seemed. She'd never told me what really went wrong, what made it so bad that he couldn't stay. I wondered where my father was now and whether he thought about me every single day, the way I thought about him.

*   *   *

Dee spent almost a month sleeping on our sofa, until a big truck from Vassett's Furniture pulled up to the house and workers in baggy gray coveralls wrestled a single bed, a small oak dresser, and one of those paper room dividers into the middle of our living room. Dee signed the order form and then asked me to help her move all the stuff to the back of the house. She pushed the mattress and box spring up against the wall, set the dresser at the foot of the bed, and then hid them both behind the hinged room divider, which was decorated with Oriental paintings of lily pads and curvy orange fish. That tiny corner of the dining area, just steps away from the back door, became her bedroom. Mom kept insisting that Dee and I trade beds, and Dee kept saying that I needed my privacy. I never argued with her logic even though Mom expected me to, out of politeness.

Every week or so Dee would gather up her laundry, and all of ours, and spend the entire day somewhere else, washing clothes. She must have been going back to her own place to do it, because the neighbors said they never saw her at the laundromat near the plaza, and Septima was the only person we knew who owned a washer and dryer. She never let anyone go with her, and eventually Mom stopped asking where she lived because she never gave a straight answer. She'd say things like "not far" or "over there," swinging her hand in no particular direction. I knew she had to live near Arts High, and I told my mother as much. If she lived out there, she wasn't even close to being poor. Every house near that school was three times as big as ours, and they all had huge green lawns that, in the desert, only the wealthy could afford. I once told Mom that I wouldn't be surprised if Dee lived in the same neighborhood where Mom used to work as a maid.

"You know where I mean? Right next to the irrigation canals."

"I *know* the neighborhood," she snapped.

She hated talking about the years when she cleaned house for Mrs. Campbell and how she used to have to stand out at the plaza, in the dirt. She used to take me with her on the days I didn't have school.

Mrs. Campbell would make Mom change into a pink uniform that had belonged to someone else and was at least two sizes too big. I wasn't old enough to understand everything Mom was feeling, but I knew she was humiliated to be seen in that baggy dress. She kept asking La

Señora if she could take it home and alter it, but Mrs. Campbell said her maids weren't allowed to take anything out of the house, ever. Mom ended up spending her own money to buy a new uniform, which Mrs. Campbell didn't even notice. The day Septima hired my mom at Frontera Street Fabrics I remember she threw that pink dress away. It was the only piece of clothing I'd ever seen her put right in the trash.

Whenever I went to Mrs. Campbell's, I'd sit in the kitchen and draw, or help out where I could. Once, I snuck into one of the back bedrooms that had a television and spread out on the bed to watch cartoons. My mother was busy cleaning some other part of the house when Mrs. Campbell came home from wherever she spent her days and discovered me. She didn't yell, but she turned off the television and said that I was old enough to be helping instead of wasting time. I was six. Mrs. Campbell told me to follow her to the garage, where she handed me a bucket and pointed me toward her semicircular gravel driveway.

"Pull out anything green that is growing between the stones," she instructed. I spent the entire afternoon in the hot sun, kneeling on rocks as sharp as thumbtacks, tweezing weeds that sliced the sides of my fingers every time I pulled. When we got home, my mother soaked my hands in iced tea and put Noxzema on my sunburn, calling Mrs. Campbell all sorts of horrible Spanish names. From then on my mom found other things for me to do at La Señora's house: fold laundry, wipe the kitchen counter, straighten the shoes in Mrs. Campbell's closet, anything to keep me out of the old woman's reach.

I knew Mom was ashamed and plenty mad the day she got fired. Mrs. Campbell called her a thief, even though she'd been working there for two years with no complaints. Mom never told me what Mrs. Campbell accused her of taking, but part of me wished that she *had* taken something good, like a gold watch or one of that old biddy's diamond rings.

"If Dee is from the Westside, that means she's rich, Mom. So what is she doing here?"

"Señor Richard isn't rich. He lives over there, too."

"He lives in a carriage house," I told her. "It's like a maid's room, except it's a little house in the backyard of a bigger house."

"How do you know that?"

"Peeps goes over there all the time."

"All the time?"

"Yeah, Richard takes him out there twice a week to practice his French horn with a quintet."

Mom shrugged. She told me that when she first met Dee she didn't trust her, but that now she'd been working at the fabric store too long to be the kind of person who was spending a couple weeks in the barrio as some kind of stupid adventure. Mom said she was even beginning to think that she and Dee were more the same than they were different.

"I think she lives in some apartment that she's ashamed to show us, or if she does live on the Westside, it's probably in one of those maid's houses like Señor Richard," Mom guessed. "Her driver's license said she was from Dallas. She probably doesn't even know what being from the Westside means in Los Cielos. If she did, she wouldn't have come down to Frontera Street to work, and she wouldn't have turned to a bunch of Mexicans to help her through the most important time of her life."

We both knew that much was true. There was a big invisible line running through the middle of Los Cielos, and it seemed that Mexicans were the only ones who ever crossed it, to work in the white people's kitchens and plant their gardens, to pick up their trash, paint their houses, mend their fences, and raise their children. If the *gringos* stepped over to our side at all, it was only for an hour or so, and in the daylight.

White women with tight-skinned tennis tans would rush in and out of the fabric shop to get fitted for one of Lettie Sanchez's beautiful gowns, or they might volunteer at the bookmobile or stand at the steps of Father Miguel's church handing out blankets and electric fans to the old people who didn't have heat or air conditioning. Then they'd go back home, feeling better about themselves. At night the only Westsiders who ventured into our neighborhoods were teenage boys in fast cars looking for trouble. Sometimes their fathers showed up too, driving around the plaza exactly the same way their wives did when they fetched their maids. But the women *they* were looking to hire weren't housekeepers. They were the leather-skirted, fishnet-stockinged, high-heeled girls their wives would never know about.

Maybe Mom was right about Dee not being from the Westside, but I didn't think so. She knew too much about the way things worked at my school not to have spent her teenage years at a place exactly like it. Peeps and I asked her all sorts of questions that even Richard, who grew up in Philadelphia, couldn't answer. She told us not to act surprised by the fact that almost every kid got a car, or a trip to Europe, for their sixteenth birthday—sometimes both. She told me, in private, that if the girls in my dance class ever planned to fly to Dallas or Houston to see one of the traveling Broadway shows, or a ballet, or anything like that, that I should go ahead and sign up, and she'd pay for the ticket. My mom said that didn't mean she was from this part of Texas. Rich people were alike, no matter where they lived.

Still, I thought Dee was keeping her background a secret. She knew all about the winter formal that Peeps got invited to by Lucinda Herndon, and she told him that if he didn't have the money, she'd rent the tuxedo he'd have to wear. She even advised him not to buy the kind of corsage he might normally get for a homecoming dance, or even the prom. She said he should get a bracelet corsage made out of tropical gardenias and dark satin ribbon, and she knew exactly where to order it. How would she know that if she wasn't from Los Cielos?

If you asked me, Dee was hiding something. She liked doing stuff for Peeps and me as long as we kept it secret. If our mothers were to ask where we were getting all the money for tickets and tuxedos and flowers and shows, Dee told us to tell them that our scholarships paid for a few extra activities. I told Peeps that was weird, but he just said, "Whatever."

Septima finally told Mom and me that we shouldn't care where Dee was from. She said we didn't have to know any more than what Dee had told us after the first night she slept on our sofa—that her husband died before she got a chance to tell him that they were going to have a baby.

Mom said she knew exactly what that was like. But that was a huge lie. My dad didn't die, he left, after I was born. I never told my mother to her face, but I knew she must have said or done something to drive him away. I knew it was her fault because she was still having nightmares about it, waking up at night screaming. Lots of times I could hear her praying to La Virgencita, begging for mercy. She never told me what her nightmares were about, and she usually told me everything.

I'd never seen my dad in person, but I knew exactly what he looked like from a few old pictures my mother gave me. Standing under a tree in the middle of a crowded park in Mexico, Paul Walker looked like someone who would run after any kind of ball that might be thrown his way. I could tell he didn't like having to keep still long enough to let the camera do its work. In my favorite photo his hands were in his pockets, and his black cowboy boots were set on the ground apart from one another, like he was shifting his weight. The short sleeves of his bright white shirt hugged his upper arms, and on his right wrist there was a bulky round-faced watch. He was laughing at my mom, or whoever took the picture, looking out from the corners of his eyes. And even though there was no real way to tell, I always imagined that she was laughing too.

Mom's never explained why he left or if she even tried to stop him.

He went to Arizona. I knew that much because for as long as I could remember, I had mailed letters to a post office box there. I sent him my school pictures, and notes about my life, mailing them all to P.O. BOX 529, SCOTTSDALE, ARIZONA.

I knew the address by heart.

Chapter 9

Dee

THE LONGER I STAYED ON FRONTERA STREET, THE LESS I needed to rely on the book of Spanish grammar that I carried with me. One month at Alma's house turned into two, and then into three; and each passing week left me in better command of the present tense. *Esta casa es mi hogar. Aquí todos somos familia.* This is my home. Here we're all family.

I managed to hold halting conversations in Spanish with Alma and Socorro about the fabric shop. Nothing deep, but they promised me that the more complicated stuff would seep in over time.

Barrio, I learned, means neighborhood, not slum. And a real neighborhood was exactly what Frontera Street turned out to be. Most of the homes were nothing but brick boxes with an occasional arch over a window or door. None of them had a basement or a second story. Their windows were decorated with curtains that may have originally been boldly colored but had been faded into meek pastels by the sun.

The street's asphalt was dotted with potholes and its sidewalks were disintegrating, but every few days parents like Petra Martinez and Albita Vargas patiently filled the cracks in the road with mud so their kids could ride their bikes up and down the block without getting hurt.

There was a steady rhythm to life on the street. On weekday mornings the schoolchildren spilled out of their houses at seven-thirty, holding paper-bag lunches in their hands. In the late afternoon the teenage girls hit the phones, and the boys congregated in Rafa Monzon's driveway to help him tinker with the engine of a hopeless old Chevy that the twenty-year-old swore he'd transform into a sweet, cherry-red lowrider.

On Friday night, the working men celebrated payday by setting up their lawn chairs in someone's front yard and contributing a few beers to the washtub filled with ice. While their wives finished the dinner dishes, they smoked cigarettes, squinted at the setting sun, and debated the Cowboys' running game or the quarterback's ongoing shoulder problem, like a group of commentators on ESPN.

On Sunday everyone went to Septima's house after church. The men sat themselves in front of the big-screen Zenith to watch football, and the women filed into the kitchen to make tamales. It was an hours-long, assembly-line affair that filled the block with the warm, musty smell of corn *masa* and green chiles. Because they did the same thing every week, each woman had her own apron hanging on a nail inside Septima's broom closet. Once they put on their aprons, they placed their jewelry in a tortilla basket next to the sink and washed their hands. Girls of all ages participated, inching up the tamale-making chain the same way their mothers had. The youngest simply watched, waiting for the day they were tall enough for Septima to station them at the kitchen sink, where the moment the mixing bowls ran empty they'd be washed and dried and made ready to be filled with yet another batch of sticky *masa* dough.

Washing was the job that initiated a girl into the tamale circle. The next job on the ladder was getting the strawlike corn husks ready. The teenagers did that. They sorted through bags of the stiff yellow fronds and selected ones that were wide enough to hold nice fat dollops of *masa*. The one time I tried it I wondered why nobody wore plastic gloves when they did their rummaging, because the husks cut like paper. After the husks were chosen, other girls dunked them into the warm water that filled half a dozen stockpots stationed underneath the kitchen table. They gave the husks a quick rinse and allowed the water to soften them up a bit.

The husks were placed in rows on the table, which itself was covered with swaths of wax paper. The older teens and the younger mothers and wives were in charge of assembly. They mixed the *masa*, shredded the pork, skinned the chiles and put each ingredient in a separate bowl. Then they approached the husks and delivered one perfectly measured spoonful of *masa* into the well of each sheaf. They topped that with a bit of meat and just enough chile to spice up the tamale but not overwhelm it. All that was finally topped with another dollop of *masa*, and the entire thing was wrapped and tied into a little bundle.

Steaming the tamales was the job reserved for veterans and the best cooks on the block. Septima led the team that layered the tamales into four Dutch ovens and kept the pots stoked with boiling water. These women knew instinctively how long to keep the pots covered and precisely how thick the steam should be to keep the tamales from becoming chewy or crumbly or hard as stone. The first two dozen to emerge were marched directly into the living room and devoured by the men. And miraculously, by five o'clock in the afternoon the kitchen was clean, the aprons were back on their nails and each lady left Septima's with two dozen tamales of her own.

Alma told me that every one of the women was capable of making her own batch at home, and it certainly would not take her all afternoon to complete. But this was a tradition, and being part of Frontera Street meant being part of the tamale cooking circle. What touched me most was that from the very first Sunday I showed up, the women worked me into the mix, letting me decide what job I felt most comfortable doing. After a couple of weeks of picking out husks, I settled on being one of the frond washers.

I tried to recall whether my mother and I ever did anything like that together when I was growing up. She tried to teach me how to play bridge, but I was never very good at it. We went shopping, but that was hardly food for the soul. She took me to her auxiliary meetings, where I learned that assigning ladies to committees was the way to stage flower and fashion shows. And, I admit, I enjoyed planning those events. But I couldn't remember ever seeing my mother's cheeks flushed by the humid heat rising from the kitchen stove. In fact, the only person I could remember ever working in our kitchen was Serita, and, yes, there were times when she would let me help her make cakes and cookies. She taught me how to separate an egg from its yolk, how to double-sift cake flour and how to grease bundt pans. As a wedding present she gave me a handwritten recipe book filled with dinner dishes that took no more than three steps to complete.

Why, I wondered, didn't people on the Westside share their lives with their neighbors the way people on Frontera Street did? It wasn't as if people over there were cold. They were friendly enough to bring a fresh pie to a newcomer. They made cordial small talk with passersby. But they kept their real lives locked inside their own four walls. Maybe the houses on Frontera Street were just too small for that.

Whatever the reason, being part of barrio life slowly pulled me out of my haze and gave me a new set of guidelines to follow. I actually looked forward to getting up early to get Socorro's lunch ready. I learned how to tell when the tomatillos and the *plátanos* at the Safeway were ripe, and—with lots of help—I even learned how to make tortillas from scratch. I felt the neighborhood's strong, steady heartbeat pump fresh blood through me. There was no question in my mind that Frontera Street was the lifeline that had rescued my baby and me, and I intended to hold on to it no matter what it took. More than anything, I wanted to become a real part of Alma and Socorro's lives, so I could say they were part of mine.

Almost everybody on Frontera Street did shift work. People would come and go, from sunup to sundown, dressed in muted-colored uniforms and sturdy shoes. Entire families worked together at Bobby O's Factory Discount Boots, tanning and stitching and packaging the cowboy footwear manufactured out of bull hide, ostrich, and eel. That was where Cece's father worked as a senior stitcher. In fact, Socorro told me one night that Cece's dad once made a pair of black lizard-skins for Governor Ann Richards, one-of-a-kind boots decorated with vines of yellow leather roses swirling up the sides.

That was the same night that Socorro pulled a Bobby O's box out of her own closet and brought it over to show me. She lifted the lid and pulled back the tissue paper, unveiling a pair of beautiful burgundy cowhides with sharply slanted riding heels and intricate stitching.

"Mr. Cardenas gave Cece and me matching pairs for our junior high graduation," she said, slowly lifting one of the boots out of the box and handing it to me. I slid my fingers over the fragrant, taut leather and followed the smooth grain as it tapered down to the narrow toe.

"See this?" She pointed to a chain of interlocking *S*'s and *C*'s stitched into the top half of the boot with glittering silver thread. I ran my palm down the descending initials, straight to the boot's smooth, slippery sole.

"You haven't worn them," I remarked.

Socorro shook her head as she put the boot back inside its box.

"Cece and I were going to wear them together on our first day at Chaparral High," she began. "But then I got the scholarship."

This wasn't the first time Socorro had hinted that she and her best friend might be losing touch.

"Are you sorry you decided to go to Arts?"

Socorro looked startled, as if she'd divulged a secret she wished I hadn't heard.

"No, of course not," she said, fumbling with the boot box and ducking back into her room to stash it inside her closet.

"It's okay, you know." I tried to console her. "You don't have to like it there just because you got a scholarship."

Without saying a word, Socorro walked out of her bedroom and into the bathroom, where she washed her ballet clothes in the sink every night. She pulled a pair of pink tights out of the soapy water and began to wring them out.

"I like the dancing," she said, leaving the other half of her thought unspoken.

She handed me the damp tights, and I draped them over the shower curtain rod. Then she drained the sink, poured another cap of Woolite into the basin, and filled it with water to soak a second pair.

"It's just that I see Cece having so much fun," she continued. "And that's what high school is supposed to be, right? The best time of your life."

I wondered what television program had convinced her of that.

"What's Cece doing that you aren't?"

"Hanging out," Socorro replied, throwing me a sideways glance to see if I understood how unfair the situation was. "It's not like she's doing this or that or anything special. It's just that she's *there*, you know, with everybody else."

I wanted to tell Socorro that I could guarantee there was nothing remotely interesting about hanging around with a bunch of listless teenagers after school, but I stopped myself.

"You've got weekends," I tried.

"Not for long," she shot back. "We're starting final rehearsals for the winter recital next week, and that means Saturdays and Sundays too."

I certainly couldn't argue with Socorro about her new school's demanding schedule. In addition to her regular classes, she attended a two-hour private dance class every weekday after school and then spent several hours doing homework. The holiday concert rehearsals would lengthen her stay on campus to well past nine o'clock.

"The thing is," Socorro sighed, "I'm pretty sure I want to be a dancer."

We looked at one another for a long moment. Inside, I was leaping for joy, happily picturing how elated Alma would be to hear the news. But on the outside I tried to stay calm, nodding my head just slightly.

"I'm really liking the ballet part of school, " Socorro continued. "It's just the other stuff, you know? The other girls think I'm out of it. And I am. I'm clueless."

I frowned.

"Half the time I don't know what they're talking about. Summer camp and cotillion and whatever. I can't even fake it."

"You don't need to fake anything," I said.

"Oh, like I'm gonna talk about the barrio with them? Like they want to hear about Rafa's lowrider?"

She's still a little girl, I thought, *a brave but frightened child.* I wanted to hold her, to stroke her beautiful brown face and tell her to just give it time. But that's not what she wanted to hear. She was asking for practical advice, and I knew I could give it to her. Finally, here was a way to repay Alma for everything she'd done for me. Here was the contribution I could make.

"Do you want help?" I asked gently.

Socorro stopped sloshing her tights through the suds in the sink. "What do you know about the Westside?"

"I know what girls like that do," I replied. "I know what they talk about."

"You do?"

I nodded. "They aren't that different from you and Cece. They just do different things. And once you know about those things, Socorro, you'll fit right in."

"You swear?"

"I swear," I said. "Now, young lady, do you have French to study?"

"No," she replied, giving me a hug. "Not tonight."

*　　*　　*

Once a week I drove all of our laundry to my house on the Westside and used that time to water the plants and read my mail.

My mother wrote to say that she planned to stay in Europe until after the baby was born. She apologized for not wanting to be part of the birth process but, she said, she was of a generation that never understood why young women considered the sweating and screaming of labor worthy of an audience. She promised she'd come home right after the big event and try to be as much help as she could. I suppose I should have seen it coming. Momma wasn't good at dealing with messy details. She had always relied on Serita and my father to do that for her. Poppa kept the cars running, kept the house painted, and kept the bank account balanced, or he hired people to do it for him. Serita was the one who did the hands-on mothering. She ironed my clothes and polished my school shoes. She got up at night and rubbed my tummy when I got sick. My mother was there, standing in the room, but Serita was the one who put the wet washcloth on my forehead.

Momma loved me, of that I had no doubt. She told me often. And, as a girl, I knew that one day I'd grow up to be a polished lady just like her. I knew I'd get to wear strings of pearls and pretty high heels to luncheons for good causes. I knew it would happen sometime after I stopped climbing trees and playing in the mud, sometime after I stopped coming home with scraped knees for Serita to kiss and bandage. I thought it would come after Mitch and I settled down and started our own family. But now she wasn't going to be around to take the first step with me.

In a way, her decision was a relief. I knew she would never have approved of my new living arrangements. She would have never understood what I had found on Frontera Street. And I'm not sure I would have been able to explain it to her. All I knew was that being with Septima, Alma, and Socorro meant more to me than anything.

I walked through the huge, quiet house and felt a hollowness I couldn't bear, and that's when I knew that I'd have to keep the fact that I grew up on the Westside a secret from the people on Frontera Street. What good would it do to tell them that I came from this? Just saying the word *Westside* would change the way they would look at me. It would alter everything they thought about me. They'd fill in the background of my life story with scenes of privilege and entitlement. And they wouldn't be able to see past that anymore.

Technically, I told myself, I wasn't being dishonest by keeping quiet. I was just buying a little more time for them to get to know me—a little more time to walk through the straight rows of their lives and deal with the rubble of my own. I needed Frontera Street and the fabric shop. They were the only places where I felt steady, like the sort of person Mitch would want the mother of his child to be.

I watered the plants and folded the laundry while it was still warm from the dryer. I gathered my things and walked out of the big house, locking the door behind me. I could honestly say I didn't consider the Westside home anymore, but my biggest fear was that my new friends wouldn't understand and they'd decide I didn't belong on Frontera Street either. If that were to happen I'd have nowhere to go, because the only other home I'd ever known was with Mitch. I had to make it work.

When I got back to Frontera Street, I looked up and down the block and smiled at how soothing the sounds and smells of the barrio had become. I set the laundry down on the brown sofa and let the walls of Alma's tiny house, our house, hug me tight.

After dinner I asked Alma if she would be my birthing partner, and two days later we made it official by writing her name on the hospital papers under the title "Coach."

Chapter 10

ALMA

"SHE CAN'T SAY NO," SEPTIMA SAID AS SHE TWISTED THE KEY IN the shop's front door and jiggled the knob.

We were standing on the sidewalk ready to walk down the mile of bad road that stretched between the store and our houses. In the summer heat the twenty-minute trip would have been too much for Dee. But it was the end of November and the cool evenings were fresh with fall. It wasn't until then, after a full day's work and six months of pregnancy, that Dee actually looked like she was going to have a baby. She was built like lots of other white women, slim in the hip and long in the leg. The baby had loaned her some curves, and even though Dee complained that she'd gotten too fat, Septima and I thought she looked wonderful.

"It's okay, I'll go," Dee grumbled as we started down the block.

"No, it's *not* okay," I protested. "She knows you are tired and she only asks you because everybody else has stopped being polite. She can sit and watch that food rot for all anybody else cares."

We were talking about Peeps's mother, Iluminada, and her crazy diets.

She'd been gaining and losing the same fifty pounds ever since Peeps was born, puffing up and then slimming back down, taking the entire neighborhood on the roller coaster with her.

We'd all been through Eat to Lose and Eat to Win, and dozens of other no-name diets that called for bananas on Tuesdays and grapefruits on Thursdays. We'd watched her Eat to Succeed and Eat More to Weigh Less, and we stood by as she set out on the Five-Day Miracle and Eight

Weeks to Total Fitness. We'd seen her buy cases of Slimfast and Dexatrim, and we laughed her off the Beverly Hills diet (*No, Iluminada, I don't think you can substitute a cheese enchilada for the two-ounce turkey sandwich*). We listened to her explain the rules of the new, easier Weight Watchers each of the six times she rejoined, and we watched her move out of her fat clothes into her thin ones and right back out of them again.

The seesawing wasn't the problem. We were used to that. The problem was that the more dedicated Iluminada was to a diet, the more crazy she became about cooking. Not for herself, but for everybody else on Frontera Street. If she couldn't eat what she wanted, she made sure everybody else did.

She used to have a schedule that she would slip into our mailboxes, a calendar showing which night you and your family would be her guest. Father Miguel had an open invitation to drop by anytime. The schedule said so.

Nobody knew how many hours into the night Iluminada stayed up cooking, but her kitchen light was always on. She had a regular job, working from dawn until one in the laundry room of the Westin Hotel a few blocks from the downtown plaza. After her shift she would walk over the bridge to the outdoor market in Mexico to get what she needed, and then she'd get right back to her cooking.

Iluminada went all out for her dinners, and they were delicious. She'd serve tortilla soup and *nopalito* salad, *móle poblano* and barbecued chicken. Once in a while she made a ham, but she usually didn't stray too far from border food—quesadillas with Chihuahua cheese, *carnitas*, and amazing *horchata*. There was always a tower of homemade flour tortillas waiting on the table, and her kitchen practically seduced you with the toasty, caramel smell of a flan cooling for dessert. And there was never a green salad or a spear of broccoli in sight.

When the whole thing started, people would show up with a six-pack or some other little offering that Iluminada's husband, Efran, would dive right into. A basket filled with tortilla chips would be on the coffee table, alongside bowls of guacamole, salsa and *chile con queso* rotating on a lazy Susan. If Efran reached for a chip first, Iluminada would give him a cold, hard glare.

"Please, it's for *you*," she'd say, sitting back and smiling as *you* and your family helped yourselves.

While you munched, she would explain her diet: what she could eat and what she couldn't. She'd lecture about proteins and sugars and carbohydrates.

When Peeps was a baby, Iluminada would bounce him on her knee and in baby talk say something like, "And *Papi* is helping *Mami* with the program, isn't he? No chips for Papa. No chips for Mama. Carrots. Carrots. Carrots."

It was funny, until you got to the actual dinner. Iluminada would have set out her prettiest tablecloth and the dishes her mother passed down to her on her wedding day. There would be a place for everyone in your family, and one ready for Father Miguel, just in case. But there was never a place for Iluminada. She never ate.

She'd orbit the table, whisking away platters and putting down new ones. She'd give people second and third helpings before they could say no, and she'd pat the stack of tortillas with the palm of her hand to make sure it was still warm. Then she'd watch you eat. She'd take in every bite with her hungry eyes, follow the fork from your plate to your lips, and just about chew along with you. Every time you swallowed, she did too. And when you moved from one part of your plate to another, she'd take a drink of water. It was so unsettling that you'd try to sneak in a few unmonitored bites while she was watching somebody else.

Efran usually slipped back into the living room during this part of the meal, hoping to get away from her eagle eye and drink some beer.

She was the perfect hostess, except she kept the table conversation confined to food: how she grated the cheese and chopped the onions, how too much meat could ruin a plate of green enchiladas, and how too little meat cheapens a stew. She'd ask if you could taste all the ingredients, and were they rich and soft on your tongue? She wanted to hear every detail. She watched you spread butter on your tortilla and then she passed you the salt.

If you asked her to join you, or if you cut a piece of *carne* and set it on a butter plate for her, she would haughtily push it away.

"*Estás loca?*" she'd gasp. "I can't eat that. Do you know how many calories are in that? How many fat grams? *Ay, Dios mió!*" Then she would serve dessert.

The dinners always disappeared when Iluminada reached her goal weight, and they were put on hold during the months she maintained. Sometimes a full year would go buy without a single invitation to supper. But Efran would warn us the moment he saw Iluminada cutting recipes out of the newspaper, and Peeps would start hoarding bags of corn chips she put in his school lunches the minute he saw a bowl of celery sticks in the fridge. They knew those were sure signs that another cooking binge was on the way.

As the years passed, every family on Frontera Street had to decide if Iluminada's invitations were worth it. I knew for a fact that Father Miguel had heard his share of confessions on the matter, from people who had invented elaborate lies to get out of going to her house and people who faked illnesses or kept their lights off all evening, pretending they weren't home.

Septima was still going because Iluminada was her best friend. But Beto refused to go back. Socorro and I had stopped attending the suppers a while ago, and we let Peeps eat at our house during her diets.

When Dee moved in, however, Iluminada was working on the last ten pounds of the Rotation Diet (tuna, sardines, cottage cheese, and berries rotated by the week), and she was cooking up a storm. When she learned that Dee was pregnant, she was convinced the weight would fly off her hips if she could keep shoveling food Dee's way. So Peeps brought over all sorts of muffins and cookies and coffee cakes, and Dee had already been to Iluminada's for dinner eight times.

"She's only got three pounds to go, so this will probably be the last one," Septima reassured Dee. "And her final-pound dinners are always the best."

"It's okay, I'll go. I just have to sit down for about half an hour, maybe take a quick nap."

"I'll go, too," Septima offered. "And I'll call Father Miguel."

There were still plenty of things about Dee we didn't know, but she had become so important to Socorro that, for the time being, I didn't care. She helped my little girl with her homework and drilled her on the French terms she had to learn for dance class. She was helping her fit in at school in a way I never could.

Dee and I both knew that Socorro's transfer to Arts High wasn't as easy as she wanted us to believe. She had lots of homework and sometimes spent hours on the telephone with Richard, wading through it.

She moaned about how everybody else was so far ahead of her in math and history, but I wasn't too worried about that. She was smart enough to catch up on the facts and figures. It was everything else that frightened me—feeling safe, having fun. She already looked different than the other kids. She didn't need anything else holding her back.

The students at Arts High had their own vocabulary—not just words, but a common knowledge that Socorro had to learn—and Dee was filling her in. She taught her what the kids meant when they said they had to choose between the Arts High and a prep. She explained how riding a horse Western style is different from riding English. And she even pulled out a map to show us where Tanglewood and Wolf Trap are, explaining that they're fancy places up East where people go to see plays and symphonies and dance concerts during their summer vacations. Dee armed Socorro with other crazy details too, like the fact that people go to Santa Fe to see the art galleries and the open-air opera, but nobody goes to Taos to do anything but ski. She suggested that Socorro agree with the girls when they complained about the low-quality shopping in Los Cielos but told her she should argue that there's not another town in all of Texas that produces better cowboy boots.

Socorro suspected that Dee had grown up on the Westside, because all the knowledge she doled out seemed like second nature. But I reminded her that the driver's license I saw at the hospital had a Dallas address, and, I said, rich people all over the country live that sort of lifestyle. Anyway, what would Dee be doing with us if she had grown up across town? People over there didn't bother with the barrio. To Westsiders the city of Los Cielos stopped at the sidewalks of the downtown plaza, and anything beyond that was nothing but a big brown blur.

Dee didn't think that way at all. In fact, she regularly made a point of telling Socorro there were things about the barrio that were just as special as skiing in Taos or summering at Tanglewood. Dee said the girls on the Westside had probably heard millions of stories about *quinceañera* parties, but the odds were they had never been to one. So, she said, Socorro and Peeps should brag about all the elaborate dance bands and banquets that they'd enjoyed. And by all means, Dee instructed, they should exaggerate.

But despite all of the coaching, I sensed Socorro was still having problems making new friends and was struggling to keep her old ones from drifting away.

Cece and Socorro were trying hard to stay as close as they'd been since nursery school, and I admired their dedication to one another. They phoned every night, and on Fridays one would sleep over at the other's house. Whenever Cece came over, Dee would huddle with both girls in Socorro's room for hours, giving them what she called white-girl makeovers. She'd wipe off the black eyeliner and red lipstick that the two favored, replacing it with two dabs of wheat-colored eye shadow, lots of face powder, and a streak of bubblegum-pink lip gloss. Sometimes she'd put tiny pearl earrings on them and pull back their hair with wide headbands.

They'd fall over laughing, chanting, "Tennis, anyone?"

Dee was twice their age, but on those nights, when she was giggling and her mind was at ease, she seemed young enough to be their sister. Sometimes, I would look at her pretty blue eyes and her funny, crooked smile, and I'd know how much her husband loved her.

I hadn't seen La Llorona since the afternoon Dee collapsed at the fabric shop, but one night when Socorro was at Cece's and Dee was eating at Iluminada's, La Llorona came back. I could feel her presence the entire evening, sense her wicked eyes watching me. I moved around the house like a hunter tracking a kill, flinching at any little sound, jumping out of my skin when a neighborhood dog began to bark.

I set La Virgencita on the bed next to me and tried to sleep.

The frigid wind that swirled around La Llorona woke me first. Then I saw her yellow eyes burning in the black shadow of her face and felt her toss a prickly shroud of hatred over me. I couldn't move. She circled my bed, saying nothing. She hovered over me and glared. She batted at my little saint with her long, ragged fingernails.

"What good is she?" La Llorona grunted. "She let you walk right into it."

I reached for my beloved statue and closed my eyes as I wrapped my fingers around it. I started to pray, to keep myself from falling apart and to try and keep from hearing what the hateful La Llorona had to say.

"You're a fool to think that lump of plaster can protect you from what's happening now." She leaned her shadowy form over my bed and hovered close to my shoulder. I tried to turn away, but her bony hand grabbed my chin and yanked it so I was looking straight into her baleful eyes.

"You've lost," she growled.

She threw her head back and burst into a guttural laugh that shook the floor and chilled my blood. I freed myself from her grip and buried my face in my hands. She screeched and cackled as I fumbled with the bedside lamp, hoping to chase her away with the glare of light.

"What do you want?" I screamed.

She bellowed louder and then blew a gust of frozen air into my face.

"I've got what I want," she gloated. "Everything's exactly the way I want it."

The next thing I knew Dee was banging on my bedroom door.

"Are you all right? Can you hear me?"

I nodded my head, not realizing that Dee was unable to see me.

"Alma? What's happening?" Dee rushed into the room, turned on the light and crawled onto the bed next to me. She slowly pulled La Virgencita out of my clenched hands.

"It's a nightmare," I said, trying to stop trembling. "A dream I have sometimes."

Dee pulled the bedsheets up over my shoulders, her face full of concern.

"No," I confessed. "It's not a dream. It's my sin."

"What?" Dee asked.

"Do you believe in spirits?"

Dee brushed a loose strand of hair off my forehead. "What are you talking about?" she murmured.

I looked into her eyes and quietly began to tell her everything about Paul and me.

I explained the legend of La Llorona to her, telling the story of the murderous mother and her eternal search for children's souls. Instead of being astonished that I believed such a vengeful spirit was haunting me, Dee seemed to almost identify with La Llorona's curse.

"I don't think she's a witch," she whispered to me. "I think she's lonely."

It was the first time I'd repeated the story to anyone other than Sepi. Maybe I let it tumble out to show Dee that I had once felt as alone as she was feeling. Or maybe I wanted her to know that Frontera Street was a refuge for me too. I can't say why I decided it was time for her to know about my past. But it was.

Socorro's father said he'd marry me, and so I told our priest that I was pregnant and begged him not to tell my father.

I introduced Paul to my family, and my father greeted him with suspicion and disdain. My mother, on the other hand, liked him right away. She was overjoyed when I explained that when he said he built hotels he meant he supervised the construction crews, not that he was a laborer. That, she promised, would make my father very happy.

Paul was so charming that he won them both over in a few weeks, and while they didn't understand why we wanted to rush into marriage, they didn't oppose our decision.

In private, Paul and I talked about moving to the United States, where our baby could be born into a good life. We planned everything out, and I was as happy as I had ever been. I thanked God for sending me such a glorious future, and I congratulated myself for waiting for such a good man.

My mother rushed invitations into the mail, and my father coaxed his fellow businessmen to set aside their six-months-in-advance requirements to order flowers, food, and a gown.

Two weeks before the wedding, Paul walked into the juice store as I was locking up. He gave me a long kiss and a loving hug. He pulled the rubber band out of my braid and spread my hair over my shoulders.

"That's how I want to remember you," he said, adding that he had to go away for a few days to plan a new project in Cancún.

The letter arrived three days later. My mother placed it in the middle of my dinner plate, serving it to me as a special treat. I opened it in front of both my parents, expecting to read about the beautiful Yucatán sunsets and how much they made Paul miss me. But that wasn't what the letter said at all. In fact, I had to read it twice, even three times, before I could believe what he had written.

My face must have paled, because my father ripped the note out of my hands before I could even think. I left the table while he read it, and then refused to leave my bedroom.

Paul wrote that he couldn't go through with it. He had a girlfriend back in the United States, somebody he'd thought he was over. But he'd realized that he still loved her, and the truth was that he had promised to marry her. Before he met me. Before I got pregnant. He said he was sorry.

My father was outraged, and my mother was stunned. I spoke to her through my locked door. I wanted to see the letter again, to hold it in my hands and prove to myself that it was real. She slid it under the door. I read it a dozen more times, hoping to find a different message buried inside the hurtful words. My father called the priest the next morning, and made me sit with them in his study.

"Tell him," he commanded.

My throat was dry, and my words came out like hiccups as I began to explain what Paul had written.

"Not that," Papi roared. "He knows that. Tell him the other thing."

I didn't know what he was talking about, and my hesitation made him shake with anger.

"Tell him how that man left you!" he shouted. "What condition he left you in!"

"He already knows," I said meekly.

"What?"

My father glared at the priest, and the man who had baptized me lowered his eyes and nodded his head. Papi took it all in like he was breathing polluted air. My mother knocked at the door and he ordered her to go away.

"I'll take care of this," he shouted.

He commanded me to leave the room while he and the priest worked things out. An hour later, he called me back in. The priest was gone and Papi told my mother to sit next to me.

"The church wants you to have the baby," he explained. "You can go to the convent in Taxco until it is born. Then you'll give it to the nuns."

My mother began to cry.

"Otherwise," Papi continued, "I know a doctor in Mexico City. We can tell the priest you miscarried."

A few days later a second letter arrived at the juice store, hand-delivered by the postman. Paul wrote that he felt terrible about how he had left things, and he had a plan that he hoped I could live with. He repeated that he could not marry me. But he was willing to provide everything we had talked about for our baby—a home in the United States and citizenship for our son or daughter. He enclosed a check, enough money to get me across the border. He said he'd already started the immigration process, had already made arrangements for me to get working papers, listing himself as my sponsor. If I wanted to go through with it, all I had to do was cash the check and get to Texas, where he would have a place waiting for me. Where our baby could be born an American.

The only thing he asked in return was that I keep it all secret. He didn't want me to look him up, or try to contact him.

I hid the letter in my room and stared at Paul's handwriting day after day, wondering why he had signed the note *"with love."*

At home, things grew worse. The priest pulled me aside one Sunday after Mass to tell me I had to get to the convent before my sin became obvious. I stopped talking to my father after he left an envelope filled with cash on my dresser, next to the name and address of his man in Mexico City. My mother couldn't look me in the face without crying, and she was humiliated by having to call the two hundred people she had invited to the wedding and inform them it was off.

It was then that the dark spirit began to haunt me. I knew that La Llorona had found strength in my worry and indecision and pounced on it like a jackal, planning to snatch my baby for herself.

I used to sit up all night trying to work out a tolerable future for myself. I couldn't give my baby to the nuns, if in her face they'd never see anything but sin. And my father's other plan repulsed me. So, I had only two choices. I could either raise my child at home or accept Paul's offer to change our lives.

I wanted to believe that my parents' embarrassment would dissolve the instant they saw their grandchild's smile. I imagined my father walking proudly through town with my baby, daring anyone to cast judgment on his good name. But I was asking too much. As the weeks passed, my father's face only hardened into stony angles of disapproval, and my mother's tears filled our house with shame. No child could be happy under such dark skies.

I phoned the number in Arizona that Paul had written in his letter and spoke to a woman who said she had been expecting my call. She told me to cash the check and take a bus, or a train, to Bandera, the

Mexican town across the border from Los Cielos. She gave me a second phone number to dial when I arrived.

At the border bridge, she said, I would be met by an American lawyer hired to bring me across legally. I packed one bag, lining the bottom with my birth certificate, my baptism papers, a photograph of my parents' wedding day, and a few snapshots of Paul. I wrapped a nightgown around La Virgencita, stashed her between two pairs of pants, and prayed that she would understand.

I told my parents I was going to have the baby at the convent in Taxco. As I lied to them I looked into their faces and wondered if somehow they knew that I'd never be back.

When I arrived in Los Cielos, the lawyer brought me here, to Frontera Street. He handed me the key to this house, which, he said, was already paid for.

Surprisingly, Paul came back just before Socorro was born. After six months of living alone, I opened the front door and saw him standing there. It was winter, and he was wrapped in a heavy sheepskin jacket. His cowboy hat was pulled down over his eyebrows, and his cheeks were red and chapped. I should have been furious. I should have turned him away, but I was too confused and lonely to do anything except take his hand and lead him inside.

He touched my belly, and then he kneeled in front of me and kissed the smooth, round swell. There was no way, he said, that he would have let me have our baby alone. I knew I was crazy to take him back, but having him there, holding me and, soon, our baby, was all I had ever wanted.

I never asked him about his other life.

He wanted to know if the little house was enough, if the cash he had been sending covered what I needed. We kept our conversations narrow, avoiding the past and never venturing too far into the future. I went back to church, to thank God for returning him to me. I introduced him to Father Miguel, who promised to baptize our baby. Every night I would turn out the light and smile into the darkness, knowing that while I was with Paul, La Llorona would have to find another victim.

Five minutes after our baby was born, Paul held her in his arms. He leaned down to kiss her round, red face and whispered something into her tiny ear. He massaged her pudgy feet and smiled when she wrapped her five fingers around his one. It was his idea to name her Socorro, which in English means *help*. No, more than that. It means *rescue*.

At the baptism, Paul stood next to me as Father Miguel poured holy water over Socorro's head. He held my hand, and we both prayed for family strength and enduring love in the name of the Father, the Son, and the Holy Ghost.

The next afternoon, while the baby and I were sleeping, he left.

Dee looked at me with a mix of sorrow and concern. "Does Socorro know any of this?" she asked.

"Some."

"Are you still waiting?"

"For him? No. He could be dead for all I care."

Dee lowered her eyes.

"Oh," I stammered. "I didn't mean . . ."

"It's okay," she answered. "Alma, I had no idea."

I took Dee's hand in mine and we sat for a moment in silence.

"We can talk about your husband," I eventually said. "About anything you want."

"There's not much to say, really. It's hard for me to believe Mitch is gone forever. But he is, isn't he?"

"What about the rest of your family?"

"I'm an only child and my father died a couple of years ago. My mother doesn't stay in one place for very long."

"So where's home?"

"Here," Dee said as she raised herself off the bed. "I'd like to think it's right here."

Chapter 11

DEE

DECEMBER WAS LETTIE SANCHEZ'S BUSIEST MONTH. WOMEN from the Westside needed gowns for holiday parties, and legions of beauty pageant contestants were placing orders for the Miss Texas preliminary contests in the spring. Lettie was in the store constantly, buying mountains of organza and an endless supply of pearl and rhinestone buttons. Her business was booming, actually getting too big for her to handle alone. That's why Septima asked if I wanted to take a break from the button counter and help Lettie do some hemming and sequin application.

I was seven months into my pregnancy, and my legs and ankles were perpetually swollen. The baby kicked my ribs whenever I stretched my arms over my head to reach the uppermost button drawers. I had to sit down every half hour to catch my breath. Hemming gowns at Lettie's house sounded like heaven, but I enjoyed coming into the store every day, seeing people and trying, at least for a few minutes, to focus on something other than my leg cramps. So, Septima asked Beto to set up an easy chair for me near the pattern books, and that way I could do the handwork in the shop.

The chair he delivered was huge, with plenty of room for me to shift this way and that. The only problem was when I finally found a position that eased the pressure in my lower back, my feet dangled a few inches off the floor.

"You need a footrest," Septima said.

She rolled the shop's stepping stool over to me, but it was too tall, lifting my knees above my belly.

"Maybe a phone book," I suggested.

Pilar, who was standing near the cash register, said the Yellow Pages we usually kept by the phone were missing, so Alma walked to the storage room to look for them there. Meanwhile, Septima rummaged through the fabric scraps and small boxes of expensive silk thread behind the button counter.

"What's this?"

Septima had found Alma's secret box and was examining it just as Alma stepped out from the back room with two thick phone books in her arms.

"Anybody know what this is?" Septima asked again.

It was hard for me to believe that Septima didn't remember the box from the afternoon I fainted. I certainly hadn't been able to forget it. There had been so many times I had wanted to pull it out and ask Alma about the photographs and the *milagro* medal and the unmailed letters inside. But something told me that no matter how close we'd become, it still wasn't close enough to ask about that box.

Alma rushed over to me and slid the phone books under my feet, saying nothing.

"Pilar, is this yours?" Septima persisted.

I thought back to my first few weeks at the shop, when Alma and I believed our worlds spun in opposite directions. It was Septima who kept pushing us together, pairing us up behind the button counter and then again in Alma's home. Somehow, from the very start, Septima knew that if Alma and I looked at each other hard enough, we would see that we were more the same than we were different.

Still, I had no idea why the things inside that box were so menacing to Alma that she couldn't step forward to claim them. But I saw panic fill her eyes as Septima moved her hand toward the lid.

"It's mine," I blurted out.

Alma's eyes darted my way, her face relaxed a bit. I tried to stand up as I spoke, but one of my feet slid on the unstable stack of phone books and I tumbled back into the big chair, knocking over a saucer of Austrian crystal beads that had been balanced on the armrest. Everyone froze as the tiny crystals ricocheted across the floor and I floundered in the chair like a fish on deck. Septima scurried out from behind the counter to take hold of my elbow as I struggled, once again, to steady myself.

Alma dashed to the counter and grabbed the box.

"Know what?" I called over to Alma. "We might as well take that home with us tonight."

Alma nodded and set the box next to my jacket and the lunch bag full of fruit and cheese she packed for me every day.

Pilar grabbed the broom and swept the scattered crystals toward the middle of the floor. She pushed the little beads and bits of dust and loose threads into a dustpan and then began to pick the expensive crystals out of the mess one by one.

"I'll go wash these," she announced to no one in particular.

Septima resumed her place at the front of the shop, and Alma stacked the phone books at my feet, whispering, "Thank you" as she gently placed my ankles on the small tower of Yellow Pages.

It was early afternoon and business was slow, which concerned Septima. Usually, she said, downtown shoppers wandered over to the fabric shop after spending the morning at Schuster's Department Store. Especially in December, because for as long as anyone could remember Schuster's had the monopoly on the best Santa Claus in town. As sponsor of the Los Cielos Thanksgiving Day parade, Schuster's could count on all of the kids at the parade following Santa directly from his giant float into the store, where he sat on a huge gold throne ringed by cardboard glaciers and a North Pole that was dripping with plastic icicles. At least four generations of children had insisted that the Santa at Schuster's was the real thing, and all the others were hopeless impostors.

But this year a Bloomingdale's store had opened at the Westside Mall, and right after Halloween the store began constructing a high-tech Santa's Village. For weeks the newspaper ran stories about the saw-and-hammer construction going on behind the plywood partition, counting down the days to Santa's arrival, which was cunningly scheduled exactly one day before Schuster's Thanksgiving parade.

Of course, Schuster's tried to fight back by offering free cookies and hot chocolate to kids in line to see its Santa, and by raffling off a pair of Rollerblades every hour. But it was too late. There was no way the old-fashioned department store could compete with Bloomingdale's in-house Alpine village, stocked with a herd of microchip-controlled reindeer, life-size dancing bears, a puppy petting zoo, and a make-your-own-ice-cream-sundae bar hosted by a jolly Mrs. Claus inside a mammoth igloo.

In fact, Septima said, she'd heard that Bloomingdale's had stolen so much of Schuster's holiday business that it might be forced to close for good.

"How much would that hurt us?" Alma asked.

Septima shrugged her shoulders nonchalantly, but the worry in her face told us she knew exactly how deeply it would damage our business and she didn't want to say.

That night we went to see the holiday concert at Arts High.

Alma wore a deep-purple pantsuit that Lettie had made for her and carried a dozen long-stem roses that Dolores of Flores by Dolores gave her free of charge. Peeps's parents dressed up, too, with Iluminada showing off the results of her most recent diet in a black velvet dress with a red satin belt. Efran and Beto both walked tall in dark wool suits.

Lettie had offered to make a dress for me as well, but I told her it would be a waste of time. It's impossible to make a woman entering her third trimester look elegant, and I had a long-sleeved maternity dress that would do.

Cece insisted on putting my hair up and hanging Christmas ball earrings from my lobes. She tried to convince me that I looked pretty, but I knew that I looked like a lumpy balloon animal.

Richard told us that a friend of his had reserved a dozen seats in the third row for us, and all we had to do was tell the student usher that we were the Frontera Street party.

We gathered on Septima's front porch an hour before the show and decided who would ride with whom, and then Richard and Father Miguel led our four-car caravan out of the barrio to the Westside.

We knew the musical program would include a bit of Handel's *Messiah* because the entire street had heard Peeps practicing it for weeks. But Socorro had kept her role a secret from the rest of us, except Cece, who was the only one who knew what Socorro was going to dance.

Since I was riding with Cece, in the the backseat of her parents' car, I grilled her every mile of the way.

"Is it a big role?"

"I'm not gonna say."

"She's just a beginner," I reasoned, "so it's not a big part, right?"

"It's a surprise."

Cece's father jumped in. "I know! She's a tree," he teased. "Or a lamp!"

"Nooo, Dad," Cece groaned.

We pulled into the parking lot, already crowded with dozens of dark European sedans, and followed a steady stream of parents and siblings into the softly lit auditorium.

Peeps smiled at us from his seat deep inside the orchestra's semicircle, and Richard explained that it was a big accomplishment for a freshman to sit in the French horn section's third-chair position. As we filed into our reserved seats, Richard asked if I would mind taking the chair on the aisle so he could sit next to Alma. I had sensed chemistry between those two. He always made a point of stopping by to chat after driving Peeps home from their chamber music sessions. I had teased Alma relentlessly about his visits, pointing out that he didn't seem to take the same sort of interest in the mothers of his other students. Socorro noticed his behavior too, and she kept pushing her mother to invite Richard to dinner, but Alma resisted.

"I'm a lot older," she argued.

Still, I was sure I heard more than a hint of hope in her blustery constraint. And I knew for a fact that her face lit up whenever he spent time with her.

I wondered if she knew that she was showing all the signs of falling in love, and whether she noticed how Richard made a point of leaning into her shoulder to whisper something about each piece of music and how he tenderly touched her arm every chance he got. I took a long look at all the proud families sitting together in the dark and felt my baby shift inside me. I thought of our row, filled with the familiar faces of Frontera Street, and realized I was sitting with my family, too.

When the curtain lifted, the audience gasped. The stage was set like an elaborate winter woods with eight flocked pine trees, a real ice pond on which a skater was doing twirls, and a garland-draped sleigh being pulled by a skittish horse dressed in bells. The scenery alone won an appreciative round of applause.

When the audience settled down, the violins trilled and a group of dancers swept onto the stage in white ankle-length tutus that fluttered with their every move. The music was from *The Nutcracker*. The Dance of the Snowflakes.

With their hair pulled back exactly the same way and identical halos of glittery tinsel on all of their heads, it was hard to distinguish one dancer from another. But the parents had no problem. Mothers pointed out their daughters to whoever was sitting next to them, while the proud fathers, armed with video cameras, raced each other to the front of the auditorium to get the best shots.

We sat on the edge of our seats, searching for Socorro. She wasn't in the first group doing intricate footwork to the flowing music. Before long, a second group of six joined the first, and the dozen graceful snowflakes continued to dance, moving their arms and feet in unison. We still didn't see Socorro.

I recognized some of the steps from the vocabulary sessions Socorro and I had carried out at our kitchen table. The dancers *brisé'd* and *piqué'd* with anxious smiles frozen onto their faces. Still, their steps were so assured and sophisticated that it was hard to believe they were only high school students.

Eventually, the music swelled to a crescendo and the twelve dancers moved into a **V**-formation, drawing our eyes to the back of the stage where another girl wearing a classic tutu stepped into the blue-tinted spotlight. The sparkling tiara on her head let us know she was the Snow Queen. She raised herself onto her toes and began to glide across the stage like a skittering top. It was Socorro.

I glanced at Alma, who was astonished. She had one hand over her mouth and the other in Richard's gentle grip. The intense stage lights and the sleek pink satin toe shoes made Socorro's legs seem miles long, and because the elastic straps on the white tutu were almost invisible, Socorro's elegant neck and shoulders appeared bare.

She was stunning.

Alma and I had never seen Socorro really dance at home. She practiced little steps here and there, but never linked them into anything you would consider actual ballet. Sometimes I would walk into the living room to find her balancing on one leg with the other stretched out shoulder high. She would time how long she could hold the pose and complain that her right leg was stronger than her left. She practiced her pirouettes on the kitchen linoleum, keeping her eyes glued to one spot to keep from getting dizzy, and she would often clown by doing dainty combinations in bulky tennis shoes. Sometimes she drove Alma crazy by moving her arms through an entire routine at the dinner table.

Her mother and I both knew Socorro had plenty of natural grace, but nothing could have ever prepared us to see her up on that stage performing double turns and split-leg leaps, landing without a sound and moving straight on to even more difficult steps.

Shortly after her entrance, a boy joined her onstage and they began to dance a pas de deux. He lifted her over his head, setting her on his shoulder and leaving her posed there as he walked across the stage with both his arms outstretched, proving to the audience that nothing was keeping her up but balance.

"Who's that?" asked an anonymous voice in the row behind me.

"Don't recognize her," another voice answered.

The dance ended with Socorro spinning across the stage toward the boy and then tipping sideways as he lunged to catch her. The music stopped, and everybody in the Frontera Street row jumped to their feet, applauding wildly. The roses Alma had perched on her lap fell to the floor, and Richard didn't miss his chance to retrieve them for her.

The concert moved on to a couple of tap numbers and a strange modern dance piece that made Beto and Efran squirm in their chairs like boys in church.

During intermission we made our way to the lobby, where the student ushers, who had forgotten to hand out programs before the show, were now passing them around like hors d'oeuvres.

The second half of the show, according to the program, belonged to the voice department, with the last piece being the *Messiah* sing-along. Richard couldn't help but laugh when he saw that the words to the Hallelujah Chorus were printed on the back.

"Pretty tough to remember, eh?" he joked as he elbowed Father Miguel.

For a few moments I worried that some of the Westsiders at the concert might recognize me, but everyone was preoccupied with their own families. And when they hit the lobby, the Frontera Street gang immediately broke into loud Spanish, solidly guaranteeing that nobody I might know would even glance our way.

When the lights blinked twice, announcing the second half, Efran and Beto said they couldn't take any more and ducked out, driving home in one of our four cars.

After the concert, Alma and I went backstage with all the other mothers. Socorro had already changed out of her tutu back into jeans and a sweatshirt, but she still had on her stage makeup, including a pair of flamboyant false eyelashes. Alma presented the roses to her with a long, tearful hug and then begged her to put her costume back on so we could snap some photos. At first Socorro refused, but as soon as she saw that lots of other girls were being forced to do the same, she complied. We walked her back onto the stage and made her strike all sorts of poses that we remembered from her dance while we proudly clicked away.

Alma saw the boy dancer standing nearby with his parents and asked Socorro to call him over. His name was Gerard, and up close he looked too thin to lift anyone. His parents told us they were from Belgium and were living in Los Cielos for a couple of years while Mr. Lacotte helped set up a pharmaceutical plant across the border.

"Gerard has been dancing for six years," his mother said. "Your daughter?"

"Four months," Alma replied.

The Lacottes laughed. "You are not serious?" Gerard's father asked in a lilting accent.

"Well, maybe five," Alma added matter-of-factly.

At that moment Socorro's ballet teacher rushed over and gave Socorro an enormous hug. Mrs. Polikoff was a tall woman who walked with a cane for no apparent reason. Her hair was an unnatural carrot color, and her face was powdered porcelain white, which made her age indecipherable.

"You are ze mother?" she asked me.

"No," Socorro said, a bit perturbed. "*This* is my mother."

The teacher turned toward Alma and then stepped back to study her from head to toe. "Ze father is tall, no?"

Alma chuckled and nodded her head.

Mrs. Polikoff, whose accent seemed theatrically thick, proceeded to gush about Socorro's rare natural gift and exceptional concentration.

"But," she said sternly, "she must grow. Grow! Two more inches. Like ze weed."

Without another word she turned to Gerard's parents and shifted into French. The three of them were speaking so fast I couldn't make out much of what they said, except that Mrs. Polikoff was confirming that *oui, oui,* it was true, Socorro was indeed an astonishing beginner.

We made Gerard lift Socorro again so we could take more pictures.

As Alma played photographer, I noticed that the other girls were posing for group photos with their arms draped around one another and their cheeks pressed together. They laughed and joked as they switched positions and changed places.

"You want one with them?" I asked Socorro.

Her eyes darted over toward the group and then back again.

"No, that's all right," she said.

She struck one more pose with Gerard, then gave him a good-night hug. She took off her toe shoes and began walking back to the dressing room.

"Mom?" She stopped a few paces away from us. "Will you get double prints? I want to send these to Dad."

A week later, Socorro handed Alma a thick envelope before she headed out for school. It was addressed to Paul Walker, and Socorro had drawn a funny stick-figure ballerina on the front. Alma set it on the kitchen counter and forgot about it by the time we were ready to leave for work.

"The pictures," I reminded her before we stepped outside.

"Oh, right," she said.

I waited in the doorway as Alma returned to the kitchen to get the envelope. But once she had it, she slid inside her bedroom instead of joining me at the front door. Not really thinking, I followed her.

I stood just outside her bedroom and watched, a bit confused, as Alma pulled her secret box out from under her bed and calmly placed Socorro's letter inside it.

"What are you doing?" I asked.

My voice startled her.

"You scared me!" she sighed, quickly closing the lid.

"Alma," I said, taking a step toward her. "What are you doing?"

She looked puzzled, as if I should have understood what I had just seen.

"What?" she asked.

"Aren't you going to mail the pictures?"

Alma answered me by standing up and sliding the box back under the bed. She kept her eyes down as she hurried out of the bedroom and made her way toward the front door. "We're going to be late," she said.

We walked a few blocks before I simply stopped and stared at her. It was time for an explanation, I told her.

"Everything in that box is a broken promise." She was clearly riled. "You know that *milagro*? The little hammer? Father Miguel gave that to me when Paul left us, and I prayed to every saint I could think of to bring him back. But have you seen him lately? I sure haven't."

Her voice was trembling and her fists were clenched.

"What about the letters?" I asked.

"I'm not going to let him break Socorro's heart, too," she fumed.

I couldn't believe what I was hearing. Alma didn't keep secrets from Socorro. They were a mother-daughter team, and that was what I admired about their relationship. I'd never known another mother to give so much, certainly not my own. So what Alma was telling me didn't make sense.

"But," I stammered, "Socorro said he writes to her."

"Wrote." Alma scowled. "He *wrote* to her for a while, and then he stopped, and all it did was make her ask more questions. What am I supposed to tell her? That her father promised her the world and then left her with nothing?"

I considered my own baby and how I would give anything for him or her to have something as simple and wonderful as a box of letters from his father. I thought of Socorro and the innocent trust she'd placed in her mother to pass along her words of love to Paul. It seemed wrong, even cruel, for Alma to decide that he had no right to be a parent.

"He's her father," I began. "He has a right to—"

"No," Alma cut me off. Her face was flushed, simmering in a slow, hateful rage. "He has a right to nothing."

Alma's nightmares were getting worse. At least two nights a week I would wake up and hear her thrashing and crying in the dark.

"Didn't you see her?" she'd ask after I'd rush into her room and flip on the light. I never saw a thing, except the torment in her face and the way she clutched her little Virgin statue against her heart.

Trembling and breathless, Alma would try to explain what the spirit had said.

"It's happening," she cried. "La Llorona says it's happening."

"No," I assured her. "Socorro's here. Right here. Safe and sound." I told her it was nerves. We'd all been through so much. "Alma," I said, "do you think I'd let anything happen to you?"

Whether she realized it or not, she had taught me how to mother. I was grateful, and I wanted to somehow pay her back. I knew how much Alma wanted Socorro to succeed, and how hard she'd worked to give her the sort of future Paul had promised. The visions of La Llorona must have been triggered by her own fear and doubt. Understandable anxiety.

"I'm going to help," I reassured her. "I'm going to make sure everything works out. And La Llorona isn't going to stop me."

Chapter 12

SOCORRO

WE NEVER RUSHED TO PUT UP CHRISTMAS DECORATIONS THE day after Thanksgiving the way people on the Westside did. We waited until December 12, the day we celebrated La Virgen de Guadalupe's appearance to Juan Diego on a hilltop in Mexico four hundred years ago, and we kept everything displayed until January 6, *el dia de los reyes,* the day the Three Wise Men brought gifts to the baby Jesus.

If *Guadalupe* didn't fall on a Sunday, Beto and Efran and all the other men and boys found an excuse to take the day off from work or school. They needed the day to make the luminarias. This year Peeps invited Richard to help. He asked my mom if she would be there too, and we had to explain that girls were not allowed to be part of the luminaria crew. That was just one of the unwritten rules of the Frontera Street tradition.

Each of the men had his role. Sometime before eight in the morning, Beto would go the lumberyard and fill the bed of his pickup truck with sand. Efran would drive to the hardware store and pick up cartons of brown paper lunch bags. By the time they got back, there would already be a dozen men waiting for them on Septima's porch. They'd all be wearing faded blue jeans, and they'd have leather gloves poking out of their back pockets and shovels resting against their legs. Septima would bring coffee and *pan dulce* out to them and then show the grandfathers and the great-grandfathers, who came up from Mexico for the holidays, into her kitchen. They would be in charge of making lunch, which Peeps told me was always a big pot of Texas red chili topped with chopped onions, sliced jalapeños, and shredded cheddar cheese.

Septima complained that for years the old men left her kitchen in such a jumble that she had started taping plastic trash bags to her countertops so she could just roll the whole mess up and throw it away. And at the end of the day she made the *viejitos* wash the pots and pans with a hose in the backyard so they wouldn't drench her floor.

Outside, the younger men were given jobs according to their strength. The biggest guys shoveled and helped heave buckets of sand onto the rooftops. The others set up the paper bags, and the littlest boys ran around plopping votive candles into the finished luminarias.

Every family on Frontera Street paid one-sixteenth of the total bill, which entitled their house to as many bags as it took to outline the front yard, the driveway, the street-side roofline, and any porch railing or windowsill. But the rule was that anyone who wanted to make a cross or a star in the middle of their yard had to do it on their own.

Septima always laid out a big circle in the middle of her lawn, which only her friends could tell was supposed to be the miracle muffin. And there were a couple of years when the Campeches, who lived on the far end of the street, bought a hundred extra bags and rearranged them every single night to make a different eight-sided snowflake. But that was a while back, when their son, Arturo, was in high school. After he graduated and moved to Austin to open his own hair salon, the Campeches went back to the basic outline.

The men always decorated Saint Joseph's for free, setting the bags on the church's slanted roof in whatever design Father Miguel wanted. Usually, he had them spell out *Feliz Navidad* on one side of the church, and *Peace* on the other.

I liked to sit by our front window and watch the men work. They never stood with their feet entirely together or their arms flat against their sides. They grunted when they lifted the heavy buckets, and they wiped their sweaty foreheads with their dirty forearms. They spoke to one another in sharp commands and spit to punctuate their sentences. I would have loved to be out there with them, feeling the muscles in my shoulders and thighs heat up like a fever as I shoveled, letting my thoughts disappear into the hypnotic beat of my own deep and steady breathing. I liked how they worked together without having to speak, and I admired the bond they built in that silence.

I wondered what it must be like to have a man living in the house all the time. I tried to picture male things lying on the coffee table and taking up space in the medicine cabinet, but I had a hard time imagining what those things might be. That's why whenever Dee talked about Mitch, I asked about every tiny detail. She was like a big sister, or maybe an aunt, who had been to some faraway place that I had never seen. Men were definitely foreign territory, and Dee was my only guide to the way they lived.

"The first time I ever saw Mitch's apartment," she once told me, "he had greasy motorcycle engine parts spread out across the living room floor and a set of barbells where the kitchen table should have been. The only furniture he owned was a mattress, a beanbag chair, a stereo and a color television.

"He didn't even own a chest of drawers," she said. "He kept his clean clothes in a white plastic laundry basket and his dirty clothes in a blue one."

Most men, Dee explained to me, believe they would be happier living without women. Until they fall in love. Then, she said, they realize that women can soften their edges, and they even seem happy to let down their resistance.

The great thing about Dee was that she was willing to tell me anything I wanted to know about her love affair with Mitch, and she told it to me straight. My mother, on the other hand, hated answering questions about my father. Sometimes I'd try to ask her what his sweat smelled like or if he liked to curse, but she never gave me real answers.

"What's that got to do with anything?" she'd say.

She didn't understand that I needed to know so I could piece him together in my mind, so I could look out the window at the men of Frontera Street and picture him working alongside them.

Whenever I asked Mom to show me how Paul walked or how he sat, she would tell me I was being ridiculous. She didn't see how vital the information was, how those were the sort of details I had to have if I was ever going to be able to recognize him on the street, or identify him in a crowded shopping mall. She didn't know that for as long as I could remember, I had made plans to find him, that I had already spent hundreds of nights squinting at the few photographs I had of him, trying to add fifteen years to his face by widening his cheeks and broadening his chest in my imagination.

In my letters, I had asked him to send me new pictures of himself, but he never did. In fact, the only mail I got from Arizona was a sappy birthday card that arrived every February 23.

"Three weeks wizout class? No. No good."

Mrs. Polikoff was asking where I was going to study during the Christmas break. She was going to Vermont for three weeks and wouldn't be around to give me private lessons.

I didn't have an answer.

She draped her arm across my shoulders and cocked her head until it touched the top of mine. We stood side by side in front of the dance studio's floor-to-ceiling mirrors, looking at our reflections. Then, speaking to everyone in class that day, Mrs. Polikoff slowly warned: "One day without class and you can tell. Two days and your teacher can tell. Three days without class, my dears, and the audience can tell."

Most of the other girls planned to take class at the West Texas Dance Academy, a studio about forty minutes outside of town that was run by one of Mrs. Polikoff's former students. The flyer Mrs. Polikoff had handed to us said that three weeks of classes at the academy would cost three hundred fifty dollars. There was no way I could ask my mom to pay that kind of money, especially when I had already told her that all I wanted for Christmas was three pairs of new toe shoes, the kind made in England, which cost sixty-two dollars a pair. Mrs. Polikoff had given me a pair to wear for the holiday concert, and the moment I stood up on them I could tell why the other girls stayed away from the boxy Capezios I'd been using.

My scholarship, which covered transportation to Arts High and my private lessons with Mrs. Polikoff, allowed me to spend fifty dollars on shoes every two months, and even the rock-hard Capezios rarely lasted that long.

I tried everything to make them hold out. I stuffed paper inside them after class to help them keep their shape. I coated them with floor wax to harden the vamps. But the shoes always stopped supporting me after three or four weeks. At first I thought I was dancing the wrong way—overarching my feet or pushing my weight down instead of pulling up. But Mrs. Polikoff said all toe shoes soften and bend until they just don't work anymore, no matter how strong of a dancer you are. She told me that sometimes famous dancers go through one pair of shoes during the first half of a performance and a second pair after intermission. Instantly, I pictured a sweaty ballerina sitting backstage in her tutu, hurling limp toe shoes over her shoulder like a miner shoveling coal.

I wanted to tell Mrs. Polikoff that I'd take class every day over the Christmas break, but there was no way I could ask Mom, or even Dee, to pay that kind of tuition. Especially since Septima was having trouble making ends meet at the fabric store.

"I'll practice at home," I said apologetically.

"No. No good," Mrs. Polikoff scoffed, stepping away from me and proceeding with our classwork.

I was ashamed. I knew the other students never had to worry about how much lessons cost, and Mrs. Polikoff probably thought I didn't care enough to find a way to practice.

For the rest of the hour I tried to avoid her disapproving gaze. When the bell finally rang, she dismissed the others and asked me to stay. When we were alone, she motioned me toward the piano, where she stood holding what looked like a letter.

"Christmas surprise!" she chimed. "Look, look! For you!"

I took the envelope and began to open it.

"Boston Ballet!" Mrs. Polikoff gushed before I could read the message inside. "Company class!"

I had no idea what she was talking about.

She explained that a small group of professional dancers from the Boston Ballet was spending the winter at a private college two hours away, using the school as a secret hideaway to set a new ballet.

"That's great," I said, still clueless.

She threw back her head and laughed. "My dear," she started again, this time cupping my chin in her strong fingers, "you will dance with them."

I looked at the letter again, keeping my eyes focused on each word until its meaning sank in. Mrs. Polikoff had arranged for me to take classes with the professionals three days a week. I read and reread the final sentence, which said, *Please consider her our guest.*

"Just you," Mrs. Polikoff said. "You tell no one, yes?"

I was too astounded to do anything but nod, and when Mrs. Polikoff kissed me on the cheek, I kissed her right back.

Chapter 13

ALMA

AT CHRISTMAS WE BOUGHT A LITTLE TREE AND BAKED DOZENS of cookies. We explained to Dee how everybody on the street would participate in *las posadas* and how we'd draw an address out of a hat to determine which house would be the holy manger on Nochebuena.

Lettie took the Mary and Joseph costumes out of storage and delivered them to Father Miguel, who was in charge of picking a girl and boy from his catechism class to play the starring roles.

Peeps announced that Richard and the rest of the chamber music group had agreed to play at the Nochebuena Mass, and Septima got to work sewing new robes for the *santos*, using the plushest velvets and the most regal tassels that the shop had to offer.

The flickering luminarias, lit every night just after sunset, bathed Frontera Street in a golden, hopeful glow.

We carried out every tradition and honored every ritual, but nothing could make the uneasy truth disappear from our thoughts. The fabric shop was sinking.

Dee pulled herself off Septima's payroll to save money. She told me not to worry, but I knew we'd really feel the loss of her little paycheck, especially during the holidays. Pilar tried dropping her work schedule down to three days a week but couldn't make ends meet, and she eventually told Septima she was looking for another job.

When Schuster's officially filed for bankruptcy, it didn't surprise anyone. But that same afternoon we were caught completely off guard when Lettie Sanchez rushed into the shop with even worse news.

"It's *how* big?" Septima asked in disbelief.

"At least three times the size of your shop," Lettie repeated.

She tried to downplay the attributes of the giant new fabric store that had popped up practically overnight on the Westside, but I could tell the place had impressed her. She pulled a magazine-size brochure out of her tote bag and handed it to Septima.

"What's it called, again?" Septima sighed.

"Textile Village," Lettie replied. "It's got fabrics from all over the world, really unusual things. It's got one of those plastic bubble rooms where the kids can play while you take sewing classes, and you can buy sewing machines there, too.

"See that?" Lettie said, grabbing the flyer back. "They've got this area filled with books and sofas, and you can go buy coffee and—"

Lettie stopped, realizing that she'd gone too far when Septima buried her head in her hands and groaned. She tried to give Sepi a sympathetic hug, but Septima turned away and stormed into the back room.

"Well, *I'm* not going to shop there," Lettie cried out, hoping her words would reach all the way to the back. There was no response.

I began to pull button drawers in and out to keep myself from yelling at Lettie, and Pilar busied herself by rolling out a bolt of floral-patterned rayon that she had sold to no one. Lettie was left standing by herself in the middle of the shop, still holding the fancy brochure and trying to decide if she should leave or stay. She took a step toward the back room and then changed her mind.

"I'm really sorry," she mumbled as she walked out the front door.

When Septima came out of the back room, her eyes were red and swollen, and she called us to her side. She set a ledger book down on the button counter and opened it so we could see her calculations.

"We're down sixty percent from last year," she said in a defeated monotone.

Pilar snapped the ledger shut, trapping Sepi's hand between the pages.

"I can't believe Lettie came in here and said all that to your face!"

Septima lifted her hand, signaling Pilar to please stop.

"It's not her fault," she said wearily.

"*No te preocupes*," I added, "you have lots of customers who live around here, and they won't go to the Westside."

Septima nodded. But she said, "That won't be enough."

She spent the next two mornings meeting with loan officers at Los Cielos National Bank. They told her there wasn't much she could do. She and Beto couldn't even take out a second mortgage on their house because they still owed more than half of Elena's college tuition.

In fact, the bankers said things were looking bad for all the small businesses near the plaza because there didn't seem to be one single department store interested in moving into the soon-to-be-empty Schuster's building.

Dee and Socorro tried to persuade me to go hear Richard and Peeps play at Nochebuena Mass, but I told them that even though I loved Richard and Peeps, an evening of their music wasn't enough to get me to step inside any church.

When I met up with them afterward, Socorro told me that Father Miguel had asked people to pray for Septima's shop and Flores by Dolores and La Indita luncheonette, which were all facing hard times. As we stood outside the church in the cold, Richard kissed me on the forehead, and then he took my hand and we walked with all of our neighbors to Peeps's house to start *las posadas*.

Father Miguel distributed the candles and the lyric sheets. He got Mary and Joseph to stand in front of the group, and we all headed toward the first house. At the door we sang our part, asking if there was any lodging for God's humble servants. Mr. Campeche darted out of the crowd to play his role as the innkeeper, standing squarely in his doorway and brusquely turning Mary and Joseph away. We continued from door to door, pleading for shelter in Spanish.

When we came to Septima's house, we expected her to be waiting for us because Father said she went straight home after church. We climbed the porch stairs and began to sing, but when we finished nobody came to the door. We sang our lines a second time and waited for an answer. Nothing. The little girl dressed as Mary grew so impatient that she rang the doorbell, which made us all laugh.

Beto finally stepped outside and quickly shut the door behind him. "She's too upset," he said, essentially asking us to leave.

Father Miguel ushered Mary and Joseph off the porch and pointed them toward Cece's house, which had been selected as the holy manger. That's where Mary and Joseph would be welcomed inside and everybody would join the party.

Dee, Richard, and I lagged behind.

"She wanted to wait at least until February," Beto said. "But the bankers said she can't. She has to close the shop by New Year's Day."

Cece got her *quinceañera* gown for Christmas and she ran over to show it to us. It was a magnificent white dress with a puffy tulle skirt and off-the-shoulder sleeves. Lettie Sanchez didn't make it, but she helped Cece's parents order it, taking advantage of the newest arm of her business, a mail-order catalog.

"Lettie says when she's finished with alterations, it will fit like it was custom-made," Cece exclaimed.

She slipped the dress on in Socorro's room and then twirled down the hallway toward us. Socorro hopped off the sofa and gave her a congratulatory hug.

"I don't want to wait until April!" Cece sighed. "You are *so* lucky your birthday is in February."

She was all smiles and good wishes.

"I told Daddy I didn't want those stupid doll-skirt centerpieces from Flores by Dolores. I want something sharp, like white daisies in green baskets."

She was completely wound up.

"And, Mrs. Cruz, if you want to get that DJ, Treble Cliff, for Socorro's party, you'd better call right now, because Daddy said he almost didn't have a Saturday left in April for us."

I nodded, and tried to turn the conversation in another direction. "Did you see what Socorro got for Christmas?"

Cece scanned the three boxes of toe shoes, the five new leotards, and the two delicate chiffon skirts with velvet ribbon waistbands that Septima had made.

"Nice," she lied.

"Look at this!" Socorro picked up one of the larger boxes under the tree and set it on the floor.

Cece sat down next to it, making her skirt balloon out like a parachute. Her eyebrows rose as Socorro pulled out a leather bag the size of a small suitcase. Socorro showed Cece the heavy brass zippers and the various storage compartments.

"Dee got it for me," she boasted. "It's exactly like the ones the dancers at the Boston Ballet use. "

"It's really great," Cece said unconvincingly.

On days with no ballet class, Socorro tried to spend time with Cece and her new girlfriends from Chaparral High, who, Socorro told us, always did the same thing. First, they'd meet at one of the girls' houses and take all morning to fix their hair. Then, they'd borrow one another's clothes until they found the perfect combination of tight jeans and clingy sweaters to wear to the basketball courts, where they watched the boys play. When they got to the courts, the guys would act as if they didn't notice the girls standing in a clump on the sidelines. So the girls would pretend that they didn't care that the boys didn't care, and then they'd walk to Walgreen's to page through magazines.

Socorro, who had thought she was missing out on all sorts of fun, eventually admitted that she didn't quite understand the point of the outings. But she wanted to fit in with the barrio girls, so she went whenever she could.

On the weekends, Cece would take Socorro to house parties thrown by juniors and seniors whose families I didn't know, and the only reason I let her attend was because Cece's father issued a strict eleven o'clock curfew that he made sure the girls kept by going to pick them up himself. Cece complained that her father was embarrassing them both *para siempre*, but to me Socorro seemed happy to have an excuse to leave the fiestas. From my bedroom I often heard her telling Dee that all the kids talked about at those parties was football or how drunk so-and-so got across the bridge in Mexico. Socorro felt comfortable telling Dee lots of things she would never tell me, and I could tell that Dee listened and then tried to figure out what sort of advice she might give to her own child one day.

About halfway through the Christmas break, Peeps's friend Lucinda Herndon, who played the flute at Arts High, began riding into the neighborhood with Richard to spend long afternoons playing music at Peeps's house. Socorro began to go over to listen and invited Cece to hang out with her and Peeps instead of the basketball girls.

Cece tried, once. But she didn't go back.

Socorro and Cece promised to continue their Friday night sleep-overs when school started up again. But I wondered how much longer they would last.

Only eight customers came to the close-out sale.

One lady bought every packet of elastic that we had on hand, and another lady took all the pearl-head pins. The leader of the local Brownie troop left with our entire stock of child-size Quick-N-Easy patterns, and a teacher from the vocational high school arrived during his lunch break to pile the long, heavy rolls of upholstery vinyl into the back of his van.

At five o'clock, when Septima closed the doors for good, there was lots of merchandise left over.

Dee stopped by the shop after picking up Socorro from ballet. Septima let them both in just before she locked the door and turned the OPEN sign around so it said CLOSED. We all stood near the cash register and watched the sign slowly sway from side to side. Septima pressed her hand against the glass to make it stop, leaving a half-moon palm print on the door. She leaned one shoulder against the hinges and gazed out toward the street.

"I've got something for you," Pilar announced cheerfully. We all turned to see her holding up a small ice chest like it was a trophy.

"Iluminada dropped it off at my house this morning with a note that said we should open it at the end of the day."

Pilar set the chest down on one of the pattern-book tables, and Septima walked back into the heart of the store. We formed a tight circle around the cooler and leaned forward to look inside as Septima pushed back the side clasps and lifted the lid.

We began to laugh when we saw five pints of ice cream, a bag of M&M's, jars of chocolate, butterscotch, and strawberry syrup, and a tub of Cool Whip set on top of long-lasting bricks of blue ice. Iluminada had tucked a stack of paper bowls and half-a-dozen plastic spoons into one corner and had even included a mound of paper napkins sealed inside a plastic bag.

There was an envelope taped to the top of one of the ice cream cartons, and Dee read the note out loud: "Efran said to send tequila, but what does he know?"

We waited for Septima's reaction, a little worried that Iluminada's sense of humor might have stepped on Sepi's toes. I noticed her lips begin to quiver as she battled a wave of tears. She lifted the cartons out of the chest and lined them up on the table.

"What are we waiting for?" she said.

We twirled the cartons around so we could see the labels and pick our favorite flavors, and that's when we noticed that Iluminada had given us all Rocky Road.

The ice cream definitely helped. While we were eating it, Septima began to tell Dee and Pilar how when she first opened the shop she signed up for night classes at Chaparral High to learn how to keep the books.

Then I began to tell the story about the time Sepi decided to sell yarn as well as fabric, and as I spoke, Sepi started to laugh so hard she had to hold her ribs.

"She ordered all this mohair and chenille, and nobody bought one pitiful ball of it," I explained.

"That's right," Septima admitted with a playful grin. "I could never figure it out. I even took a bunch of skeins over to the church, where Doña Rosa and the other old ladies meet to crochet and watch *telenovelas*."

Septima said she was sure the *viejitas* would prefer the plush, exotic yarns at her shop over the synthetic lime-green and ugly yellow stuff they got at Walgreen's.

"They oohed and ahhed and said *sí, sí, muy bonito* when I told them to hold my yarn up to their cheeks," Septima continued, shaking her head as she remembered her confusion. "But, nothing."

"It wasn't until she went into Walgreen's one day that she found out what was happening," I said to move the story along.

"Yeah, I ended up behind one of the old ladies at the checkout," Sepi continued. "She had sixteen balls of yarn and the cashier only charged her seven dollars! Well, on my way out I asked the manager if the yarn was on sale. She said no, but when Walgreen's first opened, it offered crocheting lessons, and to get people to sign up it promised to sell them yarn at half price for life."

Septima collapsed with laughter. "Those *viejitas* had been buying yarn there for thirty years!" she howled.

We were laughing so hard that we didn't know how long the man at the door had been rapping his knuckles against the glass before we heard him.

Septima stood and wiped her mouth with one of the napkins, and then quickly cleaned her hands on her apron. None of us recognized the *gringo*, who was wearing a blue sport jacket and a wide paisley necktie that arced over his generous paunch like a bookmark.

Septima pointed to the CLOSED sign and shook her head.

He smiled and held up a narrow piece of paper, waving it like a flag.

"Probably from the bank," Pilar reasoned.

We quieted down as Septima opened the door.

"Hello," the man said as he took a huge, uninvited step into the shop.

"We're closed," Septima said curtly.

"I know," the man affirmed, letting his strong Texas drawl take the words for a stroll.

"You the owner?" he asked, continuing to push his way inside.

Septima nodded, but he didn't see her because he had already begun to walk in circles around himself, looking at the tables still stocked with dozens of bolts of fabric. When his eyes landed on us, he dipped his head in a silent greeting. We sat in front of our melting ice cream and stared at him. He was wearing black cowboy boots underneath flare-legged gray slacks, and his pale bald head had a ring of short black hair encircling it.

" 'Scuse me," he said, quickly turning back toward Septima. "Did you say you're the owner?"

"I am until midnight," Septima tried to joke.

"Yes, ma'am," he chuckled with phony friendliness.

"Can I help you?"

"Well, ma'am, that's what I should be asking you."

Septima crossed her arms to let him know he'd better get to the point.

"I'm gonna buy your surplus," he boomed, sweeping his hand through the air. "All of it. Tables, chairs, everything."

Septima cocked her head, demanding more information.

"Got my truck right around the corner. And I'm gonna give you this check right here." He held up his hand to show her.

"Who are you?" Pilar asked.

The man glanced at our table looking a bit perturbed, but one second later he began to chuckle again.

"Lord have mercy, did I walk right in here without introducing myself?"

Nobody answered.

"I'm Jim Grove," he announced directly to Septima, turning his back on us.

"Mr. Grove."

"Yes, ma'am. Well, let's see. I'm prepared to write this check out for three thousand dollars. And I'm prepared to make it out to you personally."

Septima kept her distance, but I could tell the money sounded good to her.

When we opened that last day, she told me that she didn't care about not being able to pay the final month's rent, but there were a few suppliers who had stood by her until the end, and she was hoping to make enough at the clearance sale to pay them in full. We hadn't even come close.

"How about it, Mrs. . . . . ?" The man prompted.

"I don't know," Septima shot back. I could tell by her tone that she was ready to deal. "I've got some imported silk over there and at least seven bolts of Ultra Suede."

The man nodded his head.

"Forty-five hundred."

Septima sighed like she was disappointed in him.

She walked over to the button counter and pulled out the drawers filled with the most expensive mother-of-pearls, the handcrafted Navajo silvers, and the delicately carved rosewoods. I could tell she was almost enjoying the shrewd tug-of-war, daring the man to keep his cool.

"Beautiful, ma'am. Right nice," he said as she fanned the buttons out onto the counter.

"I could sell these to the dressmaker down the street—" Septima continued.

"Yes, ma'am, I get your point," the man interrupted. "Well, I see I'm dealing with a quick mind here, so I'm gonna cut right to the chase."

Septima scooped up the buttons and began putting them back into the drawers, trying to act like she wasn't listening.

Mr. Grove walked behind the button counter until he was standing shoulder to shoulder with Septima, and then he pulled on various drawers and peered inside.

"Umm-hmmm," he murmured.

Sepi waited.

"Five thousand. That's the best I can do, Mrs. . . . ."

"Guzman," Septima said, extending her hand in acceptance.

"Good, Mrs. Gooseman," he purred.

He leaned over the counter and flattened the check underneath his beefy hands. Then he reached into the chest pocket of his sport jacket and pulled out a shiny silver pen, the kind men get for Christmas.

Septima shot us a proud wink as he filled out the check, spelling her name correctly with her guidance.

He straightened up and walked toward the front door, leaving the check on top of the counter.

"I'll get the truck," he said gruffly, his voice suddenly drained of all its previous graciousness.

We jumped up from the table and rushed to Septima's side. She was as happy as we'd seen her all day, until she lifted the check and read the block letters in the left-hand corner.

At that very moment, a big white truck pulled up to the curb and we saw the words TEXTILE VILLAGE emblazoned on its side.

Two men in khaki coveralls rushed into the shop and walked straight over to the pattern-book table where our ice cream was dissolving into a sticky mess. One of the men pulled a crumpled plastic bag out of his front pants pocket and slid the cartons and jars and candy into the bag with a swipe of his sleeve. Once the top was cleared, he and his partner turned the table over and unscrewed its legs. Then they rolled the table-top out the door and into the back of the truck.

We stood behind the button counter like suspects in a lineup, turning to the right and then to the left as we watched the two workers dismantle every table and remove every chair, plowing through the shop like bulldozers.

The sun had already set and the cold evening air blew in through the open door, sending a shiver down my back. It was too cold to continue standing there without a sweater or a jacket, but none of us moved until the workers came for the buttons.

They pulled each drawer out of the wall and set them inside one of three cardboard boxes. They weren't just taking the buttons, they were taking the drawers as well! Dee reached for my hand, and I reached for Septima's. I could feel the stiff paper check folded up inside her palm.

Father Miguel ran in and asked what was going on.

"Father!" Septima cried as she rushed to him. Socorro put her arm around my waist and buried her eyes into my shoulder.

The workers grunted and coughed as they scooped up heavy bolts of fabric and carried them to the truck four at a time.

We huddled around Septima as she stood helplessly by, watching the men in khaki carry away pieces of her store. Just like the ants and the miracle muffin.

Chapter 14

DEE

WHEN SOCORRO RETURNED TO SCHOOL IN JANUARY, HER CLASS-mates treated her differently. The girls in her dance class invited her to sit with them during lunch, and they also began to flirt with Peeps, telling him how adorable he'd look with a punk haircut and cool glasses.

She couldn't figure out the switch.

"What do they want?" she asked.

"To be you," I said.

My theory was that Peeps's friend Lucinda had gone back to the Westside and spread the word about Socorro's invitation to dance with the Boston Ballet.

"They're impressed," I explained.

"Why? They see me dance every day."

I lifted my eyebrows and gave her a conspiratorial smile.

"Status," I said.

"What?"

"Look, they knew you're good, especially for somebody who just started. But they didn't know whether to admit it," I continued. "The Boston Ballet made it official, and now it's okay for them to think you're okay."

"That's real open-minded," Socorro scoffed.

"Hey, it's a start, right? You've been wishing they'd make an effort to get to know you better. This is their way of opening the door. Maybe you'll find out they're actually nice."

"Maybe."

Within a few weeks, Socorro had become a full partner in the Arts High gang, and it wasn't much longer before two of the girls—Ellen Rimyard and Holly Severson—became her closest pals. Soon they were inviting her to have midweek dinners at their homes, and Saturday afternoon swims at the Westside Country Club's indoor pool.

The first time Socorro set out for the club, I had to stop Alma from packing a brown bag lunch for her.

"She'll get hungry," Alma argued matter-of-factly.

"She'll get food there."

"We don't have money for that."

"She doesn't pay," I explained. "The parents have a tab and the kids order what they want."

Alma and Socorro looked at me with wide eyes, as if I had revealed one of the world's deepest secrets. Alma put the peanut butter sandwich she had just assembled into the refrigerator.

"Don't order anything," she said somberly.

"Mom!"

"A Coke, that's it," Alma commanded.

"Dee . . ." Socorro groaned.

"Nothing's very expensive," I assured Alma. "Ice cream, French fries, things like that."

Alma shot Socorro a final, threatening glance and then dropped the subject.

I drove Socorro to Holly's rambling Spanish hacienda–style house and gently tugged on her arm before she jumped out of the passenger seat.

"Order what you want," I said. "They expect you to."

It was impossible for Alma to find work in January, when most of the area stores were cutting loose their holiday help. She applied at the few hotels and restaurants near the downtown plaza, but they said they were waiting to see what impact the closing of Schuster's was going to have before adding to their staffs.

I offered to teach her how to drive so she could expand her search, but she said she'd be so worried about making a mistake and hurting my baby that she wouldn't be able to concentrate on the lessons.

Cece's father asked about openings at Bobby O's Factory Discount

Boots, but found nothing. In fact, the only decent offer that Alma got came in a letter that turned out to be from Jim Grove at Textile Village. He not only offered to set her up at *his* button counter but said he'd pay her bus fare, too. Alma ripped the letter into shreds, saying she'd rather starve than take money from him.

I kept slipping her twenty-dollar bills that I said I'd stashed away before Mitch died, but I knew I couldn't keep that up for much longer without triggering suspicion. I had waited and waited for the perfect time to introduce this new family of mine to the real me, but it had never come. Now I was in over my head. I knew my money could be a big help, but how was I supposed to tell them about it without looking like I'd been pretending to be somebody I wasn't? I couldn't tell them that I'd kept quiet for so long because I loved them. Which is exactly what I had done. But now that explanation sounded absurd.

There had been so many nights when I had sat at the dinner table on the verge of laying it all out. But then I'd remember how Alma took me in because she was convinced I had nothing, and how she would have never done that if she'd known I grew up on the Westside. I had convinced myself that even though things were getting tough, it was best for me to stay quiet. Because if I lost Alma and Socorro now, if I lost the trust of everyone on Frontera Street, then I really *would* have nothing, and the thought of being that lonely again terrified me. I knew I had painted myself into a horrible corner, but I wanted to believe that things would get better and that I'd have time to figure out a good way to clean up my mess.

The problem is that real life doesn't work that way.

Lettie Sanchez was the only person whose business was humming, and she wound up hiring everyone—everyone, that is, except Pilar, who'd found a job working the lunch shift at Luby's cafeteria and was already pushing for a promotion to the dinner crew.

I accepted a part-time position doing hems and small alterations for Lettie three days a week. She hired Septima as the full-time buyer for the mail-order segment of the business. There was only one full-time job left—taking dress orders by phone and packing the gowns for shipment. Lettie offered it to Alma, all but apologizing that she couldn't pay much above minimum wage and couldn't even promise to keep her employed when orders slowed down. Alma took it anyway.

To make things more efficient, Lettie moved her mail-order inventory into Alma's house, where she had arranged for the toll-free telephone line to ring. It wasn't long before the place looked like a warehouse, with four rolling racks of dresses crowded into the living room and six stacks of flat cardboard boxes of various depths and sizes lining the hallway. The dinner table was so overrun with order forms and shipping labels that we usually ended up eating our meals off the kitchen counter.

Lettie told us she had her eye on some office and storage space, but she still didn't have enough for a down payment. She offered to pay Alma's mortgage in the meantime, but found out that Paul Walker had given Alma the house, paid in full, as a gift. Still, Alma told Lettie, she could use some help with the taxes, and Lettie said to consider them paid.

By pooling our wages, Alma and I managed to cover the utility bills, buy groceries, and keep Socorro supplied for school and ballet. But we knew that once the pageant season was over, Alma would be out of work.

One evening, Socorro offered to help out by quitting Arts High.

"How's that going to solve anything?" Alma snapped.

"You won't have to pay for extra toe shoes and tights and stuff," Socorro mumbled.

Alma narrowed her eyes in anger and shook her head no. I looked at Socorro, hoping she knew that her mother wasn't annoyed at her for offering to make the sacrifice but at the fact that she had to even consider such a thing. Alma was so proud of Socorro's dancing that I knew she would do whatever she had to to keep her in school.

My stomach twisted as I listened to them. Things had finally come to a point where my silence was doing more harm than good, if it had ever done any good at all.

"You are staying at Arts," Alma insisted. Then she leaned across the table and took her daughter's hand. I knew what was coming next. Alma had been trying to prepare Socorro for the bad news since Christmas, hinting at the possibility but never saying it straight out.

"But *mija*," she sighed. "About your *quinceañera* . . . I wish there was something else I could do."

Maybe, I thought, *now is the time*. Maybe I could tell them about the

Westside and offer to pay for the *quinceañera*. Then the sting of my lie might at least be balanced by Socorro's happiness.

"Alma," I began, but she and Socorro were already deep into their own conversation and I wasn't heard.

"It's okay," Socorro said. "I sort of knew it wasn't going to happen."

"I need to say something," I tried again.

Socorro hugged Alma and they began to sway. Then Socorro straightened out her arm, inviting me into the family hug. My heart was breaking, and I ached to tell them the truth, but the instant the hug was over I knew that my chance to gracefully come clean had already slipped away. I had to figure something else out, and I had to do it before everything I cherished about Frontera Street crumbled before my eyes.

Chapter 15

SOCORRO

CECE AND I HAD BEEN PLANNING OUR *QUINCEAÑERAS* SINCE WE were in kindergarten, sketching dress designs in crayon, adding and deleting names to our imaginary guest lists and dreaming about our dates.

Every year we listened to the older girls describe their parties, and as they spoke we let our imaginations soar. They'd tell us that when it was our turn, we would feel like Cinderella, Snow White, and a fairy princess all rolled into one. We had waited for so long that it was hard to believe our time had finally come. But it had.

Since Cece got her dress at Christmas, we started to plan her party first. With the biggest concern out of the way, we immediately turned our attention to the smaller details like shoes and hair and earrings.

We'd both had a good laugh when Cece said that my mother had waited so long to start planning my party that I'd get stuck hiring Los Más Machos, the dorky barrio band that pushed its equipment around in a stolen shopping cart, and that I would have to settle for a bean burrito buffet from La Indita luncheonette. That's probably why Cece thought I was joking when I told her that the latest news was that I wasn't getting a *quinceañera* at all.

We were sitting in her bedroom, where she kept her beautiful dress hanging from a hook attached to the back of the door, so it would be the last thing she saw every night before she fell to sleep.

"Yeah, sure!" she said.

She knew it couldn't be true because even though there wasn't a single person on Frontera Street with money to burn, there were a few things—First Holy Communions, *quinceañeras*, and weddings—that no family scrimped on. No matter what. We had never heard of anyone simply not having a *quinceañera*. Never.

She laughed pretty hard, until she noticed that I wasn't fooling. Her smile tightened before it fell, and then her eyes searched mine for an explanation.

"The shop," I said.

"That's impossible! It's not fair!"

"It's no big deal," I mumbled.

"Yes, it is!"

Her parents must have heard us, because they knocked on the door immediately and Cece shot up to let them in. She repeated what I'd said, and Mrs. Cardenas gasped. Mr. Cardenas stood perfectly still and shook his head, like he had to sift the bad news through his brain before he could believe it.

I rolled my eyes and shrugged my shoulders, trying to pretend like I couldn't care less. I promised myself I wouldn't cry.

"It's just a party," I said, my voice pinched and wobbly. "Just a dress."

Cece yanked three pink tissues from the box on top of her dresser and handed them to me without saying a word. I crumpled them up and dug my fingernails into the heels of my hands. I had to make myself believe that I didn't care.

I wanted Cece to say she didn't care, either. But when I looked around her bubblegum-pink bedroom and saw her entire family feeling so sorry for me that they didn't know what to say, I fell completely apart.

I buried my face into one of Cece's pillows and wailed. I felt hot blood pool inside my cheeks and then spread like fire to the tips of my ears. The more I fought the jagged swells, the stronger they fought back. I tried to pull myself together by running my fingers through my hair, raking through the tangles until I felt strands break loose at the roots.

It wasn't the party I was crying about, really. It was everything that was happening. Arts High, Mom's job, and my father. Where was my father? I was so sure that he'd write back to me after I mailed the pictures of my ballet recital that I searched the mail every day for a month, making up excuses for him every time I found nothing. I wrote to him about Mom losing her job, and I half expected to get a check in the mail to help pay for my *quinceañera,* along with a note that said he couldn't believe his baby had grown up so fast. Why was I so stupid? Why didn't I just admit that he hated me?

"It's her fault," I blubbered.

"Whose fault?" Mrs. Cardenas asked.

I'd forgotten where I was, forgotten that Cece and her family were standing beside me. I tried to catch my breath, and I shook my head to tell Mrs. Cardenas that she should ignore whatever I'd just said. But Cece's family just stood there, speechless, linked together like beads on a gold chain. The perfect little trio. Didn't I deserve a family like that, with a father who would give me a gown for Christmas and candy hearts for Valentine's? Why didn't I get to live in a house with a man in charge, instead of one overflowing with confused women?

Iluminada had a husband, and so did Septima and Mrs. Cardenas. Dee even had one, if you looked at it a certain way. Everyone but my mom. She'd ruined her chance with Paul Walker. She'd ruined everything.

"She could have tried, at least tried!" I shouted, looking into Cece's face and seeing total confusion.

"Who?" Mrs. Cardenas asked again.

"My mother!" I screamed. "My mother, that's who!"

Mrs. Cardenas pulled me into her arms. "Shhh, shhhh," she purred.

Cece took my hand, and then her father draped his arm around us all.

Mr. Cardenas proclaimed it the perfect solution. Cece and I would have a joint *quinceañera* and he'd foot the bill.

"Ay, no," my mother protested, shooting me an accusing glance. "Did Socorro ask you to . . . ?"

"*Calmate,* Alma," Mr. Cardenas cut her off. "Cece thought of it."

We were sitting in what was left of our living room, Mr. Cardenas and Cece wedged onto the sofa next to the ever-expanding Dee, who excused herself when the toll-free line rang in the other room.

"I'll get it," she said, slowly lifting herself up, stomach first, from the sofa. "You talk."

Cece patted the now empty space, inviting me to sit beside her. She was jittery with pride.

"Isn't it great?" she squealed.

I had no idea how to react.

My mother rolled one of the dress racks into the hall and took a seat in the secondhand rocking chair that we had painted duckling yellow as a Christmas gift for Dee.

"We'll pick out everything together, okay?" Cece exclaimed.

"Okay," I answered automatically.

My mother gave me another look.

"No, Javier," she sighed. "It's too much."

"The place is already rented," Mr. Cardenas continued, ignoring my mother's rejection. "There's room for one hundred and fifty, and our list only goes to a hundred."

Cece nodded and then proudly announced: "Lettie said she would make your dress for free!"

I was afraid to look at my mother's face after that comment, convinced she would be furious at how I had embarrassed her. So I looked at my ballet bag, which was sitting, unzipped, underneath a dress rack filled with pastel pantsuits.

Just before the Cardenases had come to the door, Dee and I had been carefully removing the ribbons and elastic ankle straps from my shabby pair of Capezios. Recycling the ribbons and elastics—washing them and then sewing them onto a new set of shoes—was one way we'd found to save a few dollars. Another way was to wrap my toes with paper towels to protect against blisters instead of using the expensive lamb's wool the other girls relied on.

I thought about Holly and Ellen and how they had listened so intently whenever I'd mentioned my upcoming *quinceañera*. Lots of times, I had pictured them sitting at the tables set with fine china and long-stemmed glasses. I'd imagined them, and every other girl in my dance class, watching me glide onto the dance floor in a sleeveless sheath gown, presented to my guests by Richard, who would let go of my arm and bow respectfully before placing his right hand on my waist and swooping us both into the first steps of a grand waltz. Now I could start planning for all that again.

Dee returned, wrestling with the dress rack in the hallway as she made her way back into the living room.

"I think it's a great idea, Cece!" she declared, rustling the heavy plastic bags that cocooned expensive gowns.

Mr. Cardenas jumped to his feet to give her his space on the sofa.

"No, thanks," she said. "It's easier for me to stand."

"You'd have to celebrate in April," Cece said.

"But you'll probably get your dress by February," Dee added.

I still couldn't look at my mother, but I felt her tension start to bend.

"Well," she mumbled.

"Alma," Mr. Cardenas pressed, "let us do this. We *want* to."

Dee and I spent the next few nights drawing up lists of flowers and party favors and music selections for my first, second, and third dances.

"Simple ivory dinner plates with blue or gold trim," she suggested.

"I'm sure whatever Cece's doing is fine," my mother interjected, her voice on edge. "Mixing everything up will cost extra."

Dee kept quiet.

"Maybe Cece picked settings close to this," she eventually said.

But Cece hadn't. She'd chosen forest-green dishes to match her forest-green basket-and-daisies centerpieces, and gold-plated utensils to offset the forest-green tablecloths. I knew because weeks ago she had asked for my opinion, and I'd told her green and white was a terrific combination. I'd meant it, too, when I thought it was for *her* party. Not mine.

When Mom wasn't around, Dee told me to talk to Cece about it.

"You'll work it out," she reassured. "It'll be beautiful, and all your new schoolmates will love it."

Holly Severson's house sat across the street from the cotton fields on Valleyview Road, its enormous lawns crowded with rows of azalea bushes trimmed to look like snow cones, and stands of ancient cottonwood trees. It seemed as if all the houses on the Westside were shaded from the town's desert glare by a wide umbrella of leaves and branches. That's what made the neighborhood special. It was a lush green island floating in the sandy desert. Cece's father told me that none of those trees or bushes were natural to the area. They were all bought and paid for, no matter how long they'd stood. He said the Westsiders kept them alive by flooding their land four times a year with water from the Rio Grande that they channeled into private irrigation canals.

All I knew was that the grass in Holly's yard was soft enough to walk on with bare feet, something you could never do in our neighborhood without clusters of tumbleweed stickers cutting into your soles.

From the time she was in kindergarten until she finished eighth grade, Holly said, she went to school in the redbrick building just across the fields from her front door. If I stood on her wide-planked porch and squinted, I could see the American flag tugging on the silver flagpole in front of Sam Houston Lower and Middle School, where Holly and Ellen said they became best friends on day one.

When she was little, Holly said, she would walk through the cotton crop to get home from school. She'd stomp on the raised rows of soil that poked up like ribs and mash her shoes down on dried clumps of dirt, making them explode like little bombs under her weight. She would let so much soil seep into her shoes that her maid would order her to climb inside the big clay flowerpot next to the front door and pour out all the sod before she could walk inside.

During irrigation season, she and Ellen would pull off their shoes and socks at the end of the school day and run straight into the murky water, working their toes into the cool, grainy mud. They'd tuck the hems of their skirts into their underpants as they waded into the center. And when they came out on the other side, half their legs would be painted brown with silt.

"We'd say that was our tan!" Holly said.

"We acted like those ol' fields were big parks without swings, didn't we?" said Ellen.

"Yeah," Holly laughed. "It wasn't until third grade that I figured out that cotton didn't naturally grow in straight rows."

Ellen roared.

"It was like, all of a sudden, I noticed the tractors and baling machines out there and realized it was somebody's crop."

"Your daddy's!" Ellen snickered.

I laughed at the story with them, but I didn't believe it. I'd seen the heavy machinery that Holly was talking about. Every truck and tractor in the field had the words SEVERSON COTTON painted in white across its widest point.

We were sitting in the laundry room, which was detached from the main house, waiting for the dryer to give us back our leotards. Forty minutes earlier, Holly's live-in maid, Consuelo, had come out of her separate living quarters to set the washing machine on "Gentle" and write our names on the waistbands of our pink tights with an indelible marker. We'd gone back inside the main house to watch *Jeopardy* in Holly's room, and at some point Consuelo must have taken our stuff out of the washer and stuffed it in the dryer. Now we were standing in front of the humming white machine, waiting for the timer to hit zero. When it did, the dryer beeped, but neither Holly nor Ellen made a move toward its little door. Consuelo suddenly appeared, and the girls stepped aside as she pulled the laundry out and handed each of us a nicely folded set of warm ballet clothes.

I didn't recognize Consuelo from our neighborhood and, in a way, I was relieved. I felt uncomfortable when she was around, unsure how I was supposed to relate to her. Holly and Ellen all but ignored her when she walked into a room. They would politely say "please" when they asked her to bring snacks or when they sent her off in search of the missing *TV Guide*. And they would politely say "thank you" when she came back again. But they didn't talk to her. Not really.

Holly didn't introduce me to her, and I didn't know what she would have thought if I'd introduced myself. So I didn't. In fact, I don't think Consuelo knew my name until the day she wrote it inside my tights—doing the wash that I normally did for myself.

Part of me wanted to speak to her in Spanish, to tell her that my mom was a maid once, too, and that I didn't need her to get me things, or wash my clothes or call me "Miss." I wanted her to know that I'd never be the kind of person who would say something like "Consuelo, bring the car around." But another part of me knew that would just embarrass us both.

The Seversons weren't mean to her, not that I ever saw. They always complimented her cooking, and once I saw Holly's mother actually applaud when Consuelo carried out a basket of homemade sopapillas for dessert.

The first time I stayed at Holly's house for supper, I couldn't believe my eyes when I saw Consuelo walk though the house ringing a little crystal bell to signal that it was time to eat. Holly's big brother, Nate, who I guess didn't think the main house was big enough for him, somehow got the message in his private apartment over the three-car garage.

Holly's parents emerged from whatever room they'd been in, and everybody followed one another down a wide hall—which they called the gallery—into the informal dining room.

There, Consuelo had set colorful straw place mats, matching iced-tea glasses, and checkered cloth napkins on the long, picnic-style table that dominated the room.

Mr. Severson told me that he built the table for Mrs. Severson as a wedding gift "a thousand years ago" when they were "just starting out."

I'm not sure how I thought a rich man was supposed to act, but Mr. Severson reminded me more of Beto and Efran than the millionaires I'd seen on television shows. I liked him and I think he liked me, too.

The moment he sat down, Consuelo appeared at his side with a bottle of beer.

"Just what the doctor ordered," he announced, twisting off the cap and hoisting the long-neck up in a midair toast.

Nate, who Holly told me was home from Princeton until late January, kept the headphones of his Walkman over his ears and didn't say hello to anyone. Consuelo brought a platter of barbecued chicken and bowls of mashed potatoes, green beans, and salad to the table. Nate bopped his head to the quick beat of whatever he was listening to, and we all passed the food around. He loaded his plate with two servings of everything, and then he left. Mr. and Mrs. Severson nodded at him as he walked away, balancing his plate on his open palm.

"He's studying for exams," his mother explained.

"Yep. We just feed him and clothe him and pay that God's ransom of a tuition," Mr. Severson said between gulps. "No reason he should have to sit down and have a meal with us. Is it?"

"Stuart," Mrs. Severson said dismissively. She looked at me with a friendly smile and said: "You know how college kids are!"

I smiled back without saying that Septima's daughter, Elena, was the only college kid I'd ever known. Unless you counted Dee and Richard, who went to college way before I ever met them.

"So, what trouble are you girls stirring up tonight?" Mr. Severson asked Holly.

"Nothing," Holly answered.

"Nothing? Aw, I don't believe that for one little minute," he teased. "Two pretty girls. That's automatic trouble, isn't it, Claire?"

He threw an exaggerated wink my way, and I think I giggled.

"Socorro was invited to take class with the Boston Ballet over the Christmas holiday," Mrs. Severson informed her husband.

"That right?"

"Yes, sir," I said.

That was all Holly's mom said about me before she changed the subject to things about her own friends and whether she should fly back to Princeton with Nate to spend a few days up East for a little shopping.

The Seversons' big wooden table was made out of long narrow planks, darkened by having been put to nightly use for so long. I liked the comfortable feel of it and the rest of the informal dining room. It had a red-tile floor and cowboy-looking lanterns that dangled from a bar of wrought iron attached to the wide roof beam with a thick chain. Each person at the table sat on a little bench that Mr. Severson also must have made. There were only four of us that night, but I counted ten benches and I wondered where Mr. and Mrs. Severson put such a big piece of furniture when they were "just starting out."

Holly's mother ate her chicken with a fork and knife, but Mr. Severson picked his up with his hands and attacked it. I wasn't sure what I was supposed to do, so I decided to copy Holly. She used utensils, too, so I picked at my barbecued drumstick with my fork, wishing I'd chosen a thigh instead.

About halfway through the meal, Mrs. Severson rang a little brass bell set at the rim of her plate. Consuelo walked through the swinging kitchen door and approached the table.

"Mr. Severson is going to need another napkin."

"S'pose so," he said, wiping his big hands with the stained cloth for one last time before tossing it into the middle of his dirty plate. Consuelo silently handed him another napkin, and he rubbed his hands clean and threw that one onto the plate, too.

Consuelo cleared his spot, and then Mr. Severson pushed his chair back and sighed. "How 'bout some enchiladas tomorrow?" he said as she made her way around the table, collecting dishes.

"*Sí*, Señor."

I figured Holly's family must eat dessert every night, because they sat still until it arrived. Consuelo set down a bowl piled high with perfectly round scoops of chocolate ice cream in front of Mr. Severson first. Then me. Then Holly.

She brought Mrs. Severson a little pot of tea.

"Well, Socorro. That's one down. Four to go!" Mr. Severson said as he plunged his spoon into his two scoops.

I looked at Holly.

"You don't know?" he asked cheerfully.

"Dad!" Holly groaned, lodging a not-so-serious protest.

I shifted on my little bench, making it squeak.

"Look under your place mat," Mr. Severson said.

I didn't move.

"Don't be shy. It's what we do 'round here."

I moved my ice cream to one side and lifted the corner of the bright green place mat about one inch.

"Higher 'n that!" Mr. Severson laughed.

I turned the mat completely over to see if anything was attached to the bottom.

"The table," Holly said, pointing to the spot with her spoon.

I looked down and saw deep gouges that looked like scars. People had carved their names into the wood, but only in that one spot, small enough for the place mat to cover. Next to each name was a number, a date: Dale '78; Robin '81; Tommy '93; Ellen '85; Piper '97. There had to be at least thirty of them.

I ran my hand over the carvings as Mr. Severson spoke.

"If you eat supper with us five times, we figure we like ya enough to remember you forever," he said. "We got names that go back twenty years or more!"

"Only where the mats are, though," Holly added. "Mom doesn't want the entire table carved up."

Mr. Severson laughed and wiped his mouth with his third, clean napkin.

I put the place mat back and spent the rest of the evening enjoying Mr. Severson's corny jokes and looking forward to the day I'd get to etch "Socorro" into the hard old wood.

Chapter 16

ALMA

DEE KEPT ASKING ABOUT THE LETTERS, ABOUT KEEPING THE truth from Socorro, about my choices, and I could hear more than a touch of judgment in each of her questions.

Every time she brought up the subject, I gave her the same answer I'd given her before: "It's for the best." But what I really wanted to say was that the way I was raising my daughter was none of her business.

"I'm just wondering whether what you're doing really is best for Socorro," Dee said as she fed a taffeta hem through the sewing machine on the dining room table across from me. Folds of pink fabric draped over her belly like a toga, and when she pressed the machine's pedal it began to bob—*thwat, thwat, thwat, thwat*—chugging along like a tiny train forging new tracks.

"She wonders, you know," Dee continued. "She doesn't understand why he doesn't write back. She has a father, and she should get a chance to figure out how she feels about him. How *she* feels, Alma. Not how *you* feel."

"Oh, I see," I answered sarcastically. "You want me to be totally honest, like you." I wasn't sure she could hear me over the sewing machine's loud clicks and clacks, but she took her foot off the pedal and sat still for a moment, focusing her eyes on something over my shoulder instead of my face.

Dee had been living in my house for months and still had not revealed a single clue about her past. It was as if she'd had no life before her husband died, at least not one she was willing to tell me about. I knew nothing about her parents, what she was like as a girl, or even if she'd had a happy childhood. She'd kept everything about her background as secret as I'd kept the things inside that box. But unlike her, I refused to pry.

On the days I lived up to the role of a tactful mother, I told Socorro that where Dee originally came from shouldn't matter to any of us because geography doesn't determine what kind of person you are, character does. But I didn't actually believe that myself. Dee's history did matter, and on that afternoon my patience with her evasiveness was running out. I didn't want to fight. But I was tired of her dishing out advice concerning things she knew nothing about.

Of course I knew Socorro wanted more details about her father, but she wasn't ready to hear the ugly twist the real story took. A girl her age should be allowed to picture her father as a good man, and the truth about Paul Walker would do nothing but tarnish that fiction.

"Maybe you should let me handle it my way, Dee," I said.

"Maybe." She stepped on the pedal again.

My little house had become unbearably crowded because Lettie continued to bring in more racks of dresses and stacks of boxes and bulky file cabinets every day. There was barely enough room to breathe.

"The baby's making you emotional," I said. "Let's just stop right now, all right?"

I was trying to keep my cool. I told myself that Dee's worries were really more about her own child than Socorro. She was thinking about Mitch, and trying to figure out how she was going to keep the memory of him alive for her son or daughter.

"I see Socorro looking at that old picture of you and Paul that she keeps on her dresser, and I know she's thinking that she's missing half of who she is," Dee pushed on. "Think of what La Llorona said. She told you that the path is set, and Socorro is already following it. What do you think she's talking about, Alma? If you don't let Socorro get to know her father, one day she's going to go looking for him with or without your permission."

I wanted the phone to ring so I wouldn't have to listen to any more of Dee's nonsense. I lifted the receiver to make sure it was working.

Business had been strong, and Lettie said it would stay that way until the end of the month, when it would, she knew for certain, drop off dramatically. I tried not to think about what might happen then.

How we didn't have enough money to get through a single extra month. How I'd have to go back to being a maid to pay the bills. How I had no way to help Socorro stay in her ballet class.

I slammed down the telephone receiver and stared at Dee until she felt my anger. She stopped the sewing machine and calmly lifted her eyes until they met mine.

"Neither of us can be a dad," she said softly. "My baby isn't ever going to know how much Mitch would have loved him, no matter what I say. And Alma, Socorro won't ever stop searching for the other half of herself, no matter how much you wish she might. She's not going to forget about Paul just because you don't want anything to do with him. You can't protect her from the truth forever. You just can't."

Chapter 17

DEE

MONEY WORRIES WERE MAKING EVERYONE TENSE. ALMA TOLD Lettie to take the cost of Socorro's *quinceañera* gown out of her weekly pay, but Lettie refused. One of her handmade dresses usually sold for anywhere from three hundred to eight hundred dollars, and the mail-ordered gowns ran twice that high. It would have taken Alma years to pay.

"It's my gift," Lettie insisted.

"No," Alma replied gruffly. "I'll figure something out."

Alma was fiercely proud of how she'd managed on her own for the past fifteen years. She'd arrived with nothing but the hope that Paul would keep his word of creating a better life for her and Socorro, and was grateful for the help she got from her friends when he didn't.

For a while, she told me, she worked as a maid, cleaning for a woman she hated but who allowed her to bring Socorro into the house. When that woman fired her, Lettie unselfishly stepped aside so Septima could give Alma a job at the fabric store. In gratitude, Alma said that every day she worked at Septima's shop, she prayed that La Virgencita would make Lettie's pageant business a success. She thought her debt had finally been paid.

But suddenly all the hardships had resurrected. The joblessness. The panic. The humiliating charity. In Alma's eyes, accepting help from Lettie would sweep away what little self-respect she had left. So there was no way I could casually reveal that I had been pretending to have nothing when I really had enough money to take care of all of us. What sort of blow would that be to her pride?

I looked into the faces of the women who had given me so much and I felt sick. I was only weeks away from giving birth, and Alma had never asked what I intended to do after the baby was born, where I planned to live or how I expected to make ends meet. She assumed that I meant to stay with her on Frontera Street, adding an infant's needs to her grocery list and yet another soul to her roster of responsibilities.

How could I have let it get so out of hand?

I thought of my house, sitting wide and empty on the Westside, and I knew the time had come to claim it.

At first Cece and Socorro's party planning shored up their eroding friendship. They worked together, paging through gown catalogs and fashion magazines, gleefully narrowing down Socorro's selection to three similar-looking dresses. Then, as the girls peered impatiently over her shoulder, Lettie sketched out an original design—creating a snug and sophisticated evening dress that accentuated Socorro's long legs and flawless, narrow back.

The girls discussed where they would go to get their hair done and debated whether they should spend an extra thirty dollars for a set of acrylic nails or settle for a basic manicure that cost ten. It was a pleasure to see them getting along so well, a chance for me to see how close they had been before I met them, before they had to grope for a topic of conversation to get them through their Friday night sleep-overs.

I could tell they felt it slipping too, and I reminded Socorro that it wasn't anybody's fault. Their lives were just very different now.

Cece had become a high school sports fan or, more precisely, a fan of the athletes. She took up smoking. And, because the sleep-overs fell on football nights, she insisted that Socorro come with her to Chaparral High stadium where, Socorro said, they never sat still long enough to watch the game. Cece and her buddies spent the evening walking between, behind, and underneath the bleachers, their cigarettes jammed into the front pockets of their jeans and their hairbrushes into the back. Some of the girls paired up with boys and disappeared into the dark parking lot, where, Socorro told me, couples draped themselves like bedspreads over the widest car hoods they could find.

As soon as the game was over, the girls made their way to the football players' locker room and waited patiently for the home team to emerge—showered, slick-haired and hungry. The players would spend a few moments joking and winking at their freshman admirers, but they'd walk away with the prettiest juniors and seniors.

Socorro contended that Cece wasn't nearly as aggressive as some of the other girls. But I had noticed that an unmistakable sexual sway had crept into Cece's hips, and I recognized a knowing tone in the how-to-catch-a-boy advice she eagerly imparted, which made me think that it had been a while since she'd told Socorro everything.

Of course, Socorro kept things from Cece, too. Including how she had been avidly adding up her dinners with Holly, and how thrilled she was the night Mr. Severson snapped a Polaroid picture of her carving her name into his table. She had taped the photo onto the mirror over her dresser, and despite its prominent position, I was certain Socorro never bothered to tell Cece anything about it.

Still I had no doubt that there had been a time when they had identical visions of the perfect *quinceañera*; back when they were dressing their Barbie dolls in frilly lace gowns, back when they daydreamed about fairy-tale opulence and elegance while they groomed the manes of their toy ponies. It was somewhere between Cinderella's castle and Arts High that their expectations began to drift apart.

Cece had turned her back on all the customary ribbons and bows. She told Socorro she intended to follow only two of the unbreakable *quinceañera* traditions—wearing a white dress and being presented to the crowd by her father. But after that first dance, her party was going to take on a sharp-edged nightclub atmosphere. She wanted balloons tied to the backs of all the chairs, she wanted shoeless dancing to high-voltage rock, and a booth where her guests could get temporary tattoos painted onto their faces and bodies. She told Socorro she even planned to change clothes halfway through the event, ditching her cloud of tulle for a halter top and a mini skirt.

Socorro, on the other hand, prized the ritual and ceremony, especially after listening to Holly and Ellen describe the lavish debutante balls they intended to have when they reached eighteen. Socorro said her part of the *quinceañera* wouldn't reach perfection unless there were clusters of votive candles flickering on the tabletops, buffet stations decorated with coral roses and towering ice sculptures, and Peeps's quintet serenely playing Vivaldi, Mozart, and Strauss.

"It's just three extra guys," she pleaded with her mother. "And Mr. Cardenas doesn't have to pay them, just give them dinner."

She was fighting a losing battle.

Alma had decreed that Socorro was not to order anything extra for her half of the *quinceañera*. And she refused to back down. Whatever Cece planned would have to do. Her music. Her menu. Her decorations. Which meant the quintet was out of the question, even if Peeps and Richard were two of its members and were already on the guest list. The only way Socorro would ever get to hear Mozart or Strauss at her party was if she could convince Cece to request classical music. And that was unlikely to happen, since Cece had already rejected all of Socorro's other suggestions, except for one—ice sculptures.

I slipped the key into the lock and swung the door of the Westside house wide open. The air inside was stale and the furniture was dusty.

The baby had grown so heavy that every move I made was an exertion. I had to sit down after trimming the withered leaves from the ficus's spindly limbs, and catch my breath after bending down to clean the lint out of the dryer.

I shuffled through the mail and leaned on the piano for a rest. Then I began to look around. I studied the little collection of family photos, framed and arranged on the broad back of the Steinway. There was a time when I was very happy here. Despite Momma's arm's-length mothering, I had always felt safe and cared for. I could vividly recall how Poppa filled the place with humor, and how he made me believe I could do anything in the world that I wanted. I wondered if, as a mother, I would have the ability to do the same for his grandchild.

For an instant I pictured Poppa standing next to me at the piano, like he used to during his parties. I watched as he introduced himself to Alma and Socorro and Septima, whom I knew he would love. I thought how much I would have liked my child to see that, to see the two parts of my life come together under one happy roof.

I lifted the lid of the piano bench and leafed through the sheet music inside. Gershwin, Beethoven, Joplin's rags. I found Mozart's *Eine kleine Nachtmusik*, Poppa's favorite. I positioned the music above the keyboard and began to play for the first time since those dark, horrible days in Dallas. My fingers were swollen and sluggish, but I pushed them up to tempo and soon the notes felt like old friends. I played the joyful melody of the opening Allegro louder and louder. I closed my eyes and continued the piece from memory, each bar coming back to me like a dream. The baby, startled by the sound, gave me a quick kick and then settled down as the cadence gently embraced us. This was music written to celebrate life and great love, the sort of music Socorro wanted for her party. The kind she deserved.

I made my way through the serenades, movement by movement, imagining Alma and Socorro and everyone else from the barrio dancing in the living room with my father and even my mother. I saw their dark eyes gleaming with joy and their gentle faces finally free of worry. And I saw Mitch dancing with them, twirling Alma in his arms, leading Socorro through the minuet, sweeping Septima through the triumphant finale. Everyone looked so happy that I didn't want the music to end.

When I reached the final note, I kept my fingers on the keys so it would linger. And that is when I felt Mitch's presence take hold like a mighty anchor. Suddenly, I knew he'd settled himself inside that room, inside the entire house, where five months earlier I never thought I'd find him. Knowing he was there made everything about the place feel different—safe and loving.

Why not? I heard him say. Why not start a new life with your new family here?

I told Richard first.

I knew it was safest to start with him because his reaction would give me a clue of what Alma's might be. And, I thought, it might even let me know if this idea to try and undo what I'd done was hopelessly insane.

His carriage house was only a few streets away, and when I phoned I was certain he was getting ready for what had become a standing Saturday night date with Alma.

"Is everything okay?" he asked, a bit surprised to hear from me.

"I need to tell you something," I said. "Could you come over?"

"I'll be there in half an hour," he replied. "Did you need me to pick—?"

"No," I interrupted. "I'm not at Alma's."

"Is everything all right?"

"Yeah, I just need to talk to you."

He waited, unsure where the conversation was headed.

"Do you know where Tierra Fina Avenue is?"

"Yes . . ." I heard a dose of uncertainty in his voice.

"Meet me at 913 Tierra Fina."

"What?"

"Just meet me there, okay? Ten minutes."

I set the phone down, lowered myself into one of the rattan chairs, and waited. When I heard Richard's car tires crunch on the gravel driveway, I stepped outside to greet him. As he pulled around the semicircle, I noticed that weeds had pushed up through the loose pebbles. In my absence, scores of rangy green and yellow sprouts had infiltrated the gravel drive, something my mother never would have allowed. She prided herself on how staunchly she battled the desert's natural forces, regularly sending her maid out to the driveway to pluck out any trace of plant life that dared to prosper.

Richard kept his car's engine running as I approached the passenger-side window. He leaned across the seats and cranked the glass open.

"What are you doing here?" he asked.

"Come on in," I said.

"What?"

"Turn off the car and just come in."

He cut the engine but didn't move.

"Dee, what are we doing here?" he said, impatient to be told what was going on.

"This is my house."

I was standing in the entryway, my arm outstretched, inviting Richard in.

He got out of the car slowly, making me repeat what I'd just said. Over his shoulder I could see the orange winter sun setting behind the flat desert mesas in the distance. I knew Alma would be wondering where I had gone, and worrying that I might not get back in time to cook dinner for Socorro and Peeps like I had promised.

Richard cocked his head and exhaled in astonishment, still wary, I could tell, that I might be pulling a practical joke.

"Really," I assured him. "Come in."

*   *   *

No, he said, he didn't know how Alma would react to the news.

"What about you?"

"Huh?" he stammered.

"Does this make you mad?"

"Mad?"

"At me. Does it make you mad at me?"

It wasn't a fair question. I had just spent twenty minutes pelting him with every secret detail of my life. And now I wanted a simple answer, an instant assessment of how much damage I had done.

He pulled off his glasses and rubbed his eyes. The rattan he was sitting on rustled.

"I don't know," he sighed, his fingers pinching the bridge of his nose, his eyes still shut.

My pulse quickened, and the baby protested with a punch.

Richard put his glasses back on and stood. He was dressed for a night out, with a leather bomber jacket pulled over a white golf shirt that was neatly tucked into a pair of dark blue jeans. The brown of his burnished leather belt exactly matched the just-polished boots he had on his feet. I was afraid he was going to turn his back and leave. But he didn't.

He took a second survey of the surroundings, this time scrutinizing every item his eyes fell upon. He considered the rattan coffee table where I'd placed the glass of water that he asked for but didn't drink, and took a long, slow look at the baby grand piano by the sliding glass doors. He pondered the kiva-style fireplace in the far corner of the dining room and the dried mesquite wood piled like a pyramid next to it. His face was locked in an unreadable expression.

He moved toward the wall where four Gorman paintings were displayed under spotlights like gallery pieces, and then he looked back over his shoulder to the rattan sofa, where I was sitting.

I tilted my head, begging for an answer. "Please," I sighed. "Say *something*."

"It's hard to grasp," was all he could muster.

I made him promise to let me tell Alma in my own way.

He made me promise that I would do it soon.

"Tonight," he prodded.

"No!"

I needed time to work my story out, to come up with a way to convince Alma that moving to the Westside could help us all.

Richard responded with a disapproving look. I prayed he wouldn't actually tell me what he was thinking of me at that moment. I couldn't bear to hear it.

"If you don't tell her, I will," he warned. "I won't keep something like this from her."

"Give me twenty-four hours," I begged.

He searched my face for a clearer explanation of what had just been laid out before him, but all I could do was silently mouth the word *please.*

He helped me up from the sofa and out to my car, and we agreed that arriving at Frontera Street at the same time might look suspicious. So I drove away from Tierra Fina first, and fifteen minutes later he followed.

I could tell Socorro was angry over yet another of Cece's *quinceañera* decisions, but I waited until Alma and Richard were gone before I asked her about it. She had been trying to keep her complaints to a minimum, but she wasn't very good at hiding her disappointment.

Peeps was over for the evening, and I had no idea what I was going to feed them for dinner. I didn't have the energy to chop or bake or boil anything, and the prospect of letting them cook made me feel even more tired. In fact, the only meal I could think about at all was a steaming hot dog with sweet relish and a double-thick strawberry milkshake, which I'd been craving for two days.

"You feel like burgers?" I asked.

"La Indita isn't open on the weekends," Peeps replied, instantly ruling out the only restaurant, other than the takeout taco hut, in the neighborhood.

"I know another place," I said to them, jingling my car keys to let them know we were on our way.

In the car, Peeps broke into a playfully sinister laugh and Socorro reached into the backseat to swat at him.

"It's not funny!" she whined.

"Yes, it is," he laughed.

"What?" I asked.

Peeps pulled himself up against the back of my seat and spoke through the headrest in a coarse whisper. "Guess what kind of ice sculptures Cece ordered?"

He barely finished the question before he melted into a fit of laughter. Socorro refused to look at him, defiantly devoting her attention to the darkness outside her window.

Peeps took a deep breath and continued. "Martini glasses!" he shouted.

Socorro whipped her head around to gauge my reaction, and I bit my lip to keep from snickering. Peeps, however, broke into another rash of laughter.

Socorro slumped down in her seat and turned on the radio. She punched the dashboard buttons until the dial leaped to her favorite station, and then she fiddled with the balance until the bass pounded like a nervous pulse.

Peeps slid back into his seat, defeated by her counterattack, and I let the music blare until the end of the first song. When it was done, I reached over and turned the volume down.

"I'm giving the fifty seats back," she protested, still staring out the window at absolutely nothing. "No way I'm going to invite anybody from Arts now."

"It's not that bad," Peeps maintained, trying to apologize without saying he was sorry.

Socorro swiveled in her seat and glared at him, emphatically declaring the matter closed. I knew she was feeling like she was caught in quicksand, unable to admit to Cece or Mr. Cardenas or, least of all, her mother, that after wanting so badly to be included in the party, all she wanted now was out. I had watched her initial enthusiasm turn into resignation, and now into embarrassment.

It was the perfect moment to tell her.

"Where are we going?" Socorro finally asked, noticing that we'd passed Arts High and were quickly heading toward the Westside cotton fields.

"Someplace I used to go to all the time."

I felt Peeps pulling himself back up so he could see out the front windshield.

I turned onto Valleyview Road and stepped on the accelerator.

We passed the Seversons' land and swept alongside six other cotton crops, which in the cloud-covered moonlight looked like wide, flat pools of emptiness. I turned left onto Country Club Lane, and for a few seconds the tires lost traction on the road's red-clay surface, which, I happened to know, the families on that street preferred over asphalt because it was easier on their horses' legs.

I had no way of knowing whether any of Peeps's or Socorro's new friends had already introduced them to the Grillbarn. But based on the curious looks they were giving me, I suspected they hadn't. Maybe it wasn't as popular with the high school crowd as it used to be. Not that it made any difference to me. All I wanted was a strawberry milkshake and a place where I would feel comfortable telling Socorro everything.

We rolled past mansions, lit up like desert mirages at the far end of long, dark driveways.

"What if you could live over here?" I posed the question mildly, like I was talking about the moon. Neither of them answered.

I pulled the car through the wrought-iron gates of the Westside Country Club and slowly cruised past the main building. Beyond the sheer curtains we could see the shadowy outlines of people mingling in the formal dining room.

"What if you could have your *quinceañera* in there?"

Still no answer.

The doorman, dressed in a double-breasted uniform far too heavy for a West Texas winter, began walking toward our car as it slowly approached the front door. I shook my head no, and he stepped back from the curb with a polite nod as we taxied past him.

"I'm serious," I said as we pulled away. "What if you could?"

We were parked inside one of the stalls at the Grillbarn, a drive-in fast-food joint converted from actual horse stables. Our hot dogs and hamburgers were balancing on the metal trays that the teenage carhop had clipped onto the windows. The strawberry milkshake I ordered was as thick as I remembered, impossible to negotiate through a straw, and fat with chunks of frozen fruit. We were one of only three cars at the restaurant, but it was too early for the regular Saturday night crowd, which traditionally roared in after nine o'clock.

"I knew you were from the Westside," Socorro exclaimed. "I just *knew* it!"

I told Socorro that the country club could handle everything, and I apologized for not offering it earlier. She ate her French fries nervously, not sure how to answer.

My thoughts were jumbled. Maybe this was a terrible idea. Here I was dangling what Alma could never give Socorro in front of her face, promising that it could be hers in a blink of an eye. What did I expect her to say?

Maybe I should have just moved back to the Westside by myself, simply slipped out of Socorro and Alma's lives as mysteriously as I'd slipped in. But what good would that have done? Alma would still need work, and Socorro would still be going to class every day knowing that her mother was struggling to keep her there. I couldn't abandon them like that, not when I knew that my house could be a help, even a blessing.

Moving would allow Alma to rent her entire place to Lettie, who could use it for storage until she saved enough to rent a dress salon. The money that Lettie paid Alma in rent would save her from having to go back to the Pick-and-Pray. In fact, I could make sure Alma wouldn't have to work at all, if she didn't want to. And we'd have lots more room, which we'd need once the baby arrived.

I ran each of my arguments past Socorro, hoping to gauge Alma's reaction by her own. But she had already made the move in her mind and was barely listening. Peeps, who was working on his second cheeseburger, his back propped up against the door and his legs stretched out in front of him, cleared his throat.

"Sounds fine now, but Alma hates the Westside," he said. "She hates everything about it."

He was right.

Alma wouldn't care about the *quinceañera* at the country club, and she probably didn't give a damn about the extra space. But she did care that her neighbors had begun to pity her, and she had begun to doubt whether she could afford to keep Socorro at Arts High for much longer. If moving to the Westside was the only way to help Socorro make it into the ballet world, I knew she'd do it. What I wanted to do was convince her that I wasn't asking her to make yet another sacrifice—or competing with her for her daughter's affection. All I wanted to do was thank her for helping me get my life back on track, to repay her kindness with the only thing I had to offer. But maybe Peeps was right. Maybe getting Alma to see the Westside as a gift was not only ridiculous but impossible.

Chapter 18

ALMA

IT WAS LATE, WELL PAST MIDNIGHT, AND I WAS SURPRISED TO see Dee still awake when Richard brought me home. Socorro was asleep, and the house was warm and still. It seemed like the perfect end to a pleasant evening.

Richard took my coat and was on his way to hang it in my bedroom closet when he gave Dee a long look and said: "Now would be good."

Dee held out her hand, inviting me to sit next to her on the sofa, and I turned to see Richard nodding his head in agreement. The living room was dark, except for a pool of yellow light falling from the one and only lamp Dee had on. Richard returned from the bedroom and sat in a chair across from us. They both looked so serious that I began to feel frightened.

"Is the baby all right?" I gasped.

Dee cupped my hands into both of hers and smiled nervously. "It's nothing like that," she said.

She looked as if she was about to cry.

"I'm not sure how to tell you this," she began.

"Well, you'd better say something, because I can't take the suspense," I replied, trying to cut the tension in the air.

"Alma," Dee started again, "I'm not exactly who you think I am."

I looked at Richard, but he kept his focus on Dee.

"I'm not from Dallas. Not originally," she continued. "I'm from here. From Los Cielos. Born and bred."

I slipped my hands out of her grasp and heard myself inhale.

"I grew up on the Westside. And I still have a house over there."

I was sure she was joking, and I even let out a little laugh.

"Yeah," she said warily, "I suppose it sounds a little funny."

It quickly occurred to me that she was serious, and that's when I began to cough, to choke actually. Richard jumped up from his chair and began to slap his palm against my back.

Dee kept talking, letting her words spill into the darkness, but because I was taking loud, deep breaths I only heard parts of what she said.

". . . just never seemed right . . . scared, I suppose . . . and it might be better."

I put my hands over my ears, and she stopped in midsentence. Everything about the moment felt like the day I found her looking through my secret box at the fabric shop. She had the same look of fear in her eyes, and I could feel the same wave of anger welling up inside me. After all this time, after everything that had happened to us, we were right back where we started, with Dee helping herself to my things, to my life, and giving me nothing but lies in return.

"When did you intend to tell us?" I snarled. "Or did you plan to just sneak out one night and leave a folded twenty on the nightstand as a little tip?"

"I'm so sorry," Dee replied. "I thought if you knew, everything between us would change."

"Change?" I scoffed. "Why would you think that? You thought I'd look at you differently if I knew you had a big house and a couple of cars and even a few prized horses that you could go home to whenever you got bored of roughing it?"

"I don't have . . ."

I stood up and began to leave the room. I had no intention of sitting there and listening to anything else she had to say. But by the time I reached the hallway, my anger had become unchained.

"You let us all feel so sorry for you," I shouted. "Poor Dee, all alone in the world. Worse off than even us. Was that your idea of a fun little game to play?"

"I needed the help," Dee said, barely above a whisper. "I really did."

"Oh, sure you did. Everyone knows that moving in with a bunch of poor people is a great cure for depression. It's a laugh a minute. If you were lonely, why didn't you just hire somebody to keep you company?

Some maid standing at the downtown plaza. One *Mexicáno* is just as good as another, isn't that right?"

I saw Richard flinch, and I could tell he was having a hard time staying out of it.

"That's not fair!" Dee said. "Alma, I care about you and Socorro, and you know it."

"No." I scowled back at her. "I don't know anything about you."

Of course Socorro wanted to go. *Y por qué no?* In her eyes, Dee had not only swung open the door to liberty and justice for us all, but had come through with the *quinceañera* of her dreams.

And what was I supposed to say about that? I couldn't tell her the real reasons I hated everything about the idea without sounding exactly like the *gringos* I used to accuse of being narrow-minded. *Because those people aren't like us. Because it's not a place where we belong. Because in a border town the lines are clear even if they aren't visible.*

Dee left my house after making her confession, and when she called, I ignored her pleas to speak with me. The first eight times I hung up on her. After that I simply handed the telephone to Socorro and walked away.

Two days passed and Socorro spent every moment trying to convince me that I was looking at Dee's offer the wrong way.

Septima agreed with Socorro, telling me that saying yes didn't mean I had to go over there forever. It just meant that Socorro would get the sort of *quinceañera* she had always dreamed about.

"No," I argued. "Not the kind she always dreamed about, the kind she started wanting after she met Dee and those snobby girls from the Westside. She's ashamed of me and of everything about Frontera Street."

Septima insisted I was wrong.

"Have some faith in the love that you taught your girl to show," she said to me. "She's doing what you prayed she'd do, Alma. She's looking right past the lines that you and I could never cross. She's accepting a gift that Dee is offering from her heart and inviting you to walk across with her, instead of going there without you."

Deep down I knew there was nothing I could do about the fact that the ballet world Socorro wanted so badly to belong to was mainly white. And rich. And demanding. I knew I would never feel as comfortable in it as she might become. But if my daughter wanted me to try and live Dee's life, the way Dee had lived ours, if that was her American dream, then *por qué no?*

I told Richard to tell Dee that I'd stay until the *quinceañera,* but I didn't want to see her until we were ready to move in.

Two weeks later we were having a farewell dinner at Septima's house, our boxes and suitcases already piled in the back of Beto's pickup truck, ready for the next morning's move.

Everyone was there—Cece and her parents, Peeps and his, Richard, Lettie, Pilar, and Father Miguel. We squeezed the adults around Septima's table and lined the kids along the kitchen counter nearby. Iluminada, who had gained twelve pounds over Christmas, provided most of the food.

"You won't find this on the Westside," she said, spooning her homemade *molé* sauce over a giant serving of rice and chicken.

"The house is only seven miles away," Richard protested mildly. "It's not at the other end of the earth."

Iluminada looked at him blankly, and then smiled as she handed him the plate. I could tell that inside she was silently answering him, gently saying, "Oh, Señor Richard, it is so much farther than you think."

If Cece and Peeps were upset about Socorro moving across town, they didn't show it. In fact, throughout dinner I overheard the girls making plans to turn their Friday night sleep-overs into slumber parties for all three of them. And Cece was enthusiastically backing every one of Socorro's new party plans, now that she had been set free from her promise to share her *quinceañera.*

"So," Pilar asked as Iluminada doled out servings of *tres leches* for dessert, "what's the house look like?"

Richard answered her with an uncomfortable look and mumbled something in reply.

"We don't know," Socorro chimed in. "He's keeping it secret until tomorrow."

"Actually," he said, "Dee wanted to get the place cleaned up a bit. Get the floors washed, the weeds pulled out of the lawn, things like that."

"What street is it on?" Beto asked.

"Tierra Fina Avenue," he replied.

His answer jarred me. That was the same road Mrs. Campbell lived on. The conversation moved on, but my thoughts stalled. Tierra Fina. Tierra Fina. I fought to stay calm. There are lots of houses on that street, I told myself. Plenty of them.

After dessert, Septima led everyone into the living room, and I knew we'd come to the part of the evening that was going to swirl me through an ocean of conflicting emotions.

Socorro was sitting on the floor at my feet, and out of nervousness I reached down and began to stroke her long hair.

Beto stood and began to speak. "Almita, we can still remember when you first got here."

"Speak for yourself, *viejo!*" Pilar joked. "Some of us were still in diapers way back when."

Everybody laughed, but it was the sort of laughter that stops short because people know the words that will follow are ones they'll want to remember.

"We refuse to say good-bye," Beto continued, "because you can never leave Frontera Street and it will never, ever leave you."

I felt Socorro lean her back against my legs, and when I looked down at her, she took my hand from her shoulder and held it against her heart. We both began to cry.

"So no *adióses* for you. Only *hasta luego*. Or, like the kids say, 'later.' "

Beto blew us a kiss and Septima held us both in a tight hug.

"Don't get all dramatic yet," Cece said cheerfully. "We're not finished." She stood and scampered back to the dining room, where she produced two small gifts from somewhere inside the china cabinet. Iluminada took the moment to run to the kitchen and get Socorro and me some water. Cece brought the packages into the living room and handed me the one that was the size of a wallet. She placed the other package in Socorro's lap.

"We wanted to give you driving lessons," Father Miguel said with a wink. "But nobody was willing to volunteer!"

"No," Septima laughed. "We decided this would be better."

I untied the gold velvet ribbon that was wrapped around the little box, and lifted its square lid. Inside, was a city bus pass. Good for six months.

Septima patted my back, and Lettie planted a kiss on my cheek.

"And last but not least," Cece said, sitting herself next to Socorro, "this is from all of us who love to see you dance."

The rectangular shape of the box was unmistakable. Socorro locked eyes with Cece and kept saying "thank you" as she tore the yellow wrapping paper off a pair of her favorite brand of toe shoes, imported from England.

Richard spent the night.

The house was empty, except for the furniture we planned to leave behind. We were both exhausted from all the packing, and a little tipsy from the party. Richard fell into a deep sleep after we made love. But I couldn't relax. My mind was swimming with wild thoughts. I kept thinking about Tierra Fina Avenue and the ridiculous irony of its name—*fine ground.* I thought about how I was crossing Frontera Street, *border street,* to get to *fine ground.* Soon the names began to wrestle with one another in my head, Frontera tumbling over Tierra, avenue pouncing on top of street. The images wouldn't fade, and before long I was dreaming.

Socorro and I had all our possessions piled into a little red wagon, with the yellow rocking chair that we gave Dee perched unsteadily on top. Richard was trying to keep the boxes from falling as we pulled the wagon over an uneven road.

We walked to the edge of a lush green forest, and Socorro said she could hear birds singing from the tops of the trees. But there was no path leading into the woods, and the trees were so thick that even in the daylight the forest was dark. I looked down and found La Virgencita in my hand. Socorro began to pull the wagon into the woods, and I told her to stop. Richard looked over his shoulder and pointed to a dark tornado churning across the desert toward us. I knew it was La Llorona and I began to shout.

"You are too late. Too late to take my girl!"

La Llorona howled like a coyote as she moved closer and closer. Then I felt her bony hand reach over me to try and snatch La Virgencita from my grip. I reached out and clenched her ice-cold fingers so hard that they burned my hand, and I yanked the base of my little statue with all my strength.

"Let go!" I screamed.

Richard flipped on the light and La Llorona was gone.

I sat up and saw Socorro, standing in the doorway of my bedroom, groggy and not at all surprised to see Richard in my bed. He put his hand under my chin and told me to look into his eyes.

"Nobody's stealing anything. See? Here's Saint Mary. Shhh."

I was numb.

"We're all here. And we're all safe," Richard whispered. He kissed my forehead and then my mouth.

"I love you," he sighed. "We all love you."

The next morning, Beto met us at the curb with a box of *pan dulce* and three Styrofoam cups of coffee. Dee was outside, too, quietly standing by her car, drinking a small carton of chocolate milk.

My eyes were glazed from lying awake half the night, my head still reeling from the dream about La Llorona. I saw my beautiful daughter beaming with joy as she hugged Cece and Peeps good-bye and then climbed into Dee's car.

Beto set the not-yet-empty box of pastry on the hood of his truck, and I told him I'd take it to Septima, who was watching us from her front porch. I looked into Sepi's eyes and tried to absorb the strength I knew she was offering. She handed me a rosary that she was holding and said, "The forest only looks dark until you make a path." I gasped and she smiled calmly, planting a tender kiss on my forehead.

Then she gently took me by the shoulders and turned me around so I was looking out at the cars, lined up with engines running, ready to go.

Richard waved to hurry me along.

"Look," Septima said. "Look at the love that's waiting for you."

As we stopped and started at the traffic lights along Main Street, I tried to describe my dream to Richard.

"Sounds like I wasn't the only one who got heartburn from Ilumi-nada's *molé* sauce," he joked.

I knew he wouldn't take it seriously.

"Sweetheart," he said, "this is a big move. Lots of stress for you and Socorro both."

Normally, I would have been furious that he had reduced the awe-some power of nature's evil to something as stupid as stress. But I desperately wanted to believe that the dream foretold nothing. So I told myself he was right.

I closed my eyes and heard the car wheels hum. Richard took my hand and kissed it. I loved him very much.

"Put the seat back," he said, "and try to relax."

I felt the car cruising over the smooth asphalt, and I remembered sitting in the backseat of Mrs. Campbell's car making the same drive. It was hardly a calming recollection. When I put the seat back up and I opened my eyes, I saw the cotton fields that she used to chauffeur me past. Richard slowed down to follow Beto's truck, which followed Dee's cranberry-colored sedan as it turned onto Tierra Fina Avenue. My pulse begin to pound like a hammer in the back of my throat.

It was a cloudless morning, and the sky was an electric blue. We passed a girl riding a tall brown horse bareback, with two yellow Labradors running happily behind her. I pictured Socorro riding a bicycle underneath the very same canopy of tree branches in the spring, headed toward the levy to dip her toes in the muddy Rio Grande. Maybe she *did* belong here. Maybe times *had* changed.

We continued down the avenue, past upright mailboxes standing at the mouths of long driveways. It was a beautiful neighborhood, that was a fact, and Socorro had just as much right to live in a pretty place as any other little girl.

Suddenly, I saw Mrs. Campbell's house ahead of us, on the left. I turned my eyes toward the other side of the street and focused on the red-tile roofs, the trimmed hedges, and the tall chimneys mixed in with the trees.

"Ready?" Richard asked as he slowed the car down.

I leaned over to kiss his cheek but ended up gripping the dashboard with both hands when I saw where he was turning—into the gravel driveway that I had spent endless afternoons raking and weeding.

I sat back in my seat, trying to catch my breath.

"Are you okay?" Richard asked, stepping on the brakes.

I couldn't answer because my head was swimming. Paxton, I thought to myself, Dee's last name is *Paxton,* not Campbell. This had to be a mistake.

"Who lives here?" I asked in a panic.

Richard slowly moved his foot back to the gas pedal.

"You do, *mi amor,*" he said. "With Socorro and Dee."

Chapter 19

SOCORRO

I COULDN'T BEGIN TO IMAGINE WHAT MY MOTHER WAS THINKING. I twisted around to get a glimpse of her through the back windshield, but Richard's car was hidden behind Beto's truck.

"Do you think she's as surprised as you?" Dee asked, completely misreading my alarm. My stomach tensed, and the sound of loose gravel shifting and popping underneath Dee's tires made me think of hot oil in a pan. Dee aimed a brilliant smile my way, and I wondered how I was going to tell her that of all the houses in all of Los Cielos, there wasn't one my mother could possibly hate more than the giant Spanish colonial standing right before us.

Beto parked his truck by the wide front door and began honking his horn in celebration. He jumped out from behind the wheel and began making crazy faces and exaggerated hand gestures to show Dee how impressed he was. Dee watched him in her rearview mirror and honked back with glee.

"Hey," she said, playfully poking me in the ribs. "You'll get a better view if you get *out* of the car."

Dee was practically floating with joy. She was convinced that once my mother saw this house, all her past resentment would disappear. She shut off the car engine and unlocked her seat belt, eager to usher everybody inside her home.

I couldn't move.

For a moment I considered keeping quiet about Mom, letting Dee find out on her own. But I couldn't let her get sideswiped by such a powerful blow, not when she was feeling so good about what she'd done. I knew that I had to warn her about Mom's reaction, and I had to do it before she stepped out of the car.

I heard the rumble of Richard's old Toyota behind us, and I wondered what Mom was telling him. And what he saying to her. Richard didn't turn off the engine after coming to a stop, which wasn't a good sign, and neither of them looked like they were getting ready to step out.

Dee yanked her door handle and the automatic locks popped up like breakfast toast, making me flinch. She pushed her door open with her elbow, and as she swung her knees across the driver's seat, I reached over and grabbed her other arm to keep her from bounding out onto the driveway.

"Wait a minute," I said.

I made her shut the door and then I told her everything. I explained how Mrs. Campbell used to make my mom wear humiliating uniforms and how after good and loyal service, she turned around and accused my mother of stealing. As I spoke, I watched every emotion—from bewilderment to dismay—slide across Dee's face. When I was done, my throat was dry and Dee sat stunned, her belly wedged behind the steering wheel and her hand still on the door handle.

I could feel Mom's and Richard's eyes drilling into the back of my head all the way from the Toyota. They hadn't moved a muscle.

Dee took a deep breath and then pulled herself out of the sedan, moving her arms and legs as if they weighed more than lead. I bolted out of the car and rushed to her side, grabbing her shoulder to help her get steady. But as I slid my hand down to hold her forearm and we began to walk toward Richard's car, I saw Mom staring at me through the greenish tint of the car's windshield, and I knew I had made the wrong decision. I should have gone right to *her* side instead. I should have rushed to comfort *her* first, and now it was too late.

Richard stood and tried to secretly communicate with Dee from across the car's roof, raising his eyebrows and shaking his head. My mom wasn't budging. Not one single inch. That was what he was saying.

Dee handed Richard the house keys, and he walked over to the front door to lead Beto inside. Dee and I leaned against the Toyota, and began speaking to my mother through the window she refused to roll down.

"Alma," Dee sighed, "I had no idea. You never said . . ."

She might as well have been talking to a block of stone.

In my head, I tried to play back all the conversations that we'd had with Dee about the years my mother worked as a maid. I couldn't be certain whether Mrs. Campbell's name had, in fact, ever come up. But Dee could be right. Mom had a habit of not calling Mrs. Campbell by name, but just saying "that woman"—*esa mujer.*

Dee's face was completely drained of the pink-cheeked pride that had lit it up only moments earlier. Now she looked pale and rattled. She had no idea what she was supposed to say, so she just stood on the gravel, awkwardly attempting to find a way to bend down closer to my mother's ear without tipping over, belly first.

I wanted to tell Mom that, in a way, she should feel great about what was happening. I wanted to convince her that if she took a minute to consider how everything had turned around, she would see that Cinderella was taking over the castle. I wanted her to imagine what a huge laugh Septima would get out of the situation, and how funny the story would be at next year's Thanksgiving table.

I wanted to point out all those things, but I couldn't make my mouth form the words, and all I wound up saying was: "Mom, *esa mujer* doesn't live here anymore."

"You won't recognize a single thing inside," Dee added hastily. "I promise. All the old furniture is in storage."

Beto and Richard kept lifting boxes off the back of the truck and carrying them inside. My mother sat in the car and watched them, her chin pointed straight ahead and her eyes intentionally focused on anything but us.

Dee and I stood next to the car for what felt like half an hour, waiting for any sort of reaction from my mother. Eventually, Richard walked over and gently led Dee away from the Toyota.

"Come on," he said to her. "They need to talk."

I walked around to the driver's side and slid into the seat next to my mom.

"Are you sure you want to do this?" she asked.

"Yes," I said. "Positive."

"Well . . ." she answered, her voice quavering, "I'm not."

The dark circles under her eyes looked almost blue, and her nose was turning crimson as she tried to hold back her tears. I knew she hadn't slept all night, and whatever nightmare had kept her awake seemed to have followed her straight up Dee's driveway.

She turned toward me, her eyes narrow with suspicion, and asked why I wanted to live with Dee so badly.

"What did she say to you?" she demanded. "What did she promise?"

I had never seen her look so shaken or act so unsure of herself, and it began to scare me. She was talking as if Dee had tricked her on purpose, and her tone made me feel like she expected me to choose—between Dee and herself, between the barrio and the Westside—when I believed there was a way to love them both.

I was too afraid to tell her how I really felt, so I said we could turn around and go straight back to Frontera Street if she wanted to. I told her I didn't mind living in the house surrounded by Lettie's gowns, and I didn't care if I had to give up Arts High or even the *quinceañera*.

Mom closed her eyes and sighed. Then she put her hand on my neck and drew me in until my ear was resting on her shoulder. Her hand was cold and I could feel her trembling. She moved her palm to the side of my face and began to rock me like a baby.

"What about Dee?" she asked, her voice strained and edgy.

"I love her," I said, "*pero* you're my mother, Mom, and if you want to go back, we will."

She wrapped both her arms around me and clasped them so tight that I couldn't breathe. I didn't say anything at first, figuring she'd ease up, but she didn't.

"Don't be scared," my mother whispered. "I won't let her take you."

"Mom," I finally said, "you have to loosen your grip." But she refused to let me go. I could feel her heart pounding like crazy against my rib cage.

"Mom," I said more firmly, "let me go!"

She finally pulled away, astonished and disoriented, her hands still clamped to the hem of my shirt.

"I'm sorry," she whispered. Then she gently pressed her lips against my cheek, and I felt them flutter as she mumbled something.

"What?"

"Nothing," she said, allowing her hands to fall back into her lap.

She rolled down the window and let a rush of cool morning air sweep over us.

"Do you really want to live here?"

She wanted me to say that I didn't, and I was about to—for her sake—when I saw Beto lift the yellow rocking chair off the back of his truck. I watched him hand it down to Richard, who carried it past Dee as she stood in the doorway looking like the letter that began her name.

I thought of how that baby, still asleep next to Dee's heart, had brought us all so far. Not just out of the barrio. Not just across town. But so much further than Mom had thought we'd ever go. So far that it scared her and now I had to be the one to show her that everything we loved about Frontera Street was still inside us and could grow like transplanted seeds right here on the Westside.

"It's going to be all right," I said. "I'll do all the work. You won't have to clean a single thing. I promise."

That at least made her chuckle, and I thanked God that I'd managed to pull her out of the dark cave she had been trapped inside.

"Mom," I said, looking into her eyes as confidently as I knew how, "this is where all your hard work has led us."

"*Sí, hija,*" she answered softly. "I see."

Chapter 20

ALMA

THE MOMENT I REALIZED WHERE WE WERE, I ASKED RICHARD to turn his car around to take me back to Frontera Street. After all, how long was I expected to put up with Dee's jolting surprises—her never-ending revelations that only seemed to prove just how little I'd made out of my own life and how much she had been handed in hers? How could he or Socorro expect me to stay?

If they didn't get it, Dee did. After Socorro and I sat in the Toyota for a bit, she approached the car and gently tapped on the window. Pale and tight-lipped, she spoke in a remorseful monotone.

"We can put everything back on the truck. Alma, I swear I had no idea. Beto can take it all back. I didn't know."

I nodded my head, and Dee said she'd tell Richard.

Socorro shifted in her seat, and when our eyes met, I saw something worse than regret, worse than sadness. I saw disappointment. Without uttering a word, she let me know that I had let her down. My little girl had expected me to be strong enough to turn my back on the painful memories of Mrs. Campbell and leap into Dee's world without hesitation, the way she had.

I knew what she was thinking. She was asking herself if I honestly wanted a better life for her or if what I'd told her for years in the barrio—that the only thing separating them from us was opportunity—was empty talk. In a way, I was wondering the same thing, asking myself if what I saw in Socorro's eyes meant that she had stepped so far out of my familiar borders that she was beyond my reach.

I thought about standing firm, but who exactly would I be proving my point to? Nobody on Frontera Street needed me to tell them that life wasn't fair. And I knew Septima would be the first to remind me that every bouquet of roses comes with thorns. So I swallowed my pride and told my daughter I'd stay until the *quinceañera*.

Dee was right about the furniture. It was different from what I remembered, but the new chairs and tables couldn't change the old feelings that met me at the entrance of every room. Memories of afternoons spent scrubbing the terra-cotta floor, of hot summer mornings spent waxing the furniture, and of the endless cycle of stripping the beds, making beds, and stripping them again, made my knees feel weak.

Socorro stayed by my side, smiling a tense smile and exchanging guarded glances with Richard and Dee as I walked farther inside.

The muscles between my shoulders clenched into a painful knot the instant I opened the coat closet and smelled the strong ammonia of mothballs and saw old coats hanging in the space where Mrs. Campbell used to keep the baggy pink uniforms she made me wear. My stomach twisted itself into an even tighter knot when I stepped into the kitchen, peeked inside the cabinets underneath the sink, and saw the same blue plastic bucket I had set there years ago.

In the dining room, I noticed Beto running his dark brown hand over the smooth white adobe of the kiva fireplace, and I remembered how Mrs. Campbell made me scrub its sides with a smelly mix of saltwater and bleach to erase any sign of smoke or ash. I walked past the wall filled with art and wondered if *esa mujer* still insisted that her maids dust only the outside of the picture frames, figuring they were too stupid to keep their fingers off the canvases, even after being told the paintings were originals.

Socorro tried to dampen her enthusiasm over what she found inside, but I could see that the expensive furniture and fine artwork delighted her. I watched as she slid herself onto the slippery, polished piano bench and carefully lifted the keyboard cover to expose beautiful ivory keys that gleamed in the morning sun.

"Peeps is gonna love this!" she said to Richard. He was standing at the far end of the baby grand, studying a collection of framed photographs set on top of an antique silk shawl draped across the piano.

"Take a look at this," he said.

Richard picked up a silver-framed, eight-by-ten photo of Dee as a girl, aged seven or eight. Her two blond pigtails were dangling out from beneath the rim of a powder-blue cowboy hat that exactly matched the hue of the rest of her gunslinger outfit, except for her boots, which were red. She was holding two toy six-shooters, pulled out of their holsters and aimed directly at the camera, and her little face was scrunched up as if she'd just yelled, "Draw!"

I didn't have to cross the room to see the picture as clear as day. I'd run across it before, on the first day I ever worked for Mrs. Campbell. I remembered picking it up and asking La Señora if the adorable little girl was her grandbaby. She answered in what she thought passed for Spanish, telling me it was her daughter, who was, at the time, off at college. But her reply didn't sound right to me, because Mrs. Campbell looked to be about sixty years old. So I made matters worse by shaking my head and saying, "No, no *hija, nieta,*" insisting that she had confused the Spanish words and had actually meant to say "granddaughter." Her face tightened as she set me straight, telling me again in a high and deliberately haughty pitch, "Nooo, *es mi hija.*" I could tell by the razor-sharp edge she put on each of her words that I had not only insulted her but had stepped way out of place. Which, of course, guaranteed that she considered me a smart-mouthed troublemaker.

I studied Dee's face from across the living room. Her cheeks were as red and chubby now as they were back then, and it was almost impossible not to recognize the little girl in the mother-to-be. I tried to think back to the day she walked into the fabric shop, tried to remember how I reacted to her face the first time I saw it. I should have instantly recognized the thin-lipped mouth that she and her mother shared, or been immediately tipped off by the narrow **J** curve of her nose.

Socorro rose, moved to Dee's side, and asked her to explain who was who in the family photographs. As Dee spoke, I noticed that she angled her head slightly to the left, exactly the way Mrs. Campbell did when she posed a question, and that she also punctuated her sentences with little stops and starts, just like her mother. Suddenly, the resemblance was overwhelming. It was in the bold arch of her eyebrows. The flatness of her chin. It was in the way she rubbed her palms together as she searched for the perfect word. I couldn't believe I had never made the connection.

Richard's eyes locked on mine, and I saw him take a nervous swallow. Beto stepped around me to stand next to him, and Dee set down the picture frame she was holding and leaned against the piano, as if any wrong move might throw her off balance. Socorro was the only one speaking at a normal pitch, and I could tell that she felt the need to keep the air inside the place filled with sound. She walked over to me and took my hand. She led me to the piano, where we all stood looking at one another, unsure what to do or say.

Dee's baby was positioned low inside her now, and no matter what time of day it was, she looked flushed and tired. She was only three weeks away from her due date, and I knew she was having trouble sleeping.

Socorro placed herself between us, slid her right arm around my waist and her left around Dee's wide middle.

"I think Dee's right, Mom, don't you?" she said cautiously. "The place seems completely different. Doesn't it?"

Beto wiped his brow with his shirtsleeve and looked at me for an uncomfortable moment before he fixed his gaze on the cactus and rock garden outside the back window. Socorro gave me a squeeze for reassurance, and Richard bit his lip. We all knew that whatever was going to happen next depended on my answer.

The truth, of course, was that nothing about the house had changed since I'd walked out of it years ago. The front door, I was certain, still swelled in April and got hot to the touch in August. There were, I knew, sets of cedar-lined storage drawers built into the base of every bed frame, with blankets neatly folded and tucked inside the units in the first spare bedroom, extra pillows in the second, and off-season clothes in the third. The doorbell still buzzed instead of chimed. And the air conditioner still shuddered to a squeaky halt whenever the inside temperature slid down to seventy-eight.

No, I wanted to say, the house wasn't different at all. What was different was the family standing inside it. Me, in love with a man I could completely trust and depend on. Dee and Socorro, linked like sisters by the crazy belief that the past had nothing to do with the future. None of them completely aware of the emotional distance they were asking me to leap. I felt them bracing themselves for what I might say.

Was the life Dee was offering Socorro really her dream come true, or was it La Llorona's threat come to pass? I ran my thumb over Septima's rosary beads, which I still had wrapped around my hand, and I prayed that if I stayed, my beloved Virgencita would keep Socorro by my side.

"You're right," I said, using all my strength to smile and look cheerfully into each of the faces I loved. "The place feels completely different."

Beto and Richard left after they carried the heaviest boxes—filled with clothes and shoes and the one old sewing machine that Lettie had given us—into the rooms Dee and Socorro directed them to. I was the one who told them to put the cartons filled with my linens and kitchen supplies into the garage, where I knew they would stay unopened. There wasn't any need to pull out my flimsy sheets and pillowcases when I knew there were thick, imported cotton ones already tucked tightly underneath Mrs. Campbell's bedspreads and goose-down pillows. I winced when I thought of how carefully I had wrapped each piece of my worthless Corelle—all eight dinner plates, ten soup bowls, and one dozen cups and saucers—to keep it from shattering.

It would have been ridiculous to unpack my rickety collection of garage-sale Silverstone and scratched-up Teflon, since I already knew where Mrs. Campbell kept her French copper-bottomed pots and pans. So I stood alone in the kitchen with nothing to do, except start some water boiling for a spaghetti dinner. I reached for the stockpot, instinctively opening the second cabinet to the right of the sink, and then headed directly to the lowest shelf inside the pantry for salt and olive oil. Cans of tomato paste were two shelves up, and the garlic was dangling in a fat braid of papery bulbs next to the stove.

I could, I thought, walk down the main hallway and find out which one of the five bedrooms Socorro had picked as hers and which she had designated as mine. Although I couldn't hear either of their voices from the other side of the house, I imagined Dee and Socorro transferring their belongings from boxes into their new closets and chests of drawers. I tried to picture myself doing the same, making idle chitchat while reaching into a box marked "Alma's room" and pulling out my old, mended socks and cheap half slips and sliding them into the paper-lined drawers of one of Mrs. Campbell's antique bureaus. But I couldn't bear the thought.

I pulled the built-in chopping block out from under the granite countertop and crushed three cloves of garlic with a knife blade and the heel of my hand. I loathed the fact that I knew exactly where the cracked pepper was kept and that I was certain there would be a jar of mixed Italian herbs on the spice rack next to the rust-colored curry powder.

As I stirred the sauce and tossed a fistful of dry pasta into the bubbling water, I realized there was at least one thing packed inside my boxes that I would need. I rushed into the garage and ripped the wide brown tape off the waist-high carton marked "kitchen." I worked my hand around the dinnerware, and underneath the stainless-steel cutlery that I had wrapped inside dish towels. I leaned down into the mouth of the big box until my shoulder was halfway inside and my cheek was pressed against the wads of stiff paper piled at the top. My fingers tested everything they came across, feeling the shape and texture of each item and then moving on. Past the iced-tea glasses and the measuring cups. Past the tamale steamer and the rolling pin. I threaded my arm all the way down to the bottom of the box, where I knew I had packed the pot holders and place mats, and ran my fingertips over each of the fabrics. When I felt the rough cotton weave of what I was after, I clasped my hand shut and pulled, hard. I'd found it. The one and only useful thing I could bring from Frontera Street into Mrs. Campbell's fancy kitchen. My apron.

The men left, and by the time I put dinner on the table, the place was ours.

We ate in the dining room, where Socorro set three places at the end of the long, formal table. Deciding who would sit at its head turned into an awkward, ridiculous scene that we would have laughed about had it happened to anybody but us.

We each made big circles around the place setting, trying to avoid the top spot. Socorro and I approached the same chair at the same time, and I put my hand on it first, like a six-year-old staking her claim during a round of musical chairs. Dee seated herself on the other side and refused to make eye contact with either of us, trying instead to devote her full concentration to the unfolding of her napkin. I expected Socorro to understand that there was no way I could sit at the head of

Mrs. Campbell's table. But she didn't. She leaned against me and whispered, "Please, Mom, it'll make Dee feel better. Show her that you might like it here."

She tried to nudge me toward the empty seat with her hip. I knew she wanted me to accept Dee's subtle invitation to assume the role as head of the house. But I didn't have it in me.

After waiting a few moments, Socorro stepped away from the spot we'd both tried to claim and let me sit down. She glowered at me as she moved toward the third place setting and pulled the chair out. But then she didn't sit.

She plopped the still-folded linen napkin and the silverware into the center of the pretty white dinner plate. She picked it up with her left hand and grabbed the short-stemmed water glass with her right. Then, without saying a word, she took a few more steps and set everything back down at a new place for herself, next to Dee.

I didn't say a word, but I knew exactly what she meant by it. And even though I couldn't feel the cold, misty air or hear her scratchy, haunted cackle, I was sure La Llorona was lurking in some corner of Dee's big house, laughing at me.

"I'm starving!" Dee broke in, trying to keep the charged silence from exploding like dynamite.

"Alma," she said, reaching for the bowl of spaghetti, "this looks fabulous!"

Chapter 21

Dee

 WE HAD TWO WEEKS TO PULL THE PARTY TOGETHER AND A MIL-
lion things to do.

Every afternoon Alma and I presented Socorro with her options—
knee-length or floor-length tablecloths? Waiters or buffet? Chocolate
cake or white? Beef or chicken? And the following morning we set off
to get it done.

Alma wouldn't tell me how she honestly felt about staying in the
Westside house, but I could tell it didn't feel right for her. It didn't feel
right for me to be there either. There was too much of my mother left
in every corner. I had hoped, with all my heart, that the alliance Alma
and I had built on Frontera Street would sweep the house clean. Together, I thought, we might be able to discover the Westside that I remembered from when I was a girl. Then we could both take
advantage of what it had to offer and use it to help our children blos-
som. But it was clear that Alma was struggling to get through each
day, which made me more determined to help her the way she'd
helped me.

I made sure that she stayed in control of all the preparations. I
stepped back when she discussed the menu with the caterers at the
country club. I kept my mouth shut as the facility supervisor asked her
to select her favorite floor plan from diagrams of how the tables might
be set up in the banquet hall. But I could tell she was suspicious of their
pleasantries. And I was too. If I hadn't been there with her, would they
have doted on her the way they did?

"*Ms. Cruz* has requested two sculptures in *this* design," the supervisor informed the head of catering, presenting him with a pencil drawing of a ballerina that Socorro had made.

"Ah, yes," the other man nodded. "That should be no problem, *Ms. Cruz.* No problem at all."

I could remember my mother planning parties with these same two men, and I recalled how she felt completely entitled to their overblown civility and exaggerated graciousness. It seemed ridiculous to me now, and I told Alma as much when we drove home from one of the planning sessions. It was the first time we'd laughed together since the move, and it felt good.

"We don't have to do everything Socorro wants," Alma said. "She can do with less."

"No," I answered. "It's why we came here in the first place, so let's make the party worth it."

At the next meeting, Alma said yes to valet parking, and I suggested two attendants for the coat-check room since the event was in late February and the mothers of Socorro's new friends would undoubtedly show up wearing furs.

"And which florist will you be using?" the supervisor asked. "Westside Flowers is excellent."

"Flores by Dolores," Alma answered matter-of-factly.

He cocked his head. "I'm not familiar with—"

"Oh, come on, Vincent," I chided. "I thought you kept up. All the girls are using Dolores."

Alma shot me a conspiratorial smile.

"I haven't had anyone book her," Vincent mumbled as he thumbed through his oversized appointment calendar.

"You will," I answered. "Trust me."

He arched his eyebrows and wrote Flores by Dolores on the page that he had reserved for the black-tie dinner in honor of one Miss Socorro Cruz.

Socorro lifted one of the elegant invitations out of the box and ran her fingers over the embossed letters that read, "*You are cordially invited to attend.*"

"Your mom had a heck of a time getting them to put that *ñ* in *quinceañera*," Richard said. Two days after we moved in, he became a regular at dinner, settling into the seat at the head of the dining table. "That's what held them up for so long."

We were supposed to have mailed the invitations exactly one month before the party, according to the note about etiquette the printer had enclosed. Of course, we hadn't even placed the order until two weeks prior, and the job took six days instead of three like the printer had promised. So, there we were, addressing envelopes on the Sunday before the big Saturday night.

"That doesn't matter," Alma declared, emerging from the kitchen holding a damp sponge on a saucer. "Everyone already knows what time and where."

Socorro set her guest list next to the stack of cream-colored envelopes.

"I could just hand them out at school and, Mom, you could go down to Frontera Street and give them out there," she said, a bit disappointed.

"No," I insisted. "Let's do it right. If we get them in the mail tomorrow morning, they'll be delivered in plenty of time."

I had encouraged Socorro to invite as many people as she wanted, but she added only a few girls from her dance class, the boy who partnered her in the winter concert, and Mrs. Polikoff to the original list of everyone on Frontera Street. So, even with a table reserved for Father Miguel and all the Holy Sisters of Saint Joseph, the final tally didn't reach one hundred.

"You should have padded it a little," Richard teased with a sly wink. "More presents!"

Alma playfully smacked his arm with the sponge, and he retaliated by wadding up some of the tissue paper squares and throwing them at her. Alma looked happy, and I knew Richard had a lot to do with that. He was by now spending every evening with us. He showed up after work, gave us daily updates on the old neighborhood, helped with dinner, and then took Alma out for moonlight walks that Socorro and I both knew sometimes ended at his apartment. On weekend mornings he took Alma out on the flat dirt roads along the riverbank to teach her how to drive, just in case he wasn't around when the baby arrived. And on Saturday nights he played music in the living room with Peeps and Lucinda, who, along with Holly and Ellen, would often stay the night.

When we had first selected the off-white invitations, I told Socorro I could hire a calligrapher to address them in an old-fashioned hand with an old-fashioned fountain pen. Socorro asked if that was the sort of presentation Westsiders expected. People did it for weddings and sometimes for debutante balls, but since hers was the first *quinceañera* I'd ever been invited to, I had no idea what they'd expect.

If that was the case, she said, she wanted to write the names herself. She practiced for a few nights, drawing the alphabet on the blue-lined pages of her spiral notebook with a calligraphy pen. She added loops and curves to every letter, using a copy of the Declaration of Independence in the back of her history book as her guide.

That Sunday we created an assembly line.

After Socorro addressed an envelope, she passed it to me. I slipped an invitation and a wisp of tissue paper into its mouth and passed it on to Richard. He added the little card with directions to the country club. And Alma, armed with the damp sponge and two sheets of postage stamps, sealed.

We proceeded down the guest list, and after two hours of stuffing and sealing there was a stack of ready-to-mail envelopes piled high on Alma's side of the table. When we were done, Socorro ran off to telephone Holly, and Richard suggested that instead of cooking dinner we should pick up a pizza.

I hoisted myself out of my chair to clear the table of the empty boxes, the sponge, and Socorro's pens, and Alma moved the stack of invitations to the coffee table.

While I was in the kitchen, I found a plastic bag, and I thought it would be a good idea to put the invitations inside it so we wouldn't drop any on our way to the post office the next morning. I took the bag over to the coffee table and held it open as Alma slid the envelopes inside. All except one, which I noticed she had separated from the others. The writing on the front was especially ornate, almost hard to read.

But the name and address were unmistakable: *Paul Walker, P.O. Box 529, Scottsdale, Arizona.*

I looked Alma squarely in the eye. She said nothing.

"Come on," Richard called out, jingling his car keys as he stood by the front door. "You can practice driving in the parking lot while we wait for the pizza. Dee, you wanna come?"

I looked toward Richard. "No, you two go ahead," I replied, returning my gaze to Alma. "Getting in and out of cars is hell these days."

"Ready?" he asked Alma.

"*Un momento,*" she said calmly. "Let me get a jacket."

I closed the plastic bag as she reached down to pick up Paul Walker's invitation. She headed for her bedroom, where I knew she would put the envelope inside her secret box. I also knew that she expected me to keep my mouth shut, like I had on Frontera Street. But something inside me bucked. Something I couldn't control.

Alma believed she was doing what was best. But Paul Walker was Socorro's father, and she deserved to know him. Yes, he was a coward for running out, and Alma had every right to hate him. But Socorro was still too young to understand how a mother, any mother, will use bricks molded out of her own pain to build a fortress around her child.

All Socorro knew was that she came from the love of two people, not just one. And no matter how much Alma wanted her to forget her father, she never would. I thought of my own Poppa and how, if I was Socorro, I would want to make him feel welcome. Not allowing her to communicate with Paul would only make her craving to find him grow stronger. It would pull Alma's daughter away from her.

Alma was so afraid that I was the one that La Llorona was using to steal Socorro, she couldn't see that what the dark spirit had really done was pit Socorro's drive to know her father against her. And I had no intention of letting La Llorona win.

When Alma and Richard left, I walked straight into Alma's bedroom and took Paul Walker's invitation out of the box. For a moment I considered taking out the other letters as well.

I imagined myself writing an anonymous note to Paul, to try and explain everything: *Dear Mr. Walker: Your daughter loves you. Read these and see for yourself. She is beautiful and smart and talented. Be proud.*

Then I imagined Alma discovering me, just like she did in the fabric shop. Only this time I wouldn't faint. This time I'd argue back. It's been wrong to keep Paul away when he might want to be near, I'd say, wrong to Socorro her believe he's hard-hearted.

I thought of La Llorona and wondered if the hateful spirit was in the room with me. Then I saw La Virgencita on the table next to Alma's bed, her broken fingers and chipped veil lending sorrowful power to the love she offered through her benevolent eyes. I waited to hear her voice telling me that mailing the invitation was the right thing to do.

Before living on Frontera Street, my belief in spirits and saints stretched no further than campground ghost stories and churches' stained-glass windows. But there I was, in Alma's room, asking God whether a spirit or a saint was guiding my hand. I took the invitation and placed the other letters back inside the secret box. As I slid the envelope into the plastic bag, I pushed it into the middle of the stack so Alma wouldn't notice it when she dropped the bundle into the wide blue mailbox marked IN TOWN ONLY.

The way I figured it, Paul wouldn't have time to make arrangements to come. The post office people would have to separate his out-of-state invitation from the local mail, which might take a day. Then they'd have to forward it to Arizona. That would take three days minimum, which would put the envelope inside Paul Walker's post office box no earlier than Thursday, maybe Friday. The *quinceañera* was on Saturday and hundreds of miles away from Arizona and Paul's everyday life.

I heard Socorro rustling in her bedroom, and then I heard her footsteps coming down the hall.

"Mom? Dee?"

I closed the box and slid it back underneath Alma's bed. I tried to rise from my knees in a hurry, but I got only as far as the edge of the bed.

"Are you okay?" Socorro gasped when she saw me in Alma's room.

"Just a little dizzy," I answered. "I thought I'd better sit down."

My dreams became intense in the final stage of pregnancy, and every one of my senses went into overdrive. When I slept I felt the soft, pudgy bottoms of my baby's feet, smelled the mild perfume of the dusty white powder and the pale pink lotion that I envisioned myself rubbing onto its tiny belly. I heard Mitch cooing mixed-up nursery rhymes into our baby's ear—allowing Little Jack Horner and Mary, Mary Quite Contrary to run away with the dish and the spoon.

In my dreams he held our baby under his chin like a Buddha, his large, strong hands forming a solid foundation, his soft, full lips speaking words I couldn't comprehend. When they both closed their eyes, I could see how much they looked alike.

I told him I was ready. That he could hand our baby to me now. I looked into his beautiful face, and when he slowly opened his eyes they sparkled like stars.

I wanted to wrap my arms around both of them and hold on tight. I wanted to feel their eyelashes against my cheek and press their shoulders square against my chest. But every time I thought I had a firm grip, I wound up holding nothing. I looked up from my empty arms and saw them floating in front of me again. Smiling.

I had the same dream every night, and it always ended the same way, with me stretching my arms into a blue-black darkness and suddenly realizing that Socorro was standing beside me with her arms outstretched, too.

Chapter 22

SOCORRO

EVERY *QUINCEAÑERA* BEGINS WITH A CATHOLIC MASS. IN FACT, the entire first half of the celebration takes place at church.

The *quinceañera* girl walks down the aisle holding flowers given to her by her aunt, or godmother, or someone like that, and she places them at the feet of La Virgen de Guadalupe. Then she sits on a chair in front of the altar and stays there throughout the Mass. In some ceremonies, she enters the church following fourteen attendants—seven girls and seven boys—who represent the fourteen years of her life so far. I've even been to some where a mariachi band follows her up the aisle and some others where, instead of sitting in a chair, she sits on a quilt stitched by her family.

After Mass, the priest usually escorts the girl's mother to the front of the church, and the mom exchanges the crown of baby's breath on the girl's head for a sparkling jeweled tiara. Then they both give thanks to the Holy Mother, and the party begins. In some ceremonies, the father takes the flat shoes off his daughter's feet and replaces them with high heels, and some *quinceañeras* include a part where the grandmother takes the crucifix presented to the girl at her First Holy Communion and replaces it with a new gold cross, or some other piece of jewelry handed down from generation to generation.

There are all sorts of old traditions, and plenty that I think some girls invent on the spot. Cece once told me about a girl who displayed a portable color TV and a six-disk CD player that she got from her parents on the altar, like she was the winner of *Wheel of Fortune*.

I didn't need attendants or jewelry or even a rhinestone tiara for my *quinceañera,* but part of me felt it wouldn't be real without some sort of church service. I wasn't exactly clear on the rules of getting a Catholic Mass for somebody like me, who was baptized but never had a First Holy Communion. But I knew that if I asked, Father Miguel would do something nice just the same.

The problem was that Mom refused to step inside a church, any church, even if it was Father Miguel's, and even if it was for just one day. She said she'd gone inside right after I was born to get me baptized, but never planned to go back. And as usual, she never explained why.

"If it means that much to you, we can do all that stuff at home," she said. "I'll put La Virgencita in front of the fireplace and you can set some flowers at her feet before we head over to the country club for the dance." She laughed like it was a big joke, and that ticked me off. I mean, I was grateful that she and Dee had worked so hard planning the party, but what was the point of following tradition if you weren't going to do it right?

I think Mom had begun to believe that just because I liked the West-side, I was embarrassed by her, by her heavy accent, her dark skin, everything. But I wasn't, and I wanted the *quinceañera* to be totally *Mexicáno* so I could prove it. If we had the church service in the barrio and the reception at the country club, it would be a coming-out party that stretched from one end of Los Cielos to the other.

"If you don't believe in the church, then why do you even have that statue of La Virgen?" I asked sarcastically.

"That's different," she said.

It was the night before the *quinceañera,* and we were going over the entire issue one more time because Father Miguel had called to say that if we changed our minds, he'd be happy to perform some sort of serv-ice in the adult Sunday school classroom instead of the main sanctuary, or even on Septima's porch, where he used to preach to the followers of the miracle muffin.

Richard thought the classroom was a good compromise, but I said it was stupid to pretend you weren't at church when you really were. "It's just as stupid as pretending your life hasn't changed when it has," I re-marked.

My mother glared at me from across the dinner table, and I saw Dee and Richard grow tense.

"Isn't this enough for you?" she asked as she slammed her fork down beside her dinner plate. She threw the question at me in lightning-quick Spanish, trying, I suppose, to rush it past Dee and Richard, who, I could tell, understood her anyway.

"This party at the *gringo* country club? The valet parking *y los* waiters in tuxedos? Excuse me if they aren't change enough for you. Do you think I'm thrilled at the thought of seeing *esas mujeres* who used to drive right past me at the downtown plaza sitting at those tables, looking at you and saying: 'Isn't it wonderful that she won't end up like her mother?' Isn't that enough?"

Dee shot a nervous glance my way, one that warned me to keep my mouth shut. But I couldn't.

"Yeah, it's enough," I shouted back. "In fact, it's *everything*. That's why I want to go inside a real church and thank God for making my life different. I want to pray and sing and thank the Lord that he made me open-minded enough to see the good things about change, instead of making me as narrow-minded as you!"

"Just one minute, young lady," Richard protested.

"No," my mother said, her voice strained. "If that's what she believes . . ."

I left the table, stormed into my room, and slammed the door. This was not the way I wanted my mother and I to feel about each other on the eve of my *quinceañera*, but I still refused to answer when Dee knocked and asked if she could come in.

I looked at the long white dress hanging in my closet. It was exactly like the drawing Cece and I had conjured up that night a couple of months back, before we left the barrio, before everything changed. Maybe I should have had the double *quinceañera* like we'd planned, with the martini-glass ice sculptures and the balloons Cece wanted. Maybe my mother was right. Maybe having my *quinceañera* at the country club was just a way for me to show off. I couldn't deny that I was eager for Septima and Beto and all the others to see how classy the place was, and I'd be lying if I said that I didn't want my new friends to see me there, at the center of an extravagant celebration.

I looked at my ballet bag, set on the floor just below the hem of my gown. It was lumpy, stuffed almost full with shiny new pairs of expensive toe shoes, so many that I could toss a pair into the garbage the moment they began to soften. I dug inside the bag until I felt the envelope I knew was at the bottom, beneath rolls of ribbon, leg warmers, and extra pairs of tights and leotards. It was another invitation from the Boston Ballet, which Mrs. Polikoff had presented to me a few days after our move to Dee's.

She'd handed me the letter in front of the class, and I immediately opened it. I had been accepted to the ballet company's eight-week summer apprentice program in Boston. On scholarship. The entire class applauded, and I gave Mrs. Polikoff a hug. But as she placed her cheek against mine she whispered, "There is a leetle problem. We talk after class."

The moment she dismissed us, I ran into her office and waited.

"It is free only for scholarship students," she said apprehensively. "Others pay."

Her voice told me something was wrong, but I couldn't figure out what it could possibly be. I was a scholarship student.

"School tells me you have new address. Tierra Fina Avenue, no?"

I nodded.

"No scholarships for girls from Westside," she began. "Not exactly a needy neighborhood."

"It's okay," I lied. "I don't think my mother would let me go to Boston for eight weeks anyway. Free or not."

"Darling," Mrs. Polikoff sighed, "ask the lady from Westside to pay. She wants to help you, yes?"

There was no way I could ask Dee to pay for the summer session without my mother totally flipping out. If we were still on Frontera Street, she would have been ecstatic about a trip to Boston, would have considered it my reward for working so hard at Arts High. She would have beamed with pride when I showed her the letter and been convinced that my talent had made the Boston ballet master look beyond my past to see my future.

But if Dee paid the tuition, all my mother would see was the check. And she'd think I was trying to be like every other rich girl who paid her way to success.

"I don't think that's a good idea," I replied.

Mrs. Polikoff shook her head in disappointment. I slipped the letter inside my bag and decided it wasn't worth mentioning to anyone at home.

I told Peeps about it, though, and during the conversation I wondered where all of Dee's money came from, and how much she actually had. She probably would have told me if I had asked, but it seemed like a rude thing to bring up, particularly since she had said yes to every single thing I'd asked for concerning the *quinceañera*.

"People like her have stocks and trusts and things like that," Peeps reasoned. "They have money that just sits around and makes more money."

A week later, Peeps showed up at school with a note from Richard. It said he wanted to talk and that I should go with Peeps to the chamber music practice at his apartment after school.

"Oh, my God," I gasped. "You told him?"

"No," Peeps argued. "Well, not everything."

How stupid could Peeps be? Didn't he know that telling Richard was just like telling my mom?

"What exactly did you say?"

"I just said your scholarship is in danger," Peeps said, defending himself. "That's all. I swear."

When we got to Richard's place, he got the quintet started and then took me into another room as they played. I told him about the letter, about the address, and about the scholarship. And then I begged him to keep it quiet.

"I don't like keeping secrets from your mom, but that one isn't going to make much of a difference anyway," he said. "Not if what I have planned works out."

"What?"

"Socorro," he continued, "you know you and your mother can't stay at Dee's house forever, right? It's hard enough for her to live there now."

"Yeah, I know."

"How would you feel about moving back to Frontera Street?"

"I wouldn't mind, I guess."

"Honestly, Socorro. Tell me the truth."

"Honestly?" I hesitated because I wasn't sure what he wanted me to say. I knew what the appropriate answer was. That where we lived didn't matter as long as we were together. But that's not how I *really* felt. Yeah, I loved the people on Frontera Street, but I didn't think there was anything wrong in accepting what Dee was giving us, either.

"Just say what you're thinking," Richard said. "Whatever it is."

"I like the way we live on the Westside. Okay? I know I'm not supposed to feel like that, but what's so wrong about it? I'm just as American as Holly or Ellen, or anybody else who grew up on the Westside. And I'm just Mexican as the people on Frontera Street. So why do I have to be only one or the other, when I'm both?"

"Okay," Richard said. "I'm glad you feel that way. I think you have just answered my question."

I had no idea how what I'd just said could answer anything, but he promised to keep what I'd told him secret, and at the moment that was all I cared about.

That conversation and everything else that had happened since we moved were spinning around in my head. The scholarship. My mother. Holly and Ellen. Dee. And Paul Walker.

I knew the truth about him was something very different from the stories Mom had been spinning for years. She liked to make it sound like were a happy little trio and then one day, poof, he was gone. Like some sort of disappearing rabbit.

I wanted to know what really happened. Did Mom do something to make him leave? Or did he leave because of me?

I used to ask him in my letters, but I never got an answer. Not from him. Not from her. Not from Dee. All she ever said was that Paul and my mother realized they couldn't stay together, but she went no further than that.

Once I told Dee that I knew my mother's nightmares were about Paul, about her guilt over whatever had happened. And she told me that I was wrong. She said my mother's visions of La Llorona were about me and about her fear of losing me forever.

I must have fallen asleep thinking about all those things, because I found myself still in my clothes when I awoke to hear my mother screaming.

I dashed into the hallway and saw Dee racing out of her room.

By the look of disorientation on her face, I figured it was sometime after midnight. We both stood in front of my mother's bedroom door for a few moments without speaking. This was the first time La Llorona had appeared to her inside Dee's house, the first time in a long while that I had heard her sound so terrified.

Before Dee came to live with us on Frontera Street, I'd never made any real effort to help my mother get through her night attacks. I'd listen to her cry and tell myself she was having nightmares about my father. In a way, I guess, I thought she deserved them.

Dee placed her hand on the doorknob. She took a deep breath, preparing herself for the scene she knew awaited her.

"Just a minute," I said, setting my hand over hers. "Let me."

I flipped on the light and saw my mother cowering in her bed, her knees pulled up to her chest and her eyes focused on something nobody else could see. For the first time in my life, I saw how small she really was, thin and almost girl-like in her features. Her long hair, which she almost always kept tied in a braid, spilled over her shoulders, making her narrow face look even slimmer. She was only twenty years old when I was born, only five years older than me. Suddenly, being thirty-five seemed younger than I ever imagined.

If Richard had been in bed with her, she wouldn't have felt so scared. But my mother wouldn't allow him to sleep with her at Dee's house.

I picked up La Virgencita from the top of my mother's nightstand and handed the little saint to her as I climbed onto the bed. She took the statue, gave Mary's veil a quick kiss, and held her against her heart.

"Everything's okay," I whispered as I settled in beside her and draped my arm around her shivering shoulders. I felt her lean into me. She set the Holy Virgin down between us and squeezed my hand with both of hers.

"*Mijita*," she began, "I love you so much, *mi vida*, I don't want anyone to ever hurt you."

"Nothing's going to happen, Mom," I said softly. "I'm not going anywhere without you. I promise." She buried her head into my shoulder. "We belong to both sides of Los Cielos now," I whispered in her ear. "Just like Dee and Richard. It hasn't changed them, and it won't change us."

She sat up and looked at me straight on. Her eyes were red and her cheeks were glistening. As I held her, I thought about the meaning of my *quinceañera*, how it was supposed to symbolize my entry into womanhood, and I felt as if it really would—as if, maybe, it already had.

"I wanted . . ." my mother began. "I wanted you to be born in the United States so your life could be different than mine."

"Mami," I said, "look at what you've given me."

She shook her head in denial.

"This is Dee's," she answered.

"No," I said. "Not the house. Not the party. Not any of that. I mean what *you've* given me."

My mother shrugged her shoulders.

"You've given me the courage to walk into all of this without fear or shame or guilt," I said. "You're the one who taught me that borders are meant to be stepped over, because they're nothing but invisible fences somebody decided should keep people apart."

Tears fell down her cheeks, and as I spoke she held La Virgencita even tighter.

"Mom," I said, "you think you only crossed one border for me, but really you crossed two."

Chapter 23

ALMA

 FATHER MIGUEL SAID HE WASN'T AT ALL SURPRISED TO GET MY call.

In fact, he said, Septima had already come by the church to ask if he had heard from me yet. I smiled at the thought of her predicting my change of heart about letting Socorro have a Mass before it even happened, and trooping from her house to the rectory to inform the priest of what God had in store.

"Dee's gone to get flowers," I told him, glancing at my wristwatch. It was nine a.m. "She'll drop them by later. Is there anything else she should bring?"

"Some of the girls prefer to change into their dresses here at the church," Father said. "You could bring the gown here. But it's up to you."

"I think I'll have her get dressed at home, so I can take some pictures before they head over."

"You can take pictures here."

"Richard will do that."

I could almost hear Father Miguel forming the next question in his mind.

"You're attending this Mass, right?"

"No, Father. I'm not."

He paused. "Alma," he cautioned, "you'll regret that."

He probably was right, and for an instant I felt the tug of indecision persuading me to change my mind. But then I tried to picture myself celebrating my daughter's coming-of-age under the same roof of the religion that fifteen years ago wanted me to turn my back on her. I was willing to let her celebrate with a Mass, since that was what she wanted, but the only thing the church could offer me was ugly memories of my father's cold heart and the priest back in Cuernavaca who left me with no choice but to leave.

I remembered the last time I was inside Father Miguel's sanctuary, the day Socorro was baptized, and how right it felt for the three of us to be under God's watch as a solid little family. On that day I allowed the distrust I'd nurtured in Mexico to float away on the reassuring stream of Father Miguel's blessing. I let myself believe that by standing beside me, Paul was devoting himself to us for good. I didn't even question why he wanted to give his baby my last name. He'd said Socorro Cruz sounded like music, while Socorro Walker thumped along like a flat tire, and I believed him. So on that winter morning I smiled as Paul's strong, wide hands cradled our baby girl in a snug and steady grip, and for the first time since I had crossed the border, I envisioned a better life for us all.

Hardly aware that I was still on the phone with Father Miguel, I thought of my own father in Cuernavaca and wondered if he ever looked at his calendar to count the years and days and hours that his family had been torn apart. Did he ever feel regret? I envisioned him inside the old cathedral on the far side of the *zócalo* in Cuernavaca, with my mother at his side. I saw them both so clearly, seated in their usual spot, in the fifth pew on the left-hand side, standing and kneeling and making the sign of the cross as Father Felipe delivered the eight o'clock Mass in Latin. I imagined my mother silently praying for deliverance, while my father allowed his mind to wander, happily letting it drift toward anything but the memory of me.

"You should be there," Father Miguel pressed, and for a moment I was certain he had read my thoughts.

"Father," I replied, "I just can't."

I told him that Septima and Dee would both be on hand to make sure everything ran smoothly. And Richard could perform whatever rituals the father of the *quinceañera* girl normally would.

"Does she know you aren't going to be there?"

I chuckled. "She doesn't even know *she's* going to be there," I said. "I'm going to tell her when she gets up."

We agreed the service would begin at four o'clock, which would give people plenty of time to mingle afterward, or run home to freshen up before heading over to the Westside Country Club at seven.

Richard arrived at the front door at ten, ringing the bell instead of letting himself in as usual. He posed proudly beside the bright red twelve-speed mountain bike he had selected as Socorro's gift, a giant blue bow tied onto its sleek black handlebars. A rush of cool air pushed its way into the house as I stood in the doorway and listened to him rattle off the bicycle's special features: gel-injected seat, adjustable shock absorbers, single-piece frame, toolkit.

Outside, the sky was turquoise and the rocky mesa on the horizon was so free of shadows that it looked like a paper postage stamp. The cottonwoods in Dee's front yard were still holding on to more than a few dead leaves, which rustled like candy wrappers when the late February wind whipped through the branches. It was going to be a beautiful day.

The bicycle's wide rubber tires squealed as Richard rolled them over the ceramic tiles, steering the gift past the piano. When he got across the room, he carefully leaned it against the kiva fireplace.

"No kickstand?" I asked.

"They don't even come with kickstands anymore." He shrugged. "So, where is she?"

"Still asleep. Coffee?"

Richard followed me into the kitchen, where I had already set a carton of eggs and a bag of flour on top of the counter, ready to make pancakes the moment Socorro stirred.

I told him about everything that had happened the night before, about La Llorona and Socorro's tender words, and about my decision concerning the Mass.

"You," he said, wrapping his arms around my waist and drawing me to his chest, "are a strong and surprising woman." He softly touched his lips to my forehead and my nose. Then he gently pressed his hands against the small of my back and pulled my hips against his, landing a firm and glorious kiss on my mouth.

"Let's do it on the counter," he playfully whispered in my ear. "Right here, next to the eggs." I pretended to push him away, but didn't push too hard. I even let him lift me up onto the countertop to take the joke as far as I dared.

Sitting on the smooth granite, I was suddenly eye to eye with the man who had injected my heart with the kind of desire I'd never thought I would know again. I felt my chest swell as he buried his chin into the curve of my neck. I finally had to stop him, stop the both of us, as his lips began to wander from behind my chin to my ribs and down my torso.

"Richard!" I complained unconvincingly.

He laughed but didn't stop.

If it had been seven or even eight in the morning, he might have been able to talk me into taking such a crazy risk. But I looked at the minutes blinking away in green numbers on the microwave screen, and I knew we were pushing our luck.

I planted my shoe on his thigh and delivered a good, firm shove.

"Coffee's getting cold," I said, hopping down from the counter and taking a wide step around him.

He pulled his shoulders back and opened his eyes. His lips were full and flushed, and he took one long breath to compose himself. His eyes, still a bit unfocused, locked onto mine for a few silent moments, and I wanted to rush right back into his arms.

Luckily, the telephone rang, jolting us both back into the moment.

When I picked up the receiver, Socorro was already on the extension in my bedroom, where she had fallen asleep next to me. I heard her giggle as the deep, mellow strains of Peeps's French horn played an elaborate rendition of "Happy Birthday." I hung up before the song was over.

"Come on," I said to Richard, who by this time had poured himself the cup of coffee that I'd never managed to serve him. "She's up."

We moved into the living room.

"Oh!" Richard said, slapping the palm of his hand against his right temple. "I left the bicycle helmet in the car."

As I watched him slip out the front door, I let the promise of the day take hold of me. I felt a charge in the air that I knew would spark into pure joy the moment I saw my daughter smile. I looked forward to feeling the wave of love that would sweep over me when she put on her gown. I was truly happy.

When Richard returned, he held the purple helmet in one hand and a plastic-handled shopping bag in the other. Dee walked in beside him. She was balancing a stack of clear plastic boxes between her significant belly and her chin.

I heard my bedroom door creak open, and then the *shhhhh* of the shower in Socorro's bathroom. Richard slid the helmet's chin strap over the bicycle's handlebars, keeping a tight grip on the shopping bag in his other hand. I left him to that while I helped Dee slide the boxes off her stomach onto the dining room table.

"You should see the incredible arrangements Dolores made for the altar. Birds of paradise and white gladiolas!" she exclaimed, a bit out of breath. "And she's going to trim the pews with white carnations and accents of holly twigs full of berries!"

Richard joined us at the table, setting the shopping bag next to the boxes.

"This," she said, handing one of the smaller ones to Richard, "is for you."

Inside was a tight white rosebud, its stem pierced by a long pearl-head pin.

"And this is for you," Dee said, handing me a larger box containing a dewy orchid resting on a bed of baby's breath.

"I got the same thing for Septima and myself, but I left hers in the refrigerator at the church," she continued enthusiastically.

I opened my mouth to speak, but Dee wasn't finished.

"Dolores told me I'm supposed to present Socorro with the bouquet at the church, so that is there, too. Wait until you see it! Two dozen white sweetheart roses with tiny red carnations and lilies of the valley." Dee's eyes were brimming with excitement, and I could tell she was running on a rush of adrenaline, because no normal woman in her ninth month of pregnancy would be so invigorated after such early-morning errands.

I felt a pang of jealousy, and for an instant I considered telling her that I would go to Mass after all. But the hate I had for the church was just too strong.

"What's in here?" Richard asked, sliding the shopping bag toward her.

"Oh!" she buzzed. "I got this from Lettie."

She lifted a wooden box the size of a camera case out of the bag and smiled at us before she opened the lid. Inside was a dazzling rhinestone crown. Slowly, she raised it out of the box's satin-lined interior. It was surprisingly small. Its brilliant bits of glass were set inside prongs of polished silver and rose into three separate peaks, each topped with a pear-shaped crystal that captured and played with the light like a prism.

"It's a replica of the official Miss America crown," Dee gushed. "Lettie got it during her last trip to Atlantic City. She says there's a huge black market for these at the pageant."

"There's no way I'm wearing *that*." It was Socorro, pitching her protest from the hallway. I turned and saw her walking toward the table, her hands defiantly clamped onto her slim hips. She was wearing a pair of faded blue jeans and a simple pink T-shirt. Her hair was still wet from the shower. Her green-gray eyes dominated her face, and I noticed that the shirt's scoop neck played, in a surprisingly flattering way, against the straight lines of her strong collarbone. She was, I thought to myself, a beautiful young woman.

After breakfast, Dee went to her bedroom to lie down, and Socorro rolled out the door on her new bike. She had already called Holly and Ellen, and they'd made plans to meet beside the river and take a ride along the winter-hardened levee.

"Just don't fall and scrape your knee or anything," I warned as she pedaled over the gravel driveway, dismissing me with a quick wave over her shoulder.

Richard stood in the doorway, waiting for me to come back inside. But I lingered a few steps away from him, watching Socorro until she reached the end of the driveway and then turned onto Tierra Fina Avenue, picking up speed on the smooth asphalt.

"Feeling a little sentimental?" Richard asked.

I shook my head but couldn't answer because there was a lump in my throat.

I walked back into the house, and Richard followed me into the kitchen once again.

"Let's go for a drive!" he suggested.

"I don't think I should leave Dee alone."

"She'll be okay," he insisted. "We'll leave her a note."

I gave him a sideways glance, and wondered what he was after. "Richard, I don't think this is the right time to . . ."

He laughed. "Aw, come on," he smirked. "You think that's the only thing on my mind?"

I replied with a wink.

"No, I'm serious. Let's just go for a spin. It's a pretty day, and you should have some time for yourself before all the craziness begins."

We drove out to Panorama Drive, the winding, narrow road that climbs up the city's one and only mountain. At the top is a roadside park that juts out over the bluff. Without the help of binoculars, you can easily see how Texas wanders into Mexico on one side of Los Cielos, and how New Mexico kisses its border on the other side. At night the place is crowded with teenagers locked in passionate embraces, oblivious to the incredible expanse of land. But on that morning, in the bright, crisp sunshine, Richard and I were alone, standing next to one another on the breezy ridge, silently marveling at what stretched out before us.

"Are you sure you don't want to go to church?" he asked.

I said nothing and he took my hand.

A few moments later he gently added, "I think she'd really consider it special if you were there."

"Please don't," I said, dislodging my hand from his. "I want her to do what she wants, but I can't do it with her. I just don't believe."

"Don't believe in what?" he argued. "In the goodness of God? I know that's not true."

"I don't want to talk about it."

"Alma"—Richard led me to a cement bench and we both sat down—"why won't you allow this to be a new beginning?"

Strong gusts of wind began to swirl around us, chilly but not raw. The view was spectacular. Winter bathes the desert in silver light, and the sun dips so close to the earth that you can't help but see things more clearly than you might at any other time of the year.

Richard kissed my cheek, and I felt the cold tip of his nose press against my own.

"It would be nice to sit in the front pew as a family," he whispered.

"Hey, there's gonna be a pregnant woman right next to you. What more of a family do you want?" I attempted to joke.

"I'm serious, *mi amor.*" Richard's voice was deep and full of emotion.

"Since when have you been so devoted to the church?"

"I guess I thought about what Socorro said yesterday, about following tradition and doing things right," he answered. "Everyone needs a family, and it doesn't really matter if it isn't made up of the original players."

I was beginning to resent his implication that I was a bad mother for not going to church. "Socorro seems fine with Dee and Septima acting as her *madrinas* at the Mass," I said curtly. "It's not like I'm sitting out of the entire celebration. I'll be at the party, and you don't have to worry about me showing off my little girl. I'm more proud of her than any of you can possibly know."

"That's not what I'm talking about," Richard replied. "I know how proud you are, and I know how much you love her. Probably as much as I love the both of you."

I had no response.

"Have you ever thought of what you will do when she goes off to college?" he asked.

The question caught me off guard, and I turned and looked straight into his eyes. "Why are you asking me this?"

"I'm just saying that when the baby is born, Mrs. Campbell will come back into Dee's life and things are bound to change."

"Why do you want to get into that now?" I asked, angry that he was bringing up issues I certainly didn't want to think about on Socorro's *quinceañera* day.

Suddenly the wind seemed harsher than before, and I told Richard I wanted to head back.

"Oh, God," he groaned as I stood. "I'm doing this all wrong. I didn't mean to get you upset."

He kissed my hand and pulled me over to one of the coin-operated viewfinders posted along the ridge.

"I'm cold," I protested.

"Alma, I love you," he said. "And I love Socorro."

I smiled.

"I want us to be a family."

I felt a chill creep down my back.

Richard dropped to his knee and took my left hand. He fished inside the pocket of his leather jacket and pulled out a tiny velvet box.

I couldn't believe what was happening.

He popped open the lid and carefully removed a diamond ring that, in the morning sunshine, glistened like pirates' treasure. As the wind whipped through his hair, he carefully slipped the ring onto my finger.

"Alma, will you marry me?"

I'm not sure if I officially said yes, but I know the way I kissed him gave him his answer.

He rose back to his feet and then fed a quarter into the viewing machine. It began to whir. He held my hand as he placed his eyes against it and slowly pointed it to a spot exactly between the barrio and the Westside.

"Look," he said, stepping aside. "Look right through there."

I peered at the magnified landscape.

"What do you see?" he asked.

"Town houses for sale," I said.

"Look for the one with white balloons tied to the SALE PENDING sign," he continued. "That one belongs to us."

During the drive home, Richard admitted that he hadn't planned on proposing until the end of the evening. "It is supposed to be Socorro's day, and I wasn't going to even ask until after the last dance. But when you told me about the Mass—"

I was still trying to make sense of what had just happened, and was skeptically staring at the gem on my hand, waiting for it to suddenly disappear. He continued to speak, saying he hadn't yet signed any final papers on the town house because he wanted to make sure it was exactly what I wanted. We had an appointment later in the week, he said, to walk through the place together. My mind was racing.

"So, I'll drop you off at Dee's and come back to take you to church," he said as he maneuvered the car down the mountain. "Say, three-thirty?"

"Fine," I said. "Three-thirty. We'll take pictures and then you can head over."

"*We* will head over," he said firmly.

When he said that I felt my back tense, and an unexpected wave of anger swept through me.

"You think this ring gives you the right to tell me what to do?" I snapped. I knew I was overreacting, but I couldn't stop myself. All of a sudden I felt as if I was caught in the middle of a blinding sandstorm, unable to see where I was headed and wanting to do nothing else but run the other way.

Richard cocked his head and took his eyes off the road just long enough to dart them my way.

"I told you, I'm not going," I huffed.

"But I thought . . ."

"Well, you thought wrong."

He pulled into the gravel driveway and turned the engine off. I couldn't tell if he was angry or just stunned. We both sat perfectly still, listening to the car engine pop and whine as it cooled.

"Alma," Richard said to the front windshield, "I'm not going to leave you."

I played with the ring, my eyes cast downward.

"I'm not going to church," I whispered.

"You are the most stubborn woman I've ever known," he said, lifting my chin with his palm. "And I am crazy about you."

As we kissed, I heard the crunch of bicycle tires burrowing through the gravel, and I quickly pulled the engagement ring off my finger.

"Let's not tell anybody else today," I suggested.

Richard nodded in agreement and I put the ring back inside its velvet box.

Socorro changed her mind about the Miss America crown the moment Holly and Ellen began to gush over it.

"It's like something the ballerina in *Aurora's Wedding* would wear," Holly exclaimed. "Or Audrey Hepburn in *My Fair Lady!*"

"You don't think it's too . . . ?" Socorro tested.

"Oh, my God, no!" Ellen squealed. "It's so beautiful, and with your hair up—you're putting your hair up, right?"

I couldn't help but smile at the sight of them. They had mud splattered on the backs of their legs and ragged strands of tangled hair fell haphazardly into their dust-covered faces. Their cheeks glowed red from being slapped by the winter wind, and their lips were as dry and prickly as tumbleweeds. And yet each of them was standing there, happily imagining herself wearing that crown, just like Cinderella.

Dee woke up to find the girls scurrying into Socorro's bedroom, eager to place the circle of rhinestones on their heads. Even with the door shut we could hear them giggling and carrying on their conversation at three hundred miles a minute.

"Where's Richard?" Dee asked, still a bit groggy from her long nap.

"He went home to change. He'll be back to get you at three-thirty."

For a moment I considered telling her the news, but as she slowly awoke, she began to speak.

"Alma, I can't even begin to tell you what being Socorro's *madrina* means to me. Septima explained that, technically, it makes me Socorro's godmother. And I am so touched . . ."

"Well, it's you and Sepi both," I said, trying to lighten the moment. The last stage of pregnancy was wearing on Dee, making her overtired and overemotional, and I knew that's where she was coming from. Still, I was moved by what she said.

We embraced, clutching one another's shoulders, and as I held her I felt the baby push against her belly with remarkably strong hands and feet, eager to be set free.

Richard phoned me from the church. "You should see Peeps," he reported. "He's already in his tux."

"Where's Socorro?"

"Father Miguel took her into the bridal dressing room, along with Septima and Dee."

I could hear the hum of people mingling in the background, and I tried to picture exactly where the church's pay phone was located.

Richard continued to fill me in. "Peeps introduced Holly and Ellen to Cece, who I think is actually here as his date!"

That, I thought to myself, had to be wrong.

"What's Pilar wearing?"

"Lettie!" I heard Richard call out. "It's Alma. Tell her what Pilar's wearing."

I heard shuffling as he handed her the receiver.

"*Ay, mija,* why aren't you here?"

I didn't answer.

"Okay," Lettie continued. "Pilar is in a gunmetal-gray day suit that she must have made using one of those Vogue Vintage patterns. *Bien Eva Perón,* you know?"

I smiled and thought how much I missed gossiping with Lettie at the fabric shop.

"All the *viejitas* from the knitting circle are here *también,* draped in crocheted shawls and sweaters *en colores tan horrorosos!* They look like a living box of Popsicles."

"Have you seen Socorro?"

"No, *mija,* they're keeping her hidden in the back, *tu sabes.* But don't worry about her, because Iluminada—who is *gordita* again, you know—put three trays of sandwiches back there in case she's starving."

I was laughing so hard my eyes were beginning to blur.

"Okay, Almita, I'm gonna go now 'cause I want to get a seat up front, near the good *santos.*"

Richard came back on the line.

"I can still come and get you," he urged. "Father Miguel would wait."

I looked at my watch. It was four-thirty on the dot.

"Go," I said softly. "Tell me all about it later."

I hung up the phone and walked into the dining room. The house was silent and menacing, and I wondered where La Llorona was lurking now. I couldn't stay in the place one more minute. It felt too big and too empty, and everything I set my eyes on reminded me of Mrs. Campbell.

I decided to go to Richard's apartment and make some cookies to leave for him as a surprise. I changed into a dress, just in case I came across any Westsiders who might otherwise mistake me for a cleaning lady breaking into his place.

My plan was to walk over, but when I saw the keys to Dee's car on the dining room table, the challenge of driving alone for the first time was irresistible.

I started the engine and felt it rumble the driver's seat. I turned it off and told myself I was acting crazy. Glancing over my shoulder, I fully expected to see a police cruiser careening up the driveway to stop me. But there was no one, so I started the engine again.

The car lunged forward when I shifted into "Drive." Startled, I stomped on the brakes so hard that I buried the back tires deep into the gravel. I had no idea what to do, so I stepped on the gas a few times and tried to keep the steering wheel steady as I plowed through the pebbles. At the end of the driveway, I made the same turn onto Tierra Fina Avenue that I had watched Socorro make on her bike, and I sighed in relief when I felt the tires get a firm grip on the asphalt.

I was driving! And I was a nervous wreck.

Everything, from the trees in people's yards to the white lines in the middle of the road threatened to jump out in front of me, and I kept tapping the brakes to make sure they worked. But after a few moments of disaster-free motoring, I began to enjoy the steady whine of the wheels and the scenery that unfolded before me.

I turned onto Richard's street, but passed right by his place. I wasn't ready to stop. I aimed the car toward Valleyview Road and the cotton fields, and I cruised, practically alone on the streets, past horse stables and old barns, past homes that sprawled over thousands of square feet like giant, lazy dogs stretched out on the grass. I drove past a white-brick Baptist church where the bells were ringing, and it felt as if they were trilling just for me. I felt so powerful behind the wheel, free to point myself in any direction and simply sail away. I could drive to the town house, *my* new house, if I felt like it. I could circle around the downtown plaza and honk the horn. I could, I realized, take myself back to the barrio whenever I pleased.

I directed Dee's sedan along a tangle of back roads and laughed out loud when I found myself in front of the gates to the Westside Country Club. I stopped at the foot of the long driveway and thought for a moment. Then I turned the car around, my mind made up. I found Main Street after two wrong turns. From there it was a straight shot to Frontera Street.

By the time I got to the church, all the parking spaces on both sides of the street were taken. So I swung around to Septima's house, parked in her driveway, and walked.

Once inside, I could smell the sweet perfume of the lilies and roses. It took a few moments for my eyes to adjust to the dimness of the sanctuary. From where I was standing in the vestibule, I could see Socorro sitting on a chair in front of the altar, and I marveled at her elegant neck and shoulders and her straight, beautiful back.

"You are fortunate to have such strong women in your life—role models who will guide you through womanhood," Father Miguel was saying, clearly nearing the end of his message.

Maybe, I thought, *I should just slip back out before anybody sees me.*

"Is there anything you'd like to say before giving final thanks to our Holy Mother?" Father asked Socorro.

I watched her stand, and I took a step back, to make sure I was safely in the shadows.

"First," Socorro said. Her voice was soft, and I could tell she was nervous, standing in front of the entire congregation. I imagined she was grateful to have the bouquet of roses to keep her hands occupied.

She coughed and began again. "First, I want to thank my mother and Dee for making all of this possible." Socorro glanced toward the front pew. "And I want to tell her, and my other *madrina*, that I love them."

She looked like an angel from heaven in her white dress. I could see how her ballet training had made her body sleek and strong, and I noticed how she didn't fidget or wiggle like other girls her age. She kept her shoulders perfectly square and her chin held high like an elegant statue.

"At this point," Father Miguel said, "Richard or any of the *madrinas* who have special gifts for Socorro may bring them to the altar to be blessed."

I knew this was the part of the ceremony where the girl's mother or grandmother usually passed along a piece of heirloom jewelry, and I wished to God that I had something to give her.

I saw Septima rise from the front pew and walk over to Father Miguel. He lifted a rosary out of her palm and proceeded to bless it.

"Let us pray," he said, and I watched everyone bow their heads.

That's when I decided to make my way up the left side of the church, walking on my tiptoes so my shoes wouldn't echo. I saw Richard seated next to Dee, in the middle of the pew, and I took a deep breath as I proceeded toward him. I knew I was taking Septima's seat, but I slid in beside him anyway. He lifted his head with a start, his eyes wide open to see who had so rudely brushed up against him during prayer.

I held my finger to my lips, begging him to stay quiet. He tapped Dee's shoulder, and her face lit up when she saw me. I was happy that I had come, that I'd made our family complete.

Father Miguel handed the rosary back to Septima, who then coiled it inside Socorro's hand and kissed her fingers.

When Septima saw me sitting in her spot, she gasped, and then I heard a ripple of whispers flow through the rest of the congregation like an ocean wave.

Father Miguel smiled and said, "Is there anything you'd like to give Socorro, Alma?"

I saw my daughter's face register surprise, and then I saw tears well in her eyes. I began to shake my head to indicate to Father Miguel that I had nothing to give, but Richard took my hand and pulled me up alongside him.

"Yes, Father," Richard replied. "Socorro's mother and I have something."

He held up a beautiful gold medal carved with the image of La Virgencita that dangled on the end of a delicate gold chain. "I ordered it," he whispered to me. "All the way from Cuernavaca."

Chapter 24

DEE

AFTER MASS, RICHARD TOOK PEEPS AND ALMA DIRECTLY TO the country club.

Alma wanted make sure everything was set up properly, and Peeps had to take his place in the quintet. The rest of us, including Socorro and her Westside friends, trooped down Frontera Street to Septima's house, carrying the three trays of sandwiches with us.

Septima handed each of the girls one of Beto's big work shirts, which they slipped over their dresses to stay clean. Dolores took the wreath of baby's breath off Socorro's head and placed it in the refrigerator, to keep it fresh until the party, when Alma would replace it with the tiara. The men loosened their neckties and the women kicked off their high heels. The smokers huddled on the front porch, and in a matter of minutes the house was full of people snapping pictures of Socorro, Socorro with Father Miguel, Socorro with themselves and Socorro with her *madrinas*. Beaming like a Hollywood starlet, Socorro accepted the attention with grace. I, on the other hand, began to feel overheated and faint as we stood trapped in the middle of Septima's living room, posing for what must have been eighty-six photographs in a row.

"I think I need a glass of water," I finally said, bringing all conversations to an abrupt halt.

"Is it time?" Father Miguel asked.

Socorro clutched my elbow and led me to the sofa. People lifted my ankles onto the coffee table, and by the time I'd taken a few deep breaths to clear my head, four glasses of water were being handed to me at once.

Everyone watched nervously as I gulped down the first glass and quickly began on the second.

"You okay?" somebody asked.

"Fine," I exhaled. "It's just really hot in here, isn't it?"

"A little stuffy, yeah," Beto said.

He reached behind me to crack open a window, and the party continued. Iluminada emerged from the kitchen to set two huge pans of enchiladas on the dinner table, and the warm, spicy fragrance lured everyone into the other room.

I appreciated getting a few moments alone because I was, in fact, feeling odd. At this stage of the game I was used to being unsteady on my feet, but during the walk from the church to Septima's, my hip bones felt like they'd become unhinged. I was as loose-jointed as a Halloween skeleton, and I knew that had to be a sign that something was happening. I closed my eyes and tried to relax.

After a while, Septima sat down beside me and placed her hand on my belly. "Mmmm," she pondered. "Tomorrow, I'd say."

I knew her prediction was as unreliable as anyone else's, but there was something about the conviction in her voice that made me believe her.

"Girl or boy?" I quipped.

"I'm not going to say." She grinned.

Suddenly, I sensed she wasn't being sly. "You know?"

Septima took my hand and patted it gently. Leaning close to my ear, she whispered, "Don't you?"

When we got to the club, the quintet was playing Mozart, and Mrs. Polikoff, who must have been the first to arrive, was gliding over the dance floor by herself with a glass of champagne in her hand.

Father Miguel led Socorro to an anteroom, where she would wait until all the guests arrived. She was supposed to make a grand entrance, escorted onto the dance floor by Richard, who had spent the last three evenings practicing his waltz step in our living room, growing stiffer every time Socorro urged him to let loose. That dance was the single moment Richard feared most. Socorro, on the other hand, had a clear and beautiful picture in her mind of how the father-daughter dance would go. The music would be Strauss, and their steps would start out small. As the music crescendoed, their steps would lengthen and their momentum would build, until they were sweeping across the floor in wide, majestic circles. I'd heard her describe the scene to Richard during their final practice session. He told her not to expect so much, and she told him to relax and follow her lead.

The room was softly lit and the tables looked regal, draped with long white tablecloths that were topped with sheer pieces of tulle that fell to the floor in stiff peaks, like old-fashioned crinolines. Candles flickered from the center of the coral rose arrangements set on each table and from the two dozen wrought-iron candelabras that lined the perimeter of the dance floor. I'd never seen anything like them before, each standing at least six feet high, with impressive pyramids of twenty or more votive candles inside tiny cups of frosted glass. They made the reception hall look like a marble-walled ballroom in a Viennese castle, which was exactly what Socorro had wanted.

Six waiters in white dinner jackets orbited the floor with trays of hors d'oeuvres: salmon mousse and dill on toast points, crab-stuffed mushrooms, tiny quiches and caviar. It appeared that six other waiters had the job of simply replacing empty glasses of champagne with full ones.

I spotted Alma standing at the far end of the long buffet table, speaking to Vincent, the facility supervisor, who had pulled together the entire event. As I walked across the room, I noticed something strikingly different about her, and I tried to figure out what it was, eliminating clues with each step I took. She was wearing a black pantsuit with a beaded top that accentuated an hourglass figure I'd never realized she had, but that wasn't it. Her makeup gave her eyes a deep, sexy look and her lips a full, sumptuous roundness, but that wasn't it either. There was something else, a softness I rarely saw. Not until I approached her, and gave her a tight and soulful hug, did I realize it was her hair.

It was flowing lavishly over her smooth shoulders, with curls cascading down her back. She had the front portion pulled away from her face and gathered loosely in a barrette that Dolores must have decorated with fresh white magnolias.

"You look fabulous," I gushed as we embraced.

"So do you," she beamed.

I knew that wasn't true, not if I looked as bad as I felt. My back ached with a deep, dull pain, and my ankles burned. I intended to sit down as soon as would be polite, and stay in my chair until the party was over. The thought that I might be in the first stages of labor crossed my mind, but Septima's assessment earlier in the evening was enough to convince me that I must be reading the symptoms all wrong and the only thing I was, was tired.

"I was telling Vincent how beautiful everything looks," Alma said.

"I'm glad you approve, ma'am," he replied.

"Where's your wife? Didn't you bring her?"

He shook his head. "Oh, no, ma'am. I don't intend to stay. I just stopped in to make sure everything was to your satisfaction."

The three of us surveyed the room, which by now was humming with the small talk of about one hundred beautifully dressed people. I knew that Alma had feared her friends from Frontera Street might think she was trying to put on airs by hosting such an elaborate affair, but from what I could see, they appeared to be enjoying every detail. I saw Pilar and Iluminada talking to the Seversons in what seemed to be more than cordial conversation. I also saw Beto discussing something with Ellen's father, and whatever the topic was, it caused them both to throw back their heads in a twin set of belly laughs.

"I should go talk to people," Alma said somewhat reluctantly.

"Yes, ma'am," Vincent conceded.

She thanked him again and then turned to me, silently asking that I mingle alongside her.

"I'll go as far as the tables," I said. "Then you're on your own."

"Ladies and gentlemen," Father Miguel announced about forty-five minutes into the evening, tapping his finger on a portable microphone. "May I have your attention, please?" The noise had risen to a level that forced him to repeat the request before people stopped talking.

"For those of you who have never been to a *quinceañera*, let me welcome you to one of the most important events in a Latina girl's life. Her coming-out party, if you will. Her first social event as a young woman."

Everyone was standing in a semicircle around Father Miguel, who was in the center of the dance floor. I stayed seated at the table closest to his right side and could see people from Frontera Street nodding as he spoke and people from the Westside listening intently.

"If you would be kind enough to take your seats at the tables, we'll proceed with the ceremony, which will consist of a symbolic presentation by Socorro's mother, and the first waltz by our honored guest and her escort. That will be followed by dinner, dancing and the presentation of the birthday cake, which, if I do say so myself, is a sight to behold!"

People laughed politely and began to shuffle around the tables looking for their names on the place cards. The quintet was taking a break and would resume playing—as a quartet, of course—when Richard presented Socorro in her debut.

Peeps came to sit next to me, and Cece, dressed in a strapless blue gown that had undoubtedly once been someone's prom dress, sat next to him.

"You two an item?" I asked.

"Maybe," Cece said, giving Peeps what I hoped wasn't phony encouragement.

The truth was that Cece, like everyone else, had noticed how attending Arts High was beginning to change Peeps. He seemed more confident of himself, and that evening, dressed in his tuxedo, he certainly looked less like an outcast than he had at the start of the school year. In the past few weeks he'd cut his hair so short he looked like he was ready for combat in Normandy, and somewhere in his house he'd discovered an old pair of Buddy Holly eyeglasses that he told me once belonged to his uncle Pancho. Peeps put his own prescription inside the rims, and while he would never be football-player handsome, he had managed to make himself avant-garde, or at least what passed for avant-garde in Los Cielos. But I still wondered if he was ready to surrender his heart to a girl as far ahead of him as Cece.

"Ladies and gentlemen," Father Miguel began again, "if you've all found your seats . . ."

Chairs scraped along the floorboards and water glasses clinked against bone china.

"Are we ready?" he asked as the room settled into silence.

"I gotta go," Peeps whispered as he scurried from our table back to his place with the musicians.

"It is my great honor," Father Miguel continued, "to present to you this evening, *la señorita* Socorro Cruz."

Every head in the place turned to see Socorro and Richard enter the room, walking in perfectly measured steps. Beto was the first to stand and applaud, and within seconds everyone else was on their feet.

Socorro looked like a runway model, with her hair piled high on her head and her perfect carriage. Her dress, a spaghetti-strapped sheath of ivory satin cut on the bias, showed off every one of her angles and curves without revealing too much skin. It veered into a tasteful **V** at the small of her back, where a fishtail train, just long enough to give the gown an aristocratic look, trailed behind her. She held a single calla lily in her right hand, which I knew Septima had given her, and her left hand rested on Richard's raised wrist.

The next thing I knew, Alma was by my side, pressing what was already a soggy handkerchief to the corners of her eyes. I reached for her hand and she squeezed hard as Socorro and Richard proceeded, like royalty, toward the dance floor. Dozens of flashbulbs popped, and people continued to applaud.

When they reached the middle of the floor, Father Miguel stood next to them, and they turned to face the crowd.

"Now," he said, cuing everyone to take their seats, "Socorro's mother will ceremoniously preside over the official declaration of her daughter's coming-of-age."

I looked at Alma, who seemed unable to take in the moment. I let go of her hand and placed it on the box she'd set on the table.

She looked at the box like she'd never seen it before.

"The tiara," I whispered to her. "Take it up there."

She moved like she was in a trance, slowly pulling the tiara out of the box and carrying it onto the dance floor. You could hear the silence deepen as she handed the rhinestones to Richard and lifted herself onto her tiptoes to reach the wreath of baby's breath on Socorro's head. Richard took the flowers and handed Alma the little crown, which in the candlelight sparkled like a handful of diamonds. Socorro bent her knees, just like all the Miss Americas do on television, so her mother could pin the crown to the top of her head. When Socorro straightened up, Alma stepped aside. Richard put his arm around Alma and kissed her quickly on the lips.

Father Miguel stepped in as the guests applauded and cheered, and then he led us all in prayer. After saying "amen," he and Alma returned to the table, leaving Richard and Socorro to their dance.

The musicians eased into the familiar strains of the *Blue Danube* as Richard bowed and Socorro curtsied, gracefully lifting her train. By the fourth one-two-three, Richard had stopped counting out loud to himself and actually appeared to have surrendered to the music. I chuckled at the thought of an orchestra teacher struggling to keep time, but then I remembered how terrified Mitch had been when he found out he had to do a simple box step at our wedding reception. Richard's nervous smile made me yearn for Mitch, and imagine how much he would have loved to have seen his ready-to-burst wife waddle onto the dance floor, determined to drag him through at least one slow dance. I had been dreaming about him a lot lately, watching him in what seemed like home movies, being the perfect father to the child he would never know.

"Dance?" Father Miguel was asking Alma, who was still mopping tears. She nodded, and together they stepped onto the dance floor and joined the honored couple.

Traditionally, Cece told me, the *quinceañera* girl dances the entire waltz with her father, and the girl's mother dances with the grandfather. Nobody else is supposed to join them until the second number. The rule seemed self-evident, but it appeared that at least one of the West-siders didn't understand the tradition because, near the end of the waltz, a man I didn't recognize stepped onto the floor and tapped Richard on the shoulder, asking to cut in.

He appeared to be in his forties, was tall, and had a rugged, unpampered attractiveness about him. He was also the only man in the place who wasn't wearing a tuxedo, dressed instead in a white collarless shirt, dark suit jacket, slim-cut pants, and a pair of shiny black cowboy boots. His hair was a handsome salt-and-pepper gray that showed off his deep copper tan. I wondered who he might be, and I tried to recall the names of the various husbands and fathers I'd met earlier, the parents of Socorro's school friends. I couldn't place him.

Still, there he was, catching both Socorro and Richard completely off guard, and surprising Alma so much that she stopped in midstep and literally stood next to an equally dumbfounded Father Miguel with her mouth wide open.

Richard, unsure how to handle the situation, stopped dancing and then awkwardly stepped aside, casting a confused glance toward Alma.

The music continued to play. One-two-three, one-two-three, and the man picked up the beat and began to swirl Socorro around in wide, assertive circles. She looked stunned, but she followed the man's lead and soon seemed to enjoy his confident footwork.

Alma rushed back to the table, her face panic-stricken, and then I knew. A paralyzing chill ran through me as Richard and Father Miguel dashed to the table, to find out what was happening.

"What is *he* doing here?" Alma growled. Her neck was red, and I could see the look of undiluted hatred blazing in her eyes.

"Oh, my God," I gasped. "I didn't think . . ."

"What? *You* invited him!" She looked at me as if I'd set her house on fire.

The music ended and the guests exploded into another round of applause. Alma ran out of the room before Socorro got back, and Richard began to berate me as the quartet segued into a another selection.

"What in God's name have you done?" he hissed.

I stammered and shook my head. There was no explaining that I'd never thought he would come.

Cece hovered nearby, and other guests began to walk past us, making their way to the buffet or onto the dance floor to join Socorro and the man that she, by now, must have learned was her father.

"I'm sure there's an explanation," Father Miguel murmured.

"Yeah?" Richard shot back. "Well, I'd sure like to hear it. What the hell is going on here, Dee?"

I felt nauseous, hot and faint. "I mailed the invitation," I finally said, feeling almost as startled by the words as they were. Richard slammed his hand on the table in anger.

"I didn't think he'd show up. I—"

"You didn't think at *all*!" Richard scowled. Disgusted with me, he turned on his heel and marched off to find Alma.

I broke down and Father Miguel asked if I wanted to get some fresh air.

"Oh, Father," I blubbered, "I never thought he'd actually. . . .I just wanted him to know . . ."

"Come on," he urged. "Let's step outside for a minute."

I pulled myself up and felt waves of pain shoot across my pelvis. "Give me a minute," I said.

The music stopped and Socorro bounded over to us, her eyes wide in astonishment and her hand clasped firmly in his.

"Dee!" she squealed. "This is my father! This is Paul Walker!"

The man seemed uncomfortable, as if he had only just realized where he was and how much chaos he was about to create.

"Where's Mom?"

I could tell that now Paul wanted out. He began to avert his eyes.

"Mr. Walker," Father Miguel began, "could I speak to you alone for a moment?"

Paul nodded and nervously followed Father Miguel to another part of the noisy room, hoping, I suppose, to find a quick getaway. Most of the guests were oblivious to the crisis spinning out of control before them. They dutifully lined up at the buffet tables, where the waiters were carving prime rib and leg of lamb. Before I had a chance to say anything to Socorro, Septima stormed over to us in an uproar.

"*Por Dios!*" she gasped, sweeping Socorro into her arms, giving her a crushing hug. "I'm sorry he ruined this beautiful night for you, *mijita!* Just pretend this didn't happen okay, *muñeca?* Go on with the party. Father Miguel is asking him to leave."

Socorro wrestled herself out of Septima's grip. The instant she broke loose, she headed toward the party room's entrance, where Father Miguel and Paul were standing with their heads tilted toward one another in serious conversation. They moved into the reception area, and Socorro followed them.

I rose as quickly as I could to make my way toward the door. The pain in my pelvis seemed milder, but I suspected that was only because the mortification I was feeling had left me numb.

"Why is this such a big deal?" I heard Socorro ask Father Miguel. She had stopped them at the cloak room. "I *sent* him an invitation."

"It's the first piece of mail I've gotten from her," Paul added. "I thought it meant that Alma was all right with me being here . . ."

Father Miguel shook his head in confusion, and I knew I should say something, anything. But I hesitated, because I knew that the moment I began to speak, Socorro's beautiful party would come crashing down around her.

"It was me," I confessed. "I invited him."

Socorro turned to me and scowled. "That's a lie! You saw me write out the invitation. I did it right in front of you!"

Paul cast his eyes down, realizing he was caught in someone else's ugly web. I quickly searched the area for any sign of Alma or Richard, but there was none. I tried to imagine where they were and how much they hated me right now.

Septima must have read my thoughts because she appeared out of nowhere and said, "I don't know, but I'll try and find them."

"Look," Paul said, "I don't want to cause trouble. I'll just go."

"No!" Socorro whimpered, her voice trembling.

"That might be best," Father Miguel replied. "Under the circumstances."

"Give us a minute, though, won't you?"

Socorro looked into Paul's face and she broke into tears. He held her in his arms, allowing her to collapse against him. She sobbed into his chest, and he began to gently rock her, bending his broad shoulders over her slender frame and whispering something in her ear. She nodded as he spoke, hungrily accepting every word as if it were the last she'd hear.

It was such a private moment that we should have turned our heads, but instead Father Miguel and I stood and stared, and before I knew it, Ellen and Holly were standing beside us, too, listening to Cece whisper, "It's her father!"

Socorro followed Paul outside and stayed there for almost half an hour after he left. Her friends took turns trying to coax her back into the party, but each of them returned shaking their head, indicating that she wouldn't budge.

What, I wondered, must be racing through her mind? She had not only to come to grips with the shock of meeting her father for the first time she could remember—taking in his face, weighing his integrity, hoping he could love her—but she also had to be asking a million questions: Why did he come back now? Why did he leave back then? Why did he do that to their family?

If anyone owed her an explanation, it was me. I was the one who had dropped this bomb of confusion into the middle of what was supposed to be a magical night. I was the one who had paved the way for Socorro's unsettled past to walk right up to her on the day she was supposed to be thinking only about a bright future.

What had I done? I wanted to somehow explain how much I loved her and how I longed for her to know her father, the way my baby never would know his. But the thought of telling her about Alma's secret box, and all the unmailed letters, made my stomach clench. I confided in Father Miguel, begging him to tell me that I'd done the right thing. But he wouldn't answer.

"Do you want me to go outside with you?" he finally said in a tone that was practically a shove out the door.

Fortunately, all the commotion hadn't disturbed most of the guests, or kept them from enjoying the dinner and dancing. As I made my way out, I was stopped by several Westsiders who, with drinks in hand, purred about the affair. I smiled politely and told them I'd pass their compliments on to Alma when I saw her. Then I pressed on, trying to prepare myself for the horrible task ahead. When I found Socorro, she was walking along the edge of the club's long driveway with the jacket of the doorman's military-looking uniform draped over her shoulders.

"I tried to get her to go back inside, ma'am, " he reported with concern. "But she just wouldn't. I barely got her to take the jacket."

"Thank you," I answered.

"Socorro," I began when I reached her side.

She refused to look at me. "I figured it out," she muttered. "He told me he never got any of my letters. How dumb does she think I am?"

"She?"

"My mom!" Socorro said, breaking into tears again. "What did she do, throw them out like trash? Is that what she thought, that they were trash?"

I had to take big steps to keep up with her, and the loose-pebbled driveway forced me to quicken my stride for balance. The walking relieved some of the tension in my back, and the cool night air felt good against my skin. I was beginning to regain my strength and told myself that what I'd felt earlier wasn't labor, just nerves.

"She didn't throw them out," I said. "She kept them. All of them. In a box. For your own good."

Socorro took one last step and then stood perfectly still. She wrapped the doorman's jacket tightly around herself and looked up at the hazy three-quarter moon. I stayed a few feet away from her, and from inside the club I heard the quartet begin to play Mozart's night music.

Chapter 25

ALMA

I TOLD RICHARD TO TAKE ME TO DEE'S HOUSE, AND THE minute I got there I began packing.

"I'm not saying she was right," he argued as I threw pants and shirts and shoes into the backpack Socorro had used for her ballet things before Dee gave her the fancy leather bag.

"Are you listening to me?" Richard asked.

I kicked off the ridiculous high heels I was wearing and tossed them into the closet. I stripped off my outfit and let it spill like a puddle around my ankles. Then I stood, in my bra and panties, in front of Richard and screamed back at him.

"Don't you see what's happened here? Are you blind?"

"What I see is that Dee made a terrible mistake, and you have a right to be angry. But you are only making things worse by doing this. You need to go back there and talk to your daughter!"

"*My* daughter? How is she my daughter when I don't have a say over what she does or who runs her life? Dee wants her to live in a rich girl's house, she lives in a rich girl's house. Dee wants her to have a country club party, she has a country club party. Dee decides Paul should come back and destroy everything. Well, she gets that, too, doesn't she?"

"I'm not saying Dee wasn't out of line."

"Then what *are* you saying, Richard? That I'm overreacting? That I shouldn't be furious that the one thing I had the right to explain to my daughter in my own way was thrown in my face on the very night I was supposed to be able to take pride in how I raised my baby?" I pulled a sweatshirt over my head and stepped into a pair of leggings, and then I yanked open the top dresser drawer and shoved socks and underwear into the backpack.

"So you leave her there?" Richard shouted back. "You leave her alone so Dee can take charge? What is *wrong* with you? You tell me all this nonsense about La Llorona being out to get Socorro since day one, and now you just run the other way? Looks to me like she won, Alma! Like you didn't even put up a fight."

"You get out of here!" I screamed.

"Fine," Richard huffed. "I'm going back to the country club to try and act like a responsible parent and get Socorro through the rest of the night."

I felt my knees begin to melt underneath my own weight, and I held on to the dresser for support. Richard stepped toward me, his expression switching from anger to concern.

"Can we discuss this later?" he asked. "We really should get back there. Put on some shoes."

"I'm not going anywhere, except away from this house!"

"Look, I'll take you to my place, but you need to come back to the club with me first."

I knew that was exactly what I should do, that I should walk back into that party with my head held high and find my little girl and tell her that I did what I did to keep her from getting hurt. I needed to tell her that Paul Walker wasn't the man she'd built him up to be, and that no matter what he might have promised on that dance floor, he'd end up leaving her empty-handed and brokenhearted. I slumped onto my bed and buried my face in my pillow.

Richard sat next to me and slid the statue of La Virgencita to the edge of the nightstand. "You can do it," he whispered. "She'll help you."

"No," I said. "She can't do anything now. Please, just take me to your place, okay? And bring Socorro there. I'll talk to her there. I promise."

"All right," he said.

I stood up and swung the heavy backpack over my shoulder, accidentally knocking La Virgencita against the closet door and onto the floor. Richard lunged toward her, but too late to save the little saint.

"She's broken," he said, staring at the pieces.

I looked down at Saint Mary, snapped in two like an old broom, lying helpless at my feet. I wanted to scoop her into my arms and tell her I would save her. But I didn't have the strength, or the confidence that her sweet light could set things right anymore.

"Never mind," I muttered as I walked out of the bedroom. "Let's just go."

Sitting inside Richard's apartment alone and enraged, I dared La Llorona to show herself.

"Come on!" I screamed. "Come on and I'll rip your head off!"

I paced across the floor, one minute regretting my decision to stay away from the party and the next minute convincing myself it was the only way to handle the outrageous situation. By now all the guests would know who Paul Walker was and the gossip would be thick. So, why should I go back and give all those Westsiders a chance to laugh at me? I knew they were telling each other that they knew something was wrong with the barrio people Dee took in like stray dogs. They would have already put two and two together and figured out that I wasn't even married to Paul when Socorro was born, and they'd think: "Thank God that little girl has someone like Dee to show her how to live a *respectable* life."

But then I thought maybe I should go back. Maybe I should stand in front of all of them and ask who the hell they think they are. Maybe I wasn't as respectable as them, but did they know that Dee's "respectable" mother couldn't be bothered to come home and be a good grandmother? That she was still traipsing through Europe, sending faxes to remind Dee to contact her by intercontinental beeper when the time came?

I'd ask how come none of them ever bothered to help Dee when she needed it. Why I never saw even one of them drop by her house to see if she was doing all right. What had the oh-so-perfect Westsiders done to help? *Nada,* that's what. Not one damn thing.

"Come on!" I screamed again into the darkness. "Show your goddamned face, *bruja!* I have a deal to make with you!" I waited to feel La Llorona's bile in the air, but I felt nothing. Why wasn't she answering my call? Where was she hiding?

"Don't think you've won, because you haven't," I shouted. "Socorro's a woman now, not a child. It's too late! She won't get you back to your own children. You need a *child's* soul. You waited too long, Llorona!" There was still no sign of the witch. But I knew I was right, and I knew that she knew it. I kept talking.

"What good is Socorro going to do for you now? Why do you want to hold on to her when there's a baby for you to take?" I waited for any sign that she might be near, certain she was listening.

"Give me my daughter back," I said into the blackness. "And I'll give you Dee's baby the minute it's born. I'll hand it right to you."

When I answered the knock, I found Sepi standing there, holding my high heels and fancy pantsuit. I closed the door in her face and told her to go away, but she began speaking through the wood.

"Almita," she said in Spanish, "your baby needs her mother. That's the only thing that matters now, *verdad?*"

I leaned my shoulder against the wall and listened as she repeated herself over and over. That *was* all that mattered. What was I doing hiding in this apartment? There was no way I could allow my beautiful girl to get torn apart by the same sort of lies and selfishness that had scarred my life. I had to put what Paul did behind me. Whatever pain I was feeling couldn't compare to the hurt she was facing. I had to get back right away.

"Get dressed," said Septima, who had somehow sensed that I was ready to act. "I've got Beto's truck."

On our way to the country club, Septima told me that Paul had left the party and Dee had told Socorro about the letters and the box.

Was there anything that woman didn't stick her nose into? There was no end to the depth of bitterness I felt toward her. No words to describe my contempt.

When we stepped into the party, I saw Father Miguel rolling the birthday cake onto the dance floor. The guests cheerfully sang "Happy Birthday," and Socorro sliced the top tier listlessly. People lined up to shake her hand and get a piece of cake. She smiled insincerely as they shuffled past, wishing her the best. When her eyes met mine, I saw her expression harden.

"Would you excuse us for one moment?" I asked the lady who was about to plant a polite kiss on Socorro's cheek. I slipped my arm around her waist, but she pulled away. I stepped closer, took a firm grip of her elbow and led her from the reception line to the coatroom. A member of the country club staff saw us and said there was an office next to the men's lounge where we could be alone.

"I need you to listen to me," I said the moment I closed the door.

"So you can lie some more? I don't need to listen to that, Mom." Her voice was piqued and her shoulders were rigid.

"I never lied to you," I said, reaching out to touch her.

"You are so full of it!" Her harsh language slapped me harder than she knew. "You threw my letters out like garbage!"

"No. I didn't throw them out. I put them away."

"That's *better*?"

"I had reasons, Socorro, you were too young to—" She turned her back on me and yanked the office door wide open.

"*Reasons?*" she scoffed. "Well, they couldn't have been very good if they couldn't even convince Dee to keep your little secret. And in case you haven't noticed, Mom, I'm not a baby anymore!"

"Close that door, *mija*. Please, I love you. We are not finished here."

"Maybe you aren't," she said indignantly, "but I am."

Chapter 26

SOCORRO

THE PARTY WAS ENDLESS. THE ONLY THING THAT MADE IT bearable was that Cece and Peeps and Holly and Ellen stayed at my side for the rest of the night, shielding me from the adults.

When the guests finally began to leave, I asked Father Miguel to take me to Dee's. I knew my mother and Richard would have to stay and say good-bye to the last straggler, and slipping out while they were busy was the only way I could get away from them.

When I got to the house Dee was already there. The secret box was on the coffee table in front of her, next to La Virgencita, who was broken in two. I walked past without a word and went into my room. What I wanted most was for the entire night to start all over again so my father could walk into the party the way he was supposed to. I wanted him to place the tiara on my head and to whisper in my ear that I was his beautiful princess. I wanted that first waltz back, and I wanted to continue dancing with him all night long.

The telephone began to ring.

"Don't answer it!" I shouted. But she did.

"Yes, she's here . . . In her room . . . Richard, could I speak to Alma?"

I cracked the door to listen more closely, but the conversation didn't last, and the next thing I heard was Dee crying. I knew I should go and tell her that I was grateful for what she'd done, that she was the only person who cared enough about me to tell the truth. But I knew she would start trying to excuse what my mother had done, and I didn't want to hear it.

*   *   *

The next morning Dee let herself into my room. She looked pasty and worn-out, and I'm sure I looked the same.

"Your mother is at Septima's house. I'll take you over there."

I pulled the bedsheet over my head and ignored her.

"Look, Socorro, what I did was wrong. I had no right."

I turned my back to her.

"You two need to talk this through. Get up and I'll drive you."

"Drive yourself there!" I said, sitting up. "I'm not going any—"

Dee stumbled and grabbed onto the doorknob to steady herself. She was grimacing in pain.

"Are you okay?"

"Just a cramp," she said, rubbing her back.

But I could see it was more than that. Every drop of color had drained from her face, and her hands began to clench. She squeezed her eyes shut and began to falter like she was going to faint.

"Dee . . . are you all right?."

"I think so," she said, holding out her arm for support. I helped her over to the bed and she lowered herself onto the mattress.

"Should I call someone?"

She took a few deep breaths. "No," she insisted. "It's just a cramp, really. It's going away now. I'm fine."

I went to the kitchen to get her a glass of water, and as I returned I saw Richard walk through the front door.

"I'm going to Septima's," he said.

"Something's wrong with Dee," I replied anxiously.

In my bedroom Dee had already begun to look and feel better. Maybe it *was* just a cramp. I took the water to her and rubbed her back as she put it to her lips.

"Socorro," Richard said, "come with me."

"No."

Richard stood still for a long moment, wondering, I suppose, if he had the right to command me to go with him, and then he walked out the door as quietly as he'd walked in.

If it had been any other day, any other issue, I would have done what he said because I liked the way he played dad to me. But this was about my *real* father, and he knew that made everything different.

"You need to get some rest," I told Dee after Richard left. "Why don't you lie down?"

I pulled the bedspread over Dee's shoulders and made her close her eyes. In an instant she was out, and even though her sleep seemed fitful and I didn't want to leave her alone, I knew what I had to do.

Paul Walker was staying at the Desert Motel on Main Street. That's what he'd told me before he left the *quinceañera.*

I took the box of unsent letters from the coffee table and tied one of my old toe shoe ribbons around it to keep it shut. I used a second ribbon to secure the box to the handlebars of my bike and tried to think of what else I should take to him. I grabbed a couple of the Polaroids off the dining room table, where they'd been fanned out since Mom snapped them before the *quinceañera* Mass.

The air outside smelled like chimney smoke, and my hands and cheeks grew numb as I pushed my bike through swells of winter wind. I churned the pedals and shifted gears until I found one that made the bike move as fast as possible. Then I pressed the pedals harder, feeling the muscles in my thighs tighten against the fabric of my jeans.

Main Street was as empty as you'd expect it to be on a chilly Sunday morning. The few cars on the road had plenty of room to make wide circles around me as they whizzed past. When I glanced inside the windows, I saw people dressed for church, chatting with children in the backseat, kids who turned their heads to take a closer look at me. That could have been us, I thought. Mom and Paul and me, riding in a car like a real family. It *should* have been us, and I wanted to ask my father why it wasn't.

My breathing grew heavy and rhythmic as I passed Arts High and continued down the street toward the center of town. The Desert Motel was not quite as far as the downtown plaza, but it was at least a couple of miles from my school. I leaned into the wind and felt trickles of sweat begin to slither down my back.

I tried to remember the advice I'd read in magazine articles about children finding their biological parents, stories that I'd never told my mother I had cut out and saved. I kept them in the same place that I kept the birthday cards my father had sent me, thinking that when I turned eighteen, and was legally an adult, I would go to one of those investigative places and start searching for him.

Of course, that was when I thought my letters were going unanswered because he had disappeared, or had decided that he didn't want to have a daughter anymore. That was before I knew my own mother was keeping me from knowing him.

She said she had reasons, but as I rode through Los Cielos, past the supermarket and the fire station, past the skating rink and the hamburger hut, I couldn't think of a single reason that made sense. Not one.

My legs were tingling when I coasted into the hotel parking lot, and the cold wind had bitten my fingers to the point that they ached when I lifted them from the handlebars. I leaned my bike against a brick wall and shook my hair out from under my helmet as I walked into the front lobby. Soft music was playing and I could smell bacon being served for breakfast in the dining room.

"He just checked out," the lady told me, holding up a room key as evidence. "I mean, not even three minutes ago. He might still be in the parking lot."

I dashed back outside and ran around to the side of the hotel, where fewer than a dozen cars were parked. I noticed a white sedan slowly easing out of a space, turning toward the far end of the lot, where a little sign with an arrow said EXIT.

I ran after the car, yelling, "Dad! Dad!" at the top of my lungs.

The brake lights flickered, and I caught up with him at the exit.

"Wait!" I screamed, tapping the passenger-side window wildly. Paul turned his head with a jolt, apparently surprised to see me. He looked different than I remembered. His wide smile and the gentle wrinkles around his bright green eyes were gone, and instead of greeting me with the same joy he had on the dance floor, he looked at me with a hard edge that made me think, for an instant, that I'd flagged down the wrong man.

I ran over to the driver's side as he rolled down the window and leaned out to speak to me. He kept the motor running and all the doors locked.

"You said you'd be here today," I said, surprised to find myself trembling uncontrollably.

"This was a huge mistake," he replied, speaking so softly that I almost couldn't hear him over the engine's rumble.

"No!" I cried, moving my forehead down so it was only inches away from his. I tried to look him in the eye, but he shifted his focus to the front windshield and kept it there while he turned off the engine and continued to speak.

"I got things all wrong," he said. "I thought that after all these years your mother had accepted the agreement. I thought that was why I got the invitation. Otherwise, I never would have . . ."

"What agreement?"

He pounded the heel of his hand against the steering wheel and shook his head in frustration. "Look, I'm just making things worse," he said, reaching down toward the ignition with his right hand.

I pounded on the hood of the car. "Wait! Talk to me!" I screamed, desperate to keep him from pulling away. He slumped his forehead against the steering wheel and said nothing for a few moments. I pressed my back against the side of the car and slid down until I was sitting on my ankles, crying.

I heard the door lock click, and I jumped to my feet as he pushed his door open and stepped out, his eyes still not meeting mine straight on but darting hesitantly between my face and his feet. He took my hand and led me to the car's hood, where we both sat looking out at the morning traffic.

"I have a family," he began.

My heart jumped and I turned toward him in excitement. I wanted to tell him that I didn't care about the past, or why he'd taken so long to tell me about my half sisters or brothers. I could love them, I *would* love them the instant I met them. He didn't have to worry about that!

But he held up his hand like a stop sign as I began to speak.

"Let me finish," he said. "I have a family that doesn't know about you, or your mother."

My stomach tightened, but I thought, that was okay. We'd all get used to each other with time. Once we got past the initial shock and all the questions.

"And, Socorro," Paul said, looking me in the eye, "I'd like to keep it that way."

I didn't think I heard him right, and my expression must have shown it.

"Can you understand that?" he asked, lifting my wrist into his wide palm.

I jerked my hand back to my side, astonished by what he'd just said.

"I told your mother the same thing years ago," he continued. "When I gave her the post office box address. I told her that as long as I continued to get letters from you, I would send money, to support you both, with the understanding that neither of you should ever try to find me, or try to reach me any other way."

I struggled to remember what my mother had told me about Paul's address, but my mind was blank and all I could recall was her saying that she was sure my father treasured every photograph and card and letter that I mailed to him.

"I sent you cards for your birthday. Did you get them?" he asked.

I nodded my head, still trying to comprehend what he was saying to me.

"I knew your mother wasn't ready to accept my terms," he said, "since I never heard from you."

"I wrote," I said, thinking how stupid that must have sounded to him, wondering if he even cared.

My mind flashed back to the box that I had tied to the handlebars of my bike, and for an instant I considered telling Paul to wait while I ran over to get it. But I thought about the little crayon drawings of our house on Frontera Street that I'd made for him so long ago, all the construction-paper Valentines and the Popsicle-stick picture frame I'd pieced together, and I remembered how I'd signed every single item with showers of little hearts and the words "I love you." And I realized that the man I'd thought I was mailing those things to wasn't the man sitting beside me. The father I had imagined for all these years never would have traded love for such a twisted ransom. And it occurred to me that my mother had let me think that he loved me no matter what. That she had let me keep writing letters to the father I'd invented, the one who was a king and a safari hunter and whatever else I dared to imagine.

"I don't know if you can comprehend," he started again.

"Oh, I comprehend," I said. "I comprehend just fine."

He held his arms apart as if he wanted a hug.

I slid off the hood of the car and backed away from him.

"We can stay in touch, through the post office box, if you'd like," he said.

My head felt like it was about to explode, and my eyes burned from the tears welling up inside them. I blinked and felt them fall onto my cheeks, starting another crying jag that I knew I wouldn't be able to control. I began to make wheezing sounds that came out like something between a laugh and a howl.

"You're right," I managed to say as I watched him climb back into the driver's seat. "Coming here was a big mistake."

I walked back to my bicycle and heard his car pull out of the lot. I untied the ribbon securing the box and opened it. Inside was a picture of my grandparents from Mexico, the letters, and a little *milagro* medal. There was also a picture of me smiling. I could still remember when it was taken, before Dee showed up, before Richard and my mom fell in love. Back when it was just my mother and me.

I got on my bike and pointed the front wheel toward Septima's house.

Chapter 27

ALMA

WHAT DEE DID WAS WRONG, SEPTIMA SAID. AND HOW SHE DID it was even worse. "But that's not who you should be thinking about right now, Alma. You should be thinking about the girl caught in the middle of all of this."

Of course I was thinking about Socorro. She was the *only* one I'd been thinking of, of how much she was hurting. Richard held my hand as Septima spoke and slipped another cup of coffee across the kitchen counter to me. I had been awake all night, fighting my urge to storm into Dee's house and comfort my daughter, even if she was angry at me.

"All I wanted to do was protect her," I said. "Why should she have to know her father is ashamed of her? That's too much for a little girl to handle."

"Did you plan to ever tell her?" Richard asked.

"Of course," I snapped. "Of course I did. As soon as she was old enough to understand. It wasn't up to Dee."

"Well, now you have to let her decide how she feels about him," Septima said. "On her own terms. You can't tell her what she can and can't forgive."

I stepped to the sink and poured out my coffee. I didn't want to listen to Septima's God talk. But she continued. "Almita, think of the gifts that God has given you. For so long it was just you and Socorro, and look how wide the circle has grown. Even Dee did what she did out of love."

I looked at Richard, who nodded in agreement.

"She is about to be the mother of a fatherless child," Sepi continued.

"And, Alma, she looks up to you. She wants to be the kind of mother you are to Socorro. But, think about it—her own mother never showed her how to do that. And the two men in her life, her father and her husband, are gone forever. She is petrified."

"What's that have to do with inviting Paul Walker?"

"It's mixed up, but I think Dee believed that Socorro would resent you for keeping Paul a secret. She was convinced you were going to lose your baby to the lure of the perfect daddy she'd invented in her head. You and Richard and Socorro are the only family Dee knows. And she thought if Socorro met Paul someday, if she saw that he's a man with flaws and guilt and human weaknesses, then her need to find the perfect father would disappear, and she would understand that her true family is made up of the people who stand beside her every single day."

At that moment, Beto walked into the kitchen with Socorro at his side. She held the secret box in her hands and dropped it on the floor when she saw me. The letters spilled out and she stepped on them as she ran into my arms. I held her tight and smoothed her hair. I kissed her cold face and wiped away the warm tears. I told her that I loved her.

"He didn't even want to talk to me."

"I'm sorry, *mijita*. I'm sorry."

"Mom, he has a whole other family. Kids he doesn't want us to know."

My heart was breaking. "I should have told you," I said. "I should have let you know. I wanted to protect you, sweetheart. That's all I wanted."

"I know," she said. "But I thought he loved me."

"Socorro," I answered, "I'll tell you everything whenever you want to hear it. What happened before and after you were born. Everything, *mijita,* whenever you want to know."

"All I need to know is that you love me, Mom, and that we'll always be together."

"Always."

The telephone rang and Beto dashed to answer it.

"It's Mr. Severson," he called out from the living room. "He's taking Dee to the hospital."

"Mom," Socorro said, "she's having her baby."

I looked deep into my daughter's eyes and saw that she was counting on me to show her how to respond.

"What Dee did was wrong, but she did it out of love for you. You know that, don't you?" I said. I saw Septima smile. "She's about to be in the same spot that we once were, honey. Alone and scared. She probably could use some friends."

Septima and Beto grabbed their coats.

"Come on," Richard said. Septima picked up her purse and a small gift tied with a bow. Beto herded us out the door and into Richard's Toyota. Nobody spoke as Richard drove the same route that Septima and I had used the day Dee collapsed in the shop.

"This is for you," Septima said from the backseat. I turned to see her handing me the gift.

"Dee and I were going to give it to you last night."

I took the package and set it on my lap.

"Open it," she said. "You need to open it now."

I glanced at Richard, and he shrugged his shoulders to indicate that he didn't know anything about it.

I pulled the bow and lifted the lid. Inside was a key chain decorated with a dangling crown just like the tiara Socorro wore at the party. Nice, but hardly something I needed to see that very minute.

"Lift the cotton," Septima said.

I pinched the bed of cotton at the bottom of the box and peeled it back to reveal a shiny brass key.

"It's to the shop," Septima told me. "Dee got it back."

Beto jumped in to explain that Dee and Septima had been planning the surprise for weeks. Dee had somehow managed, through lawyers and God knew what else, to buy the shop back from the Textile Village man, who hadn't done anything with the property but board it up. He sold it to her with the stipulation that it would not be used as a fabric store, so Dee and Septima decided to turn it into a full-blown beauty-pageant-gown emporium called Frontera Street Fashions.

"The key," Septima added, "means you're one of the owners."

Richard made the final turn into the hospital parking lot, and I was the first one out of the car, running to the front door.

When we got to Dee's room, I heard a nurse telling her to push.

"I'm the coach," I said, putting my things down in a chair and hurrying to Dee's bedside.

Dee took my hand and began to cry. "Alma," she said, "I'm so sorry—"

"Shhh," I replied, feeding her a spoonful of crushed ice from a cup the nurse handed to me. "We'll talk later. We've got something else to do right now."

The room was crowded with equipment, beeping monitors that flashed yellow and green lights, and other machines that kept track of Dee's heartbeat and the heartbeat of the baby. There was a scale ready and waiting, and a nurse standing shoulder to shoulder with the doctor, who was telling Dee that he could see the head.

I heard Septima and the others in the hall, and then I saw Socorro standing in the doorway.

"Can she come in?" Dee asked the nurse, who said it would be all right if Socorro put on a pink paper gown. The nurse slipped gowns on both of us, and then Socorro walked up to Dee and hugged her shoulders.

"It's okay," Socorro said as Dee began to weep.

"Ladies, can we get back to business here?" the doctor said. Dee slid into another painful contraction. When it subsided she rested her head on the three pillows piled up behind her.

"Look in my bag," she said to Socorro, "and take it out for me, please."

As Socorro stepped away from the bed Dee held out her right hand, which had an IV in it, and pulled me toward her. Her hair was damp and her skin felt hot to the touch.

"I'm so sorry," she repeated.

"It doesn't matter," I answered.

One of the machines began to whine and the doctor cleared his throat.

"Here we go again!" he said.

Dee began to pant and I wiped her forehead with a washcloth.

"Bear down," the doctor ordered.

"Push," I said. "Puushh!"

Socorro found what Dee had asked for, La Virgencita, held together with a scarf. Dee had insisted on bringing my statue to the hospital. She placed the bandaged Holy Mother on the pillow next to Dee's head.

"Good," the doctor coaxed.

Dee's face glowed red, and she began her deep breathing as the contraction fell away.

"That was excellent," the doctor said. "The next one could do it."

Dee collapsed into the pillows and held her mouth open for more ice.

"I was out of line," she mumbled between swallows.

"Shhh," I said, pushing strands of sweaty hair away from her eyes. "I'm the one who was wrong, about the letters—"

"Excuse me," the doctor interrupted, "but you'll have to do your female bonding some other time. Right now it looks like we are about to have a baby."

The monitor began to whir again, and Dee sat up, preparing for the pain.

"*Mira!*" I heard Septima say from the door, where she was leaning in to watch. She pointed to a round mirror hanging in the corner of the room. "I can see the baby!"

Dee groaned and let out a scream as the doctor huddled closer and furrowed his brow in concentration.

"Here it comes," he said. "Keep pushing, Dee. Keep pushing."

I saw the doctor give the nurse a worried glance as he pulled the baby out. She dashed to his side with a sponge in her hand and a little rubber contraption shaped like an onion. Dee fell back and closed her eyes, exhausted from the effort. The doctor cut the cord.

I expected to hear him slap the newborn on the rump and then happily announce whether Dee had a son or daughter. I anticipated seeing Dee's eyes sparkle with the incredible feeling of love I knew would wash over her the instant she took the baby in her arms. I could still remember holding Socorro to my chest and thinking no love in the world could be stronger than what I felt for her. Dee was about to know that same feeling.

But the doctor didn't present the baby to Dee. He kept it down low and handed it to the nurse straight away. The monitor that kept track of the baby's heart began to scream with alarm.

"Oh, my God!" Dee gasped. "What's wrong?"

I felt an icy gust of wind sweep through the room as the nurse urgently placed the baby inside an incubator and began to turn knobs and dials.

Dee looked as pale as the hospital bedsheets, and I heard Septima begin to pray. I watched the doctor rush to the baby's side, ordering the nurse to bring him this and that as he massaged the infant's tiny chest. Dee was too exhausted to do more than lie back and listen to all the commotion. Socorro looked at me with panic in her eyes.

I turned and saw La Llorona hovering over the incubator, her dark robe floating like a black cloud, her yellow eyes burning like hot poison.

The monitors beeped and squealed and I heard the dark witch begin to laugh.

Dee looked into my eyes, and I could see that she had no energy to fight the hateful spirit. Socorro placed the mended Virgencita on Dee's chest, and they both began to pray for God's help.

"You will not take this child!" I blared at La Llorona, who stretched her skeleton arms toward the tiny infant. "This baby is part of *my* family! And you will not have power over us any longer!"

I thought of the months Dee had spent under my roof and how she had calmed me with her quiet strength when La Llorona shook me to my bones. Nothing, she would say to me, is strong enough to steal a daughter from a mother who loves her with a pure heart. And now I understood that I could use my love, our love, as a shield as well as a hammer.

I felt a rush of tremendous energy surge through me, and I was ready to fight La Llorona to her death. "You have no power here!" I shouted again. "God is with this family and you will never tear it apart."

Dee handed me La Virgencita and as I tightened the scarf that held her together, I noticed that she was glowing as bright as the morning sun. I wondered if I was the only one who could see the incredible beam. I stepped toward the incubator, where the doctor was too busy to pay me any mind, and I held the precious saint over my head, as close to La Llorona's cloud of darkness as possible.

I prayed harder and harder, and I then heard the deepest silence I have ever known, a profound quiet that filled my soul with an overpowering sense of calm. The baby, I thought, must be gone.

I stepped back to Dee's side and prepared to help her receive the horrible news. But when I looked toward the doctor I saw that La Llorona had vanished.

Suddenly, the monitors began flashing green lights, and the other machines began chirping like songbirds. The doctor wiped his brow and let out a little cheer.

The baby began to wail.

It took a few moments for the doctor to check everything out, but the baby's cry was all Dee needed to hear to set her mind at ease. She sat up and waited to hold her child in her arms.

"Congratulations, Mrs. Paxton," the doctor said as he delivered the tiny bundle to her. "You have a beautiful baby boy!"

She kissed her son's face and kissed his tiny hands. She rocked him and wept and pressed her lips against his little head.

"He's so beautiful," she gasped. "Alma, look how beautiful!" Socorro and I gleefully agreed.

The nurses allowed Richard and Beto to join Septima at the doorway, and they all blew kisses to Dee from across the room.

"Everyone," she said ceremoniously, "I'd like you to officially meet Mitchell Cruz Paxton."

Chapter 28

DEE

WHEN I GOT HOME FROM THE HOSPITAL THERE WERE TWO huge flower bouquets from the Paxtons on the doorstep, and a basket filled with French baby soaps and powders along with a telegram from Momma, saying she'd be home soon.

I telephoned Mitch's parents in Louisiana, and we cried together on the line as I described how much the baby looked like their precious boy. I remembered asking Momma what part of Mitch I got to keep after his death, and now every time I looked into my son's gorgeous eyes, I knew that God had given me back his heart.

The first few weeks after the birth Alma stayed with Mitch and me in the mornings and afternoons, until Septima took over for the night shift. Socorro moved her things to Alma and Richard's new town house and was immediately put back on scholarship.

The house felt strange and uncomfortable without them, not at all the sort of place I wanted little Mitch to be. It was clear that our future could never shine in a place so stuck in the past. The Westside house belonged to my mother's world, not to the Los Cielos I wanted my boy to love.

"There are plenty of town houses available in our neighborhood," Alma suggested one morning as we splashed warm water from Mitch's duck-shaped bathtub onto his chubby arms and legs.

"You don't have to say that," I said, certain that she'd had enough of living with me.

"I'm serious," she insisted. "I know Socorro wants to be near you and the baby. And so do I."

We lifted Mitch out of the water and dried him off before laying him down on the changing table.

"And," she said, "when Richard and I have our baby, it will need someone to play with."

I looked at her, wrapping a diaper around my son's legs, and she looked back at me with a wide grin.

"Alma, are you?"

"No, *por Dios!* Not yet. But believe me, *mijita,* we're working on it!"

Every member of the tamale-making circle was at Septima's house, and I could smell the corn husks steaming in the pot all the way from the front porch. As usual, Beto and the other men of the neighborhood were clustered around the big-screen Zenith, watching college basketball while the women fussed in the kitchen.

Cece, Peeps, and Socorro asked if they could play with Mitch the moment we stepped inside. He was napping, I replied, but when he woke up they were welcome to feed him his bottle. Septima took my things, and I walked to the corner of the living room where I knew the wooden cradle that Beto and Richard had built would be waiting. The head of the little bed was painted with a colorful drawing of the downtown plaza, and in the center of the square there was a fat red heart with Mitch's name and birth date written in the middle.

Alma emerged from the kitchen with an apron for me put on. She looked at Mitch and gave his tiny feet a pat. "The kids will watch him. We need you in the kitchen. The first batch is almost done."

I took my place in the tamale circle and smiled as Iluminada began to tell us about her latest diet. We washed the husks and filled them with masa. We gossiped and pressed Alma to update us on her wedding plans. We listened to the men's enthusiasm rise and fall along with the basketball score and monitored the tamales in the pots.

When the first batch was ready, Septima arranged them on a platter and carried them to the dining room table. "Eat!" she said. "Everybody eat before they get cold."

The crowd moved into the dining room, where Socorro and Cece had already arranged bowls of guacamole and *chile con queso* and stacks of flour tortillas around the tamale platter.

I heard the baby stir and saw Peeps, equipped with a bottle, rush to the cradle.

After lunch the women began to clean, and the men decided to play cards. I took the baby from Peeps, who clearly wanted to join the gin game. But before I stepped back into the kitchen, Beto turned to me and said, "Looks like you need a place to set that boy down."

"He'll be okay in the kitchen."

"The kitchen?" Beto answered with a smirk. "With the women? What's the matter with you? You know how things work on Frontera Street."

He held out his arms. "Plop that boy down right here," he said patting his knee and giving me a wink. I handed Mitch to him and he perched the baby on his thigh. Little Mitch nestled himself against Beto's broad chest, and Beto's strong hands steadied his tiny legs. Then, leaning down so his lips were next to Mitch's ears, Beto said, "You tell your mommy that this is where you belong every Sunday, rain or shine. Right here, with the men, at Tio Beto's place."

I smiled and walked back into the kitchen where the tamale circle was wating.

Tanya Maria Barrientos, a journalist for more than twenty years, is a staff writer and columnist at the *Philadelphia Inquirer*. Her fiction was awarded a 2001 fellowship by the Pennsylvania Council on the Arts and the 2001 Pew Fellowship in the Arts. Born in Guatemala and raised in El Paso, Texas, she currently lives outside Philadelphia with her husband, Jack.

FRONTERA
STREET

Tanya Maria Barrientos

This Conversation Guide is intended to enrich the
individual reading experience, as well as encourage us
to explore these topics together—because books,
and life, are meant for sharing.

FICTION FOR THE WAY WE LIVE

A CONVERSATION WITH
TANYA MARIA BARRIENTOS

Q. What inspired you to write a novel about the lives of such different women colliding in a border town?

A. Before I even considered writing a novel, I wrote a short story about Septima's miracle muffin. I also wrote a short story about Socorro as a much younger child and one about Alma when she was working for Mrs. Campbell. The short stories were really more like character-studies than anything else. So I guess the novel developed when I couldn't stop thinking about these people I had created.

Q. How did these stories turn into Frontera Street*?*

A. It took many drafts and six years of writing before work and on weekends to get it done. Along the way, I had a version that told the whole story from Socorro's point of view until I realized that a teenager would not be able to fully understand the psychological and sociological undertones of a border town like Los Cielos. So I threw out that version and had each character tell the story from her own point of view.

Q. How did you create Los Cielos? Is it based on a real place?

A. I grew up in El Paso, Texas, which isn't as racially segregated as Los Cielos. But it certainly shares an emotional divide that I think is common to all border towns. I haven't lived in El Paso since I was eighteen, but I did base some of the places in the book—the fancy high school in the Westside, the downtown plaza, the irrigated cotton fields—on my memories of life there. But naturally, after all these years, even those memories are probably not very realistic. So I'd say Los Cielos is mostly fictional.

Q. Are there any other details that are drawn from your own life?

A. I studied ballet very seriously for thirteen years and really wanted to become a professional dancer. However, I only grew to be five feet tall and very few ballet companies would even consider such small dancers.

Q. What do you consider the major theme of this novel?

A. Well, the word *frontera* means border in Spanish, and I wanted to write about crossing the invisible borders that often keep people from understanding each other. America is a place that was created, in part, to allow people to cross lines, to step from one world into the next. Here we can cross lines not just of race and ethnicity but of social class and culture. Alma knew that and chose, essentially, to put her own life on hold so that Socorro could be born in America and take advantage of this.

Q. Socorro and Alma are not the only ones who cross borders, though, are they?

A. No. The borders that Dee crosses are as important as the more obvious ones crossed by Socorro and Alma. Dee's assumptions about barrio life are shattered when she explores a world that had previously existed only parallel to hers. By stepping across that divide, she gains a true sense of community when she needs it most.

Q. What are some of the other themes of Frontera Street *and how did they evolve?*

A. I live quite far from my parents and my only brother, and I don't get to see them as often as I'd like. Over the years, though, I have developed a community of friends who are as close and dear to me as my family. I think that many people have created new families in this way and I wanted to emphasize the importance of this kind of community building. True friendship transcends racial, economic, and social divides—so I guess this circles back to the theme of borders, too!

Q. What about multiculturalism?

A. Yes, that is definitely an important theme within the novel. So often people are fearful of others' ways. Alma and Dee came from a generation that believed fitting in meant having to be just like everyone around them. But Socorro teaches them that it's possible to straddle both worlds. Embracing somebody else's culture doesn't mean you have to discard your own. It's not always easy to keep a foot in each world but it's done by millions of people from dozens of ethnic groups in America every day.

Q. What are you working on now?

A. I'm writing a novel about three generations of Guatemalan women living in the same house. I was born in Guatemala and came to the United States with my parents when I was three years old; so it's a story that is close to my heart.

QUESTIONS FOR DISCUSSION

1. Do you think Dee made the right choice in sending the invitation? Did Alma do the right thing in keeping the truth from Socorro? Is it possible to do the wrong thing for the right reasons, and are these examples of such an act?

2. Do you think La Llorona was a real apparition or merely a psychological manifestation of Alma's fears? Does it matter if La Llorona is real?

3. Discuss Socorro's role in this story. How does she serve as a bridge between old and new, Latina and American? Could Alma and Dee have crossed their personal borders without Socorro?

4. Talk about the borders you have crossed in your own life. Have there been times when you could not overcome the boundaries between yourself and someone else no matter how hard you tried? Can one person bridge a cultural divide without another's welcome?

5. Discuss the transitional moment when Alma starts to warm up to Dee. What are the factors that contributed to her ability to see past her preconceptions of Dee?

6. Are cultural differences meaningful? Discuss why they are important to our sense of identity. When do they become more burdensome than enriching? How do cultural differences affect the characters in *Frontera Street*?